Patchwork Pieces

Patchwork Pieces

D. B. Martin

Published by IM Books

www.debrahmartin.co.uk

PATCHWORK PIECES

ISBN 978-0-9929961-8-5

'For now we see through a glass, darkly; but then face to face: now I know in part; but then shall I know even as also I am known.'

1 Corinthians 13:12

Prologue

'Lawrence!'

I was staring into the leering face of the man I now realised had been following me off and on all day, wondering if he'd seen me with Margaret – and whether he was working for Jaggers or not. The flash blinded me and for a moment I was back in the ambulance, dazed and confused, the paramedic swearing loudly as the vehicle was engulfed in the smoke from my smouldering home. Pinpricks of yellow and white from the afterburn of the flash danced in front of my eyes like fireflies.

'So what's the story, Mr Juste? Replay of the big bang theory? Dissatisfied client? Or insurance scam?'

'What the …?'

The glut of Tube-goers funnelled round us as we hovered at the top of the steps.

'Make your mind up, will you?' A dark-suited businessman pushed impatiently past us, propelling my weasly assailant into me. Dark-suit could have been me six weeks ago, pressurised and irritable because he had to brave the crowds – and the Tube – in a moment of extremis when no taxi could be found.

'Daily News,' weasel-face elaborated, thrusting his press card into my face where the fireflies were slowly dying. 'Want to give us your version of the story?'

'What story?' I retorted, finally on red alert.

He smirked. 'Whatever you want it to be – before anyone else does.'

Self-preservation kicked in then, and the instincts that should have been screaming a warning to me all day but I seemed to have temporarily lost – along with my common sense, some might have argued. I took advantage of an incoming wave of Chinese tourists, gabbling incomprehensibly, and let their centrifugal force sweep me into the guts of the Tube station and away from weasel-face. Between their angular arms and excited faces I could see his exasperated one drifting into the distance as I floated out of reach. I eventually detached myself from the group at the ticket barrier just before I was swept into the bowels of hell – the London Underground.

The press! I hadn't bargained on that – but why the hell not? Fool!

I made my way cautiously back up the steps, swimming against the tide this time. Weasel-face was nowhere to be seen by then. Margaret had long since gone too, as well as the black Merc that had been stalking us. My undead wife had disappeared again, but this time, not for good, I hoped. On a news-stand just across from the steps down to the Tube station, I found out where the sly little rat had been coming from – and where the press's current take on me was going. The image of the burned and blackened facade of my home took up most of the spread on page five. The headline played on the old adage that if you played with fire you had to expect to get your fingers burnt – and right now Lawrence Juste, QC, was *smoking* … Very witty, but of course, with the possibility of controversy it presented, why wouldn't one of their number be interested in making a *real* story out of it? It didn't take much to wonder whether there was an inside scoop on the supposedly so respectable barrister who'd embroiled himself in a dodgy case, admitted to a secret past and then succeeded in burning down his home – all in the space of a few weeks. I cursed myself for being so immersed in Margaret and her tricky ways that I'd lost sight of the bigger picture as a result. I was hot news – literally. Intriguing news, controversial news – and for me, bad news.

1: Disassembling the Pieces

With the press interest explained I let my thoughts drift back to their usual inclination these days: Margaret – and by association, Danny and Jaggers. I meandered aimlessly away from the Tube entrance, unsure what to do next now I potentially had a tail. Dammit! Working out that Danny was our son even without Margaret's confessional letter had been gratifying; proof my intellect could still grapple with a complex riddle even though my emotions couldn't. But the reality – and gravity – of the situation was only just really sinking in. I was a father. I was responsible. I should be in control, protective – but whatever I did put Danny at risk. And whatever Danny did put me at risk. Add to that Margaret's position, too close to Jaggers, and that put all of us at risk. The riddle might be complex and the solving of it clever but it was all about money and murder. Not a childish game; deadly serious power play. I was like a rat in a trap – well and truly caught. I shivered involuntarily at the idea. My mobile phone rang just as the shiver reached the bottom of my spine. I jumped as if the rat trap had sprung shut round my squirming body.

'Where are you?'

'Heather! I'm on my way back right now,' I replied cautiously, already anticipating a grilling from her about my clandestine meeting with Margaret. As a business partner Heather was excellent, in court she was lethal and on a personal level she was terrifying. The prospect of being debriefed by Heather felt much like being in court – and on the wrong side of the bench. I experienced a brief but illuminating sympathy for my own clients as they faced their moment of fate and the faint possibility – despite my skills – of a guilty verdict. I'd never considered it from a personal slant before. They'd been faces, problems and outcomes – generally successful. That's why they engaged me, Lawrence Juste QC; unemotional, unremitting and unbeaten – apart from now.

'Well don't! Not until I tell you to.'

I laughed in spite of myself.

'That makes a change. You're usually ordering me to go home.'

'Not when there's press crawling all over my doorstep like ants.'

'Ah.' So they'd found my temporary bolthole too.

'Yes, ah, Lawrence. And they're not here to admire my youth and beauty, so stay away, until I tell you to get back here. Then get back here quick – and make sure no-one's following you. Lose yourself somewhere in the meantime. You're usually extremely good at that.'

The click in my ear as the line went dead was almost as irritable as Heather. Lose myself. Where could I lose myself? The only place I could think of that fitted the bill was Wimbledon Common, but that was a Tube or bus ride away and then probably as soon as I got there, Heather would be demanding I return *immediately.* In the end I sauntered down the road and found a small Turkish café on Earls Court Road, holed up in the corner and drank their version of espresso, dark and murky – like my mood. I alternated between thinking about Margaret, Danny, Jaggers and the press. The fire at my home had just been part of the game – Jaggers' game – but pawn or protagonist, I hadn't much choice but to keep playing along now. I'd thought getting Danny off the trumped-up manslaughter charge and admitting to the less savoury parts of my hidden past would deflect him. If there were no more secrets to reveal, how could they be a threat? Life would gradually resume as it had been once – minus Margaret – and Jaggers would eventually give up on trying to recover the money I'd inherited from good old Judge Wemmick, if there were no more levers to push. If I couldn't be discredited and that discredit reflected back on the Judge, then there would be no catalyst for the complicated machinery of the will trust to grind into action, require the return of the money and bankrupt me. Until my lovely wife Margaret had reappeared, that was, with her revelations about Danny's parentage and my unwitting involvement in a decade-old cover-up. Now Jaggers would be very much back on my case – *our* case – along with the police and the press – but for possibly quite different reasons. The tricky little bitch! She certainly knew how to get what she wanted.

The last thought was accompanied by wry humour, I'll admit. She'd started all this with a letter setting out my past misdemeanours, and had concluded it with one, inviting me to commit even more. It had a certain elegant, if warped, symmetry. The letter, to be opened in the event of her death, still nestled in my inside pocket. She wasn't dead, of course, and I suspected she'd enjoyed leading me by the nose before triumphantly revealing herself almost as much as the revelation itself. It explained everything – a shambles of disassembled puzzle pieces that told a deadly story, but with yet another demand attached. Reassemble them and set it all straight, or... The 'or' was Jaggers, although, frustratingly, no suggestion how to avoid him – yet. The 'or' was also implicit, but still as clear as the demand in the blackmail list she'd left me when she'd originally 'died'.

Why had I so rashly just agreed? Signed up as her willing foot soldier, rather than the fool who'd accidently swallowed the King's shilling? I thought back to the wave of passion and foolish sentiment that had engulfed me – much like the smoke from my home – immediately after her kiss. Was a kiss from her all it took – from the woman I hadn't thought I cared about at all? More fool me that I didn't understand that either, only the sudden rush of intense need that had dragged the promise out of my mouth like she'd tied a string to my tongue and pulled.

I stirred the muddy dregs of my coffee uneasily. It was as if I'd never seen the real woman behind the veneer of 'wife' all the time I'd known her. Or was it that I'd only seen what it suited me to see, as Heather always accused me of doing? Even now, I didn't know, and it was that which worried me most; my propensity to blindness even when I thought I was seeing most clearly. She seemed so different – or my response to her seemed so different – yet she was the same woman I'd taken for granted, and latterly even dismissed all these years. When did that change? Who changed the rules? Someone once told me life is a game – Lennox, perhaps, in the children's home? To win it you just need to follow the rules, but how do you know what the rules are if they change?

My second cup of overly-strong espresso was abandoned still half full when Heather rang again. I left the café and threaded my way through as many side streets as I could, back to Earls Court Square, just in case weasel-face spotted me again. Even with the detours I reached Heather's chic apartment barely twenty minutes later.

'You took your time.'

'You told me to make sure no-one followed me.'

She tutted and ushered me in impatiently. I loitered in the hallway for a moment like a naughty schoolboy awaiting punishment, then slipped away to my room while she was peering up and down the road. I felt the reverberations of the slammed front door through the shuddering walls of the apartment and closed my bedroom door as discreetly as I could, hoping she wouldn't seek me out to finish my chastisement. I'd been allocated the smallest room in her spacious home – apart from the toilet.

The larger spare bedroom was given over to her collection of shoes, permanently welcome in her house, unlike me, I suspected. I'd mistakenly detoured into it before she guided me back to my allotted cell the first night I'd stayed there, still disorientated by the after-effects of the explosion. I was simultaneously mourning the Austin Healey and being dumbfounded by row upon row of Manolo Blahniks, Jimmy Choos, Kurt Geigers and names I'd never even heard of which lined the walls, when she found me.

'But why do you need them all?' I'd asked, incredulous at the sheer volume and range.

'I don't,' she replied haughtily. 'But I can, so I do.'

Perhaps that had been where I'd gone wrong with this whole damn mess? I needn't have, but I had, because I could. If only I'd just accepted the name and fate I'd been born with, there wouldn't have been any need for pretence. Kenny Juss might not have achieved the dizzy heights of – almost – High Court judge that the manufactured man, Lawrence Juste, had, but perhaps he would have retained his integrity with his mediocre roots. The reason I'd become a barrister in the first place was because of the lofty Atticus Finch in my childhood bible, *To Kill a Mockingbird*. His grasp on the principles of justice had been true. Mine was faulty at best. Now I was reaping the reward of my years of lip service to those same principles. I'd left my past behind me because I could, but lost the essence of honour in doing so. To emulate my hero, I had to earn it back, but God only knew how!

Surprisingly Heather didn't follow me upstairs straight away. In the quiet of the guest room I spread the evidence I'd managed to save from the fire out on the bed and considered it. I'd taken it with me to show Margaret but our brief and confusing meeting hadn't given us enough time for us to do much more than kiss, agree and part. I tried to set aside for now the equally confusing jumble of emotions seeing Margaret had caused in me and concentrate on facts. I started with her letter, explaining that Danny was our child but was also entitled to the Wemmick fortune – if we came out in the open with the facts. That would certainly spring the trap Jaggers was setting round me with the damn will trust, but it wasn't that simple. It also made it clear that Jaggers wouldn't ever let that happen, so was Danny now more at risk than me? That felt wrong – that whole surmise felt wrong – why? Think, man, think!

I got it. If I'd fathered a child with Margaret – correction; stop thinking about Danny as *a child*; think about him as *your* child … OK, if

I'd fathered *our* child with Margaret, then I shouldn't be worrying about whether he was more at risk than me, or vice versa. I should be worrying about the fact that *he* was at risk at all. I'd had no choice but to commit to both him and Margaret when she'd told me and forced the promise to help out of me, but I hadn't really thought about it at the time. This was real. This wasn't merely a legal dispute or a courtroom confrontation I needed to win. Danny wasn't merely the client I'd had to clear of manslaughter to also save my sorry skin. He was a responsibility, my responsibility. The bundle of documents huddling together in my dead sister's keepsakes box, like Pandora's secret waiting to burst on the world, had confirmed that too. Fine words, yet I shied away from considering what they entailed.

But you can't do that any more, Lawrence. You can't simply ignore what you don't want to know.

That damn little imp in my head again!

I'd always maintained I would never be a father. And now I was, without even having known it had happened. How life turns on a dime! There could be no more Kat – tempting though she still was, and whereas I had to reject Kat, I would have to claim Margaret and Danny wholeheartedly now. I shivered as I had when Heather had rung me.

I wasn't ready for that yet. I temporarily shelved the problem by putting the birth certificates for Danny and Kimmy's stillborn child back in Sarah's keepsakes box. I was still good at boxing things and this time I had a genuine excuse. There was another far more important box still to be found and opened – the one Margaret implied contained the originals of the evidence she'd clandestinely sent me which could nail Jaggers for the murder of her sister, Rosemary; the case that had started this whole charade in the first place. I even had the key now, apparently, but no idea of the box's whereabouts. Margaret's rules meant she was still hugging that little secret to herself, dammit! But that had to be my first priority. If I could get Jaggers off everyone's back it would allow us to untangle the knot of the past at my pace. Emotion was an unnecessary indulgence for the moment. That was my reasoning …

With that, denial turned to annoyance. That Margaret hadn't – or wouldn't – tell me where the box was irritated me in the same way that the irksome little green light that kept blinking at the back of my mind did. It had been doing that ever since Win had been charged with Kimmy's death. It meant *something* and I remembered it from *somewhere,* but I was damned if I knew what. Luckily Heather blew further risk of having to examine my conscience out of the water with her belated arrival. She didn't knock but that didn't surprise me. She burst into the guest room in a bustle of carrier bags and consumerism.

'So, no-one *did* follow you?'

'Not as far as I know.'

'Good. I need to have my hair done and I want to look my best if the hacks are going to be beating a path to my door again.' She thrust the bags at me meaningfully. The fanciest of them carried the name and logo of one of the aforesaid designer shoes.

'Not really my style, Heather,' I commented mischievously.

'Well, I wasn't sure what style you were adopting these days, Lawrence. Nothing would surprise me currently.' She grabbed it back with a look of scorn. 'But don't play smartass with me. You won't win. *Obviously* that one's mine.'

I withered appropriately and looked inside one of the other bags as she left in a storm of expensive perfume and high dudgeon. It amazed me that Heather had such a grasp of me that I could have been forgiven for thinking I'd chosen the things myself. I piled the various shirts, trousers, ties, underwear on the bed – discomfited that she should even have got the sizes right – and was about to bundle the bags together to throw away when I noticed a receipt lying in the bottom of one of them. I ought to give it to Heather. No doubt she would be keeping a running total of 'Lawrence' costs – not that I blamed her. At least she was only counting in pounds and pence, not time and emotion. I fished it out and tossed it on the bed next to the clothes, then got up and stretched. My body still felt stiff and awkward from being dragged out of the fire that had taken the guts out of my home. Perhaps it had torn the stuffing out of me too.

I didn't bother trying any of the clothes on. Heather's customary efficiency convinced me that they would be perfect but I ought to thank her. I picked up the receipt and stuffed it in my pocket, but lingered by the window, surveying the stylish West Kensington street shimmering in the still warm early autumn afternoon. Apathy overwhelmed me – the kind that invades more because one doesn't know what to do rather than because one can't be bothered to do it. Far from hide from them, Heather must have sent the press off with fleas in their ears. Not a single stray hack littered the street. I wondered what she'd said, and the possibilities made me grin. My eyes strayed idly along the windows of the building opposite. The long casement windows set into the white stucco walls spoke of less stressful and more graceful times. One, directly facing me, was wide open, bottom section pulled up to its fullest height, allowing the voile drapes to billow out as a lazy breeze broke the humidity of the afternoon. A familiar figure moved in the shadows behind the open window. I jumped and plastered myself to the glass, straining to see the spectral figure clearly. Margaret? It couldn't be – yet … The figure sank back into the shadows but I was sure it was her. The certainty was compounded by the sound of a child's fluting protestation. Then the figure was back at the window, pulling the casement shut in one swift and violent movement. The voile drapes were dragged across and the apartment took on the same blank and abandoned look as its neighbour.

I remained transfixed for maybe thirty seconds, then sprang to life, clattering down the hallway to find Heather. She was tending the herb garden she'd set up on the window ledge of her outsized kitchen. The parsley had clearly been threatening to engulf everything else as parsley does, and was being roundly castigated by Heather and a pair of scissors. Its walking wounded lay green and bleeding on the nearby worktop.

'She's across the road, Heather! I'm sure of it!'

'Who?' She spun round, scissors in one hand and a handful of billow-leafed parsley in the other – the grim reaper and her victim. 'Who's across the road?'

'Margaret. I've just seen her at the window across the road.'

'Opposite?'

'Yes. She saw me, then she slammed it shut it and pulled the drapes across. I think I heard Danny too.'

She shook her head sadly.

'They said you might suffer some after-effects from the shock. There's no-one there. The old dear died and the kids are still arguing about who gets what.'

'Well there's someone there now and I'm sure it's Margaret. That would be so like her – to watch me from right under my nose. Come on!'

I grabbed the scissors from her and pulled her towards the hall.

'Come on, where?'

'Over the road – to find her.'

'Lawrence, my darling, I told you there's no-one there. *Really.* I *know* because I'm a key holder. Coincidentally Norton's firm are the executors and since I'm right here on the spot he asked if I would keep a key in case of emergencies. I wouldn't normally have agreed but it's always good to have a favour to call in. I checked the place only recently. It's empty. Has been for ages.'

I faltered in the doorway. 'But she could have moved in there since – rented it perhaps?'

'When I say empty, I mean uninhabitable. Upstairs, anyway. There was a leak on the second floor last spring and now it's damp as well as abandoned. The old dear's kids aren't doing themselves any favours by wrangling over it. They'll have precious little but an outer shell left if they carry on like it much longer.'

'Can we look anyway – especially as you have the key?'

She looked as if she was about to refuse, but maybe the paramedics had also told her to humour me.

'Oh come on then.' She disentangled herself and went back to the kitchen. I followed, puppy-dog style. She crossed to a rack of keys hanging on a row of hooks and collected a small ring holding the key to a deadlock and two shiny Yales. I let her lead the way, making her irritation obvious with the set of her shoulders and her bustling bird-like walk, teetering on stilettos even indoors, although I had no idea which designer these were. I followed her down the plush cream stairway that led to the ground floor reception. Heather's apartment sprawled over the first and second floors, with the bedrooms on the second floor – apart from the holding cell allocated to me, which no doubt in many others would have been a small study. I wondered if the apartment opposite had the same layout. She tip-tapped across the street and up the two steps to the front door. Numbers 27A and 27B were emblazoned on the side panel next to the door, with a small intercom to buzz.

'27A is occupied, but apparently he's abroad most of the time. In fact I've never even seen him. Certainly he hasn't been back since before the flood so who knows what state his place is in. He must have money to waste too if he can't be bothered to get it checked over while he's away. He was warned.'

She sounded peevish – as if she were a letting agent complaining about her tenant's strange proclivities.

'His funeral,' I commented, anxious to avoid delay by asking her more.

'That's in rather bad taste, Lawrence, considering,' she said over her shoulder.

'Sorry, I'm on edge,' as if that forgave me everything. Clearly it didn't with Heather but she stabbed the key in the lock anyway. She struggled with the Yale and deadlock until I came to her aid, then between us we twisted both simultaneously and the door swung open. I had a moment of déjà vu as we entered. It was like walking into the basement corridor at FFF all over again; dark and musty smelling inside, with undernotes of something more unpleasant. I could see the tell-tale signs of the now dried but mouldering damp patch from the leak on the ceiling. It was rapidly burgeoning to a dark grey-green, topped with scaly and crustaceous growth. Heather put her hand over her nose.

'Whew. It didn't smell this bad the last time I was here.'

'Do you want me to go first?' I offered.

'Too right! You wanted to come over here – here you are.' She thrust the key ring at me. 'The larger of the two Yales opens the front door. 27B's upstairs.'

I glanced around briefly as I took the bundle of keys. In the gloom 27A looked eerily like the smartly presented version of the door at FFF. The unpleasant smell seemed to be coming from there, but that wasn't my concern. I set off grimly up the stairs, gripping the stair rail then letting go as swiftly in disgust. The same scaly green mould as on the ceiling coated it.

'I see what you mean about uninhabitable, but I definitely saw something,' I commented. Heather didn't answer me. I looked over my shoulder to check she was all right. She was laboriously picking her way over the threadbare stair carpet, gingerly touching the stair rail to keep her balance. She didn't look up and her nose was wrinkled – a sure sign she was building up a head of steam to blow at me later for dragging her over here.

'Something's rotten in the state of Denmark,' she replied. 'And if my shoes are ruined by this little adventure, Lawrence, you're buying me new ones.'

'When I've got the money to,' I replied unwisely.

'With or without money,' she retorted. 'You can sell your soul to manage it if necessary. I'd better tell Norton about the state of the place though. It wasn't this bad a couple of months ago. Maybe his partner can knock some sense into those kids.' She reached the top of the stairs and stood testily beside me. By contrast to the rest of the place the front door to 27B was clean and well-maintained. I was reminded strongly of the strange sensation of something out of place that I'd had at Kat's the last time I'd been there.

'I smell a rat,' I said.

'I imagine that's what's gone off,' she grimaced.

'I meant a metaphorical rat, actually.' I twisted the front door key and the door opened smoothly. Inside 27B the noxious smell from downstairs was muted, but it still smelt stale. I explored ahead of Heather.

'Roughly the same floor plan as mine,' she called after me.

'The shoes are all in here, then?' I replied from the room that equated to her shoe heaven, topographically, before moving on to the room that faced mine.

'Ha-ha!'

She arrived a few moments after the sarcasm. As she'd said, the place was empty, but there were drapes in this room, unlike the others and significantly, whereas the other window sills had been dusty, this one wasn't. I indicated so to Heather.

'Well, you've been leaning against it.'

'No, I haven't. I haven't been any closer than this, but I can see from here that it's been wiped clean.'

'So someone likes to do their housework,' she commented, tart, but frowning nevertheless.

'In an empty apartment? Not so much likes their housework as doesn't like their fingerprints left behind, I would suggest.'

'You're becoming quite the little detective,' she remarked testily. 'Maybe you should take over from DCI Fredriks rather than avoid him.' It was my turn to say ha-ha to that. She gave me a sharp little head dip in acknowledgement and a wry thin-lipped smile. 'However, in this case I think I agree.' She bent and picked up a colouring pencil that was nestling up against the skirting board. 'Someone who likes drawing.' She held it out to me and I took it. It was unremarkable other than for the fact that it was new; freshly sharpened to a point, and significantly out of place in an empty building.

'I was right, then.'

We faced each other.

'It's minutely *possible* you were right,' she corrected. 'But more likely there are squatters.'

'Where? Where are they now, then? No, it was Margaret, with Danny.'

'What on earth would she be doing here – and how could they have left without us seeing them?' She shook her head. 'Over-wrought imagination, Lawrence.'

'And what about this?' I held out the pencil.

'It's a pencil. You'll prove nothing to Fredriks with that – but then you're not going to, because you *can't* say anything to Fredriks about this or anything else.' She watched my expression. 'Can you?'

'No,' I agreed reluctantly. 'But he knows there's more to all of this than meets the eye – just not what.'

'Then the sooner you work it out yourself, the better,' she paused. 'Lawrence,' she continued at length. 'I wasn't going to interrogate you, but I don't think I've much choice now since you're clearly obsessed – obsessed, and with a deconstructed house …'

'Damaged,' I corrected.

'No, Lawrence. Deconstructed. The police and forensics are crawling all over it right now.' I frowned at her. She elaborated. 'A little bird tells me they're wondering if you actually organised its convenient demolition – with Win, since he's out on bail now.'

My head spun with the two pieces of news – one not wholly unexpected, the other a complete surprise.

'Who says?'

'A little bird, that's all.'

'But since when? And how? There's hardly any likelihood of bail on a murder charge.'

'Well someone has obviously pulled some strings because the murder charge seems to have been withdrawn for now, and they're only charging him with withholding evidence and conspiracy to break and enter the FFF premises. *Only*!' She laughed caustically and without humour. 'That means your head's still dangling nicely over the block if they care to pursue you instead. And they've also got the car that was used to 'run' Margaret over and are muttering murder now, so don't down tools on that score just yet just because you know otherwise. I assumed *you'd* somehow worked your magic – although I did wonder how. Maybe it was Norton then?'

Noisome Norton. I laughed. Norton had given me the impression he'd wanted to wash his hands of both Win and I when we'd been pulled in by the police after the fiasco in the dungeon play palace. I doubted he'd pull strings on our behalf in that mood – fat fee or not.

'Norton's *really* good, then,' I acknowledged. 'Win was in real trouble with the evidence DCI Fredriks had.'

'I don't understand why you're representing him then.'

'Apart from my – in your opinion – unusual attitude to family loyalty, what would the press make of me abandoning my own brother when I've only just publically reclaimed him? I thought you wanted me to be *squeaky clean* in public?'

'Yes, well, maybe I'm changing my mind from squeaky clean to white-washed. I'm not an advocate of pretence, but sometimes it's necessary for the right ends. You're going to have to play the bad boy come good for the public so you'd better start by looking the part.'

'And that's the reason for the new wardrobe, is it?'

'And for *my* image, of course,' she added.

'Thanks for the concern,' I replied sarcastically, and then regretted it. She was only trying to help. My ragbag appearance, cobbled together from the brief shopping spree she'd taken me on after the explosion, wouldn't do much to cement the image of the consummate 'good guy' in place. It fit my mental state perfectly though. Perhaps smartening me up would help me intellectually too? Luckily Heather ignored the tone of my retort. She'd already moved on to what she hadn't going to interrogate me about.

'Did Margaret confess?'

'Confess to what? She hasn't done anything wrong.'

'Nothing wrong? So if I'm to believe you, there's nothing wrong with faking your own death, illegally acquiring a corpse and passing it off as yourself at your own cremation, blackmail, kidnapping a minor and planting false evidence?'

'OK, OK – but there were reasons for all of them.'

'The fair maid's champion now, are you?' She pursed her lips and rolled her eyes at me.

'I just meant she hasn't done anything so wrong – like murder – that it would warrant a confession. And Danny wasn't kidnapped. He went with her willingly.'

'But he's back now, so how could he be across the road with her then?'

'All right, maybe I overreacted a little there.'

'Hmm,' she looked appeased. 'But she *did* take him, then?'

I nodded.

'But only to keep him out of harm's way.'

'So she says …' Heather was sceptical. 'But you can't tell the police so they can close that part of their enquiries down, can you? Because she can't admit to it. She's "dead". Whereas you … are withholding evidence and involved in a conspiracy to pervert the course of justice. And talking of money to replace my ruined shoes …'

'We're not.'

'Whatever – who *did* take the money out of the partnership bank account? Her – or you?'

She had me there. I wasn't sure. It hadn't been me, so it must have been Margaret, but I knew neither answer would go down well with Heather. In the intensity of the meeting with Margaret earlier I'd forgotten to clarify that little detail. Forgotten to clarify a lot, really. I could curse myself now. It had been that kiss that had distracted me. Least said on that score, the better, for the moment. Heather could instigate criminal proceedings anytime she wanted currently – and in the mood she was in, she well might.

I retreated to a different line of defence.

'Margaret needs to lay low for now. It's difficult to talk to her.'

'Ah, going to waste more police time then?'

'Give me a break, can't you Heather? I need to find the evidence Margaret has against Jaggers first.'

'I thought I already was.' Heather replied acidly, her timing perfect as she added, 'Maybe it's in the same place as our money?' She put her hand on her hip and waited, every inch the Dom. I was tempted to tell her that but decided against it. This was Heather, after all. Best not to tempt providence.

'It will all get paid back, wherever it is,' I soothed.

'Fine promises, Lawrence, but I've noticed you have a habit of failing to follow through on them recently. For instance, like the one where you promised to stay out of trouble.'

'Trouble isn't always avoidable, Heather. Sometimes it goes hand-in-hand with the truth.'

She snorted, disdainfully.

'So, what *did* Margaret have to say, because I assume that's where you sneaked off to earlier?'

I sighed. 'We talked about bringing the truth out into the open; clearing Willy Johns of Rosemary's murder, nailing Jaggers instead, and claiming Danny.' I may not understand women but I was beginning to understand some of their caprices. It was one of Heather's – to have her skills and assistance constantly acknowledged. 'That's where you could help. Margaret said she had evidence to convict Jaggers of murder in Wilhelm Johns' place but it was hidden under Rosemary's cloak. What does that mean? It's her sister's name so there must be some significance in that – and the other clues she sent me. You said you remembered something pertinent to it? What was it?'

'Did I? I have no idea what.' She looked surprised.

'I'm sure you did – or you said something about knowing where the place was.'

'Oh, I said I'd seen a reference somewhere to where her sister, Rosemary, was buried, but whether that links to anything else, who can say? Anyway, under Rosemary's cloak is metaphorical not actual. We've already been there and established that.'

'Might it not be actual as well? Maybe it means *where* Rosemary Flowers is buried? Perhaps the evidence is secreted there too? '

She shrugged. 'I suppose it's worth a try, although I don't know what you think you're going to find there. The Deathly Hallows ghost pointing the way to the treasure? Aren't you missing the point? You need to force Margaret out into the open to get the truth, whether she wants to lie low or not. Drag her to the nearest police station if necessary. If she knows what's been going on and has evidence to prove it, you don't need to go hunting for some mysterious security box. She could simply tell you. Where is she now?'

'I don't know. There were crowds around; Jaggers too I think, or his car,' I added in my defence. 'She had to hide from him.'

'Huh! Typical.'

'Your help really would be invaluable, Heather. Can you at least remember the name of the place?'

'Not offhand,' she shrugged, before nodding reluctantly. 'Oh, all right, I'll have a look through the notes I made when I was researching the stuff to get you moving. I can't do it until tomorrow though. It's in Chambers – locked away so no-one else can tamper with it. In the meantime, it's your chance to play clothes horse. Come on, let's go.'

'Thank you.' I put on my most charming potential client-smile.

'Hmm,' she replied. 'And I know I was winding you up earlier but you do realise you're as guilty of all the crimes I was listing for Margaret as she is because you know about them and have therefore effectively condoned them. And another thing, Lawrence – even if you do manage to nail Jaggers, how are you going to explain all of that away sufficiently for Margaret to resurrect herself?' She turned and walked towards the door. 'She's dead – supposedly. And if she's not – who's the poor bitch who is? Keep that as evidence of something, though. Coming?'

She was right. I'd still not been thinking clearly. I'd been consumed by finally knowing the past history of my wife and what I could prove against my enemy, and overtaken by my unexpected response to seeing her again, but the nuts and bolts still all slotted together to make a framework of conspiracy and contempt of court. Indeed, no court would acquit anyone – no matter how well-connected – of our cumulative sum of crimes; especially not me – supposedly one of their law keepers. That was without Kimmy's murder to compound them. Despondently I shoved the pencil in my trouser pocket and it came into contact with something already in there. I pulled it out. It was the receipt I'd been about to take to Heather when I'd caught sight of the shape at the window. But it wasn't a receipt. It was a note.

From Margaret.

2: Word Association

I stuffed the note back in my pocket. Heather was clearly not well-disposed towards Margaret but she was right. Whatever I might have I couldn't do anything with it, yet. I needed to make contact with Margaret again and coax her out. If Heather had anything to do with it, it would be coercing, not coaxing, so I needed to read the note in private. In her current mood Heather was just as likely to take it straight to the police regardless of the damage it would do to me and my reputation. We locked up and left the flat. The bad smell downstairs hit us again like a wall as soon as we reached 27A.

'Shouldn't we check what that is?' I asked.

Heather wrinkled her nose and looked at her shoes, still pristine despite our expedition into the filth upstairs. 'It's not my responsibility. Only 27B – and that only to keep Norton sweet. Never know when you might need a tricky solicitor.' She looked meaningfully at me. 'I haven't got the key to it anyway.' I accepted the excuse with relief. The similarity to the children's home cellar door and its modern counterpart, the FFF basement door, spooked me, but maybe it was commonplace in period refurbishments. 'Come on Lawrence, this smell is rancid. It's going to turn my stomach soon and you wouldn't like me when I'm turned.'

I laughed. 'A little like me.'

'You're already turned, my darling,' she threw over her shoulder as she tottered down the steps at the entrance. 'Although I'm not sure which way yet. Slam the door to make sure it's properly shut and then do the deadlock, will you?' She paused at the bottom of the steps, gazing up at the first floor whilst she waited for me to follow her instructions. I turned the lock and joined her just as she exclaimed, 'Crahan House – that's where Rosemary Flowers lived as a child. It's in St Rosemary in the Marsh. That's where she's buried.' She took the keys briskly from me and cat-walked back across the road, heels leaving small pinpricks in the overheated tarmac. I caught up with her as she reached her own front door.

'You said you didn't know where she was buried – that you'd have to look it up in your notes.'

'I know. I would have if it hadn't been for that damn pencil. Crahan – crayon. It sounds similar and I just suddenly remembered. Word association – try it, why don't you? Margaret – lies – trouble. The church is called St Rosemary in the Marsh too. I think it was so-called not because Rosemary was a saint but because the boundaries of the churchyard are made of rosemary bushes. There's a mythical link between rosemary and Mary's cloak. Something to do with when she was trying to flee from Herod with baby Jesus – probably a load of rubbish though – who can disappear that completely, and pop up undiscovered elsewhere? You certainly couldn't!'

'My God, you *are* a mine of information.' I fiddled impatiently with the note and the pencil in my pocket.

She shrugged, nonchalant.

'Yeah – much good it does me. Margaret and I had a face-off over that once – her useless information. I was in the right, whereas she was wrong, but she wouldn't have it. Did a complete about-face on me and then somehow I was in the wrong!' She put on a creditable imitation of Margaret on a mission, '*Privilege obligates us to use our knowledge for good. You're just using it to argue.*' She laughed. 'Typical Margaret. I knew it was just to deflect me. Forever game-playing.'

'You really didn't like her, did you?'

She frowned, weighing up the bunch of keys in her hand.

'Actually, at times I did – once. And recently I've even occasionally been impressed with her. I mean, this manipulation of you is *smart*. She was quite likeable when she first came to Chambers – quieter and more thoughtful, but the longer she was around, the more cocky she became, and the more I realised she was all front. Like you said – complicated.' She hesitated. 'But if you're going to get things back on with her when this is all sorted out, maybe I ought to warn you that I caught her flirting with Jeremy once, so it's not just you and me she played games with. I'm sorry. Now maybe you can see why I don't think you should trust her, even if she is the mother of your child.'

I reeled. 'With Jeremy? I can't imagine that. Are you sure?'

'Sure enough, but Jeremy's out of bounds, Lawrence – however angry it makes you. He may be a tart, but he's necessary for bringing the clients in. Remember Francis is still laid up, and at this rate you could be under arrest any day for that long list of crimes I've just given you. Jeremy may be a ladies' man, but he's also a sweet-talker. You'll have to have this out with Margaret, not Jeremy – when you find her again.'

She looked too belligerent for me to argue with her, but I stored up the unwelcome new piece of information alongside the other bits I'd been gathering since Win and I had been chained up in the underground pervert's palace at Jaggers' Gods and Gargoyles Club and Margaret had first broken the cover of the grave to release us. The woman I thought I knew kept coming in and out of focus, like the evidence, and just when I thought I was starting to see clearly, the image blurred again. The emotions I'd felt when she kissed me seemed even more confusing now.

Heather ushered me upstairs and back into the kitchen where the parsley seemed to recoil as she entered. She picked the scissors up again and continued where she'd left off, shaping the parsley into a sleek bob. I watched her, fascinated, until it seemed as if she'd forgotten I was there. I was just about to melt away and read Margaret's note when she swung round just as I edging towards the kitchen door and waved the scissor points in my face.

'So what's next?'

I nervously dodged the scissors and retreated to the far end of the breakfast bar.

'Like I said, I have to somehow locate the security box with the evidence Margaret's assembled against Jaggers.'

'Then?' I knew what was expected.

'Turn it over to Fredriks and we all live happily ever after.'

'No need to be sarky,' she rebuked, viciously snipping another wayward frond of parsley. I hadn't meant it to be sarcastic, but of course it belonged in fantasy land – like everything else at the moment.

'Sorry.'

'I asked for a genuine reason.' Another piece of frilly green foliage fell to the scissors but she didn't elaborate. I was curious now.

'What's the genuine reason?'

'My darling, you have no idea what you're doing, do you? Margaret obviously has plenty, but you're rather lacking. You jump from murdered sisters, to missing children, to arch enemies, to wives who return from the grave, to teenage girlfriends who would chase you there …'

'Kat isn't a teenager,' I objected. 'Nor is she my girlfriend.'

'Not now – but she was heading that way. And does her actual age matter? It was the age *difference* I was alluding to.'

'Well, it's over before it even begun with the situation as it is with Margaret so I'd appreciate it if you'd stop caning me for it. Everyone makes mistakes at some point in their life.'

She abandoned the parsley to face me.

'But you're *still* making them, Lawrence. Do I have to list them for you?'

'No. Margaret's already done that very succinctly for me, thanks.' She looked surprised. I sighed. 'When she "died", I came home to find Danny's case folder on the desk in my study, together with a list of, shall we say, my past life errors. It was obvious I was intended to take his case as trade-off for them not being made public.'

'She blackmailed you? You didn't tell me that before.'

'Wasn't there enough to tell you already?'

She looked worried.

'But that adds another dimension to things.'

'It wasn't really blackmail – it was for justice.'

Her lips twisted disbelievingly.

'Any coercion for return is blackmail, Lawrence. You know the definition as well as I do. So what are your past life mistakes?'

'You already know them. I just didn't mention Margaret's little billet-doux.'

She considered me thoughtfully. 'Why would she do that – and risk ruining herself alongside you? Just to get you to take Danny's case. It doesn't make sense.'

'He's her – our – son. Understandably, she'd do anything for him, wouldn't she? But I didn't know then that he was mine. Maybe she thought this was the only way to *coax* me.'

She smiled wryly.

'Touché. But do you really think that?'

'It makes sense, doesn't it?'

Her lips twisted sceptically.

'And would *you* do anything for him?'

'Of course!' I sounded too emphatic to be believable. I prepared my defence but the

attack didn't come; not in the way I'd anticipated, anyway.

'Lawrence, leaving all the rest of it aside for the moment, have you thought about what you're going to do if and when this *is* all sorted out?'

I was taken aback by the complete shift in emphasis.

'As in?'

'Well, if you manage the transition I suspect you're anticipating, it won't be easy taking on a child of ten with a *past*. Have you thought about what that's going to entail?'

'Being responsible, I suppose.'

Heather crossed the room and pulled a bottle of white wine out of her outsize American-style fridge. She poured two large glasses and had half emptied hers before I even picked mine up. I watched her curiously. She was rattled by something.

'A little more than that, I think. It strikes me this is more like a game of cards where you don't hold any aces. You're accepting Margaret's claim that Danny's yours without question, I take it?'

'If Margaret says he is, he is.'

She raised her eyebrows.

'And she's been so truthful with you up until now ...'

'I have to start believing *something*.'

'But you don't have to believe *everything* ...'

'Why would she lie about it? Anyway, the rest of the paperwork seems to concur with the probability – the birth certificates in Sarah's keepsakes box ...'

'Paperwork can be altered; you know that.'

I struggled to remember what Margaret had said in those snatched moments of kaleidoscope pattern confusion.

'She said he was ours. It's in her letter too. And...'

She raised an eyebrow.

'My blood test results have the same genetic markers as his.'

'You're not a haemophiliac though.'

'My father – my *real* father – was. Margaret's father was too.'

'Damn!' she said, grimacing.

'Why are you suddenly questioning this? I know you don't trust her, but when we met she was ...' I couldn't define it. She watched me struggling. 'Different,' was all I could manage eventually.

'Different.' She looked thoughtful. 'You mean *she* was different or you *see* her differently in relation to yourself now because of the boy?' She paused, waiting for me to answer, but I couldn't. It was the same question the little imp in my head had been posing regularly ever since the possibility of her being alive had been a consideration. She continued, 'And I don't know who might have been in that apartment, if anyone, but surely if it was Margaret with Danny – your wife with your son – don't you think she'd have wanted you to find them? I think you need to be very careful.'

'Heather, I have to help her – she's my wife. I've let her down – let everyone down all the way along the line. Now I have to make amends.'

'To be squeaky clean, or white-washed?'

'To be someone decent, not a sham.'

She sighed melodramatically.

'Sometimes I forget you are an intelligent man with the ermine almost round your shoulders. Sometimes I think you're more Forrest Gump or Rain Man.'

'Cheers. I'm not a great movie buff but I know enough about those two to know you're calling me an imbecile.'

I picked up the glass of wine she'd poured for me and downed it in one. Heather pulled out one of the bar stools and perched on it like a small harpy, readying herself to tear me to shreds.

'Not an imbecile, but you've *been* blind, you *are* being blind and you're likely to *go on* being blind unless I pull the scales from your eyes. What have you got? A letter claiming to explain all, from a woman who's been lying to you for years. You tell me you're not acting like Forrest Gump!'

'So what are you suggesting I do?'

'Be cynical?'

'And you don't think I'm going to do that?'

'She's appealing to your proclivity to be a comic book hero. Stop being gooey-eyed about playing the Prince Charming to her damsel in distress. Honestly, you men – why does your dick always take precedence over your brain?'

'I didn't think it was.'

'Oh, Lawrence! Right – stay there. I'm going to show you what I mean.' She slipped off the stool, stilettos making rapid clicking sounds like one of the clackers we'd made as kids out of string and three pieces of coconut shell. She returned with an ornate hand mirror. 'Take it,' she instructed. I took it. 'Now look in it.' I positioned it so the reflection framed my whole face. 'Norton,' she said. I raised my eyebrows.

'Norton?'

'Think of this as an experiment. This is the control section – remember that from school? You set up a range of controls with a baseline response so you can monitor anomalies. This is your control experiment. Norton.'

'Poor bugger if all he ever manages is to be baseline response in a control experiment.'

'Take it seriously!'

'I am.'

'Norton,' she repeated. I watched but didn't notice any discernible difference in my expression. 'White wine.'

Approving but basically unmoved.

'I prefer red.'

'Shut up! Chambers.'

Serious expression.

'Gregory.'

Irritation. Heather smiled appreciatively.

'Kat Roumelia.' A tiny tic at the corner of my mouth. I tried to control it but it wouldn't go away. Heather's mouth twisted sardonically.

'Danny.' Fear.

'Margaret,' she said, after a long pause. My whole face jumped. 'OK. Got the idea?'

'No.' I was lying.

'Crap! Margaret has you jerking about however she wants you to – has always had you jerking about how she wants you to, I reckon. Even just saying her name makes you jump. Now do you get it? You need facts – not claims and clever little intrigues.'

I sighed. She was right. Whatever I tried to tell myself, she was right. I was jumping about at Margaret's behest again for one very uncomfortable reason. It was easier to react to a situation – and that was what Margaret kept creating – than to react to a person. And even if I was no longer ignoring Margaret and the subtle influence I now realised she'd been exerting on me ever since we'd first met, there was another person I was studiously trying to ignore. Danny.

'I'm afraid.' It was so quiet, I almost didn't believe I'd said it.

'I know,' she patted my hand and pulled the wine bottle over. She refilled my glass and topped up hers.

'I mean about Danny – not the rest of it, although that doesn't fill me with joy.'

'I know that too. Why do you think I'm helping you? It's not so you can sort out your mess of a love-life, or even to salvage your self-destructing career. It's because there's a very vulnerable child involved.'

'The problem is I don't know how to deal with a child, Heather. I never intended having one. Never wanted one. Danny has been foisted on me. I know I have to do the right thing – but I don't know what it is. And

I never had much of a role model in Pop, or the children's home.'

'You have your other siblings. How do they deal with their children?'

'Only Binnie has any and she'll barely speak to me.'

'Oh.' She fell silent, and then, 'I suppose that's to be expected. All right, you told me he has a nickname for you. You're only given a nickname when you're liked.'

'We get on in a genial, semi-professional kind of way, but that's only because I'm a novelty, and he's my …'

'… guilty conscience,' she completed for me. We stared at each other. 'But you're going to have to face it one day, Lawrence,' she said gently. 'Really face it.'

'Parenthood or conscience?'

'Both. Facts, Lawrence. Work on facts.'

I put my glass down decisively.

'I need to go to this Crahan House and St Rosemary in the Marsh and find the facts –maybe the evidence too.'

'And what facts are you focusing on?'

'I don't know. I thought I had them – from Margaret and in that letter, but now you seem to be suggesting I don't.'

She twirled her glass stem.

'Some truths are only on the inside,' she said reflectively. 'But maybe you still need to work that yourself. Eventually you're going to have to face the music with Fredriks so I guess you might as well have something worth giving him when you do. OK, forget everything you've been told and start at the beginning.'

'The very beginning? The murder eleven years ago?'

'I don't know – perhaps even before then. Perhaps at this place Rosemary Flowers is buried or somewhere else, but start asking questions instead of accepting explanations. Be what you are: a barrister. Challenge the truth until you're sure it is the truth. This is as much about yours as about Margaret's.'

It occurred to me that Win had made that point too, right at the start when he said it had to be personal to matter, and I'd ignored him whilst pretending it was. Like with my clients, it had been personal only to the extent that I'd been determined to beat my opponent. It had been to win Danny's case so I could beat Jaggers – not to discover the truth.

'Maybe you'll even find out where our money is along the way, too.' Heather's lips had a wry twist to them again but this time she was amused.

'I haven't any transport to go anywhere to find anything now, though,' I retorted moodily. I sounded like Danny when he was being truculent. I took a mouthful of the refill Heather had poured me, and hung miserably over the glass.

'I can't cope with that – here or in Chambers,' she sighed. 'You can take my car tomorrow.'

'Really?' Heather's pride and joy – more so even than my Austin Healey. I was amazed.

'Go and get it sorted so you can get back to work and stop sponging off me!' she added wryly.

The alcohol-fuelled fire of impulsiveness made my limbs twitch impatiently. Why wait until tomorrow? I wanted answers now.

'Maybe I should start straight away. I've got a lot of people and places to see.'

'Tomorrow, Lawrence. Don't compound everything else you've done by drinking and

driving too.' She fished in her handbag for her car keys. 'But look after it. It's my baby,' she added sternly. I took the keys and slid off the bar stool.

'Thanks.' I made for the door, ignoring her outraged protest but didn't get much further than that. The doorbell rang and I stopped. 'Are you expecting someone?'

Heather brushed past me in a cloud of expensive perfume and officiousness, plucking the car keys from my fingers. She gave me a look that would have withered the parsley if there had been enough of it left. She returned with the last person – but one – I wanted to see right then. DCI Fredriks.

3: Peep Show

'Lawrence Juste?' Fredriks voice preceded him along the passageway. 'I thought he might be here?' It only marginally preceded him into the kitchen. He was moving fast – much faster than me. 'Ah, I was right.' He marched in without being invited, grinning complacently. A bad move by anyone, let alone someone not necessarily welcome in Heather's home. DS Jewson paced greasily behind him, still sweating. I wondered if he over-perspired even in winter. 'We've had a bit of a development.' Fredriks gestured to the empty bar stools and made to sit on one of them. 'Shall we?' I looked over his shoulder at Heather who'd now followed them to the kitchen door and was hovering, fuming in the doorway. She gave Jewson a look of immense distaste, nodded imperceptibly as if making a decision and melted away, leaving me trapped. I hoped she was going to call Norton.

'What development might that be, Inspector?' I hedged.

'You know, for a barrister, you have a surprisingly bad memory,' he replied. '*Detective Chief* Inspector.' He grinned genially and the habitual duck pout spread across his face like a clown's mouth splitting wide open, but his eyes remained cold and hard.

'*Detective Chief* Inspector, what developments have you encountered?'

'We've got the photos back from the camera we found in the basement at that charity HQ you sent us to. Very interesting. Very interesting indeed.' The grin abruptly disappeared. 'Where's your brother?'

'Home – isn't he?' It suddenly occurred to me I didn't know where home was for Win.

'Really? We lucked out there when we paid a visit. Must be something we said when we saw him last.'

'"You're nicked" probably wouldn't have helped much.' I hoped I looked as cool as I sounded, but Heather's recent experiment threw doubt on that. Fredriks continued to observe me closely. He smiled again.

'Indeed, I'm sure it didn't. Shame we're likely to have to say it again now, isn't it?'

'The photographs?'

'Indeed again. Your brother claims to not have been anywhere near your kitchen when your sister was murdered, yet there he is, brandishing the very knife she was stabbed with.'

'Jesus!'

'No, he wasn't there, but I think your brother might be needing one of his miracles to wriggle out of a murder charge this time. So, as he's not home – where is he? You're his brief as well as his brother. I assumed you would know.'

I played for time by knocking over one of the wine glasses. It soaked Fredriks' arm. As I apologised profusely and shoved yards of kitchen roll at him to mop up, to my relief Heather quietly reappeared. Her acid tone cut across my distraction tactics.

'Are you officially interviewing Lawrence because I haven't heard a formal warning yet?' She smiled icily at Fredriks.

'More a friendly request for assistance,' Fredriks batted the challenge straight back.

'Friendly doesn't make threats or assertions, DCI Fredriks.' She came forward and held out her hand as if to shake. 'Heather Trinder, we've met before – remember?' She could have added *and I didn't like you much then either* but Fredriks' expression made it clear he'd already added the aside for her. The rough policeman became all charm.

'I *do* remember. My apologies. A little too keen to find the killer of Mr Juste's sister, but I should have observed the niceties nevertheless.' He took her hand just as she made to whisk it away. They squared up to each other like pugilists. Heather coloured. I'd never seen her blush before. I looked from her to Fredriks. The atmosphere was electric. Power play? No, if it wasn't so absurd, I would have said attraction, but I definitely couldn't trust my judgement on that score. Heather tugged at her hand and he reluctantly let go. She broke eye contact first.

'Apology accepted,' she looked flustered. 'So let's deal with the niceties then, shall we? You say you are looking for Lawrence's brother, Winston Juss, but he hasn't gone missing. He was merely not at home when you called – is that right?' Fredriks nodded, still staring unwinkingly at Heather but the icy cool QC was back in control again. 'Then it is inappropriate that you harass Lawrence about something you should simply be dealing with as an administrative matter, is it not?' Fredriks blinked. The same as my reaction to Kat in Heather's control section of the mirror experiment.

'My apologies again, but *harass*, Mrs Trinder? I was merely asking his advice,' he countered, smiling. She swept on, apparently ignoring him but I knew she hadn't.

'And he hasn't yet been charged with an offence requiring him to remain in touch with you – or be on a curfew – has he?'

'No.' He smiled again.

'Then it is obligatory that you provide his representatives with any new evidence you may be presenting against him if he is about to be charged.' Fredriks didn't reply, just waited, presumably patiently admiring the power of a beast on the attack as much as I was. 'I therefore suggest you share that with Lawrence now whilst we're waiting.' That produced a Margaret response. She didn't say "for Norton" but I could see from Fredriks' face that we'd we both inserted it this time. Heather smiled complacently.

Fredriks clearly knew when he was beaten, yet he seemed unconcerned. He nodded amusedly and gestured to DS Jewson who promptly produced a pack of photos. He'd come already prepared. Heather's eyebrows twitched and she regarded him with renewed interest. The folder of photos still displayed Jewson's damp thumb print on the glossy card cover. Her smile disappeared as he spread the photographs out across the breakfast bar and it became apparent to us how Win's fate had been sealed.

They didn't record the actual killing. They recorded the argument that appeared to lead up to it. Win and Kimmy both gesticulating angrily at each other, faces contorted with rage. Kimmy wielding one of Margaret's rapier sharp Sabatiers, and finally Win wrestling the knife off of her, raising his arm about to strike; the implication was obvious. There then followed a series of over-exposed blurred images, concluding with Kimmy on the floor – burgundy red seeping from under her hunched body.

'Jesus!' I said again, sickened but also uneasy. Win had his bad points but I couldn't believe he'd murder his own sister – yet there seemed no disputing that he might have. There was something else that made me uneasier still; the photos reminded me of a series of tableaux, set scenes – almost as if someone had carefully drawn then photographed the murder as they imagined it would happen. I'd originally wondered if the artist of the drawings I'd been sent was Danny, but he surely wouldn't have coldly drawn the murder of the woman he believed to be mother, would he? So it must be someone else. Someone who'd perhaps had a hand in these photos too.

Heather beat me to it. 'Who was the photographer?'

'We have no idea, but someone knows more than they're saying, don't they?' Fredriks looked meaningfully at me.

'So what are you doing to identify – and find – the photographer?' I asked, ignoring the implication.

'We need some help with that, so we're going back to talk to your neighbours – such as are still living in the mews after your little,' he hesitated, 'mishap.' He paused. 'We hoped one of them might have noticed some other comings and goings on the day, otherwise the only person we know was at home round about the right time was you, sir.' The beady eye was firmly on me now.

'I told you, I'd gone out before any of this happened. I was visiting my sister, Sarah.'

'Who is no longer with us ...'

'I thought we went through all this at the time. I went to see my sister because I knew she didn't have long to live. It seemed appropriate after I'd just said goodbye to my wife. At least I could say goodbye to my sister whilst she was *still* alive. The staff at the nursing home can confirm the time I was there – I had to sign in and out at reception. *Green Lawns*; part of the Green Healthcare group, near Hampton Court.' I wondered again about the possibility of a link between it, Margaret and Jaggers, given Margaret's maiden name. Another fact I would have followed up on by now if I'd been acting like Lawrence Juste: professional, and not Lawrence Juste: ingenuous fool. 'Presumably you now have an accurate time of death so you can rule me out if you corroborate my time of arrival and departure with the nursing home.' I sounded angry, and realised with surprise I was. It somehow made a mockery of Sarah's sad and lonely death that I might have to use it to fend off a murder charge myself.

'Convenient.'

'I think that's enough DCI Fredriks!' Heather sounded angry too. 'Lawrence is trying to help and now you are simply being offensive. I don't like bad manners.'

The result was dramatic. Fredriks backed off, apologised, gathered up the photographs and left, but not before he'd made it clear that he expected me to tell him as soon as Win was in touch with me, if not sooner. Jewson trudged out behind him, touching the edge of the front door as he went and leaving a slimy finger trail across it like a snail slithering away. Heather watched their departing backs like a warrior queen defending her castle until they rounded the corner of the stairs. Then she tottered back to the kitchen, took a slug of wine from the unspoilt glass and grabbed a handful of kitchen roll to wipe away the evidence of invasion.

'Ugh,' she shivered. 'Where do they get these creeps from?' She flung the paper in the waste bin and the lid shut on it with a heavy clang.

I shivered too. The photos, and what they implied, made my skin crawl too.

'Hadn't you better ring Norton to tell him he doesn't need to be the cavalry now?'

'Norton? Oh, he's not coming over. He just told me how to play it.'

'My God, Heather, you're a cool customer!' I laughed appreciatively.

'Hmm,' she smiled. 'But so is Fredriks. You'd better be careful of him.'

'I thought you won that round pretty easily.'

'He let us win.' I almost missed the flash of admiration, it was so quickly masked. 'He wanted to see what your reaction was. He didn't actually expect to get any information out of you.'

I sighed. Reaction to seeing Kimmy's body shortly after the murder and the possibility of her killer being Win had clouded my objectivity, but Fredriks wouldn't have given up so easily if he'd really thought there was information to be dragged from me.

'I hadn't thought of it that way, but you're right of course. He will have already checked up on me long ago. That was why he barged in – and overlooked the *niceties*. Fredriks isn't one to overlook anything. He just wanted to wind me up a bit, didn't he?'

'And now he wants to see what you do and where you go. He thinks you'll lead him to Win. So where is he?'

'I don't know. But I'm sure of one thing. He's not a killer, whatever those photos suggest – and didn't something strike you as odd about them?'

'Such as?'

'If you were present when you thought a murder was about to be committed – someone waving a knife around, for instance – wouldn't you run for help, not calmly photograph it? And secondly, if you'd opted to record the murder instead of prevent it, wouldn't you make damn sure you caught it all on film?'

'Some of them were blurred. Maybe the photographer lost their nerve?'

'A sociopath who misses the vital moment because of camera shake?'

'OK, you've got a point. So you think these were set up? But Win would have to have been cooperating, if so.'

'No, I think, like a lot of this, it was staged without the participants knowing. Maybe Kimmy might have joined in, engineering the argument for the photographer because Win said she wanted payback. Maybe she thought this was part of a blackmail scam that would get her it, little knowing what would happen to her afterwards. But payback for what? I know one thing now, though; it's all part of the same dirty game, and the only person who's playing dirty games with me is Jaggers. I need to find Margaret again in case she's next, and then I need to find Win.'

'But that's exactly what Fredriks wants you to do,' Heather reminded me.

'I know, but two heads are better than one, and as you said, Fredriks has a pretty smart one. Maybe I can't figure out what's going on alone, but with the combined resources of the Metropolitan Police behind me … if he's going to be on my tail anyway, why not use him to advantage?'

Heather's warning, 'Lawrence …' didn't make a lot of difference. She'd unwisely left her car keys on the hall table after relieving me of them, and I knew where I was going first.

4: Pacts

My idea was to track Win down via the same route I needed to take to find Margaret. That way Fredriks would also find Margaret – and the box of evidence – when he found Win. Maybe it was lucky Kat stopped me.

'*Lawrence!*'

Or perhaps I should say Heather stopped me because of Kat.

'Kat's on the phone for you. Danny's threatening to run away again unless he can see you.' She stood peremptorily by the kitchen door, cordless phone extended. She raised her eyebrows. 'Priorities,' she reminded me.

I temporarily gave up on my idea and retraced my steps. I took the phone from Heather, and Heather snatched the car keys back from me with a toss of her head. Ruefully I watched the keys be borne away as I listened to Danny's relayed demands, wondering how I would ever persuade Heather to relinquish them again now.

'He wants to talk to you, and he wants to go to the seaside for the day.'

I listened to the demands incredulously. 'Are children always this dictatorial?'

'No, but I think he can be forgiven for stamping his foot a bit at the moment, don't you? He's lost a mother and father in one fell swoop and he feels like he's just been abandoned in the children's home again. Not many kids have to put up with that kind of thing at only ten.'

'I remember it well,' I replied dryly.

'Oh, I'm sorry.' She went silent and I took pity on her.

'It's OK. It was a long time ago now. Maybe it's time I moved on from it.'

'Even so – I didn't mean to be so insensitive,' she sounded genuinely sorry.

Truce. We both paused, embarrassment on my part for behaving like a petulant child, God knows what on hers; unsure exactly how and where to move on to.

'Does he really mean it?' I asked in the end.

'Well, he's done it twice before … but short of keeping him in chains in his room, the children's home can't keep an eye on him every second of the day and night, can they? Given his circumstances we thought maybe it would be better if we allowed ourselves to be blackmailed this time.'

'Or allowed me to be?'

'We-ell, sorry …'

'Danny wants a day out to the seaside,' I repeated for Heather's benefit, then back to Kat, 'The problem is, Kat,' I glanced back at Heather, 'I don't have a car anymore …' Heather planted herself in front of me, lips compressed in exasperation and dangling the BMW keys in front of my nose. Who said you don't get third chances? 'Oh, I do have a car, it seems.'

'Priorities,' she hissed irritably again as I swopped the phone for the car keys once Kat had rung off. 'But do it properly. Maybe it'll be good PR for the press if they catch up with you too.' She paused, 'in fact, perhaps you *should* let them catch up with you?'

'*Heather* …'

'OK, maybe not. You'd probably say something out of turn and then I'd have to twist more arms for favours. Just don't get ice cream on the upholstery.' She headed back towards the kitchen, turning at the door. 'And make sure he has a nice time. He's a kid, remember. Not a problem.'

A kid, not a problem. True, but he was also a kid *with* a problem – me. Heather was back to trimming the parsley, albeit more kindly now. I perched back on the bar stool.

She eyed me between snips.

'And?'

'Well, what do you do on a day out to the seaside?'

She stared at me, amazed.

'What did *you* do as a kid on a day out to the seaside?'

'I didn't have days out to the seaside.'

'I thought the children's home was in Eastbourne? That's the seaside, isn't it?'

'It's on the coast, but it's not the seaside in the way kids think of the seaside. It was desolation-on-sea as far as I was concerned.'

I remembered the twisted line of trees dividing land from dunes, blasted by the cold Atlantic winds, and the iron grey sea that rolled up the dirty yellow sand the times we were allowed onto the beach. A treat, it was called. A treat to collect driftwood for the Governor's fire, marching two miles out and back along the wet sand in the direction of Beachy Head, faces freezing and fingers blue with cold. Our legs were the only warm parts of us, burning with the effort of walking on the sinking sands at the same pace we would have been expected to march on pavement. We never had the treat on a warm summer's day, only on the desperately miserable ones where the sky threatened and the wind bit. I suppose we would have come into contact with real seaside-goers if we'd been treated during the balmy-breezed days of June or July, and that would have been inappropriate in the Governor's eyes, mewling orphans that we were.

Heather frowned. 'Do you want to talk about it?'

I shook my head as I had with my sister Emm when she'd asked me the same thing.

'It makes it real to remember it aloud. If it's just in my head it doesn't dignify the experience with celebration of any sort.' It was one of the few times I'd seen Heather lost for words.

'OK,' she said eventually. 'If it hadn't been desperation-on-sea, what would you have liked to have done?'

'What we did once when I was about four and we went to visit Auntie Edie in Deal.'

'So you did have outings to the seaside!'

'One outing to the seaside.'

'And?'

'We went on a bus. A "works outing" for the family.'

'Was it so bad?'

I remembered Auntie Edie, stern but fair.

'No, not so bad. No ice cream though. No money for it.' Sandcastles, gritty sandwiches and the cool sea water trickling between my toes as the wavelets rippled up the sea-weedy shoreline we'd elected to build our fort on. Sarah collected us a bucketful of seashells to decorate the castle mound with, and Binnie had industriously studded it with them whilst Win and I dug out the moat. Georgie had watched, eyes dreamy and far-away as he often was even then. We placed the seaweed around the moat like grasslands and it looked as desolate as the beach at Eastbourne had six years later.

'The army'd make camp outside,' Win informed us authoritatively, as if he'd know. He boasted he didn't listen at school and history was boring, but maybe that was a lie. 'They'd have loads of blacksmiths and stuff to make swords too so they could chop off people's heads.' He swung a pretend sword at me and I ran away to hide behind Sarah.

'The King wouldn't allow his army to just cut off anyone's heads,' Binnie told him snootily. 'He'd be fair and honest. You don't know nothing!'

Even then, Sarah was the truce-maker, trying to stop us sliding into a squabble. She made Win the fair and honest king of the castle and was about to negotiate the truce between him and Binnie when Ma called us all back.

'Shush now,' Sarah cautioned. 'Pop won't like it.'

'Don't care! I ain't being told what to do by no girls. I'm king of the castle,' Win bragged.

'Only because we made you it,' Binnie countered.

Maybe she and Win had been at war in their own small way even then. Sarah shushed us again and then dragged us all, still quietly bickering, back up the sand to Ma and Pop and Pip and Jim, only just toddling at barely one year old.

'You kids arguing?' Pop's intervention was more forceful than Sarah's. 'Won't have arguing.' His thumbs went into his belt like they always did when we were about to come under threat from it. 'I'll have something to say about it if you are. Better things to do than listen to brats squalling.'

'No Pop,' Sarah answered for us. 'Making up games, that's all. Win's going to be the king of the castle and we're never going to war.' Win sat in the sand and sulked. I plopped down with Georgie, wary that Pop's belt might be unbuckled if we weren't careful. Being at the seaside wouldn't make any difference to whether someone got a stripe or two for annoying him. Sarah sat with the twins and poured dry sand over their podgy legs until they wriggled and laughed because it tickled. Binnie loitered the other side of Georgie, as far out of the family group as possible. Of course, I hadn't understood it then – far too young – but I saw us then as a parody of what we we'd become now.

Pop looked irritated.

'Cat got your tongues?'

The moment might have lengthened into trouble if it hadn't been for the seagull that pooped on my head. I felt like a soft patter of rain, and I looked skywards in surprise. It was clear blue from horizon to the heavens – it couldn't be raining. I patted my head where the rain had fallen and my fingers came away white and sticky. Win shouted with laughter.

'He shat on you – that one!' He pointed to the swooping gull that was by now heading back out to sea, bombs delivered. 'Kenny's a poop-head!'

I can't remember whether I laughed or cried now. It could have been either. Probably cried. Ma swept to the rescue this time, wiping away the bird's deposit with her hanky.

'Hush Win – it ain't funny,' she rebuked him, 'is it Pop?' Pop humphed in disgust at my dismayed expression.

'Toughen up, my lad. It's only shite. Get plenty more of that on you in life,' and stomped away down to the water's edge, lighting a smoke as went. I watched the thin grey trail wavering in the air above his head as he surveyed us from a distance, wondering why he seemed to dislike us all so much. Surprising he was even with us today, other than that Auntie Edie was his aunt, not Ma's.

'It's lucky,' Ma continued. 'Didn't you know it's lucky?'

'How's having a bird shit on me head lucky?' I complained.

'It's a gift.'

'Shit ain't a gift,' I argued.

'Everything in life is a gift, Kenny – even what looks like shit.'

I wasn't convinced but the threat of Pop's displeasure and the unbuckling of his belt if I complained further was enough to silence me. We ate our gritty sandwiches in silence. When Pop wandered back up to join us and brusquely demanded his lunch, Ma sent us back down the beach to our sandcastle, now sinking beneath the waves.

Win kicked it and it collapsed on one side.

'It's ruined,' I mourned.

'Yeah,' he said, moodily. He picked up a handful of pebbles and began skimming them, counting the bounces before they plopped into the sea. I watched admiringly, but conscious everyone else was subdued.

'We could mend it,' suggested Sarah after a while. 'We'd have to do it together, and maybe build a sea wall,' she added.

'Yeah – better'n ever,' enthused Win unexpectedly, whirling round all smiles.

'Binnie, what d'you think?' Sarah asked brightly.

'S'pose.' Binnie scuffed the sand and shrugged her shoulders.

'Come on then,' Win grabbed one of our brittle red spades, remnant of someone else's trip to the seaside. 'Binnie, you start digging one end,

Kenny, you do the other end. I'll build the castle up again. Sarah you can find more shells. Georgie – he's watchman. He ain't any good for anything else.'

Binnie scuffed a bigger hole in the sand.

'I ain't being told what to do by you. You ain't boss.'

'I'm king,' Win squared his shoulders and pulled himself up to his full height, inches taller than Binnie. 'And I'm oldest. I *am* boss.'

'Pop's boss and I'll tell him you're arguing again if you try to boss me around.'

Sarah leapt in again. Little Mother – perhaps more of a mother to us than Ma at times like these.

'If Win's king, why don't we all have roles in court? Binnie, you can be queen, I'll be court counsel, Kenny, you're the brave warrior because luck is on your side now, and Georgie will be our court lookout, watching for when the tide's coming in too far.'

'Yeah – and you all have to do what I say?' Win crowed. 'See?'

Sarah turned to him.

'No, Win, we all have a job to do and we'll swear to each other that we'll do it. You can't be king unless your brave warrior Kenny leads your army into battle for you, and without a lookout, you won't know when danger's coming. A king always needs a queen to look after his castle, and a wise man to give him advice when there are problems. We can't do any of that unless we have a king to serve. We're a team.'

He stared at her.

'So what do we do, then?'

It was the first time I'd ever seen Win listen to reason, even though I didn't understand that was what it was then; to me we were just playing an elaborate game Sarah was inventing to keep Win and Binnie from fighting. Do elaborate games continue all your life, changing only dependent on the game-maker?

'We swear loyalty to each other, and then we all do our jobs.'

'OK, what do we swear?'

Sarah held up her right hand and put her left hand on her chest, over her heart. 'Say after me: I swear to always look after my king and court, and my king swears to always look after me. Family sticks together.' We all solemnly made our vows and Binnie decorated each of us with a piece of seaweed denoting the royal crest. Then we toiled until we had a new and better castle and a vast wall shielding it from the sea. We worked with barely any discussion, and no bickering. When it was done, we admired it, waves trickling in over our toes as the tide continued its steady invasion but was halted – for a time – by the sea wall. Win even showed me how to skim stones before we went home and I managed my first fiver.

'See what we do when we do it together?' Sarah said.

I'd forgotten that day until now, buried in the surfeit of other memories I'd struggled to forget. Family. We had been one once – bickering and all. The memory accompanied me to the seaside with Danny and Kat. It was a different seaside, and with different people, but the theme was the same.

5: Eastbourne

Danny repeated Heather's misconception of the seaside for me when we arrived to pick him up the next day and Kat asked where in particular he wanted to go. I'd been thinking of our clandestine big wheel ride when he'd just been diagnosed with haemophilia and had run away from the hospital, landing up on my doorstep. I expected him to suggest Brighton and the accompanying fairground rides so I pre-empted by suggesting them myself but was completely taken by surprise when he shook his head vehemently.

'Where, then?'

It was an unwelcome alternate choice.

'Where you lived as a kid. She said you lived by the seaside in a big home like the one I'm in now. I want to see what it were like for you.'

I eyed Kat accusingly, forgetting our unspoken truce for the moment.

'Why did you tell him?'

'I didn't.' She frowned. 'Who told you about that, Danny?'

'*She* did. She told me lots about you and everyone when she got me from the hospital.'

There was little doubt who the *'she'* was who'd got him from the hospital. *'Margaret Juste, aunt,'* the form had brazenly stated. My gut twisted the way it always did when Margaret was involved. I was getting to know the feeling intimately now – a kind of churning, fluttering feeling, extending from my belly to my chest. I wasn't sure anymore whether it was anger, fear or desire and I didn't want to examine it too closely for the moment. Certainly not with Kat around, who I'd discovered since we'd met again that morning – truce in place – still produced the old burning inside me if I didn't consciously ignore it. I could see Kat was about to interrogate him so I jumped in first.

'Someone from the children's home. I see.' I replied casually.

'No,' he stared at me as if I was stupid. 'She came to see Mum…' he broke off and looked at me worriedly. 'Do I still talk about her as if she's alive now she's not?'

I swallowed hard – both at his use of 'mum' and the fact that Kimmy wasn't either his mum or alive. Kat was now watching me as intently as she had been Danny, waiting for me to answer – presumably deferring to the fact that Kimmy was my sister, or just plain curious how I was going to deal with this. I couldn't. All the lies I had once been able to trot out stuck in my throat and I was wordless. She frowned then answered for me.

'Of course you do, Danny – she's still your mum.'

'Ain't the same though. Ain't fair to have no-one.' His small bony face pinched to almost skeletal. The same odd feeling I felt whenever Margaret was involved invaded my chest again. I could identify it now. It wasn't desire – or fear or anger – it was … uncertainty. I felt uncertainty for him, like the uncertainty I'd felt for myself as a lost child. We were both lost.

'We'll go to Eastbourne,' I told to Kat. I owed him – at least ten years of debt, unrepayable, of course, but scourging myself to satisfy his curiosity would be a start. Her eyes widened in surprise whilst her lips mouthed *not a good idea*. Very little was a good idea at the moment – other than shouldering some of my son's uncertainty in a way I'd had no-one to help with when I'd been him almost forty years ago. I simply shrugged at her. She didn't understand, and it was best she didn't. 'But, Brighton's more fun,' I added to deflect her.

'No, Eastbourne,' he insisted, clamping his mouth into a small grimace. I found I was already doing the same and wondered if we looked alike. Heather would have told me. I made an effort to smile nonchalantly. I actually almost wished for Heather to be here instead of Kat.

Danny took place of honour in the front passenger seat of Heather's BMW, top down in deference to the sunshine. Kat squashed in the back. If I looked in the rear view mirror I could just see her corkscrew curls wriggling like small snakes fighting in the back-draught as we drove. She appeared to be in a world of her own, coolly neutral, but I suspected she was also listening carefully to my conversation with Danny, such as it was.

'This is a girl's car,' he accused me.

'True. It belongs to my business partner, Heather Trinder. She's lent it to me for the day.'

'Where's yours?'

'Off the road.'

'You crashed it?'

'No,' I hesitated, then decided to satisfy his boyish appreciation of the dramatic. 'It blew up.'

'Coo! How?'

'An accident – of a sort. I'll replace it eventually. In the meantime, this might be a girl's car but it can still go some. Shall we see how much?'

'*Oh, yeah!*'

I grinned. Uncertainty aside, boys were still boys and that was something Danny and I most certainly had in common. I put my foot down on the accelerator and watched the speedo nudge steadily up to ninety-five. It elicited the first reaction from Kat since she'd got in the car. Her face bobbed into view in the rear view mirror, cautioning. She didn't say anything but I knew what she was thinking – *irresponsible* ... I ignored her, the little imp in my head urging me on instead of holding me back for once.

'Shall we do a ton, Danny?'

He nodded vigorously, eyes glued to the road ahead.

'Yeah!'

In the rear view mirror, Kat shook her head at me, and mouthed 'no'. She catapulted backwards as the accelerating car plastered her to her seat.

'Better'n the big wheel!' Danny yelled excitedly. 'You're the best, Mr B!'

As we topped a hundred Danny whooped triumphantly. The child inside me did the same, but silently, then I allowed the speed to drop back to sixty-eight. I sensed rather than saw Kat relax, but Danny's face was fixed in a permanent grin. We continued the next ten miles or so in a buzz of Danny's chatter about speed films, car chases and getaways, with barely the need for either Kat or I to respond. The little imp had been right – even established a tentative bond between us. I left him to chatter on, suddenly more relaxed myself, despite our destination and its associated memories. Odd. I even allowed one or two of them to slip though the wall of denial – the infrequent but occasional good ones, that is. The ones I would once have recorded in my diary in sunshine yellow, not dismal black. Gradually his chatter lessened and he settled into watching the countryside rush by, grin still tacked in place. We continued in companionable silence that way for most of the rest of the journey.

'Weird name,' Danny commented suddenly as we approached the

outskirts of Eastbourne. I'd been lost, back at one day at the seaside I treasured.

'Deal? It's in Kent.'

'What?'

I flicked a quick glance at Danny to find him staring at me.

'Sorry – mind elsewhere. What's a weird name?'

'Scout. But it's in the book, isn't it? It's the girl.'

My childhood treasure – and now Danny's: *To Kill a Mockingbird*.

'Have you started reading it then?'

'Yeah. The man has a funny name too.'

'Atticus.'

'Yeah. He's like you.' I wasn't quite sure how to take that. It seemed like he was paying me a compliment. I was about to make the sort of simpering but inane response you make to compliments when he shot me down. 'He's a lawyer anyway. That makes you the same, don't it?'

'Well, similar.' I was disappointed he thought that was our only similarity. 'He's the book's hero – a lawyer who understood what was really right to do, regardless of what everyone else wanted him to do.'

'Rellyvent, you mean.' I could feel him watching me. I smiled.

'Very relevant, Danny. Makes all the difference to the way we live our lives, knowing what we *should* do rather than what we're *expected* to do – but he's a hard act to follow.'

'Do you know the right thing to do?'

'I think we all instinctively know when something's right, it's just difficult doing it at times.'

'Do you *do* the right thing?'

'I'd like to.'

He was silent again. Then, 'That ain't the same, is it?'

'No, it isn't the same,' I agreed, surprised by the perspicacity of a ten year old. I could see Kat's lips twist in amusement. *Yes, very funny.*

He nodded, still studying me, then went back to staring out of the window for the rest of the way. I wanted to ask him what had made him mention Scout so particularly but couldn't think of a way to broach it, so I remained silent too.

We arrived in Eastbourne just before lunch time and as food had always been the way to Danny's heart I suggested we start by finding somewhere to eat near the sea front. I refused McDonald's out of principle but agreed to a small café looking out over the prom. The old-fashioned gentility of the typically British seaside resort was alive and thriving here. The chintzy drapes and pristine white tablecloths of bygone years threw me back into my melting pot of memories only to emerge scarred and raw. Cafés, restaurants and most shops were banned from the boys at 'the home' but I'd sneaked into one once, curious what they were like. Memorising the inside of the small teashop I'd peeked into had enabled me to imagine Ma arriving out of the blue at the children's home, with Pop uncharacteristically good-tempered, to whisk me away from there. In the fantasy they explained it had all been a mistake and everything was going to be all right again now. This was to be our celebratory tea, in the tea shop I'd peered into.

The table was laden with plates, piled high with plump cake overstuffed with creamy fillings for the boys, dainty fairy cakes with pink frosting and silver sugar baubles for the girls. A bulging spherical teapot with matching cups like small bowls graced the centre of the table. I sat in pride of place, looking out of the window and down the promenade towards the pier and the sea. The tea shop could have been anywhere in my fantasy but now it seemed it must have been here. In my imagination, the girls slipped in opposite me, Emm and Jill shared between Sarah and Binnie's laps. Win and Georgie sat either side of me, whilst Pip and Jim played hide and seek under the table. Ma hovered over us, indulgently scolding the twins for their boisterousness and exhorting us to eat up, as she always had about even the most meagre meals. Pop leaned nonchalantly against the side wall, thumbs in his belt as usual, but smiling.

That was when I knew it wasn't real. Pop didn't smile at us. And our tea table was never laden. Lucky to have a slice of bread and a teaspoonful of dripping most of the time.

In the fantasy, I always stared at Pop at that point and then past him out the window at the prom stretching away into the sea. When I looked back there was no table, no cakes, no Ma. Just Win, Georgie and me, and the paltry high tea table at the children's home, Miss Liddell or one of the Houseparents hovering to reprimand perceived bad manners or inappropriate behaviour. There was none, but it was an opportunity too good to be missed – a small spillage, or a too healthy appetite. This time, when I looked along the pier and then back again, the scene didn't change. The promenade still stretched away to the sea but Danny remained opposite me and Kat diagonally opposite me. I sighed inaudibly and inside me something changed gear.

Danny had the café's alternative to a Big Mac; a double decker burger like a small volcano with melted cheese oozing down its slopes like flowing lava and a pool of ketchup next to the forest of chips in the valley below. He laid into his edible landscape with gusto, as I'd expected, spraying ketchup in small splatters on the snowy cloth because he insisted on eating the burger with his fingers instead of a knife and fork. By contrast, Kat ate her prawn sandwich over-daintily, wiping her mouth with the napkin in between each bite, as if she was trying to pass an exam in etiquette. And me? I had no appetite at all, having lost the calm of the journey as I now anticipated the place I knew was only a mile or so out of town, but a heartbeat away from hell.

Kat was watching me carefully in between minuscule bites.

'Penny for them?'

I shrugged, uncomfortably aware – after Heather's recent class on self-awareness – that my emotions were quite possibly already evident on my face.

'Not worth even that, Kat. How's the burger, Danny.' He beamed at me, mouth full, and nodded enthusiastically. I watched a lump of it go down his throat like a boa constrictor swallowing a small mammal. He spluttered and Kat patted him on the back.

'Is this Beachy Head?' he asked when the mammal had been assimilated.

'No this part is the Grand Parade. It leads to the pier that you can see behind you. The coastline one way is called Pevensey Bay and the other way, Beachy Head. It always felt cold to me on Beachy Head. Probably because it's so exposed. You can see almost a hundred miles of coastline from it – all along the Kent coast one way and towards Brighton the other.'

'Cool! Were there spies here during the war? They said at school that there are gun place things on the cliffs so they could machine gun the Germans.'

'Gun emplacements, you mean? Probably. I wasn't here during the war – either of them. Not *quite* old enough.' Kat giggled. Danny glowered at her.

'It's not funny, Miss. It was serious stuff.'

'I'm sorry, Danny, I was laughing at Mr Juste saying he wasn't quite old enough to be in the war.'

We exchanged glances. The inclination to tease back was intense – one of those casually intimate moments that I'd never experienced before I'd met Kat. Don't, the imp instructed. She's off-limits, remember? You still have a wife. I bit my lip. Danny silenced her mirth for me by studiously and obviously ignoring her like Win would have ignored Binnie when she taunted him as a child. The family likenesses – ah, the family likenesses. Now I knew they would be there, I could see them so easily. They must be in me too. I changed the subject.

'Pevensey Bay has a real castle, you know – Pevensey Castle. It was originally a Roman fort and then William the Conqueror built a castle there after the Battle of Hastings. There's definitely a gun emplacement there that was used in the Second World War.'

Danny's face lit up.

'Can we go there after Beachy Head and your place?'

'Wouldn't you rather just go there? More interesting, and amazing views along the coast.'

He shook his head.

'I want to see where you lived and if it's like where I do.'

I should have known when I noticed his likeness to my siblings and me that he wouldn't give up easily. I accepted defeat and we walked along the beach for a while after lunch, but Danny didn't want to go on the pier, or find somewhere for an ice cream, or build sandcastles.

'I can't do that no more,' he looked distressed.

'Why not,' I asked.

'That's what you do with your mum and dad. I ain't got none.'

So they'd told him Hewson wasn't his father? What else had they said? My mouth opened and shut. Kat got there before me again.

'Do you want to talk about it?' she ventured.

'Not to you. Sorry, Miss, you're nice an' all, but you don't understand.'

She linked arms with him.

'My dad died when I was fourteen, Danny. I might do.'

'What about your mum?'

'She died when I was twenty.'

'You were grown up then.'

'I still lost both of them.'

'But you had a mum 'til you were grown up?'

'Well, yes, but I have no mum or dad now.'

'But you aren't a kid. I am.'

He detached himself from her. He jabbed a finger at me.

'But you ...'

For a moment I thought he was accusing me. My skin crawled. I wasn't prepared for this. Then he shrugged despondently. It seemed I was off the hook. The coward in me was relieved, but simultaneously Heather's words still pricked my conscience. I shouldn't just walk away from him, even if I could. I was his father, even if for now, it was still my secret, and emotionally scourging myself with a visit to the home in Eastbourne didn't actually do anything for Danny. Helping him deal with what was happening to him right now, until I found the courage to share my secret with him, could.

Kat was looking offended and Danny truculent. Suddenly I realised it was up to me to deal with the situation before the day went completely off the rails. Ownership of Sarah's box must be rubbing off on me. Little Mother, and her wise counsel. How, though? Danny kicked a stone and it slithered down the top covering of shingle on the beach. It resurrected the memory I'd been preoccupied with on the way here – the sunshine ink memory – and an idea how to help Danny without letting Kat know what I was doing in case I still couldn't quite trust her. I patted my pockets in pretended sudden alarm, hoping I'd assimilated Heather's lesson as well as Danny had assimilated his burger.

'Kat, I think I might have left my wallet at the café after paying the bill.' I looked aghast – or so I hoped. 'It's got all my credit cards in it.'

'Oh, God! No! We'd better run back and see if they've found it!'

Now it was the turn of frustration. I practised looking apologetic.

'Damn! It could be picked up by anyone by the time I get there.' I grimaced and rubbed my side. 'My ribs – they were cracked or bruised in the fire. Either way I'm a wreck. I'm so sorry, we're going to take ages walking back there and probably lose all of Danny's time on the beach.'

'Oh dear,' she was genuinely concerned – the Kat I remembered; the real Kat, not the manipulated Kat. 'It's all right. You two stay here and collect shells or something. I'll run back for it.'

She glanced across at Danny, now miserably throwing pebbles into the sea a short distance from us. I almost laughed – perfect, even down to the pebbles. Instead I grinned my thanks – and let her go. Danny didn't seem to notice, lost in his world of childish dejection. I watched Kat, trudging back along the beach, head down doggedly as if wading through sludge, remembering so many similar walks long ago with no prize at the end of them – assumed or real, other than avoiding a caning for laziness. I felt mean for tricking her but not so mean as to call her back. She'd easily take thirty minutes or so, there and back, even though her legs were longer than my scabby little sticks had been.

I waited until she was about a hundred feet away before addressing Danny, not entirely sure how much or what to say yet. I could lengthen the distance and time before Kat returned though, giving myself more time to think.

'Come on, Danny. Shall we wander on? She'll find us as long as we stay on the beach.'

He tossed another stone angrily into the water and it made a plopping sound and the water spurted up in a small fountain where it sunk.

'Tony Jones can make them bounce on the water,' he replied irritably. 'Another thing I can't do.'

The sunshine ink memory blossomed from idea to words.

'It's called skimming and I can show you how to skim stones. Do you want me to? Your Uncle Win taught me – at the beach.' He turned round then. 'My brothers and I used to do it all the time when we were kids – mainly on the duck pond in the park even though it was banned in case we hit a duck. If we had, your Uncle Win would have waded in and brought it home for tea, I reckon.'

He laughed but then stopped abruptly.

'But is he me Uncle Win, and are you me uncle too?'

My skin crawled again and the little imp in my head urged, *'Go on. Now's your chance.'* But how could I? How could I explain all the lies to him, and that I was the biggest liar of them all, and still expect him to trust me?

'Why do you say that?'

'They told me not to think about you that way at the home. Said we'd need to talk about everything when it was sorted out but in the meantime I had to stay there with Mum gone, and me dad not me dad after all.'

Inwardly I heaved a sigh. They'd only told him about Hewson then, not the rest. That was yet to come.

'Was Miss Roumelia there when they talked to you?'

'No, not then. I think she knows about it though. She still calls you me uncle.'

'We sometimes call someone uncle or aunt even though they're not that really, but people are who you make them, Danny. And you make them close by allowing them to be so.' The irony of my wise words didn't escape me but sometimes lessons are slow in being learnt, and I was clearly a stubborn learner.

'But who'd I make close for me, now?

'Who do you want to be close for you?'

'You, even if you aren't me uncle.'

'Well, then I am.' I smiled encouragingly. He grinned back and the laughing child from the car journey here was back, only to disappear just as suddenly.

'But I still have to go back there without a mum and a dad, don't I? If I had a mum or a dad, I wouldn't have to – and it ain't a home, whatever they call it.' He kicked another pebble and it skittered into a clump of seaweed.

'Home is relative Danny. By that I mean, home can be lots of places for lots of reasons. For example, the fire at my home means technically I have no home now, until it's repaired. On the other hand, I do, because one of the people I work with – who pretends to be fierce, but isn't really,' I couldn't contain the smile when I pictured Heather, scissors in hand, massacring the parsley whilst simultaneously mothering me, 'has given me a home until then. I could say it's merely somewhere to stay, or it could be somewhere I go to feel safe and cared for. I can choose how I see it, even though I haven't got a choice where or what it is.'

'I only got the children's home. No-one gave me that, they just told me I had to go there.'

I hated myself then. Really hated.

'Then for the moment – like my temporary home – that could be your safe place.'

'But I don't like it there. There ain't no-one to talk to – no-one I like, anyway. If you was there I could talk to you, but you ain't.'

'What about your little sisters? They're there with you, aren't they?'

'Yeah, but,' he was disdainful, 'they're just babies.' He thought for a moment and then added awkwardly. 'I don't like having no-one to talk to, I mean *really* talk to. I ain't ever thought about that before. I always thought there was someone, even if they didn't listen all that much.'

I stared out to sea, unsure how to answer him. I hadn't had anyone to talk to either. I'd taken Lennox's advice and boxed everything, including my thoughts and my need for affection. That was how I'd got to here, as lonely as I'd been then. The only measure of comfort I'd had was in my multi-coloured pen and the words I wrote with it – long since destroyed so no-one else could read them. A burnt and dismantled box. The ashes of a lost childhood I had no desire to reconstitute or share, but this was my son – even if I was too much a coward to acknowledge him openly as such – and he deserved some comfort from me.

'I didn't either, Danny. I had two brothers in the same home as me but couldn't talk to either of them. Georgie was …' I hesitated. Did I tell him Georgie was an addict, probably already past saving even then, and Win a self-serving bully at the time? No, it was too bleak a prospect for a child facing the same situation as me. 'Georgie was ill and it was difficult to get through to him. My other brother – your Uncle Win – was out of reach in a different way. I had to rely on myself, so I talked to myself.'

'You was mad?' He looked incredulous, 'Like Mum said Aunt Mary is?'

'No, not mad.' I laughed ruefully – although my secret psychedelic diary might have been construed as such if anyone had seen it: mad – or bad. 'I kept a diary. I had a special pen to write it in – different coloured inks. I used red for things I was angry about, blue for my special thoughts, and yellow for the things I hoped would happen or that made me happy. Black was what happened every day. It was my rainbow, and the future was my pot of gold at the end of it because I knew one day, I'd leave there and be able to choose what I wanted to do. You could do the same.'

'I ain't got a diary or a multi-coloured pen.'

'You could have Danny. You just need a pen to write with. Anything will do – and it doesn't have to be in colours. Of course, that was just my way. You should do things your way, but things *will* change in the future, like they did for me. For the time being, you could talk to your diary when you can't talk to me.'

'And what will happen to me in the future?'

'I don't know. Like I don't know for myself. There are no certainties in life, only possibilities.'

'But I ain't got no possibilities either. I got nothing.'

He tossed another stone and it sank dismally, like the first one. I scoured the shoreline and picked out three smooth, flat pebbles, like tiny discuses.

'Here,' I beckoned him to me, rolling my sleeves up. He came, a trace unwillingly, mouth turned down at the corners. I manoeuvred him gently into position, and put the stone into the curve between forefinger and thumb. 'Loosen up and relax. We're going to swing your arm like you are polishing the top of a table. When your hand is as far forward as it will swing, let go of the stone.'

His small body felt frail curved into mine. An uncomfortable ache filled my chest cavity, different to the discomfort of cracked ribs, or the feeling of uncertainty Margaret caused. I guided his arm backwards into the position to swing and then propelled it forward, imagining our two arms a scythe and swinging through waving grass to make a clean cut. He let go of the stone slightly too early but it still bounced twice across the water.

'Oh wow!' he turned to me, face split wide in a grin. 'I did it! Can we do it again?'

'Of course. Do you want to try it on your own this time?' He looked uncertain. 'Come on then, we'll do it together again this time. There are plenty more on the beach for you to skim on your own.'

He curved back into me and grasped the stone. The salt tang in the air bit and the cry of the gulls overhead sounded like cheering. The waves rolled in and out, leaving a spumy tide mark on the smooth sand. I remembered the water trickling over my toes and Win, Binnie, Sarah and I digging and moulding, shaping and creating our castle as Georgie shouted excitedly whenever the sea tried, unsuccessfully, to breach our defences. The aching in my chest cavity turned to a bubble about to explode. I could almost have told him there and then. Maybe there were possibilities – even when you were sure there were none. Danny's arm guided mine this time, back in a long arc and forward, slicing the air. The stone flew long and low, skipping over the blue-grey undulations of the incoming tide, bouncing four times before sliding into the depths. He was jubilant. No stopping him this time – and he didn't need my help. The despondent child had gone. My child saw there were possibilities too.

We spent much of the remainder of our thirty minutes collecting pebbles for Danny to hurl back into the ocean, counting the bounces, and triumphantly celebrating each leap across the meniscus of the sea, until I spotted a speck that could be Kat, far off in the distance but making her way doggedly back towards us along the beach.

'What do you think about the future now, Danny?'

'What?'

'Well, do you see how things can change for the better when you least expect them to?'

'Yeah, s'pose they can.'

He grinned and we stood companionably looking out to sea where the last stone we'd skimmed had sunk into the sea.

'Mr B,' he broke the silence first, 'will I know what the right thing is to do, like Atticus?'

'I hope so, Danny.'

'How?'

'I guess you just have to keep trying to make the right choices and be brave enough to follow them through.'

'Is that what you do?'

'It's what I should do.' His mouth turned down at the corners again and I felt as if I'd let him down. 'Tell you what, shall we make a pact about the future and what to do with it?'

'Yeah! Like blood brothers! They did that in *Slipping the Chains.*' I shook my head, bemused. 'The DVD I was nicked with.'

'Ah, that.'

'Yeah – it was brilliant! They cut their palms and let their blood mingle. We could do that too, couldn't we?' His face fell suddenly. 'But I'd probably bleed out before I could make the pact, wouldn't I?'

I could barely keep a straight face. Danny hadn't seen the black humour, but I had – all too clearly in far too many ways since we were already far closer than blood brothers.

'Maybe not quite that bad, but the palm cutting probably wouldn't be such a good idea. How about we take an oath like in court.' I took the stance Sarah had made us take all those years ago, on another beach in Kent, right hand held high, palm outwards. 'I swear to make my choices good ones, and have the courage to follow them through.' He repeated it solemnly after me, and then we clasped hands. I added the final words that Sarah had insisted on in my head, "family sticks together". Danny was entitled to it, even if I was still struggling to uphold my oath to it. A gull flew overhead, cawing in applause – pinning the moment forever in my memory alongside that other day at the seaside. I loosened my grip on Danny's hand but he held onto mine, staring. Where I'd rolled up my sleeves before showing him how to skim stones I'd exposed the birthmark Sarah and Ma called my guardian angel. It showed purplish red on the inner wrist of my right arm.

'You got one too. Weird.' He dropped my hand and rolled his sleeve up. His birthmark wasn't identical, but it was too similar for coincidence. He frowned and peered at mine again. I tried to make light of it.

'Funny things, birthmarks – aren't they? My mother called it my guardian angel when I was teased about it as a kid. See, it has wings.' He examined it, and then scrutinised his.

'So's mine – sort of.'

'Then maybe yours is a guardian angel too. Doubly lucky – a blood brother *and* a guardian angel.' I could see Kat much closer now. I wasn't sure from a distance whether she looked annoyed or anxious, but whichever it was, I hadn't a lot of time to find out the rest of what I wanted to know out of her hearing.

'And Danny, since we're now technically blood brothers, can I ask you something, just between the two of us?'

He shrugged.

'Yeah, course.'

'The lady who collected you from hospital – can you tell me about her?'

'Why?'

'I just want to make sure we're thinking about the same person.'

He considered me for a while.

'You want to know if it was Mrs Juste, don't you?' I was amazed again at his shrewdness. I knew he'd met her at least once via Kimmy. He'd told me as much when I'd first been interviewing him about the manslaughter charge.

'Was it?'

'Depends.'

'Depends on what, Danny?'

'On who's asking.'

The barrister's son – or should that now be the liar's son?

'Well, it's me asking; can you tell me?'

'OK.' He picked up another pebble and skimmed it far out to sea. He was a fast learner. 'As it's you, *maybe*. I didn't take much notice of her the first time she came to talk to … Mum, but she did draw me a picture before she left – of her and me. Like a cartoon. It was funny – and clever. The next time she came, she didn't do any drawings and she was all serious. Only wanted to talk to Mum. They had an argument and Mum sent me out the garden. Mum said afterwards that she took herself too serious now she was Mrs Juste, that's why she could be your missus. When she got me from the hospital though, she told me to call her Molly and not to call her by her other name. Then she was like she was the first time I saw her. That's why I have to say it depends.' He kicked at the shingle and scraped the sand away from another discus-like pebble, a real gem. Thrown right it would be a five or six bouncer, easily.

'Did you like her?'

'Depends again. When she was all serious – not much. When she was all glammed up and doing her drawings, real quick, like this –' he made a scrawling motion mid-air with his left hand, five star-skimming pebble still clutched in the right hand, 'yeah. She said everything should be a game, and fun.'

I supposed for a ten-year-old boy, games were fun – if not for a fifty-year-old man.

'So where did you go after she collected you from the hospital? You didn't go back to the children's home straight away, did you?'

'I'm not meant to say.' He frowned.

'We're blood brothers, remember?' I coaxed.

'I dunno. It was getting dark, and I was hungry. She got me a burger on the way there – and a shake although I didn't like that much. It tasted funny. Then I fell asleep. When I woke up it was dark and raining. She put a coat over my head to keep me dry. She called that a game too – to see if I was brave enough to let her lead me without peeking.'

Why so cautious? Danny wouldn't have known where she was taking him.

'Anything else? It would really help me, Danny.'

'We stayed indoors all day.' He shrugged. 'Funny place, though,' he added as an afterthought. 'Dark, like a hidey-hole.'

I was surprised at his naivety. I hadn't thought Danny was naive, for all his youthfulness, and today he'd twice surprised me with how sharp he was. Even before that he'd always struck me as pretty street-wise.

'Didn't you think it was odd? Being taken somewhere you didn't know by someone you hardly knew?'

'But I did know her,' he disagreed. 'She was Mrs Juste, so *you* must have sent her. That made her OK. She is, isn't she?' Now he looked worried that he'd made a mistake I would be cross about, not worried for his own safety. I suddenly understood why Heather had described him as vulnerable. It wasn't youth or helplessness, or even his condition that made him vulnerable. It was me. 'Did I do the wrong thing? We hadn't made the pact then.'

'It's OK, Danny. You didn't do the wrong thing. You did what you thought was the right thing – and you're here and fine, aren't you, so it was OK. But maybe *we'd* better have a code between us for the future so if anyone tells you to do something and you're not sure if I'd think it was the right thing to do, you can ask for the code word.'

'Oh yeah – this really is like *Slipping the Chains*! They used codes too.' He beamed.

'So what code word shall we use?'

'Eastbourne. Where we became blood brothers.'

'OK, Eastbourne it is.'

'*All right!* But not if it's Molly – Mrs Juste, right?'

'Mrs Juste too.'

'Oh,' he looked worried again.

'Mrs Juste will know the code word if she needs to, don't worry.'

He nodded slowly, pulling his mouth down at the corners again, and studying me as he did so.

'Is this like real undercover stuff? Spies and the like? I mean, your car gets blown up and Mrs Juste is supposed to be dead, but she's not. I haven't told anyone that though,' he added proudly.

'I suppose it is. Codes and spies – they go well together, don't they?'

Kat was within a few feet of us now. Close enough to imminently be able to hear our conversation.

'Did Mrs Juste say anything else?'

He skimmed another stone and it bounced five times. 'Cor!' he said appreciatively. I grinned encouragingly and waited, eyes on Kat's now rapidly approaching shape. 'She called me her go-get-it.'

'Go-get-it?'

'Yeah, like – for errands and stuff whilst she was playing dead. She kept saying that I was the one who could make you go-get-it. The drawing I had to give Auntie Emm was one of the times I made you go-get-it.'

I was speechless – and irritated at the cynicism with which Margaret had pulled Danny into her crusade, even if she was also keeping him out of harm's way – and Jaggers'. When I tracked her down, there was going to be something very close to an argument over that.

Kat reached us fresh-faced and breathless mere seconds later.

'It wasn't there. Where else could you have left it?' I stared at her blankly, momentarily forgetting the fool's errand I'd sent her on. 'Your wallet – where else could you have left it? It wasn't at the café and they hadn't had any other customers after us.'

'Oh, sorry.' I patted my trousers and grinned foolishly. 'I must have put it in the other pocket without thinking – that's why I thought I'd lost it. Easier to reach on the right-hand-side without having to twist round for it.'

'Really?' She looked unconvinced. 'Well, thanks for the wild goose chase. Shame you had to send me all the way back down the beach before you remembered. I hope you've had fun, even if I haven't.'

'Old age,' I apologised, ruefully.

'That isn't how I would put it.'

'Sorry?'

'What have you two been up to?'

I was about to protest our innocence when Danny shot me in the foot.

'That's a secret, ain't it, Mr B?' he replied winking slyly at me. Kat frowned.

'If you're up to your old tricks …'

'What tricks, Kat? The kind you play?'

The truce was broken.

'I don't play tricks,' she rounded on me furiously. Danny watched us with curiosity.

'No, perhaps you don't call them that.'

'That was different. We're both meant to be playing it straight now, remember?'

But did that include reporting in to Fredriks? I was still pretty sure Fredriks knew exactly where I was and what I was doing on our day at the seaside, without me having to tell him.

'So we are. And whatever's between me and Danny is entirely innocent.' I smiled reassuringly. 'We made a pact with each other, that's all. A friends' pact.'

'He still likes you, even if he can't get kissy with you no more,' Danny offered her. We both stared at him. 'Just saying,' he mumbled, before seeming to pay all his attention to skimming one of his potential sixers. She opened her mouth to reply but obviously thought better of it.

'Well …' We avoided each other's eyes. She pursed her lips, and abruptly changed tempo. 'If you want to go anywhere else, hadn't we better get a move on now?' She looked meaningfully up the beach. 'Get it over with.' She added quietly for my benefit.

'Yeah! So we going to see that castle then?' Danny piped up into the awkward silence.

'Castle?' Kat and I both looked confused. 'But I thought you wanted to see where Mr Juste grew up?' she asked.

'Oh no, not now. I don't need to see that now.' He beamed at me. 'Can I have an ice cream, too? One with two dollops and a flake in it?'

I couldn't help laughing, but I'm not sure which I was laughing about most – Kat's expression, Danny's appetite, which was starting to become legendary, or my reprieve.

'Go on, find the nearest, then. This time the game's called find the ice-cream kiosk.'

He flung another star skimmer into the sea and it bounced six times.

A record, even for Georgie, who somehow had the most knack when we'd been kids. He whooped excitedly and scampered off down the beach, leaving a trail of Man Friday footprints.

'Someone's remarkably happy all of a sudden. What else were you plotting in my absence?' Kat was still suspicious.

'I taught him to skim stones and we made up the code between us, to keep him safe, that's all.'

'Which is?'

'Like Danny said – it's secret. Wouldn't be a code otherwise, now, would it?'

She snorted impatiently and followed Danny at a pace just slightly too fast for me to match without suffering the sharp kick of cracked ribs. I shut the discomfort out by concentrating on what he'd told me about Margaret – Molly; the clever artist. If Margaret had also been the clever artist behind the drawings Heather, Kat and I had been sent, then she'd also either been present or watching when Kimmy was murdered.

But that could also make Margaret as much the sociopath as I'd described the photographer.

My stomach knotted. I couldn't believe that – couldn't afford to believe that; that way lay madness – and if it was true, how could I trust her? No. Simply because she'd drawn the pictures, it didn't mean she'd known about the photos or even been an observer that day. She was tricky, manipulative and enigmatic but that was purely to obtain justice. And I had to start somewhere with rebuilding trust between us, even though Heather's control experiment still nagged uncomfortably at the back of my mind. This time I wasn't going to be blind. I had her letter, her personal assurance and a code agreed with Danny. I had things under control now. Danny couldn't be manipulated in my name anymore, but the sooner I found the damn security deposit box and got everything out in the open, the better – even my own reprehensible part in things.

Danny's ice cream was reminiscent of another food mountain but he demolished it like dynamite had been threaded into the cone and the whole mass imploded. His energy seemed inexhaustible now he was happier and I marvelled at the difference our pact had made in him. Kat eventually lost her sour expression as she watched him clambering gleefully amongst the ruins and peering through the slots in what was left of the castle battlements where the archers would have placed the tip of their arrows and awaited the signal to fire. To me, he was Win, Georgie or me, playing our make-believe games of soldiers and swordsmen, heroes and kings in our long ago land of the unlost.

'Apparently there's a ghost here too – the Pale Lady of Pevensey,' Kat told him, when he scampered back between forays into the crumbling stone walls, showing him the National Trust leaflet one of the volunteers had thrust at us as we entered.

'Oh, we know who that could be, don't we, Mr B?' He winked at me and Kat shot me an uneasy glance. For a moment I shared the feeling.

'Who?' she demanded.

'Someone William the Conqueror's men must have killed. They probably slit her gizzard and let her guts spill everywhere like this – shhzzz!'

'Horrible child!'

I laughed with relief. 'I think boys often are.'

'And men,' she retorted, haughtily, yet she watched him like a mother hen would her chick as he darted off again. But it wasn't her who reacted badly to Danny's four-foot leap from the cannon that had been left on display and which all the kids were swarming over like iron filings on a magnet. It was me, heart pounding and fists clenched; like I did whenever I thought of Margaret and love and loss, and I knew the promise I'd made on this day out at the seaside was one I wouldn't now ever be able to renege on.

'I got a guardian angel, like you,' he protested when I banned a repeat jump. Kat's expression questioned me. I held up my arm by way of explanation and she nodded, with an 'ah' of understanding. She'd seen it often enough, along with the rest of my naked and lying body. 'His has got wings as well, though,' added Danny, as if that made a difference.

'A true guardian angel then,' she commented ironically, eyes mocking, yet ... The unresolved business between us was still unresolved – probably always would be now, as long as Margaret remained back from the dead.

Danny allowed himself to be led meekly back into the children's home via the gift shop when the stone walls had all been scoured. In the stationery section there was a set of coloured ink pens. I paid for them without Kat seeing and passed them quietly to Danny. His mouth formed a 'coo', and he pocketed them as swiftly and neatly as a pickpocket would have done in his bomber jacket, grinning contentedly. We made it back for the allotted time of his return, four o'clock, with minutes to spare. Kat delivered him to the dorm parent who was waiting in reception to greet us, not quite keeping Danny in chains in his room, but as wary as. I stood diffidently by the entrance to reception, cautious about being too obvious, but unable to simply watch him walk away without a tightness in my throat. It seemed I was developing a habit of finding the things I hadn't known I valued and then allowing them to slip away from me again. He turned to wave to me and patted his pocket. I raised a hand to wave back, unconsciously placing my left hand over my heart. A salute I hadn't intended making, but he mimicked it. Our pact was sealed.

***

I dropped Kat back at her office in Croydon, both of us aware we had more unsaid that said. She tried to apologise again for going behind my back to Fredriks but I waved the apology away.

'We've been there, Kat. It's in the past. Let's leave it there.'

'But I don't want it to be in the past, Lawrence. Can't we start from scratch now things are out in the open – when Danny's settled somewhere? Maybe not with you, after all. I accept that, but perhaps with one of your sisters?'

Regret moved me more than surprise.

'I don't think that will be possible as things stand, Kat.'

'But I thought you said I was forgiven?'

The curve of her cheek still had the softness of a peach. I wanted to stroke it as I had when we were lovers.

'You are, but things are different now.'

'Because I lied to you?'

'No, because I made a vow I shouldn't break now I know I'd be breaking it.'

'I don't understand?'

'Margaret.'

'Oh,' her face fell. 'So that's why Danny said we can't be kissy anymore? She really is alive then?'

'And I have to let you go because of it.'

'Only if you want to.' She waited. The little imp in my brain laughed aloud at my desperation, but I had no choice. Danny and Margaret together saw to that. 'I see,' she turned away and I cursed every principle ever made by man. I caught her hand just before she moved out of reach.

'I'm sorry.'

'It's OK, I really do understand.'

She squeezed my fingers briefly before gently disengaging hers and we parted politely, neither of us raising the question of when we might next be in contact. I couldn't deny the attraction but I'd betrayed enough people already. The more I wanted Kat, even if I did nothing about it, the more I betrayed Margaret, even if only in my head. Like the rest of my life, my emotions were a mess. The only person currently pushing me beyond the morass of sticky confusion was Margaret – and yet she was the most unreachable.

I edged back out into the traffic and made my way through the evening rush hour towards Earls Court and Heather's temporary 'home', still mulling over why Margaret had involved Danny in her scheming. It seemed an odd thing for a mother to do, yet this was no ordinary situation. She must have had her reasons. I put that part of the puzzle to one side and concentrated on a more pragmatic part of it. Where had she taken him? And was she there right now?

I was puzzling over that and not paying sufficient attention to Heather's exhortation to mind out for the press when I nearly scored full points for one. I could have scored a hat trick, in fact, because his mates were waiting on the kerb side as I slowed and called an apology before realising what he was. I pulled away swiftly but not before the flash of a camera recorded for posterity the gaunt face of Lawrence Juste QC, speeding away from his potential victim, guilt written all over him. There'd already been one hit and run in my recent past. I could well imagine the opportunities for malicious speculation now whether the driver had been me. Shit! I would doubtless be in tomorrow's papers again, and Heather's car firmly locked away in her garage and banned from my use. I could almost hear her tirade.

'When I said don't get ice cream on my seats I didn't mean blood on my bumper was allowed instead. My verdict? You're banned – and not just for three years.'

I found a quiet side road far enough away to have lost the hacks and their photographer. Jesus, I was in a state. My hands were sweating so badly they left imprints of my palms round the steering wheel. Why had I thought I was in control enough to sort this mess out when the slightest mishap threw me into a tail spin?

It must have been a full ten minutes before the shaking stopped and I could muster enough self-discipline to turn the engine over again and put the car into gear. But where was I going? Back to Heather's? I'd have to tell her about the near miss to pre-empt tomorrow's news, then she'd almost certainly reclaim the car and the car keys. I could hire a car but the press – seasoned detectives that they were – would be on to that immediately and following me from dawn till dusk. Then I'd have a veritable convoy on my tail, with Fredriks and his greasy-fingered sidekick heading it. Even to get back to Heather's I'd have to run the gauntlet of the die-hards no doubt now attending my return on her doorstep. I turned the engine off again. Think, man, think! It was time to lose the brain-freeze and work out a plan. I put my head in my hands and searched for wisdom – in vain.

Stupid fool! I'd completely forgotten with everything else going on that in my pocket was the note I'd thought was a shopping receipt, but in reality had been one of Margaret's inimitable messages. In my haste to hide it, I'd read the sign-off but not the content. 'Be in touch soon,' had been enough to identify its sender. Damn! Had I already missed an opportunity to meet? I fished around and pulled it out.

'So, you'll be wondering by now what to do next. We need a piggy bank – get it?'

A typical Margaret missive, but I was finding my way round them now.

Statement or an instruction? Whichever, think laterally. A piggy bank was akin to a security box. Whether she was teasing me or not, the hidden security box was definitely still the first thing on the list of necessary weaponry in this particular battle.

6: Family

Now I knew that it wasn't Danny who'd drawn the pictures, but possibly Margaret herself, coupled with the fact that it had been her sending the little snippets of evidence to me, Kat and Heather, there was the only place I could start my search. Family. My brain finally whirred into action. Margaret had told me she'd given Sarah the evidence to put in the safety deposit box. Kimmy had been in on most of the pretence and had wanted 'payback', but with Sarah and Kimmy dead, and Win apparently 'unavailable', it had to be Binnie I sought answers from. Binnie had been hostile all along but seemed to know more than she'd been admitting to. It was high time Binnie stopped avoiding me and started telling me why she was so cool whenever Win, Danny or I were concerned. Margaret's letter had also claimed Binnie and Sarah had made the connection between Kimmy's school friend Margaret, and the Margaret I married quite independently of anything she'd later involved Sarah in.

With that, everything started to make sense. Binnie must have decided that avoidance was better than being part of the whole sorry mess. She'd always had that about her – the inclination to stand back, add the fizz to the mix and let someone else take the force of the blast. Even on our halcyon day at the seaside the argument between us had only first bubbled up because she'd deliberately goaded Win. So if she'd made the connection then, maybe she also knew something about the murder eleven years ago, and more to the point, the other one barely more than a week ago. Maybe she even knew who Kimmy's murderer was? I couldn't ask Sarah, Kimmy or Margaret, but I could ask Binnie.

With that worked out I didn't return to Heather's. I knew I was risking Heather turning on me, but not whilst I had her 'baby' in my possession. I parked at the end of Binnie's street to maximise the advantage of surprise, but surprise took me unawares instead. The place looked the same as the last time I'd visited unannounced, but with one very obvious anomaly – the curtains were gone. Peering through the front windows, the rooms were cleared of furniture too. It was empty. The grass at the front was neatly trimmed, and the borders tended, but the place was deserted. I lingered on the doorstep, unsure what to do next. The label in the new shirt I was wearing, courtesy of Heather's original ministrations when my home was wrecked, scratched the back of my neck and I realised with irritation it was because I was sweating with anxiety. Christ, I'd be turning into DS Jewson if I wasn't careful. I kicked the glossy yellow front door in frustration and it left a black scuff mark from the sole of my shoe. Heather's warnings about my tendency to inappropriate behaviour rang in my ears but they merely served to irritate me further. It was bad enough two of my siblings were dead, and my brother about to be charged with murder, *and* missing, but now the one who I'd harboured hopes of having the answers to the mystery had taken herself off too. I stared despondently at the scuff mark. It brought with it a tumble of memories – from Sarah polishing boot soles to Win kicking the FFF basement door open just before Margaret had officially resurrected herself for me. I let the memories break over me like a wave, drowning out all but the sense of helplessness I felt in its wake. I was going to rescue Margaret and Danny from Jaggers, prove Win's innocence and lead us all back into the light? Crap. Who was I kidding? Even my stroppy older sister had given me the slip.

The honeysuckle on the side wall had gone over but intertwined with it the clematis still boasted small nodding flower heads. I watched them bouncing gently, mesmerised, as I tried to muster my thoughts. A bee buzzed angrily past my ear, making me jump. I turned and watched it land clumsily on another of the dainty blooms. Its weight made the flower droop submissively. *Buzz, buzz, buzz, buzz, honey bee! Buzz all you like but don't sting me!* Binnie's high-pitched girlish voice swam around my head like a taunt. It was one of her favourites as a child. She – unafraid of insects and wasps and bees. Me, terrified of them after a bee, and then a wasp, stung me in quick succession one summer's day when I was about seven. We'd raided the malt jar and I'd got some of it on my threadbare shirt. It was probably that which attracted the bee in the first place. Ma was out the front on the air raid mound, gossiping with Mrs Dew, and so heavily pregnant with Jill and Emm she'd probably turned a blind eye to our mischief. I hadn't considered at the time how exhausted she must have been by the sheer effort of keeping everything going. Now, with the benefit of knowing how expensive that jar of malt must have been for our family's meagre purse I could see why things had to eventually descend to the despair of that moment in 1959 when my happy harum-scarum world ended with the children's home.

For then, though, despair was red and swollen legs, throbbing like they were on fire from seven consecutive stings. The bee had stung the tender inner flesh of my thigh – exposed in my fraying summer shorts. I'd clamped my knees together and howled. The wasp was caught mid-flight between them. It was one of those moments I could never have anticipated – or orchestrated – if I'd tried. Once upon a time I would have laughed at my bad luck, considering how minor it was compared to my later runs of misfortune. With hindsight it had a peculiarly karmic sense to it. Stung, not once but many times over – exactly as now.

Ma had entrusted Sarah with Pip and Jim – then only four and full of trouble. Binnie had the – by comparison – easier task of keeping an eye on me and Mary whilst Georgie was off day-dreaming somewhere and Win out exploring. Initially she'd swung into action, wrapping my legs in a wet towel, drying my eyes and singing her buzzy bee song until my wails had dwindled to snivels and I'd even tentatively joined in the song. She could make anyone join in if she tried hard enough, she just didn't – usually. Then she'd lost interest, leaving me inside with a ragged comic, towel-swathed legs and a 'you'll be all right now – no wasps in here, see?' She'd always had the ability to step away and be separate – perhaps too separate. I compared the Binnie I remembered as a child with the Binnie I'd encountered again as an adult. She was apparently no different.

I gave the door another frustrated tap with the toe of my shoe. My avenues for enlightenment were rapidly dwindling, it seemed. I doubted Emm had any more to add to the subject, and as she was clearly the better-informed of the two, Jill was unlikely to be any better. Win had supposedly told me all he knew – or was being as tricky as Margaret about what he wasn't telling me. Apart from that, he was as annoyingly absent as Binnie at the moment. I'd hit a brick wall as well as an empty house, apart from one avenue I had no intention of exploring unless I had to.

I checked round the back before leaving, but there was nothing to suggest where the occupants had gone and the neighbouring properties looked as unhelpful. Not empty, but their residents were no doubt still out at work. I supposed I could wait around for one of them to come home but there was an air of general privacy to the road, with the majority of the homes neatly bounded by fencing or walls, and net curtains or blinds at the windows. This wasn't a road where everyone knew each other's business. It was a road of closed doors and pulled curtains – the kind of road it occurred to me suited Binnie and her dislike of being involved perfectly. In fact loitering around an empty property in this kind of neighbourhood could well get me reported as a vandal or a thief if I wasn't careful. Christ, it might even have an up-market version of Kat's neighbour, Mrs Gnome, in residence! I imagined what she would have to say to the police or the press about me. That spurred me on more than the possibility of being reported. I swiftly exited the garden, letting the gate bounce on its hinges behind me and feeling some satisfaction at having at least disturbed the peace in a small but non-criminal way. There was obviously as much of the thug in me at times as in Win, I admitted ruefully.

Back in Heather's car I contemplated what I knew I least wanted to; the sister I tried not to think about at all. Yet if I forced myself to remember, she was the one who'd stepped in where Binnie had left off when I'd been stung, re-wetting the towel over and over again to soothe my red and swollen legs and cuddling me until I got cheered up and went back outside to play, blotchy but brave once more. I had to face it, my only other option was to talk to Mary.

I shivered, remembering the origami birds swinging from the ceiling in her room at the home. *Asylum,* the little imp whispered in my ear. *Give it the proper name – what it really is.* I leant my head back against the expensive cream leather headrest and felt something close to despair. I was too old to be running around chasing my tail like a mad dog – too old, too tired, and too ragged. At times recently it felt like it was me who'd lost their sanity, not my crazy sister. For the second time in as many days I wanted to cry like I had when Heather had driven me away from my wrecked home. No amount of buzzy bee songs or reassurance would change the fact that my life was in tatters, and one day soon I was going to have to face a child I hadn't anticipated fathering and be strong and wise for him, when I had no idea how to be so for myself.

I think I would have stayed there like that for hours, exhausted by failure, if it hadn't been for the sight of the elderly couple meandering along the road, nosily studying each of the houses they passed. It was a small but pertinent reminder that a man in a parked car doing nothing was almost as suspicious as a man loitering in the garden of an empty house.

'Come on you stupid bastard,' I chastised myself aloud. 'You've gone AWOL with Heather's car and for that alone she'll have your nuts in a fruit cake. And you've almost run down a member of the press which would be the icing on it. Do it. Just do it.'

But still I couldn't.

I turned the key in the ignition, just as the elderly couple drew level and cast me a suspicious glance, revved, and headed down the road in search of the only place I could stomach being right then. Nowhere.

7: Nowhere

Nowhere wasn't a real place. It was the idea I associated the place with – Wimbledon Common. The uncultivated expanse of tree and scrub on the edge of the city – not manicured like Hyde or Green Park, but lush and natural, and for me, redolent as much of solitude as calm – what I needed most now. The only time its all-encompassing peace had been destroyed had been when Margaret and I had come across a lone piper deep in the centre of it once on one of our walks. The only time too we'd been in mutual concord other than to propel my career forward. That Margaret seemed a life-time away from the one who'd been leading me by the nose recently, although not on that day. That day she was virtually as she was the last time I'd seen her, only a day ago.

Presumably the piper had been practising for a concert or recital. We didn't ask. The mournful wail of the bagpipes rapidly dispersed wildlife and humankind alike at the time. No peace on the common that day.

'Nowhere,' Margaret had said.

'Nowhere that I want to be right now!' I'd agreed, steering us onto the path leading off the common and back to the car.

'No, the piece is called "Nowhere",' she replied, impatiently. 'It's usually a strings arrangement. Unusual for the pipes.' I raised my eyebrows in mock tribute but ignored her inclination to linger. We found the tree on the way back because I took a wrong turning on one of the circuitous pathways in my impatience to escape.

So nowhere was here, where the Margaret I'd thought I knew wasn't. And indeed, everywhere was beginning to feel like that now. On an impulse I went in search of the tree, retracing what I could remember of our trajectory off the common that day – a short way from the centre, skirting the scrubby lake overgrown with bulrushes and waving grass. It was on a track seemingly leading nowhere too; Margaret had always liked those best. Apt, in fact – then and now. It took several attempts before I found it again but I didn't mind. There was no piper today, and very few walkers. There was space to think, if only I could force my addled brain to work logically.

The last time I'd been here, I'd been talking to Heather about one of the black-edged funeral cards I'd been sent – by Margaret, I now knew. It had pointed me in the direction of her and FFF, and eventually led to her appearance in the play dungeon Jaggers had created under the Gods and Gargoyles Club. The little hanging man in the corner of the card, denoting time was running out for me, hadn't been quite complete then – swinging maniacally from the gallows arm. God, how she liked her little jokes, and I'd been missing them all along – right from the start. I'd married the mother of my child, without even knowing I'd fathered one; joke one. She'd carefully manipulated my life without me even noticing she was doing it – often even helping her to do so. Joke two. She'd brought my child and me back together in the one situation she knew I couldn't wriggle out of, professionally. Joke three. She'd danced me about like a puppet on a string – or a man on a gallows – and then enchanted me. Joke four. And joke five? I was *that* joke. The smart man who wasn't smart at all. And yet, it was her cleverness in doing it all that now reluctantly attracted me and commanded my loyalty.

The tree was at the end of an overgrown path between thick rows of shrubs – a tangle of gorse and rhododendrons, spiky with fresh thorny outcrops, bushy with this year's lustrous growth. An odd mix of sharp and smooth – like Margaret. I was about to turn back, writing the trail off as another dead end when I spotted the tree and it's strange three-rooted base nestling in the gloom. I pushed past the remaining overhanging fronds of rhododendron and stood in the clearing. It was exactly as I remembered it.

Margaret had been ecstatic with delight when we'd first come across it.

'I must paint it! It's perfect.'

'OK, paint it – on your time. When you said let's have a quick walk, I didn't agree to an expedition.'

'I thought you liked walking on the common?'

'I do – the known pathways, fine – but not the thorny undergrowth, especially dressed like this.'

It was after a tea party for one of Margaret's charities – I couldn't even remember which now. Dragged along to do my duty as she'd done hers at Francis's turgid drinks party earlier on in the week. We'd left, after swilling too much over-brewed tea and consuming the requisite number of sickly cupcakes, with me complaining of a blinder of a headache, but knowing we had still to go on to another charity event where Margaret was cutting the ribbon to open some self-congratulatory edifice or another. She'd suggested the walk as a way of clearing my head. I'd agreed – but not to this.

'Come on,' I commanded, and walked away, thrashing irritably at the shiny leaves that bounced back at me as I made my way towards the main path. I turned to check she was following. She wasn't. 'Oh for God's sake!' I called to her, but she didn't answer. I retraced my steps, head now pounding and the first jagged edges of visual disturbance splitting my vision, signifying an oncoming migraine. She was still standing in the clearing, rapt. 'Margaret if you want to get to this thing we're meant to be going to, you'll have to come on.'

She swung round and laughed.

'You look like a teapot.' I hadn't realised I'd put my hand on my hip and had one arm outstretched as if to latch on to her and drag her with me. I straightened, temper unravelling. She smiled – that smile she had for when she knew she'd irritated me and found it amusing. I could see now she was mercurial; generally the dull, dutiful, perfect barrister's wife, but occasionally springing a stunt on me like this – with that smile. That little wry twist to her mouth that irritated and interested me on the odd occasions I saw it. 'It's amazing, and look, it has a letterbox too. To leave messages for the gods,' she paused, 'or their handmaidens.' The smile twisted a little tighter.

She knelt down in the mud and put her hand in the crevasse created by the splitting of the three parts of the trunk into its roots.

'And now you're going to be filthy and insist on going home to change.'

She laughed, the tinkling of water into a well, and got up, brushing the earth from her knees dismissively.

'Life isn't always perfect, Lawrence and neither are we. Why don't you try it sometime? Not being perfect.' It was the closest she'd ever come to being critical of me. Her comments were usually veiled or obscure. I hadn't known what to say back. 'Or leave a message for the gods to show you how to be human. They're supposed to help in times of trouble.' We eyed each other antagonistically. 'Maybe not, then,' and that little twist again, 'but at least you'll know where to reach them one day, won't you?'

I'd forgotten the exchange – occurring only weeks before she'd 'died' – until now. We hadn't gone home for her to change. She'd gone to the ribbon-cutting ceremony with dirty knees, not quite hidden under the hem of her dress, and been serenely unconcerned about it; a snub for me.

I shook my head in surprised disbelief. She'd been telling me, even then; warning me that trouble was ahead. More fool me for not listening – and for disdaining Margaret and everything to do with her. But maybe I had found the one thing that might give me a direct line of communication to her – the letterbox she'd made such a point about then. She'd couched it in such a way that I'd dismissed it – knowing that one day I might need to contact her, unseen. My admiration for her grew a hundredfold. I not only had an enchantress for wife – and a seductress, going by the clothes Kat had stored for her – but a clever and far-sighted strategist. I knelt in the dust where she had and felt inside the crack in the trunk. It was empty, but it was certainly big enough to hold a note, hidden from passers-by – not that there would be passers-by here. It was a secret nook in the midst of the bustle of life, and only found if you knew where to look.

I sat, my back against the tree, uncaring that the mud was staining my pristine trousers and struggled to find a way to let Margaret know I'd figured out her poste restante. I couldn't. After a while my mind wandered – as it does when focusing so hard on one problem the stray thoughts you're not attending to slip under the radar. Inconsequential ideas, ambiguous comments, tiny elements of the whole; windblown seedlings growing like weeds on the ground I'd prepared to nurture the solution to the problem. Encyclopaedia Britannica, she'd called herself – yes she was that all right! She gathered knowledge to her like a repository gathering archives, re-using it later to get her own way, like Heather had remarked. The tree's hard bark cut into my back and I shifted to ease it. Rough and irregular like the tree, I imagined the pattern it must have imprinted on my back through my shirt and laughed inanely. If it spread across my whole body I'd become a tree-man, limbs like branches. I'd have to shed the bark-skin like a snake shedding its sheath to become a human again – if the tree god allowed me to. The abstruse thoughts suddenly combined into one. Jesus! This was the tree in the drawing Margaret had given Danny to give to Emm; Danny, the go-get-it. How stupid that I hadn't seen that earlier – or connected it to Margaret's announcement, 'I must paint it! It's perfect,' until now.

Margaret had said the drawing had been to force Emm and Danny to meet – to come out of the shadows. But it hadn't been to allow Emm to come out of the shadows, but Margaret. To make the point about the tree letterbox, and enable communication between us.

Dammit! How much else of what she'd said had I misunderstood? And if only I'd worked this out earlier I could have told Danny whilst we were on the beach and effectively already removed him from the loop as go-get-it right then.

I scrambled up from my earthy seat and fumbled for my phone, intent on ringing Kat. Contact with Danny would have to be via her. Then I stopped, mid-number. And what the hell was I supposed to say to her? *I've just figured out Margaret is in touch with me through Danny, so never mind the risk to him, put me in touch with him again so I can pass a message back to her, would you?* And I'd insisted I wasn't 'up to' anything? I put the phone back in my pocket. This wasn't right. Parents didn't put their children at risk, whatever the difficulty of the situation. So far Danny had been charged with manslaughter, abducted, and now made go-between where murder was involved. I was already failing in my responsibilities as a parent. I needed to get a message to Margaret without using my son.

I fished around in my pocket to find only the note from Margaret that I'd mistaken for a receipt. Even the cryptic 'piggy bank' made sense now. The tree was a safe repository too. I crossed it through and wrote 'tree' instead. I debated whether to simply put it in the nook in the tree, but that seemed rather pointless, so I brushed myself down and made my way back to the car.

The common was still a place of birdsong and warm breeze, but it went unappreciated by me. So did my companions in nowhere. Head down, I trudged away from the clearing and onto the main track, mulling over alternate delivery possibilities. The light was just beginning to dwindle to a watery version of the day's previous full-beam sunshine. Autumnal for the first time, the air had that early evening tang to it I hadn't noticed hitherto; the gently musky smell of old loam and decaying flowers. I rubbed my upper arms to generate some heat, wincing at the grumbling it provoked in my chest. *Serves you right*, I chastised myself. *Exploring scrubland isn't prescribed as a cure-all for cracked ribs.*

A muffled figure walking their dog meandered towards me, waiting patiently for the dog to catch up between its bouts of enthusiastic sniffing. The dog dived into the bushes about five yards away from me, nose aquiver at some newly tantalising smell and I smiled involuntarily at its enjoyment. Simple pleasures – walking the dog, savouring the evening; if only that were all I had on my mind right now. I nodded a polite greeting to the approaching figure. They responded by pulling their hood up and whistling for the dog before turning away to where it had bounded out of the undergrowth a few feet behind them. The hood would normally have made me suspicious but this figure was slight – a woman or a tall boy. Perhaps not the wisest time of the day for taking a walk on the common, but then they did have the dog with them – a large one at that, a German Shepherd. Plenty match for would-be assailants.

The owner whistled a long low call and the dog trotted past them and straight at me. I hesitated as it approached, mildly intimidated and only just avoiding it as it suddenly put a spurt on and bounded past. The dog walker whistled again and I swung round to check the dog wasn't about to take another pass at me. As I did so the dog-owner blundered into me, barging me off the path. I stumbled and swore as the rib-pain raged and by the time I'd straightened, they were way off into the distance, unconcernedly following the roaming dog.

'Damn!' I cursed under my breath. It was as if they'd deliberately barged me. A slight build didn't necessarily mean non-criminal. Instinctively I felt for my wallet. I'd been wary of a mugging, not of a pick-pocket. The wallet was still in place but I got it out to check anyway. All intact. I'd been wrong then. Puzzled I gingerly replaced the wallet and checked my other pocket. It was turned inside out. 'What the?' Emptied – including the scribbled reply to Margaret – although the pencil was still there, lead point impaled in the seam, and making it wave at me like a drowning man. If they'd wanted it, they could have easily swept it away too. They hadn't. They'd only taken the note. I stared after the disappearing figure, now merely a speck as it slipped into the gathering gloom and laughed out loud. I couldn't be sure, but it seemed that my innovative wife might have devised her own way of acquiring my reply. Was she a mind-reader too then? Or had she eyes everywhere? Uneasiness displaced the laughter like water creeping over the head of a drowning man. Compared to Margaret – alive or dead, I was very much out of my depth. I only hoped she cared enough to throw me a life jacket if it looked like I was about to go under completely.

I continued slowly back to the car, the pain in my chest dulling to a sick ache by the time I got there. I ground my teeth together in frustration at the slowness of my pace but only succeeded in giving myself a headache. The irony of the moment didn't escape me; the man with the wrecked house was rapidly disintegrating himself. I didn't laugh this time, I jumped as the phone jangled in my pocket and my head jangled with it. Struggling to retrieve it from my pocket the ring tone gave out just as I pulled it free, sweating and swearing. It was Heather – no doubt on my case for the return of 'her baby'. I wondered if she'd leave me a message. Probably. Heather rarely let the opportunity to make her point go. I waited and about a minute later the voicemail came through.

'I knew I shouldn't have trusted you. I just hope you eventually turn up, with my car intact, and when you do I'll share with you the little gem Fredriks has just shared with me. Something about a case being re-opened. Sound like fun to you? No, I didn't think it would.'

The click signalling the connection had been cut could easily have been the sound of the blade landing on my neck – or my balls. Whichever, I was about to be emasculated one way or another. Maybe the life jacket didn't matter? You can only kill a man once, can't you?

8: Road Rage

The coward's way out? Hardly. To face Heather in full flow you had to either be extremely courageous or ridiculously foolish. I was probably the latter, but the tone of the message gave me little choice. Something was going down and I needed to be acquainted with it.

I nestled in the driver's seat of Heather's car and allowed its plush leather upholstery to comfort my aching body even though its efficacy was fleeting, and entirely dissipated by the time I got off the phone with its owner. I greeted her politely and then held the phone away from my ear until the reverberating pain of her extreme displeasure had dulled to a similar level as the headache.

'So,' she finished with, 'where are you now?'

'Wimbledon Common.'

'Wimbledon Common? What the hell are you doing there?'

'Thinking, Heather.'

'Well, come and think back here. It'll be more productive than communing with nature, especially after Fredriks' return visit this afternoon.'

'So what was all that about?'

'Trouble. He's still very keen to talk to your brother, but sadly your brother seems equally reluctant to talk to him. Sadder still, it doesn't work that way when you're out on bail – does it?' I didn't answer. I'd claimed to be thinking, now I actually was. Where the hell had Win gone? It didn't make sense for him to skip bail. We'd agreed to cooperate; he, Norton and me. We had a case to make, and I was set on making it. I owed him that much and I'd thought he trusted me now. 'Lawrence? Please don't tell me you've finally gone all strong and silent on me!'

'Sorry, Heather, like I said, I was thinking. I don't know where Win is, but I can't believe for one minute he's skipped bail. He doesn't know about those photos yet so as far as he's concerned, nothing has changed. Anyway, the case against him is still arguably circumstantial – even with the photos. Does Fredriks say he's skipped?'

'No, but he's muttering that it would be a shame if he has. Fredriks still thinks you know where he is and he wants you to tell Win that he needs to make himself very obvious in the next hour or so to avoid that unfortunate assumption being made. That is the message I have to pass on to you.'

'God, I'd better try and track him down, then.'

'Yes, him and the other criminal elements you like hobnobbing with.'

I ground my teeth to stop myself taking the bait.

'Was that all he was agitating about? You made it sound as if he had something else to share?'

'Oh yes. Win is merely the hors d'oeuvre. The case he's considering re-opening in the light of potential new evidence is the entrée. And we both know which one that is, don't we?'

New evidence? What?

'The Johns case, of course.'

'Oh, my dear, I'd almost be happy if that was so. Worse. This is all to do with witness tampering and now pointing at me too, Lawrence, so you've got to stop pussy-footing around now. You said Margaret knows everything? Well, she needs to stop playing hide and seek and share it with Fredriks too. Get her to forget her little crusade now and come in from the cold. If she doesn't – well, I shall be starting to think that fire really did mess with your mind and she's just a figment of it – like the woman you said was in 27B.'

'There was someone in 27B,' I insisted, affronted. 'You thought so too.'

'Squatters perhaps – but not Margaret.' I was silent. 'Lawrence? Are you still there?'

'Yes,' I said grimly, 'I'm still here.'

'All right, how about this as an alternative, *assuming* Margaret *isn't* a figment of your imagination: why can't she give the evidence to you so *you* can present it to Fredriks with a little flourish, throw your *innocent* mistake on the court's mercy and ride on the wave of being a crusading truth-seeker, despite it not being in your best interests to do so. We'll figure out how to reintroduce Margaret to the living once due process has been satisfied. Played right it could still be a winner for you – the squeaky clean lawman who cleans up his mess, engineers a joyful reunion and plays happy families ever after – and so on. Sit on it all and you'll look like you *are* intent on a cover up.'

'Win can tell you she's not a figment of my imagination.'

'Win's not exactly highly visible either at the moment,' she reminded me. 'Bring them both in, get Margaret talking and get this settled. Stay as you are and ...'

'I need more time ...'

'You haven't got more time.'

'And what if I can't persuade Margaret to come in from the cold? It's not just my reputation at risk here. It's her life. It's dangerous.'

'Oh, and it's not for us? Francis, Jeremy and me? It's not a game, Lawrence. This is my life too – and my reputation. If you go down, I follow, and so do they. We're all on the same ship and it'll be sinking fast if witness tampering is levied at any of us – even as a malicious joke. Do we get tarred with the same brush as you just so Margaret isn't *at risk*? Has she worried about you being *at risk* all this time?'

She was right, but I couldn't deny the sequence of events that inevitably had to put me more firmly on Margaret's side than anywhere else. I attempted brisk pragmatism to hide my embarrassment.

'Well, he can't re-open it without telling me because I prosecuted it.'

'You're never here to be told, Lawrence.' Heather replied tartly. 'And I'm on the butt end of this – thank you! Bring my bloody car back immediately and *then* we'll talk about what to do next. To Chambers though. The press are camping out on my doorstep and I'm probably going to have to climb out the back window to escape.'

'Really?

'Oh for God's sake!' The phone clicked off and I wanted to laugh despite myself. Battle stations all round then, but a council of war was definitely necessary if Fredriks was about to declare hostilities too.

The BMW purred into life as I turned the key in its ignition and I allowed myself a moment of regret for my charbroiled Austin Healey. Its battle cry had been less slick and somewhat throatier than the BMW – satisfyingly rough as well as powerful – but beggars couldn't be choosers and the BMW was more than a beggar's choice. I headed sedately along The Causeway towards Parkside, mindful of the trouble too much speed combined with lack of concentration had almost got me into earlier. I still had to slow at the junction with Cannizaro Road, but there was nothing behind me so I turned the corner at a less than leisurely pace, and remained cruising at twenty, savouring the dregs of peace afforded by being amongst the wooded wealth of the area. The vehicle that came up behind me did so at such speed, I wasn't even aware of its presence until the impact. For a full minute I wasn't sure what had happened, just the bone-shaking shock as I catapulted forward and the airbag exploded in my face like a solid cloud. I bounced off it and ricocheted against the headrest, neck spasming and flinging me back at the unyielding protection of the airbag's so-called cushion. Jaw slack and mouth gaping open, I had sufficient presence of mind to ram on the brakes, only to yo-yo into the vehicle ramming me from behind like the ping-pong ball in the game of cup and ball I'd played as a kid. The airbag hampered any sight of the rear view and wing mirrors but the power of the vehicle behind me was undeniable. Even with my foot off the gas and hard on the brake, the BMW was still being propelled forward like a drift in front of a snow plough. I yelled in terror but my throat closed over and a strangled gasp battled the suffocation of the airbag for supremacy. Just as suddenly, the car lost momentum and juddered to a halt. I jolted around like a kid in a bumper car, ribs screaming pain at full pitch. Winded, I struggled for breath, hands still clamped to the steering wheel and arms hugging the airbag. My heart competed with my head for the winner in the drum roll competition and my jaw belatedly followed, crashing cymbals that made my head ring in agony. My ribs completed the job by became knives, carving up the sacrificial beast.

'Jesus Christ and fucking hell!'

But my saviour wasn't listening. As I released my grip on the steering wheel, whatever monster was rampaging behind me revved aggressively and rammed me again. I felt the BMW's wheels skid on the tarmac simultaneously with the shock of the collision. The car leapt forward like a wounded gazelle before careering into the side of the road. I lost my grip on the wheel then, sandwiched between airbag and seat and could do nothing but wait for the vehicle to stop moving of its own accord. The car and I eventually ended up at ninety degrees to the road, still upright, but with the back wheels wedged in the hedgerow and the nose pointing forlornly at the bright bursts of nodding flora opposite. Stunned and nauseous, I barely mustered enough wherewithal to spot my attacker as they swung out round the nose of the BMW, clipping the front bumper as they passed, and sending the car rocking again. It was a Range Rover, mud-splattered green, and like many around these parts, no doubt, with reinforced roll bars and bumper making a perfect battering ram for the likes of me in my 'girl's car'. The driver hooted aggressively, and gave me the V sign before speeding up and disappearing round the bend of the road in a swirl of blue exhaust.

I attempted to disengage myself from the airbag but couldn't. It was taking its job too seriously. I felt around for something to deflate it as it clung tenaciously to me and it was a shard of broken glass from the smashed rear view mirror that saved me. I savaged the airbag as I might have my attacker, swearing and shouting at it until it eventually succumbed and deflated with a noisy sigh. I copied it as I was at last able to breathe freely again, before gulping and sobbing until the shakes took over. For the moment I didn't even feel the cuts on my palm from the jagged mirror. Blood brothers floated insanely around my head until my body's faulty nerve endings and pain receptors roared back into life. Fortunately the internal locking system hadn't failed and I could open the door. I intended sliding cautiously from the driver's seat, but ended up tumbling out onto the roadside and scrabbling around on hands and knees, babbling pathetically. There I remained, huddled up, shredded left hand stuffed under my armpit to numb the stinging until I stopped trembling enough to be able to stand and see what damage had been done to the car, as well as me. It was bad. Heather's baby was fatally injured.

'Shit, shit, shit!' I kicked the wheel nearest me and wished I hadn't. The tremor from the protesting axle shook the car and me. I winced with renewed pain, and the axle collapsed. 'Fucking shit!' I added. Now what? The urge to cry swept over me again. That was more times in the last few days than I remembered as a child; Jesus! What had I come to?

I limped round to the rear of the car to check what damage had been done there, but it was too deeply embedded in the bank to be able to inspect without a contortionist's act and I was far from being able to do that. I could barely stand, but somehow I had to get myself back to Chambers and the car off the road before it was the cause of another collision.

'Bastard!' I said to my now non-existent assailant. Had it been mere road rage gone mad because I'd been ambling along, or was the reason for the attack more sinister? The latter possibility had me looking up and down the road anxiously. I didn't know, but now the evening was starting to draw in I didn't fancy being stuck here as twilight fell if Jaggers was responsible. I pulled my phone from my pocket to ring the AA but there was no signal. Typical! The only option now was to make my way into Wimbledon village and find a phone box.

It was a long and tedious walk. Not in distance – in reality it wasn't that far – but I felt as tenderised as a steak under a butcher's hammer by the time I found a phone box that hadn't been vandalised at the bottom of

Wimbledon Hill. As a kid, we'd revered the red painted boxes in the neighbourhood. They were the only means of emergency communication if you didn't have a phone at home – and we didn't. We'd had none of the trappings of luxury that were an accepted part of daily life these days. No phone, no TV, no money, only a meagre welfare state. Of course we didn't vandalise the phone boxes. We never knew when we might need one, feeding the pennies in and pressing button B on the mysterious black box the receiver was attached to in order to make the connection. It had been like casting a magic spell, if and when Ma had needed to make a phone call – an exciting occasion we all revelled in. The phone box I eventually found in working order had been pebble-dashed with chewing gum – even on the receiver – but it was still beacon-red. I missed the mullioned windows of the boxes of my childhood, and the encrusted gum made me cringe but thankfully the phone still worked its magic, albeit without button B.

The AA promised to be there within the hour. The thought of plodding back up the hill and waiting in the grey evening chill for them to arrive was sufficient for me to brave any curious locals and set up camp in the corner of The Alexandra, with a packet of painkillers bought from the local corner store and a copy of *News from the Top* that someone had left on the chair nearest.

I hung over my half of Young's Best and leafed irritably through the magazine, a society rag – Margaret's kind of thing. A load of useless self-promoting prats in my opinion, but one self-promoting prat in this edition was far from useless. A double page spread on pages twelve and thirteen sang the praises of no other than my childhood enemy. Jaggers smiled magnanimously from the glossy portrait of him *'relaxing at home'* on page twelve, trademark ring and all, sinuously charming: *'the business angel behind the corporate mask.'* He even referred to the ring as his icon, reminding him that the lion roared, but should still be able to lie down with the lamb, and he did so by championing the causes of the vulnerable children FFF helped. *Cynical bastard! Yes, after you've ripped the heart out of your objectors!* I silently accused.

The reporter went on to laud the work of FFF and proclaim the charitable perfection of Jaggers and his fellow trustees. He was heralded the *'unsung hero'* of the business world; the principled man of the boardroom and mentee of the Wemmick patriarch, George Wemmick, who'd *'adopted'* him as his named *'heir'* since George had no male descendants. The lovely Molly – or Margaret as I knew her to be – was referred to as another member of the FFF team, also campaigning tirelessly alongside him. She appeared in cameo at the bottom of page thirteen, a photo too small to see her clearly, other than in the vague likeness to my wife, masked by chin prosthesis and blonde hair.

'He's not just a man but a mission too – righting wrongs, providing opportunities for the opportunity-less, and championing justice in all its forms' the fawning reporter gushed.

So his PR campaign had begun before charges were even levied against him. I flung the magazine down in disgust, wondering where Margaret stood in relation to this little piece of manipulation, and how the popularity swell would affect my place in the public eye when the truth was revealed. Probably place me nicely as the condemned man on the gallows, I thought morosely – like the little hanged man on all the black-edged cards Margaret had sent. If I compared the tone of the article about him to the last one the press had concocted about me, there was no doubt who the darling of the people was likely to be if faced with an open competition.

I drained my half pint and put it down heavily on the table in front of me, wondering despondently if I should have another. It might not be wise but the alcohol seemed to help and the heavy pub atmosphere almost dictated it with its overwhelming smell of slopped beer and crumpled salt and vinegar crisp packets. A gout of laughter burst from the darts players at the far end of the bar. The fat one with the check shirt straining over his belly was being thumped on the back in congratulation. He lolloped over to the dartboard and retrieved his arrows. Double top and a treble to win the game. Another unsavoury man of the moment. His companions cheered him back to the bar and he downed the dregs in his glass, slapping it down heavily on the bar mat sodden with spillages – a parody of me. He the victor, me the vanquished. The bar man leaned across the bar towards the little group and I suddenly felt my lack of belonging keenly. I had the makings of a family, but no idea where most of them were at the moment – and the one I should go and talk to – Mary – I was actually afraid of. I had a wife, apparently giving me a second chance, but unreachable. And I had a son, but no idea how to be a father to him. The only person I had, in reach and indeed, waiting for me, was Heather. I shivered. A ghost had walked across my grave and returned to dance on it. Heather would join it gleefully when she knew I'd trashed her car.

I slunk over to the bar and ordered another half. It wasn't as effective as brandy but it was the next best thing. I took it back to the magazine and

Jaggers' smug leer. I ignored him and concentrated on the lovely Molly this time. Margaret hardly needed the alter ego's wardrobe Kat had kept so secretly for her to perform her parallel role as Molly Wemmick. She was clearly a skilful actress to have kept up the façade for both Jaggers and me all this time. True, it must have been difficult, never knowing whether he might suddenly turn on her, or whether I would see through the disguise and unmask her. Was it really all for the sake of justice? And for whom? I couldn't help but wonder where Danny came into the crusade since she so easily used him as part of it. I drank some of the refilled half pint, allowing it to soothe my roughened edges. Now I felt ashamed. Margaret must have felt lonely too at times – many times, in fact. She'd been out in a limb and possibly afraid, and I'd not been there to help her. And here I was, considering forcing her into more danger, merely to take the heat off myself. Demanding the evidence Margaret had so carefully hidden and kept as a hold over Jaggers for over a decade would be as bad as betraying her. The 'body' inside the Austin Healey could be real next time. No, Heather didn't understand because she wasn't emotionally involved – didn't even like Margaret. That coloured her view of things just as much as my emotions coloured mine. I could ask her, but no more than that. If Margaret wanted to remain undercover and play out the game her way, honour dictated I had to support her decision. I'd have to swing a little longer from my gallows, uncomfortable though it was.

I wondered if I'd worked out the link earlier the tree letterbox would have guided me better. How many notes had Margaret left in there in vain whilst I laboriously stumbled my way through her clues? Heather's long-time judgement of me as blind was well-deserved. I was a failure, had lost my edge – and the reason? There was no denying it – despite my previous pompous strutting – I needed Margaret. God, how I cringed now when I remembered my boast to Danny on our introduction, *'if I'm convinced, I'll defend you – and you'll get off.'* No self-doubt then; no uncertainty. The notion of failure was inconceivable then, like the possibility of not being omniscient.

'Bloody fool,' I muttered into my beer.

'All right, mate?' The barman had left his pumps on an exaggeratedly casual tour of the tables, emptying non-existent fag ash and butts from the ash trays, reminding me of my first lesson in self-knowledge on this bumpy ride to face myself. Appearances – they can win the war, or lose the battle, depending on the audience. My mutterings of self-derision hadn't gone unnoticed by him or my companions in The Alexandra, and possibly my identity might not either unless I reined in on the self-pity. The barman lingered next to my table, no doubt having me pegged as either a drunk or a weirdo. I sighed dramatically for his benefit.

'Shitty day,' I confessed. 'Just trashed the missus' car and am telling myself what a prat I am before she does.'

'Tough luck,' he commiserated. 'You got a ride home?'

'The AA are on the way to see what they can do – breakdown service probably. They'll drop me back, I expect.'

'Ah, so you can have as much as you like if you ain't driving then.'

'Yeah, and I might need it!'

He laughed and moved away. Appearances had done their job. I was the perfect caricature of the loser – and almost not a lie, because without an emotional rudder, that was exactly what I was becoming. The fling with Kat had been my middle-aged swansong but I'd even failed in that. How did you cultivate love based on lies, or a relationship based on a chasm? Neither of us had been honest enough with each other to bridge the gap, and the claim to Danny that I was invincible had been born out of the work Margaret had so diligently toiled at for me over the years. I was the perfect patchwork, painstakingly pieced together out of her good works, social steering and careful grooming. The empty space I'd acknowledged existed in my life when she went wasn't merely because her routines were no longer in place to keep me rigidly in check, it was because she was no longer there to fill it. I'd been blind about that too. I didn't just miss her, I needed her, or someone like her. Without her, my patchworked life would be no more than frayed pieces of thread before long.

9: Gathering

The AA didn't drop me at Chambers. The taxi did. Swinging through Putney and over the bridge heading towards Lincoln's Inn, we passed Battersea Bridge Road and Binnie's place again, just off the main thoroughfare. I was tempted to ask the driver to detour past it to see if the inhabitants had returned, but then – what was the point? What could have changed whatever made Binnie disappear so absolutely in such a small space of time? I tried to picture what could have made Binnie and her hard man husband run. Jaggers? But she'd studiously kept clear of him, so that was unlikely. Win? Possibly, but I knew Win to be more pussy than predator now, and I was damn sure Binnie must too. Who, or what, else, then? I was stumped.

We'd made it to Millbank and were passing the Tate by then. My ribs grumbled from the additional aggravations of the day. I gritted my teeth, ignoring the duelling complaint of headache with rib ache. At least it took my mind off the bollocking Heather was about to treat me to. I imagined Margaret's rendition of me if she'd been painting me right now. A cross between Munch's *Scream* and one of the tortured souls from Dante's *Inferno* would be a good approximation. I could see the taxi driver eyeing me from time to time in the rear view mirror and made an effort to stop grinding my teeth, focusing my attention instead on the winding river scene as we crossed Lambeth Bridge and skirted the Embankment. At least we were taking the scenic route.

'Molar?' he asked abruptly. I jumped. I'd been too intent on channelling the nagging pain into a receptacle somewhere in my mind that I could seal up and ignore – another of Margaret's little mind-tricks, like throwing away tension.

'Oh, yes.' An easy explanation for my grim expression. Back to grinding my teeth for credibility's sake now, and wincing as my whole jaw genuinely complained at the persistent aggravation.

'You prob'ly got 'n abcess. I had one of them. Bloody nightmare. He had to stick a needle in it in the end. More bloody painful than havin' the damn thing out. You're that bloke aren't you?' He waited. I didn't answer, hoping he'd get the message that I didn't want to chat. 'That barrister bloke – the one that got the kid off. You his uncle then? Really? Funny business. How'd you not know then?' My mind jumped back and forth with his questions. His eyes were more on me in the rear view mirror, than on the road ahead. Never upset a London cabbie. You rely on them to get you to where you're going. But which to respond to? The traffic snarled and we slowed almost to a stop. I was aware of his eyes now narrowing antagonistically at my lack of reply. I gave in.

'I think I might have been in the news recently with one of my cases.' A mistake. It gave him carte blanche.

'Yeah, you 'ave. Not just the thing in court – your house got blown up too didn't it? Funny business.'

'No, just extremely unfortunate.'

'Oh, right! A car crashes into your front room and it's just *unfortunate*?'

'Yes really.' I was irritated with him.

'Sure it weren't an insurance job?'

Now I was uneasy. A cabbie with far too much to say about me.

'I'd rather have my home back than the insurance, thanks. Are we going to be stuck in this much longer?'

'Depends.' He grinned.

'On what?'

'Whether I know a back route, or not.'

By the balls, even by the taxi driver.

'Do you?'

'I might, but ... so is the kid family?' No escaping this interrogation. I'd be getting it one way or another, but the quicker we got to Chambers, the less of it I'd have to dodge.

'It's being investigated. Where is the back route?'

'So why d'you not know before?'

'I haven't been in touch with my family for a long time – since I was a child.'

'That's what the papers said. So it's all true?'

'Well, I don't know what else the papers might have said but that part's true. Safest to always take whatever they say about anyone with a pinch of salt.'

'As with that smarmy bastard too?' He jerked his head as if nodding

82

at something. I was mystified until I realised I'd brought *News from the Top* with me and it was folded open at Jaggers, grinning expansively from the oversized photo on the first page of the feature.

'As with all smarmy bastards. Are we close to the back route?' The traffic had edged forward to the Southbank Centre. We funnelled onto the roundabout.

'Nah, no back routes here, but won't take five minutes now.' He grinned at me and swung round the car hovering between lanes in front of us, hooting as we passed it to take its place in the stream of traffic heading back over Waterloo Bridge. 'Bloody tourists. Don't know where the eff they're going most of the time. I'll put me foot down now. You got somewhere important to be?'

'Yes,' I agreed, thankfully.

'No problem, mate. I'll get you there. Looks like you've got enough on your plate without being late too.'

He dropped me just along from Chambers within the boasted five minutes, and tipped his forelock at me for the tip.

'Cheers, mate! And for your life story,' he grinned cheekily. 'Nice to know what the hacks don't.'

I grabbed the magazine off the seat and tucked it under my arm. No doubt he could have found a faster way through the slow-moving traffic for the whole of the route if he'd wanted to, but he'd marked me for an interesting target as soon as he recognised me. I should have remembered that about cabbies. They're the eyes and ears of London as well as the wheels. I hoped whatever he thought he'd wheedled out of me wouldn't find its way to an enthusiastic hack, not that there was much to it they didn't already know – other than that I'd just confirmed I was touchy about the insurance claim. Dammit! My grip really was going.

'Get that tooth seen to as well, mate. You look bloody awful at the moment. Need to have a grin as perfect as your pal there to look like the good guy.'

'Thanks for the advice,' I replied sarcastically. He shrugged his shoulders and lifted his hands in a gesture I'd often seen Francis do after one of his moneyed clients had declined sage legal advice, then flipped his for hire sign back on. I ground my teeth again but irritation gave way immediately to something more serious. Kat, waiting just outside Chambers' main door, and furious.

'I think it's time you told me what's really going on, Lawrence!'

'Going on? With what?'

She spotted the magazine under my arm.

'Well that's part of it. Have you read the whole article?'

'Most of it.'

'In that case, you'll know there's a lot more explanation in order.'

'About what?'

'Well it hardly corresponds with what you told me, does it? You said they were money laundering at FFF, but it's genuinely a charity – how the hell would they get something like money laundering past the Charity Commission for a start?'

'I didn't say it was money laundering for sure, I said it could be. It's certainly a nice respectable front for a wholly unrespectable set of activities.'

I could see the taxi driver slow a short distance along the road and pull over. He'd already been far too interested in me. I didn't want him witnessing an argument between me and the woman he'd probably soon identify as Danny's social worker. I unlocked the door and hastily ushered Kat inside, weighing up who was worse to face at the moment – her or Heather. I'd forgotten the worse alternative still; Ella, hovering at the bottom of the stairs as we entered reception. I groaned. For *my* sins, there was obviously no choice to be had. I was about to be treated to all three, and a council of war with Heather would have to be abandoned in favour of a battle skirmish as precursor to full scale hostilities unless I kept Kat and Ella apart. I wouldn't say Kat actually snarled, or Ella bristled, but the air crackled with animosity.

'Shall we find Heather?' I asked pathetically, without much hope of defusing the ticking bomb. Luckily Heather found us.

'Lawrence! At last – where have you been?' She appeared at the bend in the stairs, plush carpet masking her arrival and impossibly high Jimmy Choos making her ankles wobble in an effort not to sink into it. She still managed to make the entrance regal, despite the sensation of camera shake as she descended towards us, lower legs trembling with the effort of control. I wanted to laugh, but the possibility that she might take off one of the offending Choos and stab me with it was too great to risk it. Her face was stern.

'I had a bit of difficulty on the way here.'

She looked at me quizzically.

'Not with my car?' she asked suspiciously. The tension heightened.

'Can I explain later? It seems we might have other things on the agenda first.'

'Yes,' she eyed Kat with curiosity.

'Entrapment, perhaps?' Ella's voice was silkily polite but as cutting as a rapier.

'And who's entrapping who?' Kat countered. 'Seems like there are accusations flying around without any supporting evidence.'

'Learnt the meaning of the phrase from DCI Fredriks whilst you were spying for him, did you?' Ella added nastily. Heather paused and looked from Ella to Kat before continuing to the bottom of the stairs and taking up position next to Ella. In the gloomy lighting of the evening half-power in Chambers – the halfway house to powering-down completely once the cleaners' vacuums had died and their mops had swabbed their last for the day – they looked like twins, oddly separated by three decades.

'All right Ella, that doesn't help, even though it may be true,' Heather's authority shattered the sensation of mirror image and the younger woman took a step aside, acknowledging the real power base. 'But what are you doing here, Miss Roumelia?'

'I would have thought that was obvious. And I didn't withhold evidence or conspire to pervert the course of justice, but there seem to be at least two candidates for that here – you Mrs Trinder, for not turning in the package of evidence that was sent to you, and you Lawrence,' Kat swung round to me, and launched her missile full in my face, 'for doing the same with yours, trying to persuade me to do the same with mine, *and* for not telling Fredriks about your wife.' Cool. Ice-cool, and as dangerous again as I'd thought her when she'd admitted to storing the cache of Margaret's alter-ego clothes. There was none of the softness of the burnished peach I'd once seen in her, and had felt again when we'd returned Danny to the children's home earlier. 'And because of whatever secret nonsense you're feeding Danny.'

'Secret nonsense? I haven't fed anyone any secret nonsense, least of all Danny.'

'So you've been absolutely straight with me about everything, have you? Told me and everyone else the whole truth like you expect your clients to do in court?'

'Oh, and you've always been wholly truthful, Miss Roumelia, haven't you?' Ella burst in before I could reply. 'Never been lurking behind any snidey little secrets or sparking off any tricky little revelations then?'

'Ella, *please!*' Heather's attempt at holding the bitch at bay was failing. Ella had smelt blood and wanted it – especially since it was Kat's. 'Although, she has a point. One might say you've been as guilty of entrapment and conspiracy as Lawrence has been of stupidity.'

'Oh, thanks Heather,' I interjected. She threw me a look that would have withered fruit on the vine.

'Are you behind all this nonsense from Fredriks?' she continued, ignoring me. 'Providing him with evidence that makes Lawrence – and me – look like liars, when all we were doing was checking facts before turning everything over to the police. We've already had too much of playing with evidence. This time the claims need to be real, not conjecture – and I'm sure you understand what I'm getting at.' Heather's sword thrust home.

'It was different, then.'

'Why?' Heather walked across reception so she was facing Kat, five foot nothing compared to Kat's willowy stature, but intimidating nonetheless.

'Because ...' but she didn't get a chance to explain. Heather was in courtroom form.

'Because it didn't suit your game plan?'

'Your entrapment game plan,' Ella chimed in nastily.

Glowering at each other over the top of Heather's head, Kat and Ella squared up like prize-fighters. This was getting far too personal, and personal was proving to be very dangerous.

'Whoa – what are we all fighting about? We've all got the same end in mind, surely? Finding out who murdered my sister Kimmy and making sure Danny is OK. Shall we call a truce for the moment and sort out what all these accusations are that are flying around?'

Ella remained openly antagonistic, only barely restrained by Heather. Kat looked mutinous but didn't react. Her lips were set in a grim line.

'OK, I'll go first.' Heather intervened. 'Someone has been stirring – although why, I don't understand.' She continued, 'I had DCI Fredriks on the phone earlier about both the Johns and the Roumelia cases,' she swung round to include me in the fray. 'That's why *we* need to talk and *you* need to stop gadding about like a tourist on their first trip to London.'

I ignored the side-swipe and addressed the crux of the explanation.

'But why? You mentioned witness tampering? Who's been witness tampering?'

'Someone has been telling him that there's more going on behind the scenes than we've been admitting to, and that there may be anomalies which have a bearing on the validity of the original judgments. And the more he's interested in the Johns case the less he's interested in the

Roumelia case, I would guess. Isn't that so, Kat? So I wonder who's been suggesting that to him?'

'Your brother's case?' Kat nodded. 'But there's nothing wrong with your brother's case, is there? I thought that was all settled – it was just Fredriks trying scare tactics on you.'

'The reason you betrayed Lawrence, in other words, Kat?' Ella couldn't help shoving her own sword point back in; the Picador irritating the bull with their cruel little darts whilst the Toreador readied for the kill. I felt sorry for Kat. She'd had both Heather and Ella against her from the word go. I couldn't add to that, even if she did now seem to have turned on me. Besides, I was still feeding her nonsense – or starving her of the truth.

'Kat's already explained all that and apologised for any trouble it caused at the time. Why are we harping on about it again? Come on – we need to have a bit of empathy for each other, don't we? And we need to be dealing with today's problems, not raking up old wrongs.' Kat's expression softened and her eyes signalled a muted thank you to me, but Heather wasn't to be similarly moderated.

'But why would Fredriks even *think* there was cause to re-open the Roumelia case? There was nothing wrong with it.'

I'd forgotten the Roumelia case had been hers and she was unusually sensitive about suggestions of impropriety currently.

'It's not going to be re-opened, Heather. Fredriks was merely holding it over Kat to force cooperation. It really is the Johns case we've got to worry about.'

'So what's this then?' She thrust a telephone note in Louise's handwriting at me. It informed Mrs Trinder that DCI Fredriks would like to examine all Defence Counsel paperwork held on the Crown v Alfie Roumelia case, 1987, and that he would obtain a warrant for its release if it wasn't voluntarily provided. 'I beg to differ, my learned colleague.' The sarcasm could have buried me. 'It's not the Johns case I have to worry about. It's this one! It was dismissed without prejudice. Now it's being re-opened. New evidence and witness tampering.' She glared at Kat. 'Or is this just to force my cooperation too?'

The ringing in my ears blotted out Kat's reply – or maybe there wasn't one. I knew the accusations wouldn't have come from Kat though. Why would she want her brother's dismissal re-investigated? Kat cleared her throat. She looked embarrassed.

'There was a witness.'

Heather rounded on her belligerently before I could voice my surprise.

'There were several witnesses, all contradictory, but overall they cast sufficient doubt on the one claiming your brother's involvement for the case to be dismissed. I interviewed all of them.'

'… but ...' All eyes were on Kat. The burnished peach-plum woman made a reappearance.

'But?' I asked, apprehensively. Suddenly I felt light-headed and queasy.

'I don't know. They've gone – apparently. Or that was what Fredriks told me when he was pushing me to tell him about you.'

'Gone? *Gone?*' Heather began to pace around, stiletto points leaving small pecks in the plush carpet of Reception.

'I don't understand it either,' it came out in a rush. 'I don't understand it either. Mrs Juste tracked them all down for us. They were solid, she said.' Kat reminded me of a small chastised child. 'When he let up, I thought it must have simply been a mistake.'

'Bloody Margaret! She's going to ruin me too, not just you!' The kick aimed at me was metaphorical, but winded me nonetheless. I rallied, trying to appear logical, despite the stars dancing in front of my eyes and the sensation of spinning.

'That's not fair, Heather. She's not here to explain for herself. And people move around. These witnesses may simply have moved on without telling anyone. Margaret wouldn't manufacture them – why would she?'

'Why wouldn't she? She's good at manufacturing.' Heather flung round at Kat. 'How have they gone – moved on, or disappeared without trace?'

'I don't know.'

'Look, a case is only re-opened when there's probable cause. Or new evidence. This isn't new evidence, it's just old evidence mislaid. Why would Fredriks check them out again, anyway?'

'Someone told him to.'

'*Someone* ...' Heather pursed her lips at me and I knew what – or whom – she was thinking about.

'*Your wife,*' the little imp in my ear confirmed. I shook my head to silence it and the dizziness returned. For the moment all I wanted to do was sit down. I shouldn't have had that second half on an empty stomach. I struggled to concentrate.

'Your *friend*, that's who, I guess.'

I stared at her, uncomprehendingly. The logical, controlled part of me objectively dissecting the reason for my thick-headed idiocy, whilst the other part – the here and now and trying to deal with the problem part – slipped beneath the steadily rising meniscus of confusion like a drowning man bobbing up and down, gulping in lungfuls of water between snatches of air.

'My friend?'

Kat pointed to the magazine under my arm. 'Him.'

Jaggers.

The idea sunk slowly into my consciousness, and with it, the connection. He'd contacted Heather about the case some time ago and threatened her. She'd ignored the threat but it had led to her identifying the handwriting as the same as that on Wilhelm Johns' 'confession'. Tampering with evidence, indeed. But not *her* tampering with evidence, *him*.

I pulled the magazine out from under my arm and held it out to Kat.

'This man: John Wemmick?'

She nodded. Heather snatched the magazine from me and devoured the article before allowing Ella, who'd come to join us, almost conspiratorially, to take it from her.

'It sings his praises,' Heather commented at length.

'It would. It's a set-up – set him up, put me down.'

'Why? He barely knows you, even though you keep having a pop at him,' Ella accused.

'It's a long story,' I looked at Heather. She eyed me, and then the smiling face on the magazine Ella was now clutching, speculatively. She took the magazine back off of Ella and flicked through the article again.

'But not about such a bad guy as you make him out to be, Lawrence.' She looked me square in the eye and I didn't like what I saw. 'What *really* is going on between you two, now it's dragging me – and Chambers – into it too?' Ella hovered next to Heather like a miniature bodyguard, dividing her hostile glances between me and Kat. 'You know,' Heather held my gaze, 'I know what you've told me but this article implies quite a different story. Which do I believe? Especially since I now know you are so good at glossing over what you don't want known. And your little war is dragging me into it too if it's him behind this just to get at you.'

'You already know the truth, Heather. And what about the things you have on him? The letter to you, insisting the Roumelia case is reopened, which is in the same handwriting as Wilhelm Johns' statement. His fingerprints matched the unidentified ones on the murder weapon used on Kimmy too. Doesn't that make him potentially a bad guy?'

'But we don't have the Johns case file any more so there's no proof; only what I thought I saw at the time.'

'You told me you removed the file from my desk for safe-keeping and it was only a copy I had at home that got burned.'

'True. But we don't have it now.'

'Why not?'

'That's gone too, like the witnesses Kat's just told us have disappeared.'

'What do you mean, gone?'

'*Gone*, Lawrence, that's what I mean by gone. It was locked in my desk drawer. Now it's gone. Like the partnership money that's gone – apparently withdrawn by you or your dead wife. That's another thing that needs explaining ...'

We stared at each other. Dammit! I should have dealt with that, but I'd been distracted. '*By Margaret*,' the imp reminded me. Now my failure looked like indifference – or worse – deliberate avoidance.

'And Danny – that's what I came here about in the first place. He needs explaining too.' Kat's voice had a serrated edge to it. So that was why she'd been so angry with me. She must have found out, somehow. No going back now – even if I might have miraculously been allowed a chance to one day in the future.

'Danny.' It felt more like a confession than a name.

'Yes, Danny. Whatever your little secret is with him, it's set him on the run again. Where did you tell him to hide?'

'Jesus!' Life suddenly became immeasurably worse than it had been even half an hour ago – difficult thought that was. 'I didn't. I told him to stay put – even if he didn't want to.'

Kat shrugged disbelievingly.

'Well *he's* gone too and we're about to go on full alert to find him. That's why I came here. Not to crow over whatever Fredriks may have turned up on any of the cases you've had a hand in. To find out if you could help. There was no-one at Heather's and I knew you had to return her car, so where else might you both be? I've managed to stall them until now because I suspected you knew what was going on but I'll have to tell Fredriks that you and Danny had a secret conversation after you'd engineered for me to be out of hearing.'

Heather sat down at the clerk's desk and tapped her fingers on the top. Its dirty brown top was unprotesting. It had suffered a lot worse than molestation from Heather's perfectly manicured coral talons, but the tattoo they beat out set my nerves on edge.

'I think we've had enough now, Lawrence. Whatever little games you're playing, this is a vulnerable child – one *you're* responsible for, *remember*?'

Kat looked from Heather to me, frowning. Ella smiled knowingly. So it looked like Heather had told Ella about my suspect parental status, and Ella would delight in stirring the mix if it was likely to upset Kat.

'Actually the state is responsible for him.' Kat corrected, icily, 'but Lawrence is morally responsible for him, especially if he's encouraged him to run away.'

'Bloody hell! No! I wouldn't do anything to put Danny at risk.' I thought furiously. Why had he gone this time? We'd had an agreement – a pact. 'We made a promise to each other – to only make good choices and to see them through. We agreed a code word so if ever he wondered if he was being told the truth and it involved me, he'd know from the code word whether to believe it or not.'

'So what was the code word?' Kat insisted. 'And why would he need it?'

'Because I could be used by … oh, never mind. If I told you, it wouldn't be our secret would it?' I replied snappishly. 'However, I told him to stay put and he agreed. So now, we have a more important priority than re-opened cases and whatever else Fredriks is up to. Christ!' I allowed my tumbling thoughts and frustration to spill into the tension. 'What the hell is going on here? It's like we're standing on the edge of a black hole and people keep slipping into it.'

I knew my business partner after all these years. The rhythm of the tapping fingers speeded up. Heather was losing patience.

'Including your brother,' she added. 'He's another not so little thing DCI Frederiks wants to open up.' She paused, eyeing us each in turn. 'OK, here's where we are. First, Danny, do you know where he is Lawrence? No lies or excuses, just tell us what you know.' I shook my head. 'All right – next, Win. What about him?'

'Joined the ranks of the rest of the gone, it seems,' I admitted moodily, still churning over where Danny might be, and why. Everyone seemed to be 'gone': witnesses and Binnie, Danny and Margaret – but where? A glimmer of an idea formed with the last pairing.

'You must know something about his movements, you're like a pair of gloves. Are you covering for him?' I shook my head again. 'Typical!' I was about to protest, but Heather had already moved on to a subject I wanted to discuss even less. 'Oh, and where have you left my car, by the way? It's not out the front.'

'Ah ...'

The fire in the air turned to ice.

'I don't believe it! What have you done to it?'

'It wasn't my fault ...'

I thought for a moment she was going to hit me. I even cringed against the anticipated blow but my Guardian Angel must have existed after all. Dulcet tones, that in a past life I couldn't ever have imagined being grateful for, cut through the high-pitched harangue at my woeful admission and sent the furies in different direction.

'Jesus! A mother's meeting and the biggest motherfucker isn't even a woman!'

Win. At least one missing piece of the jigsaw was back in place, but it seemed like his arrival was only a sop for the loss of the others, the ones that signified the difference between destruction and salvation.

10: Dispersal

'Can't a bloke go down the bookies in peace without being pestered by nagging women?'

The bulky figure at the door moved into the relatively lesser gloom near the clerk's desk, waving a mobile phone at us. As he drew closer, it was clear the list of missed calls filled the whole screen. Heather's eyebrows hit her fringe.

'Well, you told me to keep trying till I hit pay dirt,' Ella told Heather belligerently. 'And now I have. I rang everyone else who might have known where he was too, including the brother in Australia.'

'Oh my God, Chambers' phone bill …' Heather paled.

Briefly there was silence until Ella rounded on Win, demanding where he'd been, what he'd been doing and quoting the penalties for jumping bail. I guessed she was employing the barrister's barrage as self-defence against Heather and a charge of wasting Chambers' money. The machine-gun fire of questions was only halted eventually by a violent protestation from the victim himself.

'Bloody hell! You're doing my head in! I'm here, OK? I can hear you – you don't need to shout! I know better'n the lot of you the penalties for jumping bail. You think I'm stupid? I ain't on curfew and I'll report in and shut quack face up when I know what this little unlawful assembly's all about. Can you just stop squawking now?'

If we'd been the Keystone Cops, the slapstick would have been split-timing perfect. It suddenly struck me that was what involving Fredriks in the Roumelia case was – not perfect, but equally carefully orchestrated.

'Red herrings,' I announced to their bemused expressions.

'You what?' Win stared at me as if I was mad. 'We ain't at Billingsgate now, matey.'

'No, all of this – it's designed to set us at each other, and whilst we're doing that, we're not concentrating on sorting anything out. We're allowing our efforts to be diluted – spread too thin to get to the bottom of anything, and whilst we're doing that the evidence is either slowly dissipating – 'gone' witnesses and disappearing files – or being muddled so badly it'll take us years to untangle it. That's what's happening. Yes, we are a Billingsgate, Win – one of our own making, and chock full of red herrings!'

'Explain,' demanded Heather.

'The Roumelia case. Which witnesses have mysteriously gone missing? Do we know?' I queried of Kat.

'Fredriks didn't say,' she replied slowly, 'just one of the ones who poured doubt on the charge.' She bit her lip, frowning. I turned to Heather.

'But you thought everything was above board with the Roumelia case. You were even prepared to argue the toss about that when Wemmick tried to pressurise you over it.'

'Well, of course I was. I wouldn't tamper with evidence or withhold it if it was relevant to the truth. There was nothing wrong with the witnesses, the evidence or the decision. The only thing I'd be less positive about now is whether there was something more to your Margaret's involvement, although I checked what she researched and it all looked kosher then – as she presented it.'

As she presented it. My head suddenly cleared and I saw the whole game plan as clearly as if someone had laid it out in front of me.

'Fredriks is just stirring things up, then,' I assured Heather.

'And are you suggesting there's something dodgy going on between Fredriks and Wemmick?' Heather was appalled.

'No, but Fredriks is canny. I would guess he's followed up on the leads that have been fed to him because he's a strategist. He's playing both ends against the middle. If someone plants a seed that there was something wrong with the case, the smart man gives it time to germinate and see what grows. *We* are aware there might have been something wrong with the Johns case, so we're already sensitive about the possibility. If Fredriks leaves it long enough, what he has might grow into something recognisable for him too. Fredriks leaves us to stew a little with a few choice comments. That in turn stirs us up and reinforces the paranoia Wemmick has already created by querying the validity of the decision with you. It's very clever, but then John Arthur Wemmick is a very clever man too.'

'I am not paranoid,' Heather told me thin-lipped, but she looked tentatively relieved. 'But does that mean there's nothing wrong with the

Roumelia case?'

'I'd venture to say no, but in stirring it up with you, I guess Wemmick might have realised the slip-up he made with the handwriting. In fact, aiming my car through my study window might actually have been to get rid of the files, not me!'

'But you didn't have the Roumelia file.' Heather looked confused.

'He did at one stage,' Ella contradicted. 'I saw it in his desk drawer – and then it disappeared the same time the Johns case notes did. I thought he'd taken both of them home.'

'Since when did I give you leave to poke around in my desk?' I rounded on Ella.

'Since you played your little games in court and left me running round after you like an idiot,' she retorted. 'And her, obviously, since it was her brother in the dock, then … '

'Ah,' the reason for Ella's extreme dislike of Kat suddenly became clear to me. Power play: who had it, who didn't have it and who wanted it …

'And I think you're making someone who works hard for charity into a villain, simply to take the heat off of you, actually.' She continued, 'You should simply come clean and get Chambers off the hook now, before you're forced to.'

It suddenly occurred to me that Ella might be the reason Jaggers thought I had both case files with me at home. I caught Heather's eye and could see from her expression, the idea had just occurred to her too. There was a clatter from somewhere in the basement.

'I think I may have left the back door unlocked,' Heather announced, uneasily. 'Ella, would you go and check please. We can't have anything else go missing.' Ella threw her a black look but reluctantly made for the door to the basement. When it had closed behind her, Heather got up from the reception desk and tottered across to wedge it shut. Kat smiled. Heather wiggled back and settled back behind the desk, like a judge taking their seat.

'Right, so is the Johns case another red herring?'

'No, it's the sprat to catch the mackerel.'

'Bloody hell, we're back to the fish market,' Win commented. I laughed, relieved the spy in the camp appeared to have been excluded – and surely that implied Heather was still on my side?

'No, *I'm* the fish market, Win – you're just the unlucky bystanders. I'm the mackerel, the Johns case is the sprat. Wemmick is after me. He's always been after me – and he was using Margaret to get to me because she was vulnerable. Now he's using you, Heather, and Danny too. It was because I feared something like this that I agreed a code word with Danny, and also why I asked him to stay put at the children's home, even though he didn't like it. At least he was safe there. But he's never gone missing against his will. I think each time he's gone, he's gone willingly, this time too.'

'Who the hell with?' Kat demanded angrily. 'Surely they know how dangerous it is for him to go missing like he this – with his medical condition.'

'My bet is that he's with someone who'll take good care of him – has the best reason in the world to, in fact: Margaret. He'll be fine.'

'Margaret?' Kat exclaimed. 'How do you know?'

'Has she been in touch?' Heather demanded.

'No, but …'

'Then you don't know. How can you trust someone who keeps changing her story?' Kat countered.

'Yes, how can I?' I looked her straight in the eye and she had the grace to blush, albeit angrily.

'I thought we weren't raking up old wrongs,' she snapped back.

'I was just making the point that changing a story isn't always with the intention of deceiving.'

She looked mollified. 'So what would be her reason for best reason in the world for keeping him safe? And where is she? When is she going to resurrect herself for *everyone*, not just you?'

'When it's safe for her to do so, I guess,' I replied, hoping her other question would be forgotten in deference to discussing Margaret's whereabouts. 'It's a dangerous world to be in – trying to bring a murderer to account.'

'Really? But why does that involve Danny? I don't know, Lawrence. There are times when I wonder whether you've made this whole little fiasco up, and she isn't alive at all. She's as dead as she's supposed to be and pretending she isn't is merely a convenient way to get yourself out of a different tricky situation.'

What she alluded to was clear to me, even though Heather and Win looked mystified.

I sighed. I'd been wrong assuming our post-beach admissions had resolved things between us. Water under the bridge wasn't necessarily clean water. I had to give up on Kat for the moment. It would be a very long way back for us, if we ever had the chance to test it out.

'Heather,' I appealed. 'You know I'm telling the truth.'

'To be fair, Lawrence, I've only ever known what you've told me,' Heather's lips pursed testily. 'Maybe Ella and Kat are right. You have got us all very successfully caught up in your tailspin, haven't you? Maybe *you're* the red herring.' I was aghast. Apart from Win, Heather was the loyal support I'd relied on all along. If she was turning against me now …

'All right, the letter from her, and the partnership bank account withdrawals on her card. What about them? They prove she's alive, surely?'

'You were given her bank card when she was supposedly dead. You obviously didn't cancel it and used it in her stead.' Ella pushed the basement door open and all eyes turned to her. 'And you don't need to deny that, by the way. We know it would be a lie or you would have done more to sort it out when it first happened, wouldn't he Auntie? Even you've said that to me, privately.' Ella flicked her hair out of her eyes and glared at me defiantly. Heather began to object, but then fell silent. I appealed to her pragmatism.

'The pencil in the flat opposite – you even found that, Heather. You were with me. It proves Margaret was there, and if she was there, she has to be alive.'

'No, it seemed like *someone* could have been there, but not necessarily – or even – Margaret. I said at the time that she'd have let you find her if it was her, wouldn't she? It was probably squatters and I've already warned Norton about tightening up on security.'

I flung round to Kat.

'So what about the photograph of Margaret I found in Molly Wemmick's office.'

She shook her head and I didn't wait for her answer, realising as I said it only I had seen it – not Kat. Damn! But of course Win was here now. I turned to Win. 'And you actually saw her when she got us out of the play-palace at the God's and Gargoyle's Club.'

Win shuffled his feet and his shook his head sheepishly.

'Well, I know you said it were her then, but she didn't look like Margaret – that woman. Similar, but remember I'd just been whacked and couldn't see all that well at the time with two black eyes. *You* told me it was her ...'

'Oh, *come on!*' Four pairs of eyes watched me, with various degrees of suspicion. 'What? You think I'm making this charade up? Why?'

Surely Jaggers' propaganda machine couldn't work that easily on people who actually knew me?

'It would be a way of covering up the fact that you messed up badly eleven years ago, Lawrence,' Ella looked smug. 'And playing up your wife's death is a very convenient way of getting sympathy from some quarters,' she eyed Kat and Heather. Heather bristled but still didn't jump to my defence – far from it.

'I suppose the partnership's bank could have helped out with money troubles,' she suggested, perturbed.

'I didn't have money troubles until now …' I threw back.

Ella spoke over the top of me. 'It says in the paper you do. It was maybe even the reason you got rid of your sister, if she was blackmailing you,' her smug smile was now tinged with malice. 'Then try to pretend it's all a massive plot against you.'

'That would make me a sociopath of the first order,' I snarled at her, furious at her sly twisting of the truth.

'Aren't you? Or a psychopath!' she spat back.

'Stop it!' Heather tapped a coral fingertip on the magazine, still lying on the desk face up with Jaggers smiling – triumphantly, it now seemed – at us. 'I don't believe you're a psychopath or a sociopath, but I have to admit that this guy you're painting black as black doesn't seem to be that from what I've read about him in here. And nor is his worry that the Roumelia case was a set-up quite so divisive if he knows you were involved in something else that could be construed the same way in the past. He's simply tarring Chambers with the same brush because one bent barrister could mean a whole barrel-load of them. I'm not excusing him or saying I don't still think he came across as an arsehole when he threatened me, but it would explain it. I can even see his point of view.'

I stared at her, amazed and horrified.

'OK, so you all suddenly think I'm a liar, a thief and a murderer. I thought the law said we're all innocent until proven guilty. Why does that not also apply to me?'

Heather sighed.

'It does, Lawrence. I wasn't accusing you, just saying your story isn't as credible as his. Personally, I still think we should simply hand over everything we have to Fredriks, including how to get hold of Margaret – if she's alive and well – and let him sort it all out. Whether it's all how you say it is or not, you've suffered a beating, an explosion, lost your home, possibly your wife, and your sister all in a very short space of time.

The mind can do strange things under pressure. There *is* a case to be made in your defence even if you haven't played it down the line in the past, if you'd let me help.' She was obviously trying to look sympathetic but to my mind it didn't work.

'And there's Danny to think of. What if he's not with Margaret? What if he's really missing?' Kat added anxiously.

'Kidnapping by proxy?' Ella suggested, maliciously. Kat sent her a hostile look and continued.

'He has a serious medical condition and needs to be monitored. And you *were* planning something with him on the beach, whatever you say to the contrary. That's why you sent me off on that wild goose chase,' she looked annoyed again. 'You might have been intending to keep him safe, but you haven't. We need to find him Lawrence. Now!'

I looked at my jury. Three out of four had cast their vote.

'And what do you think?' I turned on Win, studiously silent until now.

'Well,' he hesitated. 'Kimmy were invited to your place, weren't she? There weren't no-one but you to invite her there by then if Margaret was gone. I s'pose you could have waited for me to go, then ...' He looked ashamed. 'Oh, I dunno! No, you're a prat, but you're not a murderer little bruv, although I think you might be sick in the head – like Mrs ...'

'*Miss*,' Heather corrected crisply.

'Like Miss Trinder here says,' he finished awkwardly. He picked up the magazine and studied the smiling monster to avoid looking at me.

'Margaret herself set up her own "death",' I retorted. '*You* told me about that. You don't do that unless something underhand is going on. And *you* were the one who told me that I was being coerced into taking Danny's case so I'd be hooked and forced to get involved in Margaret's little crusade. I didn't know anything about Danny or who Wilhelm Johns was until you told me. Am I really so good an actor I've fooled all of you completely and I'm actually the sole villain of the piece?'

Heather made a moue of wry amusement. Win answered for her.

'No, you're shit. But that won't prove nothing to the cops.'

'Look, we have at least two murders, a missing boy, missing money, maybe missing witnesses and missing truth – but a man and a woman who I think can piece the whole damn mess back together again between them. This man,' I pointed to Jaggers' jeering face, 'and my wife. Please help me do that – for all of us.'

'Well ...' Heather's lips twisted as she considered me. I waited anxiously, the condemned man awaiting sentence. 'Whilst I don't think Lawrence is a murderer, he does owe me the contents of his bank account and – I fear – some hefty car repairs?' I hung my head. I felt disconcertingly like a naughty schoolboy. 'And he owes me and DCI Fredriks some answers about the Johns case. Unless he can do that, whether by himself, or with the lovely Margaret's help, my reputation – and our business – is down the pan. I still think it makes sense we reel Margaret in and then let the police sort it out.' I frowned at her. 'Fredriks is OK,' she added diffidently.

'That makes absolute sense to me too,' Ella butted in. 'Just hand both of them over to Fredriks and be done with them.' She smiled nastily at Win and me. 'That's why I called DCI Fredriks and told him we'd got both his bail-jumper and the man behind the witness tampering in the Johns case and the murder of Kimberley Hewson here. I expect that's him and a squad car right now.'

Outside an array of flashing blue lights flickered through the glass panels of the entrance to Chambers.

'Ella, you had no right ...' Heather sprang angrily to her feet. 'I was going to add that Lawrence has to be allowed to talk to Margaret first and then defend himself, and his brother hasn't been charged with murder yet.'

'Well, it's too late, Auntie. *He's* got a record as long as your arm already,' she nodded towards Win. 'And he's as tricky as they come,' about me. 'They're both owed their come-uppance, and they're about to get it.'

The lights settled into a rotating pattern of blue and white behind glass panels.

'This won't solve anything!' I protested angrily.

'I agree,' Heather tottered round to the front of the reception desk. 'Margaret will just disappear again if Lawrence can't get to her and draw her out – and so will the money and the evidence Lawrence thinks she has.'

'So will Danny, if he's with her,' Kat cut in.

'And me defence lawyer,' Win added despondently.

Ella shrugged and walked haughtily over to the door to let Fredriks and his posse in.

'There's only so much greasy pole you can climb before you slip back to the bottom where you belong.' She paused coolly by the door. 'And juniors you can walk all over on your way up it.' She smiled complacently at me. 'Eventually you have to pay what you owe.'

I looked helplessly from her to my now shaky allies.

'Hey!' Win called to me. 'And I owe you something for all the crap you put me through.' He looked me straight in the eye, lower jaw jutting belligerently. 'Ready?'

I didn't realise the punch was coming until it collided with my jaw, then every inferno that had ever raged in hell set my face alight and burnt into my brain, devouring my ability to stand, move and eventually stay conscious. I tasted blood through splitting lips as I sunk my teeth deep into a pillow-soft tongue before falling into a deep pit from which I doubted I'd ever rise again.

I woke in the Gents, still in Chambers, tongue swollen and the bottom half of my face throbbing like someone was inflating and deflating it in time to the beat of pain. I was propped up against the cistern, legs akimbo, astride the toilet – lid down, mercifully. The light was meagre, less even than the half gloom that we'd gathered under in reception. The reason was Win, blocking the doorway to the cubicle, and leaning nonchalantly against the frame. He was rubbing the knuckles on his right hand.

'You got a bloody hard jaw, little bruv. You been eating cement?' I mumbled a reply along the lines of *fuck off* but it sounded more like a drunk retching. 'You won't make a lot of sense until your tongue goes down, 'fraid. And you lost a tooth – sorry, but I had to get you out of there somehow. We were about to be dobbed in by that arsy little bint.'

I gargled again and he must have – miraculously – understood what I'd said – curses and all. He laughed.

'No, you know I had both a mother and a father – like you – so that ain't fair, although I am a bastard in other ways, I agree. A clever bastard. They think me and Mrs Whatserface are taking you to casualty to get your jaw fixed – it might be broken by the way. Then we're supposed to take you back to see Duck Face. Mrs Whatser's squared it with him but we got forty-eight hours max, then we're both right in the shit again. I don't think you killed Kimmy, and I know there's summat going on here. I know Jaggers. He ain't no nice smiley bastard, he's just a bastard, plain and simple. But after your forty-eight hours, time's up for both of us, so you gotta get us both off the hook by then.'

I leaned heavily against the cistern and groaned as the events of the last day or so slowly came back into focus with Win.

'Oh, wonderful! They've got photos, you know – of you threatening

Kimmy with a knife in my kitchen. They were on the camera in the basement of FFF. How do I get you off that?'

At least that's what I wanted to say. I knew what I'd said, but it sounded merely like a collection of weird guttural mutterings. Maybe it's something to do with kin, because Win understood nevertheless. We carried on our conversation with him talking plain speak and me talking caveman whilst I gingerly wiped away the blood and discovered that the tooth I'd lost was one that had plagued me on and off in the past. There was a strange sweetish tang in my mouth, mixing with the sanguine bitter of old blood, gall and regret.

'I weren't threatening her. I were trying to take the bloody thing off her. She were downright crazy that day.' He passed me more toilet paper and tossed the blood-stained lump I exchanged for it down the open pan in the next cubicle. 'No meds, I guess.'

'But it doesn't look like that and that's what the police are going to make the case on – that and the fact that the knife had your fingerprints on it and ...'

'And the bag, right?

'And the bag.'

'Yeah, well, I seen him play his little games with them till the poor bastard passes out. They don't cross him again after that. You think Jaggers killed Kimmy?'

'Who else could it be?'

'Then you got to prove it.'

He moved and the bare light in the centre of the Gents made me squint, leaving little multi-coloured lights flickering before my eyes. One was particularly annoying – the little green blink-blink-blink that could be the beginning of a detached retina, or the glimmer of an idea I had yet to nail. With it came one of the stray thoughts I'd been toying with on and off for weeks now.

'Why did you first try and get everyone back together, Win?'

'We were family. Family sticks together.'

'But we hadn't.'

'Don't mean something that happened has to stay happened. We all got choices – just have to go about them the right way.'

'Do you remember that day we went to the beach in Deal – Aunt Edie's place.'

A slow smile spread across his lumpy face.

'Yeah, I remember. Me and Binnie – we never really seen eye to eye, and never really not neither.'

'Sarah had to stop an argument between you and Binnie and then we all made a giant sandcastle together. We made a promise then too – to stick together as family. Is that where the idea came from?'

He considered for a moment, clearly reliving the old memory.

'Maybe.'

'But you never tried to find me.'

All the hurt I'd felt as a child when left out of things welled up unattractively in the man. Only the distortion of an already ruined face hid the inclination to cry – pathetic in a grown man, but real nonetheless. Win tutted at me.

'Oh, I did, little bruv. I found you all right, but I thought we'd best leave you be when I did.'

'Why?'

'Because it was obvious you didn't want to be found. No point forcing anyone. It never sticks.'

'But you force people all the time on behalf of Jaggers, and you forced me when Danny was being charged.'

'Jaggers – that's just a job, and we all know the rules – punters and pushers alike. Up to them if they choose to break 'em. I ain't ever really hurt no-one 'cos of it, only scared 'em. And I didn't force *you*. I told you about Danny, that's all.'

'Wasn't that forcing me?'

'No, only one person ever forced you.'

'And who was that?'

'You.'

I stared at him.

'Like I said, no point. You gotta choose to get involved. You're family, and if you're family, I choose to get involved for you.'

I made a supreme effort and actually understood my own words this time.

'In that case. We've got someone to find in order to help another member of ours. Where's your car?'

11: St Rosemary

Win's car was the same make as Heather's, but not a 'girl's car' this time. A man's; a wealthy man's. It was a BMW 7 series, complete with integral phone, fax, wine cooler, traction and climate control. A lounge, or office, on wheels. All in black, including the interior. No worries about making his upholstery dirty, then. I raised my eyebrows and whistled – with difficulty through my swollen lips – when I saw it parked discreetly two blocks down.

'No my dick ain't that small,' he commented. 'I just like to know when I need to put me foot down, something will happen. V8 and 4 litres,' he added. 'None of your half-ass show.' He patted the bonnet proudly – as I would have done with the Austin Healey. 'Mrs Whatsit won't like it though. Not the way she planned it.'

'I hadn't thought any of this is the way any of us planned it,' I replied dryly. 'She'll survive if this gets the job done.'

'Hope that brassy little bint don't,' Win replied, with a grin. 'Or at least gets a right bollocking from Mrs Whatser ... Where we going then?'

'I probably ought to go alone – not drag you into this any further.'

'Oh, no, matey. You ain't driving this little beauty away without me in it. I'm sticking to you like shit on a shoe from now on.'

The shakes had started to kick in now – shock most likely, and I shivered. He was probably right. I needed someone to cover my back, home and away – a minder – and who else better for that than Win? The last little fiasco had demonstrated that amply.

'OK, but I need to get to Margaret to find Danny, and that's best done on my own.'

'I been a chauffeur before, and I can do it again. Ready?'

He unlocked the driver's door and the lock automatically clicked off the passenger's side. I nodded. There was nowhere else to go and nothing else to do. It was Win's terms or nothing; by the balls again.

I slid carefully into the passenger seat, ribs grumbling as I doubled up to get in. The pounding in my head had subsided to a slow thump, followed by a sharp stab in the area of the lost tooth. The two were orchestrating themselves perfectly to create a concerto of discomfort, backed by the low rumble in my chest. At least the luxury of the leather upholstery was comforting.

'Crahan House in Kent. That's where we need to go.'

'Why?'

'It's where Margaret lived before we met. Her sister is buried in the churchyard of her namesake – St Rosemary in the Marsh. She's the other victim in all this.'

'Oh yeah – her,' he sounded offhand.

'And it's where her family came from.'

'But they won't be there now, will they? They're all dead apart from Margaret. Wha's the point?'

'I've got to start somewhere. I think it could be there.'

'I don't s'pose you're going to tell me why?'

'It won't sound very convincing,' I explained.

'Try me anyway.'

Crahan. A message in a pencil, not a bottle. Word association – like Heather said. Something I'd twice been prompted to do – or so I thought – via the abandoned pencil and the piggy bank message. Why? What was there? And why did I think it was the place to start? Something in my gut? Or a way to postpone the person and the moment I least wanted to confront?

Mary.

No, it was more to do with needing to know more about my wife's roots, I assured myself. Maybe then I would understand her and her behaviour better. And her clues.

'It's all to do with digging up the past – I think.'

I strapped in and closed my eyes, allowing the sensation of speed to carry me away to better times and places when I'd been riding high on success with a high-profile reputation and a perfect-solution wife. Or further back still – to peering through the driver's window of Mad Mike's Austin Healey, parked ostentatiously outside the Alhambra when I was nine, and imagining what life would be like for me when I owned one too. If only as children we knew what life would hold as adults. I snorted wryly. Then we'd probably elect to never grow up.

'OK? Ain't choking on your mistakes?' I opened my eyes to catch Win casting a sideways glance at me before swearing and veering off towards St Katherine's Bridge. 'Shit!' he added, 'sodding roadworks!' He changed gear, revved, and we headed over the bridge and clear of the pile-up.

'Don't we all choke on our mistakes at some stage in our lives, Win?'

'Yeah, it's OK to choke – just don't die from them.'

We drove in silence for a while and I watched the London docklands pass us by with mild interest. Refurbishment was in full swing here and I hadn't appreciated before quite how much the cityscape was changing – like the landscape of my life. I let my mind wander as Win drove, glad after all that I didn't have to concentrate.

Why had Heather gone from taking me in, shielding me from the press, even loaning me – unwisely as it turned out – her car, then doubting everything I'd ever told her about Jaggers? Admittedly the story was wild – crazy even – but she'd seen it as it happened. How could she disbelieve what she'd witnessed parts of as they happened – the evidence packages, the fire, the items in Sarah's box, Margaret's letter. Kat's mercurial changes I could accept – almost. Much of it was my fault – involving her, rejecting her, and involving her again. Heather, though … perhaps I still wasn't seeing things clearly enough – or as others saw them and me. There was change in the air and I didn't like it.

Win cut through my mêlée of confusion and self-castigation to point out we were passing Billingsgate.

'The home of the mackerel!'

'Funny,' I replied, but it was an opener. 'Why do *you* think Heather – Mrs Trinder – changed her tune about Jaggers?'

'Did she?'

'I assume she did. Why would she have gone along with me until now – taken me in – if she thought I was making up a load of rubbish about him before?'

'She was waiting.'

'What for?'

'The angles to play out – remember? Pool – or billiards if you're a posh bastard like Jaggers.'

'The angles being?'

'I dunno, matey – you know what you told her and what she knows. What do you reckon they are?'

'There are a number I suppose, from Heather's point of view. Where's the partnership money gone? What's the real truth behind the Johns case, what am I up to with Margaret … Danny too, of course.'

'Plenty of angles to play with there, then. And as far as Missus Whatserface knows…'

'Trinder.'

'OK, as far as Mrs Trinder knows, *you* ain't playing squeaky clean with any of them.'

'But I am.'

'Oh yeah? Bit tricky for a corpse to empty a bank account, ain't it?'

'Margaret's not a corpse – she did it herself using a card I thought I'd cancelled, but obviously she got hold of before I'd done it and then put it back. Then there's the Johns case. I didn't cover anything up, I just didn't question deeply enough. I'm at fault, but not criminally; morally. I did what I was paid to do, but not what I should have done.'

'And how do you think your buddy sees that?'

'I don't know. I suppose it will depend on what other evidence is being presented – this witness tampering implication, for instance.'

'Jaggers?'

'It has to be. Who else has got it in for me?'

'Dunno. Maybe you ought to make a list. Any of them three ladies tonight could start it off, I reckon – especially the bint who called the cops.' I ignored the dig. 'All right,' he continued, 'what would you do if you thought your business partner had cleaned your bank account out and broken the law and you're a barrister?'

'Hand him over, I guess,' I replied, reluctantly.

'There you go, then. Make a good detective, wouldn't you?' he grinned, enjoying his own joke far too much. 'Easy, really, then ain't it? Didn't need me to answer it. Just put yourself in someone else's shoes and it's job done.' He paused and something I'd long since forgotten, but shouldn't have, slipped back into my mind. *'You never really understand a person until you consider things from his point of view… until you climb into his skin and walk around in it.*[2] 'But she ain't yet – remember? She's the one still sweet-talking plod for us, or you'n me wouldn't be hitting the open road right now.'

'Umm,' I wondered what form sweet-talking might take between Heather and Fredriks, then dismissed the thought as ridiculous. 'They're still all red herrings, Win.'

'Bloody Billingsgate again,' he laughed.

'No, not real herrings – tricks.' I paused. 'It's Jaggers behind all of this. Margaret explained how and why in her letter. It's all to get to me and force me to hand back the money I had via Judge Wemmick's will –

plus compound interest. Heather knows that too – but I need to prove it.'

'Seems a lot of hard work for him to bother with. He usually just leans on someone a bit – physical like – and gets what he wants. Why so much extra effort to soften you up? You ain't *that* special – no offence, like.'

I did the calculations in my head – the original sum plus compound interest over more than thirty years. It was rough, but not far off.

'No, not special, expensive. Something around two and half million is the reason why.'

The car jolted and steadied.

'Fucking hell! Is that what you got?'

'No, it's what I've got plus compound interest over thirty-three years. That means interest on interest on interest ad infinitum, so the interest repayable under the terms of the will if I'm discredited or I bring Judge Wemmick's name or the family name into disrepute by association with me becomes thousands of percent – a fortune.'

'And this is all just about spondoolicks? Money?'

'Yes, pretty much so where I'm concerned. The rest of it – where Margaret's concerned – is somewhat more complicated.'

'So have you got the readies to repay if you have to? To get him off your back – and mine – if it's the only way?'

'I suppose I could. I'd have nothing left, though.'

He whistled.

'Wants to break you, then. Lucky you to have that kind of dosh.'

I grunted. 'Money isn't everything, Win. In my case it's the source of most of my problems, and all of this is his way of showing me I have no choice. Either I hand it over willingly, and be allowed to continue, but with nothing – or he'll take everything anyway, one way or another. That's why the Johns case, the money – even Kimmy's death – are all red herrings. They're just to distract everyone else away from the main issue – the money.'

'OK, so now explain where Margaret comes into this.'

'Well, she clearly has another agenda: Danny – and to see justice done for Rosemary.'

'By finding her real killer?'

'It seems so.'

'Huh – who do we both think that is?'

'I think we both *know* who that is.'

We continued in silence for a while as we both considered what that meant. Win broke it about a mile further on.

'I get the stuff about Rosemary, but what d'you mean about Danny? I thought he were just her way of getting you involved?'

I remembered then that Win – like Kat – wasn't party to the confession I'd made to Heather, although it looked like Heather may have already spilt some of the beans about it – to Ella at least, given Ella's sly remark about Danny being my responsibility. And if Ella already knew, it wouldn't be long before it was made public. I certainly owed my own brother the courtesy of knowing before everyone else did.

'Ah … umm.' I looked out the window at the docklands landscape now meandering into the outer suburbs of the city, dowdy and depressing. We dropped into the slipway entering the Blackwall tunnel and the road ahead was a dirty yellow brick road, highlighted in the cars' headlights. 'Danny's parents aren't who we thought they were …'

'Yeah? Tell me another. I know they weren't Kimmy and her bloke. Duck Face made that clear when he was going through all the reasons I might have had for topping her; cow! And after all that grief I let meself go through for her – and Jonno, poor sod.'

'Yes, it has caused an exceptional amount of grief for everyone, that little angle.'

'So … give? It was gonna be one of the first things on my list to clear up if it hadn't been for this load of shite tonight.' He laughed humourlessly. 'But at least if it weren't Kimmy then someone hasn't been bonking their sister, if you know what I mean.' He leered unattractively at me.

'No.' I measured the likely response to the truth. Whatever it was, it wasn't going to be complimentary. 'He's still your nephew though.'

'How?'

'There was some paperwork in a keepsakes box that Sarah left me. I wasn't quite sure why she would want to leave it to me at the time since we'd barely even started to get to know each other again, but now I understand. There were two birth certificates in there – a stillborn child, supposedly Rosemary Flower's child, and a live one – supposedly Kimmy's. But when I found out Danny wasn't genetically Kimmy's son, I looked at it all again. Rosemary was already dead when both children were born – in 1989 – so neither child could be hers, but if there were two birth certificates, there were two births. For Kimmy to have Danny, the two babies must have been swopped with Kimmy taking the live child, even though he wasn't hers.'

'Well, he weren't no immaculate conception, so who's his mother, then?' I hesitated, 'and don't tell me it's the Holy Ghost.' He snorted derisively. I dropped the first bombshell.

'His mother is Margaret.'

'Jesus! Now you're *really* having me on!' He turned bodily in his seat and an oncoming car flashed us as the car swerved.

'No, honestly. If there were two children, and one of them was a Flowers and one Kimmy's child – but Kimmy's child died – what's the obvious conclusion? Margaret was the one who registered both births too. She simply substituted Rosemary's name for her own and because only she was involved with registering them, no-one questioned it. The letter she left me to open in the event of her death confirmed it. I didn't open it until after the fire but I'd already pretty much worked it out by then.'

He shook his head. If he hadn't been driving I think he would have scratched it too.

'Why use her sister's name? That's sick.'

'No, smart – or possibly opportunistic. There's some tricky stuff to do with the Wemmick inheritance involved too, but it was probably more to do with the fact that Margaret would have still had Rosemary's ID to hand and this way Danny remained a Wemmick.'

I waited for the most difficult question to filter through the filing system Win was obviously delving through in his mind. It didn't take long. I was starting to realise that Win's bluff and bluster masked a pragmatic brain.

'OK, so, the thousand dollar question is – no, make that the two point five million pound question – who's the daddy if he's still me nephew? Jonno?'

'No. You don't really need me to tell you, do you?'

He was silent. I could almost hear the possibilities being tested and discarded. There weren't many.

'Not really, but you might as well make it a hat trick of crap – kid, mum and dad.'

'Me.'

'Yeah, I was right. It wasn't the fucking Holy Ghost.'

We completed the rest of the journey through the Blackwall tunnel in awkward silence, re-entering the daylight, such as it was, still in darkness between us. I waited nervously for his considered reaction. He switched the headlights to sidelights and broke the silence as we emerged from its gloomy depths.

'It figures, but why didn't you tell me sooner?'

The reply was surprisingly mild considering the second bombshell I'd just dropped.

'I didn't know.'

'You just said you worked out she was Danny's mother from the stuff in Sarah's keepsakes box. She was your wife, for God's sake. How could you not know you'd fathered a kid with her?'

'Because I was drunk, remember? You reminded me of the circumstances yourself – although then you told me my lovely party companion was my sister. It was actually Margaret. I could ask you how could you have not known Kimmy was lying?'

'It weren't Kimmy who told me.'

That surprised me.

'Who was it then?'

'Margaret.'

'Margaret?'

The suburbs were slowly giving way to countryside, grey and bleak in the dwindling light. Win switched the headlights back on and the yellow brick road continued ahead in their dipped beam, but with no magician likely to help me with my problem at the end of it, unless Crahan House housed him. 'I think it's time for us to put all our cards on the table, don't you, Win? Tell each other everything we know?'

'I already told you what I know.'

'Have you? Really?' I watched his lips curl at the sarcasm, but he didn't respond to it. I sighed. 'OK, I'll start then.'

I told him then what Margaret had written in her letter – about her family connection to Jaggers, her half-brother. And about the liaison between him and Rosemary – by then using the stage name Maria Flowers so I hadn't automatically put her and Margaret together when I'd formally met her as Margaret Green. Finally I explained how Margaret was sure that Jaggers had killed Rosemary and had the evidence to prove it but had insisted on keeping it to herself until she knew Danny was safe. Danny was the key because he was the only male now truly in line to inherit the Wemmick estate, albeit indirectly through Margaret and her illegitimate mother. Nevertheless that also made him next on the list to be disposed of when Jaggers found out because with Danny's claim proven, Jaggers would be ousted from the comfortable little niche of power he'd carved for himself as head of the Wemmick empire. He responded to my confession time with a question.

'So, why do you trust her if she even lied about all of that?'

'I haven't got much choice but to trust her for the moment. She's the only one with all the answers.'

'You don't have to trust someone to play along with them.'

'Why would you play along with them if you don't trust them?'

'To see how the angles play out.' He glanced sideways at me. In the half-light of the evening, he looked just like Ma, if only for a second. 'I don't trust no-one but meself, little bruv. I only know what's going on in me own head. That I can trust – even if it's ass about tit. What's going on in anyone else's? Pah! You gotta learn to do that too.'

We filtered off the A2 and onto the M20. Win put his foot down and the car purred into life. I watched the speedo rise to ninety, enjoying the mild sensation of G-force pinning me back in my seat as we accelerated. The speed-freak child still existed in me, and obviously in Win too. It released something less adult in me, less measured and cautious. See how the angles play out? There were a lot of angles and a lot of possible tangents they could spin off on. Win spoke my mind for me.

'Don't think you know the half of it yet, little bruv. If I'd known this a while back I might not have let meself get so far involved, but there's one angle you've got to follow through on – Danny. He's your kid.'

'He'll be with Margaret.'

'You convincing me or yourself?'

'I don't need to convince myself. What mother would put their child at risk? Margaret may be manipulative, but she's always had Danny's interests at heart.'

'If you say so – his funeral if you're wrong. Wouldn't want that on me conscience, personally.'

'Time for your cards on the table now. Maybe it would help me see how the angles are playing out if you told me what you know about Margaret.'

'Not a lot to tell you really. Margaret was always a quiet kid, serious – didn't like Kimmy much but actually got on quite well with Mary when Mary was allowed to come and see us, which wasn't often. Particularly remember her standing up for Mary when Rosemary made fun of her. Got a kind heart – I'll say that for her. Maybe you're right about Danny being OK with her. One of the reasons I went along with her plan in the first place, really – because she was good to Mary – and Jonno, of course.'

'And what exactly was the plan – the real plan? And why didn't you see fit to tell me that you'd known her all along – even when you were leaving me out of it?'

'By then *I couldn't* say nothing. Would've messed everything up. She said Danny was your kid with Kimmy, but Kimmy was in trouble again by then. That's why she got Kimmy and Danny involved with that charity.'

'FFF.'

'Yeah, that one,' he shifted in his seat and the speed wavered, then increased. 'Said it would help keep him safe and Kimmy out of more trouble. And I knew she wasn't keen on Jaggers. Well, neither was I by then. She said Kimmy was sailing too close to the wind and that was putting Danny at risk but she couldn't tell you straight out that Danny was your kid because you'd wonder how she knew and once Jaggers was mentioned, or any of your family wheeled in, you'd run a mile – maybe even divorce her. Her plan was to drip-feed you bits, gradually getting you involved and then work on you about adopting Danny. She really wanted kids, you know, even though you didn't.' I squirmed. 'When you'd seen the error of your ways, she were going to push you to re-open Jonno's case too – although she didn't tell me how she were going to do that. Just said you were *manageable* – just had to be done the right way.'

'So you'd both been scheming behind my back for years?'

'Not scheming. Figuring out how to put things right.'

'But that isn't the way it's panned out.'

'No. Kimmy got herself in too far with Jaggers before Margaret got it sorted out and he'd already done that little number on Danny like he got you to do on me in the children's home. I don't know what kind of business she was doing for him, and I didn't want to, but she could obviously make life difficult for him or he wouldn't have reacted so bad to her playing him up. All Margaret's plans went down the pan then, so she came up with this new one – like I said, playing out the angles. She said the adoption could still be swung further down the line because he'd have to be vouched for to get a suspended. Trouble was, you still wouldn't play ball; adamant you wouldn't take the case – eyes too much on the prize of the High Court by then. So she came up with the hit and run idea and a way of making you take the case – threaten to expose you while you were right slap bang in the centre of the public eye. Everyone would be watching you and you'd jump around like a cat on hot bricks to be the good guy if the press were watching. Once you were involved, that was when I came in – and all the rest of the shit until you had no other way out.'

'But how did she think she was going to make a come-back from being dead?'

'She wasn't. She weren't planning on getting killed, just a little roughed up. Unless …'

'Unless what?'

'Well, unless she wasn't planning on coming back, because if she ain't dead, then why pretend she was?'

Not planning on coming back? I let that sink in for a while. That didn't make sense. She already had – although not openly. As Molly … and where did that leave me – and Danny?

'What about her role as Molly Wemmick? Did you know about that too?'

'Yeah, course.' His lip curled sardonically. 'Hey – maybe that would solve it – her little resurrection problem. Molly and Lawrence get it on further down the line having been thrown together as good Samaritans protecting a kid. Like in the movies. Perfect!'

It had occurred to me at roughly the same time Win had suggested it. My bully-boy brother was as devious– or maybe as smart – as my 'dead' wife.

'Was she always this tricky? Even as a kid?'

'Margaret? No, like I said, quiet and serious – but stood up for the weaker ones. Rosemary was the tricky one – that's why she and Kimmy got on.'

'You weren't fond of Kimmy either?'

'She was me sister.'

'That wasn't what I asked.'

'Fond of her? No. Felt responsible for her – yes.'

'In Margaret's letter she said that Kimmy and Rosemary became bosom buddies at the Gods and Gargoyles Club. Was that true?'

'Yeah, pretty much. I didn't have any say in what Kimmy did by then – she was an adult, and a wild one. I cleared up after her because she was me kid sister, but I couldn't stop her. Kimmy and Rosemary both stripped – did Margaret tell you that too? I used to make sure I weren't there when Kimmy did it. Couldn't look. I saw Rosemary a couple of times though, by accident. Didn't like that much either but by God she could put on a show. She was like Margaret, but with attitude – bolder, brassier, right in your face, if you know what I mean. You could walk in a room and miss Margaret; you'd never miss Rosemary. She made sure of that.'

'I don't know why you couldn't just have told me all this when you first came to see me about Danny. Have you told me everything now?'

'If I'd told you, I'd have done what Margaret was trying to avoid – make you run like fuck. Would you have said, "Oh thank you Win, let me get meself right in the shit, then"? Course not! I had to get you to be desperate, so you had no choice but to get yourself *out* of the shit.'

'But it didn't matter by then. Margaret was already "dead", so I wasn't going to be running from her, was I?'

'Yeah, well, if you remember, I weren't sure whether she was or she wasn't. Had it taken out of my hands, didn't I? For all I knew she was alive and her plan was well on track. Didn't want to foul anything else up.'

'And what do you really think now? Is she alive or dead?'

'I dunno.'

'But you saw her in the, the …' I was lost temporarily for an adequate description of the dungeon we'd found ourselves in after raiding the FFF building.

'The play palace?'

'Yes, there.'

'Like I said to your lady boss, you'd given me a nice pair of black eyes by then and me eyes were never that good to start with. She didn't look the same, but she didn't look entirely different either. If you ask me, she looked more like Rosemary used to than Margaret, but *she* really is dead so that was just me being spooked.' His jaw set belligerently. I stared at the road ahead, wondering what to say to convince him he'd seen what he'd seen. He surprised me by suddenly adding quietly, 'All right. If you say it was her, then I'm going to have to believe you since you're me brother – for argument's sake, though.'

'OK.' I trod water, determining how reliable his *for argument's sake* would be when put to the test. 'So, even if you weren't sure about who you saw, why didn't you tell Heather Trinder this? You could have potentially corroborated most of my story even if you didn't say for certain that Margaret was Margaret.'

'Like I said, play out the angles, little bruv. You still got to get me off, and I still don't trust no-one but meself.' We drove another four or so miles in silence until he broke it with, 'Here we go, St Rosemary in the Marsh.'

The signpost said twenty-nine miles. It was a desolate area; not somewhere I'd choose to live. Now the light had gone the marshes stretched away from us in empty spaces full of disquiet. The empty spaces in the car felt similar and it occurred to me he hadn't confirmed yet that he'd told me everything.

'Is that all I should know?'

He grunted. 'Bloody enough, isn't it?'

Too much and not enough, not that he could make any of it less or more.

'Is there ever a way back from this for any of us, Win?'

'Way back to where?'

A good question. I didn't know. I set the tone this time by staring out of the window and letting my thoughts wander into places I would have preferred them not to, but now knew they had to. Win, it seemed, didn't believe me a murderer or a thief, partly because he was also party to some of the machinations that had led to here so knew I was mainly telling the truth, although he wasn't sure about everything. Heather, Kat, Fredriks and the public at large, however, only had what I told them – or someone else had – to go on. What I told them had been irrational or incoherent much of the time – amply reflecting how I felt. What others were beginning to tell them was calculating and measured, and conflicted dramatically with my less credible tale. The adversarial newspaper editor, throwing scorn on the likelihood of my innocence as the man in the middle of a twisted tale of intrigue and suppressed fact, and now Jaggers in the magazine article – cool, controlled and clean – were far more believable than me. Jaggers was being the kind of squeaky-clean Heather had urged me to be but I'd wilfully ignored, riding on the arrogance of presumed safety because of my lofty position as a respected man of the courts. My audience tonight had just made it very clear they were sceptics, and if people who knew me were sceptics, how much more cynical would people who didn't know me be? I'd been so up close to myself, labouring under the assumption that since I knew the facts everyone else would assume my innocence too, I'd entirely missed the alternative possibility: that I was a conman, a liar and involved in at least one murder. The intellectually intriguing mystery that was Margaret had tricked me too – into being blind. I could already see how Margaret's plan to throw me into the spotlight and force an apparently altruistic involvement in Danny's case was now being reverse-engineered against me.

I really should go on alone – no matter how tempting it was to have Win along for the ride. My rapidly tarnishing profile would soon start to infect anyone seen to be helping me too. A battle campaign had indeed been begun following the council of war I'd anticipated with Heather this evening when she'd reeled me into Chambers, but it wasn't the one I'd anticipated. This battle was developing an alarming number of fronts to be fought on, and my allies on all of them were scarce. I had to keep them out of the frontline until I needed them or they would be annihilated before I could call on them for back-up.

The road sign indicated there were now a mere five miles left to St Rosemary in the Marsh. It reflected back in the car's headlights like it was blinking at us – an SOS. It triggered a recurrence of the little blinking green light I'd first imagined when the hack had snapped me outside the Tube station, and again when I was hunched over in the Gents at Chambers. I was close, so close to remembering where I'd seen it before, and then it was gone again.

'Win, I really should do this alone.'

'Why?'

I struggled for a reason he'd accept.

'Because Margaret won't break cover unless she thinks it's safe. With me, it's merely a clandestine meet. With you around, it could be an ambush.'

'Cheers. And what about the fact that I were her partner in crime long before you? Anyway, what makes you think she's going to be here – or prepared to meet you?'

'Nothing. I don't know much about anything at the moment, but one thing I am convinced of is that she won't talk to me if you're there too. She cut you out of her plans for a reason.' I thought about the hooded figure on the common, 'But she seems to have a pretty good idea where I am and who I'm with, so she'll know you're with me. If she does want to talk to me what better time than now with no-one on my tail currently? Wouldn't you be wary if you were in as dodgy a position as she is?'

'I bloody am,' he retorted irritably. 'But you don't know what *her* angle is yet.'

I thought of the kiss and the way my head had spun and how her eyes had been soft and misty when we drew apart. Surely her angle was what it had always been: the future, and making sure she, Danny and I had one. If that was an angle it was a good one, even if it wasn't my dream come true.

'Danny,' I said decisively. 'He's her angle – via me.'

'Phwaw!' He stretched and arched his back. 'Learning fast, aren't you?' he replied sarcastically.

'I don't understand.'

'Well, you know what'll push my buttons now, don't you.'

'And mine,' I reminded him.

'You're telling me you want me to leave you at this Crahan place and bugger off?'

'Not bugger off completely…'

'What then?'

'I'll need transport to get me where I need to go afterwards, but without you in it.'

'So you need my bloody car, but not me. No way. I know what you did to the lady boss's car. I ain't letting you do that to this little bitch. Anyway, this is about family. We stick together. Like I said before, if you want me car, you get me with it.'

'But I promise I wouldn't trash it. And you need to be back smiling nicely at Fredriks as soon as possible or you'll be in trouble. It may take longer than forty-eight hours to get to the bottom of this mess. And if I'm family, why don't you trust me?'

'How'm I s'posed to trust you, little bruv, family or not, when I got good reason to know you ain't to be trusted?'

'That was a long time ago and I thought it was forgiven now?'

'Forgiven, but not forgotten.' He descended into moody silence.

'Family, Win,' I reiterated.

'You ain't behaved like family to me for a long time, even if you are.'

'That hasn't always been my fault. You chose not to make contact with me, remember? But you dragged me into all this when it suited you, nevertheless. If you'd come to me and told me the whole story right at the outset maybe none of this would have happened.'

I was pushing it but I needed his guilty conscience active. He clamped his jaw tight and I could see the tense set of his profile against the moving backdrop of grey-black trees and bushes as we ploughed through the shadowy landscape. It was an expression I remembered from childhood; Win, truculent. I'd get nowhere like this. I tried another tack.

'If Danny *is* with Margaret I can take him back to the children's home. If she won't come out into the open, we won't know. *He's* never betrayed you, even if I have. C'mon Win – I thought you said you wanted to help me. Now all of a sudden you're going back on that – or is it you'll only help me on your terms?' He didn't reply. My last shot finally got him. 'And why did you help me out back there if you don't care? That wasn't just familial obligation or to save your ass. If anything you're further in the shit now.'

'How'd I know you won't disappear off into the wide blue yonder, with me car and your Margaret and just leave me to take the rap for it all? I'm the one potentially up on a murder charge, not you.'

'And Danny, Margaret and I are potentially on a murderer's list.'

We entered the village and cruised along its main street. It was a picturesque set-up, although its best features were shrouded in gloom. The dark seemed to have fallen more thickly here than it would have in the city, with its potential for twenty-four hour artificial daylight. A light mist was billowing in the dips of the undulating street. Win parked up outside the pub, a rambling white, oversized cottage with small mullioned windows and a rickety looking tiled roof. It proclaimed its offer of B&B from the afterthought of a sign dangling under the main pub sign: 'The Highwayman'. It was situated immediately next to the church.

'Cradle to grave – via the pub. Got that right, at least!' Win commented.

The highwayman on the sign was the archetypal 'stand and deliver' type, replete with swirling black cape, rearing chestnut mare and pistol aiming straight at the clientele contemplating entering the hostelry. For a moment I was reminded of Kitchener and his pointing finger – as loaded as a gun singling out man and boy as cannon fodder for the First World War. It occurred to me I probably had as little chance of coming out of this war alive as they'd had. At least they'd entered their war with honour and acquitted themselves with pride. I was continually on the run – the absconder from justice, the objector with no conscience. And I still had a lot more running to do.

'Well?'

'I'll think on it – over a beer. Can't do anything tonight anyway.' He turned off the ignition and stretched. 'I could do with a bloody great big steak and kidney pud.' He eyed the swinging highwayman suspiciously. 'D'you think it's one of them two peas and a piece of steak you could balance on a postage stamp places?'

'Nouvelle cuisine?' I laughed. 'I don't think a highwayman would approve of that much.'

'Good,' he said as if we'd just settled a discussion. 'We'll check in here and the grub's on you.' He heaved the door open with a grunt and lumbered out. 'And the beer,' he added as an afterthought.

'OK.' I followed him, already counting off how many of my forty-eight hours we were about to waste in there. 'But we don't have much time for anything, Win. We've got two days at most before Fredriks is after us again.'

A pebble skittered across the car park and pinged against my foot. I jumped and looked over my shoulder but the car park was empty apart from us. Christ I was on edge. By contrast, Win was the epitome of calm.

'Look, we're here. We don't know where this Crahan House place is, everywhere's closed except for the pub, and I'm bloody starved. If you want me to even think about letting you drive off to God knows where in my car, I'm havin' me dinner first!'

It seemed the only terms to talk with Win right then were treaty terms. I pushed the door shut, looking uneasily over my shoulder again towards the church looming out of the shadows behind us, and the serried ranks of gravestones arranged around it. An owl screeched in the distance, on the wing and seeking prey. Better to talk terms inside. I wasn't easily spooked usually – but the dark and the possibility of rodents were two of my very particular psychoses. We found the bar and prepared to parlay. The archetypal pub sign translated into an archetypal marshes pub – plus B&B. The landlady was a sharp-nosed and equally sharp-brained woman in her mid-forties, with a lazy husband who'd taken charge of the realm of the pots and was clearly not leaving it any time soon. The rest of the kingdom had therefore devolved to Queen Landlady and she ruled it with her cash register. She waved us through to reception, relieving me of fifty quid up front for a twin room and breakfast – way over the odds for a mid-week one-nighter in this part of the world, but her practised eye roamed my battered face and detected both my uneasiness and Win's reluctance to look further afield for better terms.

'This is a decent place – no trouble here,' she warned, as she palmed my wad of cash, one of the last gifts from the partnership bank account before it was declared completely defunct. I muttered my disapproval but Win nodded our agreement. 'And I s'pose you'll be wanting supper too?' Win beamed at her as he turned to go back to the bar, leaving me to it. I nodded reluctantly, wondering how much extra that was going to cost. She eyed me speculatively before pointing out a table in what passed for the restaurant. At least I could settle terms with Win there.

'On business are you?' She eyed my battered face.

'Not exactly.'

'Oh?'

A copy of the *Evening Standard* lay open on the desk behind reception. A bad photo of me smiled grainily back from it next to an image of the smoke-scarred mews. She watched my eyes stray to it, smiling knowingly when they found their way back to her.

'Doing some research.'

'Here?'

'Well, nearby. A place called Crahan House. It is near here, isn't it?'

'Might be. Why you interested in it?'

I wished I hadn't lost my nerve and volunteered information.

'My wife used to live there, I believe. I thought I'd try and track the place down since I was passing through.'

'Bit isolated,' she commented. I wanted to laugh. The whole place was isolated. 'It's on the road out towards the coast. Been empty for years though. What was her name?'

'Green, I think.'

'You think? Thought you said it was your wife's family?'

'Or Flowers. My wife's mother was a Flowers, but her maiden name was Green.'

She looked at me curiously.

'She's in the graveyard.'

I was taken aback. 'Margaret Flowers?'

'Something like – there's a gravestone up the back near the stone wall with Flowers on it, but it never does.' She gave me a tilted smile, enjoying whatever joke she was having at my expense. 'I'll reserve you a table for dinner. Menu's on the table. Only the specials left on tonight. Pay in advance, drinks extra. Twenty each.' She waited expectantly until I handed over the appropriate notes. I slapped them down on the reception top and she swept them away, casting an amused backward glance at me before going to chivvy one of her serfs – the lazy-eyed waitress with the big bust and small waist that Win had been busy ogling whilst I was being interrogated by the landlady. I joined him at the bar.

'Hear that?'

'No,'

'We've found the right place.'

'No we ain't.' He downed the rest of his pint. 'She said there weren't no-one there – deserted.'

'I thought you weren't interested – or listening.'

'I'm always listening, just not always interested.'

'Well, whatever, it sounds like Rosemary's in the graveyard.'

'A dead body's in the graveyard – they usually are. How's that going to help?

'It's a link.'

'What to? Come on. All I'm up for right now is finding me bed and then eating me board.' He picked up the key to the room I'd just been ripped off over.

'OK, while you check that out, I'm going to check out the churchyard.'

'Suit yourself. Don't bring no vampires back with you. They ain't having *my* dinner.' He lumbered towards the stairs and made his way heavily upstairs, and round the turn in search of room number four. The creaking overhead recorded his progress. By the sound of it, number four was only a short distance along the passageway on the first floor. I heard a door bang and assumed Win and bed were about to be united. I left the bar and stood at the door to the pub, considering. I'd said I was going so I'd have to do it, but I wished I hadn't been so rash now. I clenched my fists and threw the tension away like Margaret had taught me to. It didn't work. OK, file things instead – you've got plenty of material to work on. Sort the mass of unsorted facts and questions in your head and forget it's dark and isolated. I crossed the car park towards the parish church to make my acquaintance with Margaret's sister – or not, if this turned out to be yet another red herring, wondering if the evidence could be nearby too.

The church probably dated back to Norman times. It was built of Kentish ragstone, now coated with scaly green-grey lichen. Of traditional design, it had a square tower, replete with spire – no doubt added several hundred years later, and with the chancel extended beyond what must have been the original small gathering space. The north and south walls were pierced with small arched windows that must have been cut out later too. It wasn't the church that interested me though, but the residents in the churchyard surrounding it. The God of the living was surrounded by his dead, including Rosemary Flowers, I surmised.

Surprisingly it was a relief to be on my own for a few moments, despite the eerie surroundings. I collected my straggling thoughts and attempted to order them. From merely needing to reassemble the evidence that would lay the murder of Rosemary Flowers at Jaggers door, and possibly also the murder of my sister, now I had to convince everyone I hadn't actually orchestrated the deceits myself. And if Heather no longer trusted me – the one person I'd thought had seen through the façade but still believed in the man behind it – how could I expect Fredriks or anyone else to? I'd been forced into hooking my wagon to Win's star after the debacle at Chambers, and we were all but on the run because of it. I reached the gate to the churchyard before succumbing to my irrational fear of the dark. Childish reluctance to enter a graveyard at night reigned supreme until pragmatism pushed the ridiculous paranoia aside. Finding Rosemary Flowers' grave wasn't necessarily going to solve any of my problems, but it would at least prove I was finally being fed facts, not fantasy. Maybe it even bore more of Margaret's clues to help me. I made a mental note to enforce the remainder of the reciprocal 'cards on the table' from Win over dinner, such as how Danny and his alter ego's birth certificates could have found their way to Sarah, and Win's to Mary. That particular phoenix hadn't even been touched on yet, but someone had given both of them the documents. Given Win's part in Margaret's past plotting, he was as good a candidate as any, despite his claim to ignorance.

The rickety gate creaked, and opened obligingly enough for me but slammed shut as soon as I entered. I jumped. The moon was up and full, and the air cold, eerie. Then I grinned. Get real, man. It's not a film set, even though it should be.

'Werewolves too, if you're lucky,' I told myself.

Luck was more in the fact that the full moon shed a sparse silvery light on the gravestones, making it easier to decipher the names on them. The common village names seemed to hover between Marsham and Marish, so the gravestone the landlady had referred to stood out like a sore thumb. It was in exactly the place she'd described it – on the far side of the graveyard, alongside the rough stone wall that defined the church's boundaries. It wasn't just the uncommon name that set it aside, or its position, but the fact that it was virtually the only grave that was untended. Now I got the landlady's joke. Overgrowth straggled its edges and wheat grass sprouting from the base of the churchyard wall next to it was steadily invading the plot boundary, tickling the small squat head stone with wispy ears of mock corn. Mossy grass and weeds had carpeted the main plot, without even the poor remains of a posy or a floral tribute left to suggest that once it had been cared for. This Rosemary had no flowers for remembrance. I brushed the waving fronds of grass away and let the moonlight play across the chased stone, surprised. The owl hooted again.

'Rosemary Clare Flowers. Born 3rd March 1964. Died: February 22nd 1988.' No inscription, no 'dearly beloved sister' or lamentation at the loss of her. Given Margaret's desire for justice, why not? The moon slipped behind a cloud and a swathe of the mist we'd driven through on the way in eddied around my legs. I felt suddenly icy and ill at ease. Far from mocking the idea of werewolves and the living dead, the graveyard felt as if it could be full of them. I shivered and straightened, stepping back abruptly from Rosemary's headstone.

'She's gone, never to returnnnn ...' I jumped and swung round to collide with Win, swaying gently and laughing like a demon.

'Fuck off!' I brushed imaginary grass seeds from my trousers and squared my shoulders, then winced as my ribs complained at the unwarranted exertion.

'I told you there was now't to see here.'

'That's where you're wrong and it's right in front of you.'

'Rosemary's grave – right. So you found her. So what? It ain't her you want to find, it's her sister.'

'I know, but it proves we're tracking facts now. Heather thought she was buried here. She *is* buried here. This has to be the first time I've been told something that isn't a lie. Odd that it's so overgrown though. All the rest here – even the untidy ones – have been tended recently. Margaret would be fuming. She's a stickler for appearances.'

Win frowned and squinted at the headstone. He belched loudly and then pardoned himself self-consciously. He scuffed at a tuft of dandelions bobbing at the edge of the plot and spreading generously towards the other weeds carpeting the mound that marked out the grave. 'So what you making of this then?'

'I don't know – nothing probably, but at least we've found her. Now I can start looking for more facts to prove Margaret's story and perhaps reconstitute that evidence she's got against Jaggers. Perhaps I'll even take a quick look at Crahan House now too. Might give me a clue where she and Danny are.'

'Not tonight matey. I've had me fill of moonlit sagas. And if you want to go and poke around a deserted building then you do it in the day and on your own – right? I'm having a lie-in.'

'OK.' I couldn't have asked for a better reaction. Time to consider – and if Margaret wanted to talk – a place and privacy to do so. She'd find me. The crayon; the more I thought about it, the more sure I was it was a clue – a word-clue. Ludicrously I held out my hand like I would to a client. 'It's a deal.' We shook on it, with Rosemary watching us.

'Right, now I need a slash, so you can make your goodbyes to Miss Flowers here whilst I go and have one outside – wouldn't be right in here, would it?'

'Win?'

'Yes?'

'You don't seem all that bothered by this.' I indicated the grave. 'It was a terrible murder, and you knew her.'

'Yeah. I knew her. And what she made Kimmy like. I knew the bloke who was accused of it too, remember? Me mate – and our half-brother. It was a long time ago, and I can't do anything to bring either of them back, but I can look after meself and me own and maybe clear his name one day. I ain't doing anything for her. That's her sister's job.' He made a sound like he was clearing his throat. 'That, and the weeding.' It sounded callous and I was about to call him a mean bastard but he turned away a shade too quickly. 'It's a triple room by the way,' he called over his shoulder. 'A double and a single bed. I've bagged the double. Age before stupidity.'

He shambled away, making the gravel on the path crackle like hoar frost being compressed, and leaving me considering the nature of Miss Rosemary Flowers. I watched him go, listening to the crunch of his footsteps fade away and wondering what other twisted emotions I might uproot before the weeds were all cleared from this grave.

The crunching stopped and was replaced by the tinkling of water over stone. Win having a slash outside the churchyard. I grinned into the dark. The principles of man are strange things. We can fight and lie and cheat. We can manipulate, condemn to death and betray, but we draw the line at pissing in a churchyard.

The light mist that had begun to gather around my ankles earlier was starting to drift upwards. I shivered, my mind turning back to childhood terrors, and crunched my way in Win's wake, imagining footsteps shuffling behind me and a ghostly voice calling after me to stay. I was at the gate before I realised they were real.

'Lawrence, Lawrence – wait!' She appeared out of nowhere, hair glistening with tiny droplets of water like crystals in the moonlight, tightly belted into a lilac mac. 'I've been trying to get your attention since you got here, but Win was always around.'

'Margaret!' I reached her in less than two strides, despite the complaint from my ribs. She put her hands out as if to ward me off then allowed them to settle lightly against my chest, smiling. 'I knew you'd make contact!'

'What the hell are you doing here?'

'Trying to find you.'

'Well, you've found me. I hope no-one's followed you?'

'Only Win. He brought me here.'

'Win,' she echoed. She pulled me into the shadows behind the gate. 'Then it's time we talked.'

12: Angles

'I couldn't agree more!' How's Danny?'

'Why?' She nestled closer.

'Just checking he's safe.'

'Of course he's safe. More importantly, there are things we need to get on with.' She was almost part of me, she was so close. I could smell the fresh damp of her hair and feel the warmth of her body against mine. There was no denying she stirred something in me now that had always been dormant before. I could feel my body responding to her proximity in the same way as when she'd kissed me on Fulham Broadway. She stood on tiptoes and kissed me again, lightly on the lips, and my heart raced.

'I agree – but there are so many things to sort out too.' I savoured her smell and taste. 'We didn't have time to talk about anything last time. There's so much I need to know.'

'What do you need to know?' She didn't wait for me to answer. 'You know everything of importance. You know I'm here. Danny's your son and John's your enemy. What else is there to know?'

'Who I can trust, what I tell people – and about you …' I concentrated on controlling the physical effect she had on me. 'For a start, how the hell do I explain a resurrected wife?' She raised her eyebrows questioningly. 'Well, in theory, I've cremated you. Presumably that means I've cremated someone else in your place, which in itself is a criminal offence. God knows how we're going to deal with that. How can you come back from the dead without both of us being faced with conspiracy to pervert the course of justice?'

'Cremation – ugh!' She shivered, then burst out laughing. 'Oh, Lawrence, trust you to get bogged down in the detail when the bigger picture has still to be resolved.'

'Win suggested that Molly might take her place one day – is that your plan?'

'Win again. What have you been telling him?' She frowned. It made her look angry, but I couldn't believe she was. Her body language was all wrong for anger – or why was I responding like she was seducing me?

'Only enough for him to cooperate. You'd already told him what was going on anyway. He was helping you once, wasn't he? I assumed you trusted him then; and he saw you when you helped us escape.'

The frown deepened.

'He used to work for John once; in theory he always did. I never knew whose side he was really on so I only told him what I had to. Why do you think you can trust him?'

'He's my brother – I have to.'

'John's *my* brother, or my half-brother at least, but I don't trust him. Just because you're related doesn't mean you can trust anyone. And Win's accused of murdering Kimmy.'

'Not yet,' I objected, surprised she was so well-informed. 'He's not been charged yet. Plus he didn't.'

'And how do you know that?'

'You know as well as me that he wouldn't.'

'Do I?' A bank of clouds engulfed the moon. I couldn't see her face but she sounded sharp. 'How do I know?'

'Win's not a murderer, but we both know who is.'

'Oh,' she was silent, then, 'you can't prove that though.'

'But you can. You have evidence ...'

'Where no-one will find it unless I tell them,' she replied quietly.

'Surely you trust me? I'm your husband.' I found I was holding my breath, waiting for her reply. I'd never reacted to anyone this way before – except Kat. She moved against me again and my body burned.

'Maybe. But everyone can be manipulated because of love, can't they? And if we trust someone because we love them, that makes them – and us – vulnerable. Even if Win can be trusted, if you tell him what's going on, you make him vulnerable. Do you want his death on your conscience?'

'I don't want *any* deaths on my conscience!'

'Then don't tell him anything and he won't be at risk from you or you from him. Why do you think I've told you so little?' She stroked my cheek and my skin buzzed. 'Promise me you'll keep everything I tell you only between you and me from now on?' I hesitated. I had no choice if I wanted to hear what she had to say.

'I found your post box,' I said instead.

She wriggled closer still. My head pounded.

'I know.'

Her hair brushed against my cheek and she pushed her hand between the buttons of my shirt to find bare skin. It felt like ice was invading my heart whilst hell burnt my body. My head swam with desire as she pushed her leg between my thighs and rubbed her hip against my crotch. The moon scudded in and out of the clouds, teasing, then hurrying its silvery grey half-light away with it. For the briefest moment I was back in Kat's bed and Kat's arms, feeling the flood of desire coursing through me, and the shadowy face I leant to kiss was hers. As our lips touched Kat's heady exotic taste was replaced by Margaret's sharp floral perfume. I tensed, shocked at the trick my mind had played on my body, and wondering what it meant.

'What's the matter?' She pulled away, suspicious.

'Sorry. Ribs – the after-effects of playtime in the dungeon and the explosive properties of Austin Healeys.'

I kissed the tip of her nose, heart still pounding uncertainly, and unsure who for. She grimaced sympathetically at me.

'Poor baby. We'll have to do something about that when this is all over.' She pressed her pelvis against me and wriggled, 'And this,' she giggled, then pulled away just as my stomach turned to molten lead, suddenly business-like. It left the molten lead solidifying in all the wrong places. 'We'd better get on with business now, though. Have you been following John's PR campaign so far?'

I struggled to get back on track.

'You mean the article in *News from the Top*?'

'Ah, so you have.' She sounded pleased. 'Good. But that's just the start of it. It gets better – or worse, depending on your viewpoint. There's another feature scheduled for tomorrow in *Forward Thinking* and the day after in *Court Questions*, although that's a feature solely about you – courtesy of John. And it's not going to be complimentary. That's why we've got to act fast now. Once your reputation is on the line you're going to struggle to get anyone to take you seriously.'

'What do you mean?'

'Well, Fredriks is re-opening the Roumelia case and the Johns case will follow by Friday.'

Again, I was surprised. Even I'd only just found out either was a possibility a few hours ago. Who could have told her?

'How do you know?'

'Sources,' she tapped her nose coyly at me. 'Remember; the less you know, the safer you are. Fredriks will have John's version of them, carefully edited to show how you suppressed evidence and bribed witnesses, including your sister. It will also go so far as to suggest that your sister stopped playing ball recently – with obvious consequences.'

'Christ Almighty!'

'Exactly. That works nicely against you or Win – your extremely loyal brother, keen to protect his newly found – and rich – younger brother. John's going to strip you of your good reputation and once you're discredited, he'll leak information – ostensibly from you – about Judge Wemmick. There'll be an enquiry into how the terms of the trust have been breached, and – need I say more?'

'No, I can see exactly where all of that is leading, but why is he upping the ante again now? He appeared to have backed off after the case against Danny was dropped.'

'Uncle George has been diagnosed with throat cancer – advanced. John knew about it a while ago but didn't tell me until recently. I think he thought you'd be his golden goose before he needed to flee the nest, but it hasn't quite worked out that way, has it? When Uncle George dies, the estate will be under scrutiny, and so will John's claim, so he's revised his plans. He's going to realise as much of the estate as he can immediately and transfer it into holdings that he has a majority share in. Whatever the outcome of Uncle George's will, he will still have control. The trouble is that means getting whatever he can back from you as quickly as possible too so he can syphon it off. You're a major asset of the estate, you know – probably more than the rest of it put together currently. From my point of view it means we need to get ready to secure Danny's claim, whilst still keeping Danny out of John's reach too.'

'In that case, why not just present all the evidence now and fight it out in court.'

'Oh, my God, Lawrence – you can't be so naive as to think John would let it get to court? You, I and Danny would all be joining your sister way before then. No, we have to be very clever – much cleverer than him.'

'And you have a plan?'

'Of course, darling. How did you guess?' She grinned mischievously, and the attraction was cerebral as well as physical. 'Do you think he would have bothered about you if you had nothing? He's only chasing you because you're worth chasing. If he thought you had nothing, he wouldn't bother. He's nothing if not pragmatic! But that works for us. We keep him chasing you until we've proven Danny's claim and it's out in the open. *Then* we go to court.'

'And how does this work in reality?'

'First you need to be poor – do the same as he's doing and turn it all into cash.'

I stared at her, uncomprehending. 'Why?'

'Because it will confuse him – wonder what to do next. That buys us time.'

'But cash is an asset too – and it's got to go somewhere.'

I could almost imagine myself aping Win's baffled face whenever I said something he regarded as legal speak. She laughed delightedly at me and my bewilderment.

'Yes, somewhere no-one knows about but us. Didn't you wonder where the partnership cash went?'

'With you, I imagine – and I really need to ask you about that ...'

'I bet you do,' she laughed appreciatively. 'I imagine Heather is absolutely fuming but I did her a favour if she but knew it.' She looked impish. 'The partnership is poor already, so John won't touch it. Not worth staging a take-over of a business that has nothing.' She looked smug and I couldn't help but admire her brazen audacity even as I felt sorry for Heather.

'But, it's not yours to take ...'

'Oh, it's all right,' she was impatient. 'We can give back what's not ours later. In fact I'll quite enjoy playing Lady Bountiful to Heather's Lady Supplicant.'

'She'll probably impale you with one of her stilettos before you manage that. So where *is* the cash then?'

'In the wardrobe.' She laughed at my bewilderment. 'The wardrobe with my treasures in it,' she explained patiently. My heart plummeted further than I thought it was possible.

'I know which one you mean, but you know what happened to the house.'

'Yes, your lovely little sports car got aimed at it like a missile and it went bang!'

'And so did the money then.'

'No it didn't.' She shook her head complacently and her hair swung around her face like ripe corn rippling in the fields, just before harvest. 'There's a false back on the wardrobe and inside is a fire-proof case. The money's in there. You just need to recover it.'

I stared at her.

'Well, there's fat chance of that at the moment. I wouldn't be able to get near the place. I'm under suspicion too, remember?'

'So you need to get out from under it because you've also got to liquidate the house and all your investments for this to work. If you don't John will merely wait until you break.'

'Liquidate everything? You must be joking! That would take months!'

'No it won't. It'll take a matter of days done the right way. I did Heather a favour with the partnership bank account, and John – bless him did you one too. Now there's no house to sell, only insurance to claim.'

'Rebuilding costs only. Nothing like the value of the land in that. And insurance claims of this order take months – even years – to settle.'

'No they don't if you cut them a deal they can't refuse.'

'What deal might that be?' My heart was pounding again – but not from desire this time.

'They keep the land in trust, and give you only seventy-five per cent of the rebuilding costs. If at any stage over the next five years you're found to have been involved in the blaze, you forfeit the land. That should do it.'

'And you already know how much it will amount to, I assume.' I couldn't keep the edge out of my voice, but she didn't seem bothered by it.

'Of course. Seventy-five per cent of rebuilding costs are in the region of £1.5 million after the refurbishment, the partnership money amounts to five hundred thousand and your investments another five hundred thousand. £2.5 million, Lawrence – enough to start a new life five times over. If we have to – that is.'

'But it's my current life I want back.'

'Not whilst John thinks there's that much to be squeezed out of you.'

'But he'll know the cash is still somewhere even if the assets are gone. How will that get him off my back?'

'Here's the best bit,' she giggled. 'You're going to actually give it to him.'

'What?' I was aghast. She threw her head back and laughed aloud then, eyes sparkling and whites luminous in the moonlight. 'You're going to actually give it to him,' she repeated eventually, 'at a controlled hand-over and then he's going to think it's all been destroyed. Burnt. We're going to stage it. A fire in which the money is burnt – except of course, it's not. I told you, John's nothing if not a pragmatist. He concentrates on what he needs to and moves on when it's no longer working. In the meantime, Danny's claim will have been documented, the evidence will have been retrieved and ta-dah! The trap is sprung. *Then* we can go back to life as it was – almost – but better. Danny will be heir to the Wemmick estate, and in your care as his father, and I rather like Win's idea that Molly and Lawrence fall in love. We'd have to get to know each other *properly* then – for propriety's sake, but like Win said, the fairy tale ending …'

'That has got to be the craziest idea I've ever heard.'

'It's no crazier than becoming Lawrence Juste so you could abandon Kenny once you got Judge Wemmick's money.'

'That was different. There were reasons.'

Kat had said almost exactly the same thing to Heather just a few hours ago to explain her betrayal, but sometimes reasons outweigh the betrayal.

'There are reasons now too. And one very compelling one is your son.' Her voice was harsh, determined.

'What if I don't want to go along with it?'

'Do you really have a choice? Tell me what you plan on doing to get yourself out of this mess then?'

'I don't know yet. I'm still thinking about it.'

'And while you're thinking about it, how safe do you think Danny is? My way he'll be safe with us, have new parents *and* all the money will be ours. A happy ending worth fighting for, don't you think?'

'I don't care about the money, but what if it all goes wrong, Margaret? It's too risky. I could lose everything. We all could lose everything.'

'How wrong do you think life has already going for you? Look, tomorrow there'll be another feature singing John's praises and lauding his contribution to humanity – doctored of course. It's the first of many, all focusing in on FFF and the people the charity has helped. The next step will be to focus in on the people who've tried to hinder it. You're number one on the list. The focus in *Court Questions* the day after is you – an unpleasant focus, believe me. John already has enough tame editors happy to jump on the band wagon rolling all over your reputation to keep going all year. By next week, your name will be mud, and so will your future. John will still be on your back, squeezing you, and Danny will still be under threat because John will be scrutinising all possible contenders for the estate; and he'll be ruthless. Just because Danny's gone unnoticed this far, do you really think it will stay that way once John sets his eager beavers on it? At the moment he regards me as an ally so now is the time to act. Prevention, not cure. I can't be seen to be helping you, but for the time being I'm ideally placed to make this work. This is the only way, Lawrence. For all of us – Win included.'

'Unless …' My barrister's brain finally fired on all cylinders. The blinking green light that the flickering of the headlights on the St Rosemary in the Marsh sign suddenly made sense. The saint's miraculous solution.

'Unless what?' She sounded irritated.

'Unless he overlooked new evidence.'

'New evidence? Not possible. John set him up too well. It's all documented. I've seen the photos.'

'*You* have?'

She nodded and the facts jarred.

'Then who killed Kimmy if he was taking the photos?'

She looked momentarily taken aback.

'Did I say he did? Whatever. It's a done deal now. Win's in the frame.'

'In the frame …' I smiled. 'But maybe not the same one. Remember the security cameras you had fitted? The ones I wouldn't let you use?'

She frowned, hesitating. 'I … go on.'

'Well, one of them must have been left set up and ready to run after all – or I turned it on by accident somehow. Maybe I knocked it, or flicked the switch by mistake. I was always doing that to begin with, remember? Bad design idea. Anyway, I realise now that I saw the thing blinking at me just after the police eventually let me back in after Kimmy was found. I think that in the camera is a film of exactly what happened, and unless the murder happened outside the kitchen and Kimmy's body was brought back in later, murder, murder victim and murderer will all be starring on it.'

She breathed in sharply.

'You're sure about this?'

'Not a hundred per cent, but almost. So with that and your evidence, surely we've enough to nail Jaggers several times over – assuming it would be him we'd see starring on the film with Kimmy? Even if it wasn't it would at least clear Win and lay the groundwork for some kind of conspiracy theory in my defence. I'll take the consequences of my bad judgement over Jonno's case. It will be an honest confession. It wasn't malicious or with intent – just stupid and avaricious. Ruined or not, professionally, I'll still have my assets *and* my family.' Now it was my turn to look complacent.

She whistled, a long low note of appreciation. 'That certainly does change things,' she added thoughtfully. 'But what if it's blank? Or goes AWOL in the meantime? I think we'd better check it out first, don't you? You'll look an idiot *and* ruin my plans if you're wrong. Leave it with me. I'll check it and give you the nod first before you do anything. Then you can tell Fredriks about it and recover the money at the same time, but don't tell anyone about the money yet. I need to figure out how to do this first.' She pushed away from me, and shoved her hands in her pockets, deep in thought. I was ignored. A screech owl pierced the mist with its mournful wail and I instinctively looked over my shoulder. Margaret caught my glance. 'Yes, actually we should get out of sight just in case Win gets curious why you're still out here.'

She set off briskly across the churchyard, leaving me to follow. She stopped near Rosemary's grave and settled against the wall, apparently completely indifferent to it. I studied her as she pondered the new information, trying to see the Margaret I'd assumed I'd been married to all these years in this wily minx, both cerebral and sexual – and certainly making both sides of the equation multiply to produce an unexpected response in me, even despite Kat. There were definite similarities, physically – even with the cosmetic adjustments that she'd been sporting when she'd released Win and I from the play palace. Her eyes were the same colour – bold blue – and her face shape; but overall she was edgier, more forceful. Maybe I simply hadn't seen her like this because I hadn't expected to. We see what we want to see and hear what we want to hear. I'd learnt that from childhood and had been re-learning it recently as an adult, but nevertheless, lessons are unlearnt just as easily as learnt, if there's an inclination to. Heather had been trying to show me how thought and expectation modified reaction when she'd been playing mirror, mirror with me after I'd thought I'd seen Margaret in 27B. It was high time I addressed both more logically and less reactively. And maybe her crazy plan *was* the only way out – or one even crazier. My world had been built on reputation and credibility, pragmatism and logic. The belief I now had to instil in everyone was that even if Lawrence Juste appeared guilty, he wasn't. Increasingly that looked unlikely to be achieved.

'When's Win expecting you back?' She slipped off the wall.

'Soon, I guess,' I admitted reluctantly. She pressed herself against me again, this stranger who was my wife and rapidly coiling herself around my brain, gut and heart, like a parasite, even though I couldn't understand how and why she could do that. I let her kiss me lightly on the lips, internally evaluating my response and comparing it to how I responded to Kat. *You fool – forget Kat. You have a wife again now.* I kissed her back. It seemed satisfactory, but ...

She drew away from me, tilting her head to one side. Her hair tumbled over her collar and draped softly on her shoulders. The mist had settled into small droplets cresting her head like a crown of tiny crystals and her breath created a fine vapoury drift across her face like a bride's veil. She was an ice queen, fire-ice, and it was getting cold – ice cold in hell. She examined me thoughtfully.

'Could you lie convincingly to Win?'

Could I lie convincingly to myself? No answer to either question, other than one I knew was the wrong one.

'Why would I want to? I'm trying to tell the truth now, not perpetuate deceit.'

'Because one of us has got to get back into the house and check that camera without them knowing. We need a diversion to keep them busy and away from policing you – or me by association if they know your every move.'

'What kind of diversion?'

'Win. Get him on the run. That will occupy them.'

'I can't. I've already dragged him into something he's not involved in.'

'OK, in that case, take him back and get him charged. Then they'll be busy interviewing him so they'll ignore you temporarily.'

'No! I've lied and cheated enough on him in the past. I don't want to do that again.'

'You're not cheating on him. If you're right, you're doing this to get him off too. Sometimes appearances are deceptive. You have to appear to be doing one thing in order to do something else – like I have for Heather and the business. If you won't set him on the run, Win needs to be in prison, and fighting off a murder charge for this to work.'

'Win may be dumb at times, but he's not in self-destruct mode. And why is that essential to getting one of us into the house?'

'If Win's charged, it'll also look more plausible to the insurance company and you'll be able to finalise the claim on the house.'

'I thought we weren't following that plan.'

'It's always best to have a back-up. Yours is plan A. Mine is plan B.

We follow both – just in case. You're going to have to determine the insurance claim some time anyway. If it's in hand and ready to settle, we've more flexibility in case things go wrong.'

'I still don't see how I'm going to persuade them to settle just like that. There'll be investigations, forensics to review, a guilty party to establish.'

'Not if you offer them the deal I suggested.' Still I demurred. 'This is for Danny as much as you or I,' she reminded me.

This *was* the Margaret I knew – the one who knew when to press her point and push my buttons about something I already felt guilty about. Was it more acceptable in her new guise as my son's mother? What difference did it make? I was still a rat in a trap – just a different trap for a different reason. One or the other of them would get me – Jaggers or Margaret. Better Margaret, all told. At least Danny and getting my life back would be the compensation, and perhaps this unnerving response she now produced in me might even grow into something more comforting and comfortable eventually, particularly if I actually *tried* this time. Atticus would certainly counsel that I should.

'OK, but Win would be more likely to cooperate if he thought I was trying to get hold of evidence to clear him, and not that he was simply going back to be clamped in irons.'

'All right. Tell him about the camera but nothing else. If he knows the rest and tells John – what plan do we have then?'

I didn't like it. Risk made me feel uneasy – the kind of uneasy I'd felt every day in the children's home, in case what little in life that was good might disappear without warning unless I kept a tight hold on it. My tight hold now reverted to the evidence in the security box somewhere, whatever else I agreed with Margaret. 'And what about the evidence you've got? We'll need that too.'

'When the time is right. Anyway, I can't get it at the moment.' She paused. 'I trust you, Lawrence. Don't you trust me? I even gave you the key to it. Why don't you trust me?'

'I do trust you. But I don't know where the box is that the key fits, do I?'

'You don't need to – yet. Sarah organised it all before she died. It's absolutely safe. You do your bit and then I'll do mine and we'll go and get it together. We need to check on the film whilst you're making a fuss of handing Win back over, then you can sort out the insurance claim and reveal the film to the police. I'll keep John occupied in the meantime.'

'But ...'

'No buts, Lawrence.' She put a finger on my lips. 'If there are buts, how can I believe you trust me? I'm trusting you with my life – and our son's. Can't you trust me with a little collection of evidence? It's not going anywhere.'

I was about to protest again but there was a steely quality to her and a tension in the finger pressed to my lips that suggested I was in danger of pushing her too far. I didn't know this woman, despite having been married to her for years and fathering a child with her. Nor did I have any option but to rely on her to help, given how things were developing. Jaggers' plans were already putting me out in the cold and the longer I stayed there, the less possibility there was of coming in from it. She was right. I had to take a risk – but a risk with as much security behind it as I could muster.

'And Danny, you're sure he's safe?'

'Why wouldn't he be? Look, you'd better get back to Win now before he comes looking for you again. Convince him to let you take him back to Fredriks and then sweet talk Fredriks into allowing you back into the house. I'll sort out the rest and be in touch when it's ready. Just be prepared – and don't be spooked if things happen that aren't quite what you expect. Just follow my lead. Trust me?' She stood on tiptoes and kissed me. The effect was the same as before. My head spun and the breath left my body. My face was damp but I couldn't tell afterwards if it was from the condensing mist or the sweat of fear. 'You won't let me down, will you?' she whispered. I shook my head, even as my spine tingled and my palms itched at the thought of what she wanted me to do – everything; risk everything – to gain everything. If it could be done ... She peered at me for a moment. 'The camera in the kitchen, right?' she waited for confirmation.

'Yes, under the spice rack,' I agreed.

'OK, I'll get it checked.' She kissed me lightly on the lips in farewell. 'Be in touch soon,' she teased, before stepping into the shadows. I was alone in the churchyard again with only my thoughts and fears to accompany me back to the brother I'd betrayed once, and was about to betray again. I told myself the outcome would be good even if the method was bad. It was a twisted logic, but what part of this nightmare wasn't twisted? I hesitated at the gate, perplexed at the curious idea that had just begun to form, twisting everything another turn – if that was possible. Then I set it aside for the angles to play out.

13: Family History

By the time I made my way back to the pub and into the restaurant, I'd almost convinced myself I wasn't again about to shaft the brother I'd betrayed as a child. Win was already starting the second of three large courses, including steak and kidney pie and two pints. His mood had mellowed as his belly swelled and he was reflective rather than bellicose when he greeted me, but that in itself made me feel guilty. I, on the other hand, had little appetite and my mood soured as my agitation grew. The restaurant was empty apart from us. So much for the landlady's claim that to be sure of a room I'd have to pay cash at the premium rate.

Time for persuasion tactics – an old courtroom trick; wait until after lunch when the jury is more receptive. When Win was two and a half courses and three pints into well-being, I made my pitch. If I couldn't swing this now, I wasn't likely to – ever.

'Candid camera.' He shook his head at me as if I was a bad joke. 'All right – caught on camera then. That's the evidence against you.'

'Yeah, thanks for reminding me – just when I was starting to think life was smelling of roses, not manure.' The sarcasm was as heavy as the beer, murky and at least six per cent volume. 'So they got photos of me, but I didn't do it and that's why there's not one of me killing her. Can you think of a better way to take the piss?'

I rallied, refining courtroom slick to comradely chumminess for Win's benefit.

'You're absolutely right about the photos taking the piss, Win, that's precisely what they're doing. But I've got a much better joke than that – candid camera.'

'So you keep saying,' he retorted drily.

'OK, I'll explain. Whilst we were refurbishing the house in the mews, there was a break-in a few doors along from us. It seemed to really rattle Margaret and she insisted we get security cameras installed. I thought it was going over the top but she was so insistent in the end I left her to it.

The problem came when they turned up to install them. To do that anywhere but downstairs we would have needed a whole bunch of extra wiring and all the refurbishment they'd just done upstairs to be undone. By then the major heist at our neighbour's place had turned out to be a VCR, some costume jewellery, and an insurance scam. Margaret gave in and we only got the cameras installed downstairs. After a few weeks of being filmed doing everything from picking up the post to picking my teeth I refused to even have them on, but they're there nevertheless. They're well concealed so you wouldn't even know they're there unless you knew where to look. I'd pretty much forgotten about them until now, but the one in the kitchen *might* actually have still been on.'

'What d'you mean – *might* have been on? Don't you know?'

'Well, you know how you only notice something subliminally until another trigger reminds you of it?'

'No,' he said flatly. 'That's something you smart arses do, not me.'

I tried not to smile. 'You do it too, you just haven't noticed. I only thought about it today because I *have* had a trigger. I think the light indicating that the camera was on and recording was blinking at me, and seeing stars after you hit me was the trigger, but without actually going into the house again and retrieving it, I can't be sure. If I'm right though, we may have had the evidence to clear you right under our noses all this time. It may also reveal the murderer.'

He blinked at me as the information sunk in.

'Then I'm home and dry?'

'Not necessarily. I'm not a hundred per cent sure. And I don't want to make things worse by coming up with some cock-and-bull story and then looking like an idiot. I need to check first.'

'I don't see how any cock-and-bull story is going to make things any worse right now. Tell Fredriks and get on with it.' He swigged the dregs of his pint and signalled to the waitress for a refill. 'Worst he'll make of it is that you're an arsehole. Better than me. Currently I'm a murderer.'

'Win, you don't understand. If there's nothing there, my credibility is completely gone with Fredriks, yet I've still got to try and get you off, maybe with an accusation of wasting police time to go with it. I need to get that camera checked *before* I hand it over to Fredriks, all fanfares blaring. OK?'

He grimaced at me. 'Ain't that tampering with evidence?'

'No, it's checking it exists. I'm not going to tamper with anything.'

'OK,' he shrugged. 'Enlighten me. How you gonna get to it when you ain't even allowed in?' The busty waitress delivered his replacement pint and he watched her wiggle away before downing a mouthful of treacly beer and wiping the back of his hand across his mouth.

'I – or someone else – will have to get into the house.'

'Oh yeah – that's an easy one.' He pouted and pretended to flutter his eyelashes at me. 'Don't worry officer, I may sound like I'm feeding you a load of bullshit, but I'm a good guy, really. Why's he going to believe you if your lady boss don't – or your girlfriend? They were both beginning to think otherwise when we left there. Maybe they'll be saying that to Fredriks by now too.'

'Because you're going to persuade him.'

'Me? How the fuck do you work that one out?'

'By allowing me to take you back in tomorrow – early, and then leaving me out here in the field doing the investigating – and checking.' I decided against telling him *who* would be doing the checking – mindful of Margaret's caution about telling him too much. 'That will convince Fredriks we're on the level. Goodwill between men – including policemen and their quarries. Then I'll ask for access to my home because I won't be *persona non grata* with the police after that. It should even convince Heather.'

'Not after what you done to her car,' he retorted wryly, 'and I'm a sitting duck if you don't get the goods or you're wrong.'

'You're a sitting duck anyway, Win – now or in forty-eight hours' time – but if there's a possibility of turning this around, shouldn't we see how this angle could be played out?'

He fiddled with the now empty beer glass. I waited, counting internally, like I did in court when driving a point home. So much of credibility was about timing. Make the right point at the right time, with the right emphasis and the audience does the rest – shame I so rarely managed it on a personal level currently. He picked up the glass to drain the non-existent dregs and slammed it back down irritably.

'I got me conditions.'

'And what are they?'

'You make sure Danny's OK before you do any more plotting with Margaret.'

'Who said this was anything to do with Margaret?'

'It's got her fingerprints all over it, that's why. I want to know the kid's all right. And you keep that lady boss of yours off my back whilst you're doing it. I don't mind the stuffy old coot – he knows what he's doing, and says now't while he's doing it, but her? She's a motor-mouth in designer clothes.' I was surprised Win had taken so against Heather, but then she was everything he wasn't: trim, elegant, eloquent – and in charge. Opposites don't always attract.

'OK, if that's important to you.'

'You ain't heard the last one yet – I said *conditions*.'

'What's the last one?'

'I'm thinking about that. In the meantime, mine's a pint. I won't be drinking much of this in clink if you don't do the business, gnat's piss though it is.'

I left him cradling his fourth pre-prison pint whilst I lounged against his car in the now mist-laden car park – the only place I wouldn't be overheard by the officious landlady or her nosy staff. I rang Heather to tell her to impart the good news to Fredriks. I wasn't welcomed like a long-lost prodigal but she was at least polite. I went back to Win to report.

'I still don't like it, but it's done now.' He tipped his beer glass sorrowfully to one side, watching the amber meniscus slew over with it. Then he tipped it the other way. 'Can I ask you something now?' He didn't wait for a yes. 'If Margaret was really dead, would you visit her grave?'

I was taken aback. His expression gave no clue to the reason he'd asked such a morbid question.

'But she's not.'

'But if she were, would you – even though you didn't care much for her?'

I almost challenged the *didn't care much for her*, then I remembered when I'd been laying my cards on the table I hadn't admitted to Win that my feelings might have become more ambivalent recently.

'Well, out of respect, probably.'

'Yeah, that's what I thought. You'd go it out of respect because they were family. If they weren't, then you don't give a toss, do you?'

'Well, maybe not quite so callous, but it's not personal then.'

'Yeah,' he paused. 'The thing is, after I left you roaming the graveyard looking for vampires to stick your stake into I was sitting here thinking about things, and it just don't make sense.'

'What doesn't?'

'Why her grave's like that – a trash heap?'

It had occurred to me too, but it felt disloyal to Margaret, having just told her I trusted her, to now start criticising her in her absence.

'Life gets busy?'

'Or it don't matter?'

'Maybe you're making more of this than there is, Win. People die, life moves on.'

'She wanted justice.'

'You don't get that tending a grave.'

'But Rosemary was family.'

'She had a new family – me.'

'Yeah, like that mattered.'

I was irritated, but uncomfortable too, thinking of all the graves I hadn't tended in the past – Ma, Georgie, Pip, and now Sarah and Kimmy. I picked up his empty glass to change the subject, pointedly seeking the landlady or the pigeon-chested waitress. He sat back in his chair and folded his arms across his chest, stared pugnaciously at me over the top of his rolling gut. He wasn't changing the subject just yet.

'You don't think it matters?' I prepared for a sermon on loyalty and family. Last orders sounded distantly in the empty bar. He snorted with disgust. 'Bloody hell! S'pose I'm not going to get another pint now.' I waited, resigned. 'All right, this is my beef; I kept thinking about what you said about Margaret being livid with the mess. You're right – she would be. She's respectful. Had a sense of what's right. I know she changed after Rosemary died but you don't really change inside, do you? Did I ever tell you about Mary?'

I sighed. I wasn't really in the mood for reminiscences now and especially not about Mary. She always made me feel uneasy – even at a distance. The landlady appeared at the entrance to the restaurant and hovered. She made a meaningful face at me as I caught her eye.

'I think she wants us to go.'

'Well she can sod off then. This isn't *her* last night of liberty.' He waved his empty pint glass at her and she deliberately ignored him, nose in the air. 'Bloody women!' His mouth clamped into a bad-tempered grimace and he settled back in his seat. I was clearly going to be treated to his bellicosity instead. 'Mary,' he repeated. 'She liked Margaret, but she didn't like Rosemary – or Kimmy. Can't say I blamed her. She didn't have much going for her. The times she was allowed to come and join in must have felt a bit like this – temporary reprieve. They nearly always spoilt them.'

I responded 'how' half-heartedly, knowing I had to let him ramble to keep on his good side, but hoping the lack of enthusiasm would keep it to a minimum. I was wrong.

'Sarah had a cat. Its name was Timmy or Tommy – something like that. Bloody great big tabby, tough as old boots and twice as fierce, but he loved Mary. Apart from Sarah only Mary could get near him – unless he was being fed. Anyway, one time Mary was there, the bloody thing got run over. Of all the times for it to happen! Back legs smashed to bits – and who knows what else. Even I felt sorry for it. Mary was beside herself. Cradled it in her lap like a baby, covered in blood, sobbing like the world was ending. She was like that then – always too happy or too sad. It died sometime during the afternoon but still she wouldn't let go of it. It was only when Margaret and Rosemary came over to see Kimmy and Margaret suggested they give it a funeral that she let go. So that's what we did. I had to dig the hole, Sarah found an old shopping bag for a coffin, Margaret made a posy from flowers in Sarah's garden and we buried it under the apple tree. Mary said the prayers and then we all went in for tea.'

'Nice,' I commented, shivering with distaste. Of all my childhood aversions graves were the closest to rats. Rats lived in cellars and sewers and mausoleums. Rats were closer to the dead than the living. Rats equalled death, and death equalled rats. The equation balanced perfectly in my child's mind, and my adult's logic had failed to dispel it – even after all these years.

'Actually it *were* nice until Rosemary got the devil in her and told Mary that the cat would come back and haunt her if she didn't shut up about it. Sarah told her off, but then Kimmy joined in too and there weren't no stopping them.'

I shifted impatiently, wondering how the tale of Timmy the cat was going to help me, but he ignored me and continued his monologue, face reflective and tinged with something I couldn't quite define.

'Sarah told them she'd send them home if they carried on and that shut them up. She was boss, see, even though no-one ever said it. We all thought that was it until I went out the back for a fag – Sarah wouldn't have it in the house – and there's Mary, throwing forty fits, with the bloody cat draped round her shoulders like a scarf. When we got her calmed down enough to get some sense out of her all she would say was that the cat had come back from the dead and had jumped on her. Well, course it hadn't, but someone had dug the blessed thing back up and it was obvious who the culprits were. They were pissing themselves down the side alley. Rosemary and Kimmy.'

'So neither of them were very pleasant then.'

'No,' the strange expression was on his face again.

'Where's this going, Win?''

'I'll tell you: Margaret insisted we bury the thing again and every time she came over after that, she put flowers on the spot where it was buried, buttercups and daisies, sometimes forget-me-nots – they grew like weeds in Sarah's garden. All for a bloody cat. Said the poor thing deserved respect. She kept that routine up for Mary right up until she and Rosemary went to live with Jaggers, when she were about fifteen. That's almost three years.'

'Her sister's been dead over ten. Anyway it wasn't the cat she cared about, Win – it was Mary, and her feelings.'

He studied me.

'Yeah, exactly, because Mary was like family for her by then. For family – ten years is nothing. You ought to talk to Mary you know. Yeah – that's me last demand. Talk to Mary.'

'Mary.' I pursed my lips. It was the least expected and most unwelcome demand I could have imagined. 'Win, I haven't got time to visit a mad sister. I appreciate she's had a sad life and I'm glad Margaret was nice to her, but she's got nothing to do with this and I've got far more pressing things to do right now.'

'Oh yeah – really? You should be ashamed of yourself. She ain't mad, she just got a condition.' His lower lip jutted angrily.

'OK, maybe I'm allowing stereotypes and childhood anxieties to prejudice me. She's got a condition, but I've only seen her once since childhood and she seemed pretty mad to me then.'

'Course she would. She wouldn't know whether to trust you. She puts it on if she don't know you – in case.'

I rubbed my hands over my face. I wasn't going to get anywhere with him unless I publically flogged myself for my past failings, since that was what his rambling narrative appeared to demand.

'Win, I understand I've not been good at family loyalty, whereas you all have been – even Margaret – but there's a time and a place. When I'm trying to get you off the hook, and keep my son, my wife and myself safe from a murderer, it's not the time to be cosily reacquainting myself with an estranged and … *ill* … sister.'

'You still ain't listening Kenny. That's where it all started.'

'All started? What do you mean?'

'Yeah, I reckon so. This is where it all started.' He nodded and

145

grinned triumphantly as if congratulating himself. He'd got my attention now. 'OK, confession time. Margaret used to visit Mary on the quiet after she went to live with Jaggers. They'd become close, see? Because of the cat. I turned up the same time as her once just before Jonno's trial, just by chance. I used to take Sarah because she never learned to drive. I hadn't seen Margaret in a while by then; she was grown up, but I reckon that's when it all *first* started, back when we was playing happy families.'

'I see,' my voice sounded harsh and dry. Happy families? How happy – and close? The cards were rolling – on the table and right off of it too.

'Shame I wasn't part of the happy family back then as well. What about Emm and Jill? Were they part of this too?' I couldn't believe Emm had lied to me. She'd always maintained she'd only met Margaret once – as my wife – and I'd believed her.

'No, not really. They were fostered – only saw them once in a blue moon and only then when they were old enough to decide for themselves. Foster parents said it would be *disruptive*.' He said the word as a sneer. 'Kimmy was turning tricks at the Gods and Gargoyles by then too. Certainly wasn't letting the twins anywhere near her.'

'So how did Emm and Jonno come across each other?'

'Huh,' he was rueful. 'You can't protect everyone from everything. He was like family by then, after looking out for me in clink. When Jim headed off to Oz after Pip died, Jonno came over to see him off; family get together – one the twins were actually allowed to be at because it might be the last time they saw Jim. Emm had only just had that accident that left her the burn scar on her face and the foster parents were trying to make up for it. Sarah put me wise and I steered him towards the club instead. Couldn't shut him out, but couldn't let him in either. I hadn't bargained on Kimmy, though!'

'When you say Sarah put you wise, do you mean she already knew about Jonno being your half-brother?'

'I guess so. I reckon Sarah knew everything.'

'So why the hell didn't she tell *me* everything? In fact why didn't any of you just tell me everything from the outset? You've led me a right bloody dance, the lot of you! In fact, worse; you've all been plotting and scheming behind my back for years.'

I was suddenly so angry I could barely speak. And I'd been beating myself up about lying to Win? Crap! At least I was lying to achieve a good outcome. I'd been lied to simply to be manoeuvred.

'We weren't plotting. It was … complicated.'

He looked miserable and it reminded me suddenly of him as a boy, facing Pop and the belt. The anger drained out of me, to be replaced by professional pragmatism. If Win was going for confession time, now was as good a time as any to find out exactly how much I'd been manipulated – before I did a bit of manipulation myself. I sighed noisily for his benefit.

'Go on then, why do you want me to talk to Mary?'

'OK,' he looked relieved. 'When I first came out of clink I did what Jonno suggested – kept me head down and tried to stay out of trouble. Was even a security guard for a while…' My expression must have been sceptical. 'All right – bouncer then, but it was a job, and clean. Paid shit, of course. I was never going to get out of the gutter on that wage and then up pops Jaggers. Think he must have found me through the girls, now I think on it. *"Just a bit of collection and delivery – nothing underhand, no drugs, no violence,"* he said. I agreed; stupid sod! Had a stroke of luck at the bookies on me second pay packet and thought life had taken a turn for the better when he offered me the partnership on the strength of it. *"You want to invest that, Win, not gamble it away again. Gamblers always lose in the end. Let's do each other a favour – for old time's sake."* Jonno had a knack with the cards and had a bit of spare cash from that too, so we were both in. He needed us but he made it sound like we needed him.'

I interrupted, 'I still don't see where Mary comes into this.'

'Just be patient will you! I'm trying to tell you.' He paused, rolling his eyes melodramatically at me, before turning reflective. 'None of us talked about you, apart from Mary. Mary always had a thing about you. She and Margaret had got close by then – after the cat nonsense – so she told Margaret about you, the wonderful Kenny, and the fact no-one else talked about you made you mysterious. See, I do know women. Got to be a bit of an enigma for them to be interested. You're just Joe average otherwise.' He snorted in disgust. 'Reason I ain't never got married. I ain't got no mystery. My life's an open book – a comic book!' He laughed scornfully at himself.

'Go on,' I prompted, struggling to stifle my impatience.

'I think she got as obsessed about you as Mary in the end. Knew all about you anyway – as much as I did – probably more. When I bumped into her that day at Mary's place she was still on your case. Had all sorts of ideas how to draw you back into the family circle. I said I didn't want you involved. You'd chosen a different life – let you have it. I put me head down and hoped I wouldn't run into her again until the record got unstuck, even made Sarah change her visiting days for a while, then the murder happened and you were completely forgotten.

'Kimmy went walkabout and came back a week later, saying nothing but was off her meds and being a right bitch again. Eventually she told me she was pregnant, and Jonno was the father. I went ballistic. Talk about betrayal – me mate *and* me brother, although he didn't know that. I was so bloody furious I didn't know what to do, but when Jaggers came to me complaining that Kimmy was giving him jip too, and I should shut her up if I knew what was good for her – and me – it was gut reaction. I knew we'd both be up shit creek without a paddle if I didn't get her off his back because I knew what he was capable of by then. Wasn't I meant to be his fixer? *"Even fixers can get fixed if they don't do their job"* he said. I knew what that meant. He wanted the murder sorted and plod out of the club because they were ruining business. I wanted back at Jonno, and him off me back and Kimmy's. I hated meself for suggesting we set Jonno up for it but I reckoned he could look after himself, and he'd be off the hook in no time with no real evidence. In the meantime I'd persuade Kimmy to get rid of the kid and both problems would be fixed. What I never understood – or bargained for – was that he'd say nothing. Maybe Jaggers made a bargain with him too – both ends against the middle? That'd be his style all right. I dunno. I just kept me head down again because you'd popped up by then and I had enough on me plate with Kimmy not playing ball about the kid without having you to contend with too.

'I didn't think about Margaret until I took Sarah to see Mary again, and there she was, taking me aside and telling me all kinds of shit about having stuff that might put Jonno's conviction in doubt and nail her brother instead. I said, *"Whoa there, that's too heavy for me"* because you don't take on a bloke like Jaggers without plenty of firepower. She said she needed your help. Wanted me to introduce her to you. Well, I weren't going to do anything of the sort! Christ Almighty! By then Jonno'd made it clear that he wasn't going to defend himself and I'd only be putting meself back in the shit if I asked why. I told her that and she didn't ask again. Jonno got convicted and sent down for ten years – off in five with good behaviour. Two weeks later I heard about the stabbing. Next time I went to see Mary when I knew Margaret'd be there and *I* approached her.'

'Convenient, that,' I commented. 'Him getting topped in prison.'

'Yeah, I thought so too.'

'So the plot was hatched and you, Margaret and Mary have been planning my downfall ever since?'

'Don't be so bloody paranoid! No-one's planning your downfall.'

'Other than Jaggers.'

'Other than him,' he agreed. 'And I still didn't like it much because it involved trusting you and you'd shafted me as a kid, but what could I do? You were central to it. I didn't want Jaggers to get away with setting up Jonno with murder and then getting him murdered too. Landing all the shit on you seemed a fitting reward for the pile of it you dumped on me, so I agreed.'

'So what was this first plan?' I asked, silkily polite. My head finally felt how it would if I was piecing a defence case together – cool and objective.

'I didn't have to do anything at first – just be her eyes and ears, and wait. She didn't tell me how she was going to get in with you, but she seemed convinced she would. We married Kimmy off for the kid's sake and Margaret took herself off too – to get away from the papers, she said – ghoulish bastards, wanting to know the ins and outs of everything. I thought maybe she'd had a breakdown and that was her cover for it. She seemed different, when she came back, but that was probably stress, and growing up, I s'pose. She had to stand up for herself without Rosemary around – Rosemary was always the one in charge out of the two of them as kids. Made her more like Rosemary, I guess – and get on better with Jaggers. S'pose that had to happen too given what she told me. Had to watch her back, didn't she? Be smart – sharp; like Rosemary was.'

'Margaret can be very smart,' I agreed ruefully.

'Yeah – wasn't always though. Bit of a ditherer as a kid. I guess when you met her, she was more like Rosemary than Margaret. Shovelling shit makes a difference to anyone – even a kind kid like her. After Rosemary died, there were times ...'

'Times what?'

'Oh, no; nothing – stupid idea. Anyway, Kimmy had her kid in a private nursing home, no less, arranged by Margaret. I only heard from Margaret intermittently after that and in the end I decided I was fine with that, after all. What good was raking up a whole load of trouble going to do? She got herself hitched to you, and I wanted even less to do with her then, but all of a sudden she was back on me case, wanting me to check up on Kimmy. I checked, reported in and that was it, but gradually it got more often – and more tricky. She wanted me to look after stuff – documents – and dig up stuff about you. I didn't like it. She took it all back for a while but then she wanted to give me even more and I had to hide it. It was becoming a bloody conspiracy – and I ain't no good at conspiracies, unlike some …' I ignored the barb. He'd entirely missed the point that he'd been actively conspiring whilst I was still blissfully ignorant there was anything to conspire about, and ironically he seemed better than me at it by a long chalk so far. 'So I told Sarah.'

Little Mother. 'And what did she tell you to do?'

'Leave it to her.'

'So that was how Sarah got the photos and the birth certificates that were in her keepsakes box? They were the things Margaret asked you to hide?'

'I guess so. I never looked at the stuff. I only had it when you were having your fancy place done up. She took it back for a while when it was finished, and I still can't see why I had to hide it after that. Looks like your place was pretty fancy and security conscious – with hidden cameras and stuff. Still don't know how she got them photos from the home, either. That really were a surprise. She must have known a damn sight more than I thought she did.'

And been spooked by it.

I thought of the security cameras and the fire-proofing; protection – but not against run of the mill burglars perhaps? Win dragged my attention – and speculation – back to his confession time.

'What did Sarah tell you when you went to see her?'

'Only that Margaret had visited her and they'd talked about me as a child, and about Margaret's childhood. She didn't admit that some of them would have been shared memories. Secrets – so many secrets – and you have the gall to accuse me of them.' The cynicism slipped out before I could stop it.

'It weren't all secrets. Sarah would've told you if she'd lived longer and knew she could trust you. She were as straight as a die.'

'A die waiting to be cast and with all the evidence to roll the dice and win with, but still keeping it to herself. Why did she only give me her keepsakes box and not Margaret's documents then?'

'Maybe she didn't have them.' He considered me for a moment and then added, 'but she gave *you* her keepsakes box, so *you'd* have the dice to roll. That means something – maybe even tells you where the rest of it is?' I curled my fingers around the safety deposit box key in my pocket, attached to the key ring that also held the key to Margaret's wardrobe of treasures, and considered. A key – and Margaret trusted me to have it – why? It must be very difficult to get hold of if she was so unconcerned as to let the key out of her possession like this, whereas she'd been anxious about it before. Win was watching me suspiciously. 'So where do you think it is?' he asked. 'And how you going to get round the fact that you been breaking the law almost every day since this all started.' I hesitated. 'Oh, come on. This is my head on the block,' he paused, and with extra emphasis, 'and my bloody car getting you to and from.'

'OK, I think it's all in a safety deposit box that Margaret and Sarah know, or knew, the whereabouts of. And we need to get hold of it to nail Jaggers.'

He considered. 'Well, you can't ask Sarah so what's Margaret told you?'

'She hasn't.' It came out too loud and too defensive. Win's eyes narrowed. I consciously imagined myself back in court. 'I mean I didn't ask her – I didn't have time. She seemed to confirm what I thought, and that I have the key – but not where to look for the box. If I could just find it, I wouldn't have to cash in any chips to roll the dice,' I added thoughtfully.

'Cash in your chips? That means snuffing it and I don't think for one minute you mean that. So what chips you cashing in?'

'Metaphorically speaking,' I replied hastily.

'Yeah,' he gave me a strange look which could have meant he didn't understand what metaphorical meant, or equally, he knew I was hedging.

'So ask her where it is, like the boss lady suggested.'

'She's not the boss lady. Heather Trinder is my business partner. And if Margaret wants to keep that evidence hidden for the time being then maybe it's because it's safer that way. Her head's on the block too if Jaggers finds out what she's been up to.'

'Oh boy. Women. Never trust one with your life.'

'Win, so far Margaret has killed herself off in order to make this happen, and has accumulated evidence that might seal her own death warrant. She's also the mother of my son. Priorities shift with circumstances, and belief and behaviour with them. For the moment I have to make Margaret and Danny my priority as well as getting you and me off the hook.'

'And you're going to do that by dobbing me in?'

'I'm going to do that by dobbing you in and then getting you off with the evidence I can get hold of *by* dobbing you in. Then I need to get my hands on the evidence that will dob Jaggers in instead, and I have to play along with Margaret's rules to do that. Unless someone else knows where it is.'

'Such as?'

'Binnie, maybe? Binnie knew Sarah was leaving me her keepsakes box,' I added slowly, computing the other possibilities and coming up with a blank. 'But the problem with that, Win, is that Binnie's disappeared.'

'Oh.'

'I went to try and talk to her again yesterday and her place had been cleared out. She's gone – completely. Is she running?'

'Running?' He bit his lip and fiddled with the empty glass again. 'She don't run, she walks ...'

'Win, if you know something you haven't told me until now, then now is the time to share it. Confession time, remember?' I grabbed his arm and squeezed. I never mastered the art of the Chinese burn as a child but luck must have been with me – or surprise. He yelped like a wounded dog.

'OK, OK. Binnie ... Where d'you think all this stuff would be if it weren't in Sarah's keepsakes box?'

'I don't know.'

'Where it's tucked away so tight it'd be like getting into Fort Knox to get to it.'

I nodded. 'Yes, a safety deposit box.'

'No, a safety deposit person.' I shook my head in disbelief. It *was* the booze talking after all. 'Oh bloody hell, I keep forgetting you don't know any of these in-jokes we used to have. Sarah didn't trust banks. For years after her bloke died she kept all her money under her mattress. Binnie found it when Sarah first got ill and wanted to put it in the bank for her. Sarah wouldn't have it. Said she might need it sometime, so Binnie did the next best thing – took it and told her *she'd* put it somewhere safe. Sarah called her a bleeding safety deposit box and Binne said no, she'd be a safety deposit *person*. It was their joke. Binnie even gave her a fancy key and told her whenever she wanted to take something out of her safety deposit person, she'd have to produce the key, like they do in the bank vaults. Trouble is, Binnie don't like responsibility – never has. When she gets fed up, she just clears off. Walks.'

'Is that why you don't get on?' It was almost too easy an explanation;

Win with his 'family sticks together' and Binnie with her 'just clears off', but maybe this time the simplest explanation was the real one.

'Yeah, I guess. So maybe you ain't looking for a box, you're looking for a person.'

'Jesus, Win – stop it! There's no such thing as a safety deposit person and I've got a key that's obviously to a safety deposit box. Margaret confirmed that.'

'No, you got a key, and you got someone telling you it's the key to a box. That's two different things altogether. And you got a woman who don't check on her sister's grave. I don't think you got anything at all, little brother. You just got a fancy key, like Sarah had – a pretence.'

I turned the key over in my pocket and eventually placed it and the rest of the bunch on the table between us.

'So what are you suggesting I do with this key?'

'Find someone who can tell you?'

'There were only three people who could do that. Sarah, Margaret, and maybe Binnie. I can't talk to any of them right now.'

'Then talk to Mary. She ain't going nowhere,' he replied tartly.

'Mary! Jesus, Win – what is it with you and Mary?' I exploded.

'Oh, for fuck's sake haven't you been listening to anything I've said?'

I looked at my watch. It was nearly midnight. The brain-freeze of lethargy I'd been suffering from yesterday had kicked back in again, along with the plethora of complicated family history Win had been regaling me with.

'Win, I've been listening to everything you've been telling me for hours, and I'm still no wiser about who can help me.'

He looked exasperated.

'And when did you miss the bit about Mary? OK, I'll tell you it again then; Mary and Margaret were close. Mary trusted Margaret. Margaret trusted Mary. Margaret and Sarah both used to go and see Mary. Margaret gave Sarah the stuff to hide after I wouldn't. Sarah didn't trust banks, she hid stuff in other ways so the key ain't to a deposit box. If Sarah, Margaret and Binnie can't tell you what that's the key too, I'm bloody sure Mary could. Got it? Christ Almighty – now who's the stupid one here?'

Mary. The one who'd quietly handed me the first phoenix in the form of the origami bird that turned into Win's birth certificate and back-to-back, his father's death certificate. It had proved his father – and mine – wasn't the one we'd both assumed him to be, and it had been the first step on the slippery path to identifying where our family diverged and where it met. She'd also been the one who'd wanted me to check what was in her, then, empty, box of goodies. Of course. Whether I wanted to see my mad sister again or not, and whether I wanted to believe Win's claim that she wasn't mad, I had to talk to her.

14: Distant Thunder

We drove back to London in silence the next day and reported in to Fredriks as agreed. Win accepted his fate meekly but sourly. Fredriks eyed my bruised face with secret amusement. I ignored it.

'Will he be charged?' I asked.

'He'll be checked in first, and we'll see,' he responded, duck pout tight and noncommittal. 'And you're going to be – where?' He directed at Win, ignoring me.

'Home.'

'19, Wilsdon Road, Finchley?'

'What it says, ain't it?'

'And you're taking him there?' Fredriks turned to me.

'If necessary,' I replied, curious what 19, Wilsdon Road, Finchley would be like – and why Win had kept it to himself all this time.

'And staying there with him?'

'Well,' I hadn't considered where I'd be staying on my return. Continuing in Heather's nest was probably somewhat in doubt, given what I'd done to her baby. 'Maybe. Do you need to know right now?'

'Helps to keep track of our other prime suspect,' Fredriks' lips pursed whimsically and the duck pout became trout pout.

'I'll let you know,' I retorted, joining Win in the sour stakes.

We left as soon as the formalities were completed, Win quietly jubilant he wasn't being held, me quietly surprised and wondering what Fredriks was up to.

'So what about getting this evidence you reckon you got?' Tequila sunrise broke through whisky sour as we left the station.

'I have to get into the house again for it. I don't think Fredriks is likely to agree to me just waltzing in there straight away, do you? He's still suspicious. I think I need a judicious word put in for me first.'

And for Margaret to send me one that she'd already done the job, I added silently.

'And who's going to do that?'

We were back at the car, parked in one of the widest bays on the second floor in the car park two blocks along from Chelsea police station. 'Less likelihood of door bashes here – and bloody hooligans,' Win had commented as we'd parked up. It also provided more room for Win, and his ample girth, to manoeuvre into the driver's seat.

'I'm thinking about it. In the meantime, there are other things to concentrate on.'

'Like talk to Mary,' he agreed. He turned the ignition and revved the car aggressively. It chugged and died. He swore and turned the engine over again. This time it rumbled and growled before dying. 'Shit!' His jaw set. I knew that look. It was the one he'd had on his face when he'd declared war on Jaggers and his gang at the children's home. He turned the ignition viciously again and stamped his foot on the accelerator. The engine screamed and the air in the car smelt of chemicals.

'Win!' I shouted above its screech. 'Stop! There's something wrong.' He ignored me and revved again, jaw jutting determinedly. For a moment he reminded me of myself – an older, fatter version – refusing to accept the inevitable. A cloud of blue-grey exhaust suddenly exploded behind us and the car hiccupped before purring throatily like an angry lion.

'Fucking hell!' Win announced through the fug. 'You're a bloody jinx with cars. I think the exhaust's blown.'

'Really?' I remarked dryly. 'Nothing to do with you then?'

He took his foot of the accelerator and the car slowed to a relieved idle. The air still smelled of fumes and I coughed.

'Me? I ain't a jinx. I'm the one being jinxed.' He shot me a dirty look and turned the engine off.

'It was fine on the way here. Why should it suddenly go now?'

'I don't know, but it don't sound fine now, do it?' He heaved himself out of the driver's seat and I eased myself gingerly out my side. We might have had a night's sleep at the pub in St Rosemary in the Marsh, but it hadn't been a good one. The mattresses were lumpy and I suspected mine might also have been home to an infestation of bed bugs because my sore ribs were now pebble-dashed with a rash of small itchy lumps, not that my sleep had been good either. It had been infested with strange connections that didn't connect and people asking me to do impossible things I promised to perform but knew I couldn't. I left the tightrope walk gladly on waking, with Margaret and Jaggers my avid audience, and the rats in the pit below my fate if I fell. By the time I made it round to the back of the car, Win was already on his hands and knees, fishing out what looked like a balled up blackened and oily rag from the exhaust pipe. He held it up to me like a trophy.

'Someone stuffed it up me arse,' he exclaimed, childishly incensed. 'That ain't nice. Bloody louts. I thought it'd be all right up here.' He struggled to his feet, and the bundled rag spread into a length of soiled plastic, originally a large clear bag, but now soot-blackened and pock-marked with small puncture marks. 'It's usually a spud. If it'd been a spud it would have gone pop all over our buddies over there.' He gestured to the cars parked across the way from us. 'At least they were bloody useless at it.'

I took the ragged plastic from him and examined it. Why use a plastic bag when it was so clearly not man enough for the job? Of course it wouldn't work properly. It would inevitably be expelled, albeit maybe leaving the catalytic converter damaged. But then maybe it was meant to? I passed it back to him uneasily. Maybe it was another warning, like the Land Rover that had rammed me whilst driving Heather's car; one I should be heeding on Win's behalf.

'Win, I think I ought to go and talk to Mary alone.'

'Record got stuck again, has it? Why, this time?'

'The same reason as before; because I've already dragged you far enough into this mess and Fredriks wants you home where he knows he can reel you in whenever he wants to. If you're haring off into the wild blue yonder, he's not going to be happy when he comes a-knocking and you're not there.'

'You're just trying to ditch me again.'

'No, I'm trying to protect you, Win.' His look of surprise would have been comical if it hadn't been for my sudden realisation what the warning might be. 'And if you hadn't found this and the exhaust had been partially blocked for any length of time, it wouldn't have been enough to stop the car running, but it would have impeded the release of the exhaust fumes. What do you think would have happened then?'

He scratched his head and pulled a face. 'I guess we would have been pushing up the daisies from carbon monoxide poisoning if we'd sat in it for long enough.'

'Exactly. Suffocation – with a plastic bag. Who does that remind you of?'

'He puts it round your head not up your ass,' he snapped back.

'Makes no odds to the result though, does it?'

'You think this was aimed at me?'

'I don't know. We were both in the car. It could be aimed at either of us, but whoever it was aimed at, tagging along with me can hardly be good for your health at the moment.' He began to protest but I cut across him firmly, 'Much as I appreciate you sticking by me, I have to deal with this alone. I'm not getting anyone else killed just to save my sorry skin.'

We faced each other over the shredded plastic that could have been our epitaph; killed by the back-draft of poisonous gas our toxic past had created.

'You're me family,' he said harshly.

'And you're mine.'

His face crumpled, the hardened bully beneath the sagging folds of skin suddenly merely a middle-aged man, and afraid. Not just for himself, I realised with shock, but for me too. All the bluster about trusting no-one but himself had been a bluff.

'You're my little brother. I let Georgie down back then. I let you down back then. I ain't gonna do it again.'

'We both let all of us down, and this is our legacy, Win – but it's my turn to fight this time. And whatever you say about trust – you have to trust me enough to let me do that. I think it's time to repay some of my debts – with interest.'

He gave me an odd look but didn't ask what my debts were. He made to toss the piece of ragged plastic away but I stopped him.

'Evidence,' I explained. He shrugged and tossed it in the boot instead. As it drifted gracefully onto the floor of the boot, it spread and its other message could quite clearly be seen written within its sketchy logo.

'*Snap! Job done every time by ...*' The name was defaced and unreadable.

Christ! Irony? Or a message from Margaret that she'd already accessed the camera and checked it over? Win waddled to the front of the car and climbed back in, leaving me to shut the boot. I stared at the shredded plastic bag a while longer, undecided, in the end concluding that I should regard it as exactly the kind of twisted joke Margaret would enjoy whilst imparting her message if no other was forthcoming in the meantime.

We arrived at 19, Wilsdon Road, Finchley without any further drama. It was unremarkable. A two up, two down terrace that had been subdivided and turned into two one-bedroomed flats. Downstairs a small child's scooter was propped against the wall and a doll in a toy pram was abandoned beside it. The doll peered blindly at us like Kimmy had when we'd seen her new-born before we were whisked away to the children's home. The memory still wasn't pleasant. Inside a high-pitched wail told of a childish tantrum in full swing, accompanied by an exhausted woman's voice, heavily accented.

'They got four of them,' Win commented. 'Pakis. Work hard though. Nice people. Grandparents got the corner shop but the kids live here and two doors down.'

I smiled inwardly. The hard man indeed wasn't hard – nor as prejudiced as he liked to sound. I saw him inside, unexpectedly embarrassed about seeing the cramped semi-squalor of where he lived compared to the luxurious surroundings I'd occupied until a short while ago. Even Heather's spare room, shoebox though it was, seemed more spacious than this.

'Want a cuppa?' he asked as we both stood self-consciously in the tiny kitchenette, aware that a boundary between us had been crossed and it would be impossible to redraw it now. We'd finally claimed each other. He pulled the top down on the kitchen cupboard to provide a work surface. It was faced with blue sticky-back plastic, lightly checked and tea-stained.

'Before I go, then …'

He nodded. It seemed we'd agreed I'd continue alone and he'd remain here although we hadn't said so in words. He dropped a teabag with a small Liptons tag attached to the end of its string into each of two mismatched mugs and waited patiently for the kettle to boil. It was an old-fashioned job, squat and iron grey, perched on the back ring of the chipped enamel hob. He dropped the cap on its spout and the rumbling of the simmering water inside made it vibrate.

'Like we used to have.'

He snorted. 'Old-fashioned, me.'

'I gathered.'

We smiled at each other, and the awkwardness dissipated a little.

'So you're actually going to see Mary then?'

'Who else is there to talk to?'

He shrugged. 'And what about the camera stuff?'

'I'm going to ask Heather to put a good word in for me.'

'Hah! Rather you than me.'

'Unless you want to ask her to help?'

'Me?' His expression was one of astonished hilarity.

'Well, you managed to persuade her to let us go on the run in the first place – how the hell did you do that? You must have used some kind of magic charm then.'

He looked like a schoolboy caught out in a prank.

'I told her we were going to get the money back that you'd stashed.'

'Oh my God!'

'Well I couldn't think of anything else to get round her. She kept on and on about it after I'd knocked you out – you were out for ages, you know. Thought I might have hit you a bit too hard to begin with but then you started mumbling about keeping promises so I knew you were going to be OK. Whenever a brief mentions promises you know he's got his wits about him. Don't give nothing away without getting summat back, briefs don't.' He winked.

'Cheers,' I replied sarcastically.

'Fact of life.' The kettle began to rattle urgently on the hob. He grabbed a tea towel and whisked it off just as it started to whistle, expertly pouring the boiling water into the mugs as the steam billowed upwards, temporarily engulfing us both and softening the impoverished kitchenette in its vignette of misty white. He fished an aged bottle of milk out of the fridge, sniffed it and grunted his approval before slopping it into the mugs and yanking the teabags out by their strings. They lay, in a pooling brown stain on the plastic covered worktop. He offered me one of the mugs, keeping the one with the chip in its rim for himself.

'We're not always tricky,' I replied mildly, but somehow I no longer associated myself with my peers. They belonged to another life I was leaving behind.

'No, I s'pose not. Everyone has a job to do.' He sipped his tea daintily and I watched, bemused, forgetting my own until the heat of the liquid burnt through the china and scalded my hand. I put it down quickly, briefly catching sight of myself in the now clearing glass of the steamy kitchen unit. I looked different too. Less Lawrence, more – what? Not Kenny. He was long gone. Maybe a mix of Kenny and Lawrence. Win broke through my reverie with another surprise.

'All right. I'll give her a bell. I'll tell her you're getting the money back but you need her to keep Fredriks sweet so you can get it sorted. Then you'd better come up with the goods or you'll have to explain to her why I lied for you because I ain't dealing with that she-devil all on me own – OK?'

I laughed. I didn't blame him. The consequences were dire – but they seemed too far distant to worry about for now. They say situations create necessities. The consequence of this situation was a necessity I'd survive or die from once I'd survived everything else. I hoped in the meantime, Margaret had indeed got the 'job done'.

I didn't finish the tea. Seeing myself in the reflection of the glass reminded me that time was fast running out for Lawrence if he was to complete the transformation required of him to beat Jaggers at his own game. Visiting Mary was but a step along the way. If Sarah had been given access to everything by Margaret, and had needed somewhere safe to deposit it, maybe *Mary* was that deposit box – or person as Win insisted – not Binnie. Increasingly the finger was pointing towards Mary being the key to the mystery, rather than the key itself. It would also explain the source of Win's birth certificate and why Margaret said she couldn't reach it for the moment.

It was already mid-afternoon by the time I took the M4 out of London in Win's car – surrendered with his absolute trust in me – and a mock threat of what he'd do if it came back harmed. Leaving the city actually lifted my spirits, even though I'd always loved the buzz of the place. In the past, the pulse of the traffic and the throb of the masses, heading for something – anything – in their daily routine, had always filled me with purpose. I'd felt an active part of the pulsating life-force that was the city and its people. But that was on a good day – and in the past. On a down day it left me jaded and worn-out. Recently life seemed to be made up only of down days and now the atmosphere felt stifling, as much from the mêlée of problems I was facing as the last dregs of the unexpectedly lingering hot summer. The fresh green of the countryside and its open spaces were a relief even if they did also bring sad associations with Sarah and what I imagined might have been her last view of the world; the banks of green interspersed with the variegated drifts of flowers she'd found so soothing.

The rapeseed fields on the way to Mary's care home had been in full bloom the last time I'd visited – great swathes of acid yellow, blinding me as I hugged the road cutting through them. In the short while since then, the crops had gone over, transforming the rape stalks from fluffy yellow lollipops to untidy brown frizz. The humidity that had stuck my shirt to me now presaged a storm. They should harvest before the weather broke. Clear blue sky was already deepening to sullen grey as I drove on through the sunburnt wreck of the rape crop. The impending downpour increased my sense of urgency too – the need to be somewhere and doing something that the London masses seemed to have. I set aside the frustration of being out of control of my life and put my foot down on the accelerator. At least I had control of the effortless power Win's outsized BMW wielded.

My hunch about the impending storm proved to be right. The first spots of rain had already started to fall as I reached High Wycombe and it was pelting down by the time I'd travelled the remaining twenty miles and was drawing into the gravelled drive of the institution where Mary lived. It still looked too grand and luxurious for what was little more than an asylum, and I was still curious who might be paying its fees, although the possibility that it was Margaret now seemed more than likely. I pulled into the parking area and waited a while for the rain to ease before getting out – putting off the moment if I was truthful. It didn't. Hammering down on the roof of the BMW like beats on a drum, it made my head pound too. The paramedic had been right in what he'd said to Heather, not so much in the possibility of disorientation and confusion – God knows I didn't need my home to have been burnt down to feel that – but in my over-sensitivity to noise. If it didn't stop soon I'd have to brave the downpour just to escape the din before my head exploded like my car had. After another five minutes of tympanic accompaniment with no sign of it easing off I gave up and made a dash for the main entrance. The cool of the rain on my face was soothing even if it pebble-dashed my clothes whilst my shoes were sodden from splashing through the puddles on the way to it. I swept the plastered hair away from my forehead and paused to look around on the threshold of reception. There was no-one there. Should I wait and report in, as I had before? Or should I simply try to find Mary's room on my own?

The uneasiness Mary always produced in me – even as a child – took over. I hesitated, half-tempted to simply leave and drive back to London, return the car and seek out Heather. I could apologise profusely for trashing her car and tearing off and beg for her to once again allow me to hide myself away in her little guest room until I could bring myself to do what I knew I had to do. It was the coward's way out, though. Was I really so scared of facing Mary that I had driven all this way, only to run away again because there was no receptionist to check me in? What was there to fear, other than fear itself? Or was it a darkness in her that I also feared might be in me that worried me so?

As I dithered, the storm outside intensified. I peered through the glass of the door. The drive was rapidly turning into a lake. Some isolated islands of gravel still remained between the puddles but were rapidly being subsumed into the whole. A sudden crackle of lightning followed closely by the ear-splitting boom of thunder made me jump. I automatically counted as Georgie had always done as a child. Five – one mile away. Close. I weighed up staying and going again; not such a good idea to be driving in a thunder storm and the rain was now torrential. I'd barely be able to see a hand's distance in front of me. Perhaps God, or fate – whichever existed, if either – was making my decision for me. Lightning streaked the sky again and the thunder crack was almost simultaneous as I counted. One. The reception area sunk into darkness. Overhead. There must have been a direct hit on the power lines. That pretty much did it. In darkness or not, this was definitely the safer place to be. I may as well face all the darkness I feared in one go.

I made my way unsteadily towards the cluster of exit points leading away from reception that I remembered from my first visit. There were three, one for each of two separate wings with the central hub of the building in between. Mary's had been the one on the right the last time. I took the same one and it led me into the depths of a darkened corridor – almost pitch-black without its internal lighting. I faltered barely two steps in, visions of rats and other unseen terrors making me shiver nervously.

'Don't be so stupid. This is a nursing home. No rats or thugs here,' I told myself aloud, casting a look over my shoulder in case anyone had appeared in the plush reception area behind me to hear. It was still deserted.

But what about lunatics? Like your sister … the little voice whispered. *Your crazy sister.* An icy finger trailed down my spine.

'She's not crazy, she's bi-polar.' I replied aloud again, then laughed at myself. If anyone sounded crazy, it was me. The tingle ran down my spine again.

'Keep to the wall. That way you'll follow the corridor.'

Jesus, why did I keep talking to myself?

I edged along the wall, sliding my palm along the glossy dado rail and over the bumps of doors and door frames. I counted them as I went. We'd passed four – maybe five – on the way to Mary's room before we'd turned off into the smaller corridor last time. Her room had been at the end of it. My eyes started to accustom to the half-light and I breathed a little easier. There was a window part-way down another side corridor I calculated must lead to Mary's room and I focused on the glimmer of light coming from it, the frame starkly outlined from time to time as the lightning sparked, although the thunder seemed to be moving away. I counted six between the next round of thunder and lightning, and then eight. The storm would probably ease soon, but I was here now, and committed to staying. Typical though, that I should arrive to visit my 'ill' sister when there was a lightning storm and the power had failed. The absurdity of the situation caught up with me then and I leant against the wall just before it turned the corner and led towards Mary's room and laughed hysterically this time.

'*What's so funny?*'

I jumped.

'Who's there?'

'*No-one. There's no-one here. You're imagining it.*'

'Where are you; who are you?'

'*Perhaps I'm your conscience?*'

I breathed deeply and consciously calmed myself. Fool! It was all in my head – paranoia – like Win had accused me of. Another lightning flash lit the corridor. It was empty, but I remained hugging the wall until the power surged back on and the bright white of the overhead lights blinded me. Just as suddenly paralysis left me. I turned the corner and ran down the corridor towards Mary's room, stopping just short at her door. It was closed and the corridor was still empty. I hesitated. I was too spooked to face Mary now. I retraced my steps to reception and found the desk manned again now. The receptionist threw a barrage of questions at me as I approached, expression frozen in that officious way receptionists have of making you feel guilty for simply existing.

'Can I help you? Who are you visiting? Did you get lost when the power went off?'

There was no avoiding her. I mumbled my apologies and went over to suffer the inquisition. She thrust the visitors' book at me and I signed it obediently. She looked at my entry.

'To see Mary Juss. Do you know where you're going, or shall I get someone to take you there?'

'It's OK to just turn up unannounced, then?'

'Of course.' She looked at me strangely.

'It's just, the reason for the patients being here ...'

'Residents. Not patients, thank you.'

'Yes, of course.' I was embarrassed. I hoped the hacks didn't track me here and ask the receptionist for a comment. It wouldn't be flattering. 'I think I can find my own way there.'

'All right, remember to sign out when you go. It's fire regulations. If I'm not here, the book will be on the desk.'

I returned to the corridor, now brilliantly lit, irritated by both the receptionist and my response to her and made my way along the corridor, counting off the doors again as I did so and marvelling how different things looked in the light. Maybe what I'd said to Heather was right – I'd lost objectivity because it was all too close to me. The idea encouraged me. My head cleared with the possibility of clarity rather than continual confusion. Get this meeting over with and review the facts objectively and logically. Yes, that was the way to do it. It occurred to me that was precisely what Heather had been urging me to do with her little mirror experiment too. I turned the corner and the door to Mary's room was straight ahead of me again. It was ajar. With Kimmy murdered, Binnie disappeared and Margaret in hiding, a feeling of inevitable disaster lurked beyond every doorway at the moment. I didn't want to find out why the door was ajar, but I had to. This was why I'd come here – in search of answers, no matter how unpalatable. I walked slowly towards the door, hairs on the back of my neck standing to attention and skin crawling. Keeping at arm's distance, I pushed at the door with my fingertips. They left a sweaty mark like DS Jewson's hand had on Heather's front door. The door swung open effortlessly but I remained on the threshold, nerves jangling. My stomach knotted uneasily.

'Mary?' The room appeared to be abandoned, apart from the flock of origami birds still hanging from the ceiling on long strands of cotton. They flapped and swung in the draught from the opened door. 'Hello?' Still no answer. I entered cautiously, ducking under the fluttering birds and calling her name again. I could see the tip of a shoe poking out from the end of the bed at the far end of the room, as if someone was lying on the floor there. The instinct that something was wrong heightened. I paused in the middle of the room, birds fluttering behind me. The image of Kimmy's body on the floor in the photographs Fredriks had shown me flashed before my eyes. One of her legs had been sprawling awkwardly, shoe half off, whilst the rest of her body hunched round the knife and the blood. *Oh my God.* The words spiralled in my head, like the blood had pooled around the knife. I edged towards the bed.

'Mary? Is that you? It's Kenny. I've come to see you again. Are you all right?'

I kept the shoe firmly in my sights as I approached. There was no movement. I couldn't see over the top of the bed, but nor could I bring myself to walk round it. Instead I leant across it as I strained to see who the shoe belonged to. There was nothing, just the shoe, and then arms wrapping themselves round me like rope; binding me tight and squeezing me until the breath erupted from me in a harsh groan and my ribs screamed pain. I collapsed face down on the bed, too winded to shout for help. My assailant fell on top of me, simultaneously throwing something over my head and turning my world grey and airless. I gasped and writhed as I sucked the sticky mass into my mouth. It smelt over-poweringly of chemicals. The arms squeezed tighter, forcing the breath out of me and the grey stuff forced my eyelashes into my eyes. My eyes watered and my nose ran as I writhed in terror, but my attacker simply held on tighter. I was back in the home; the frightened boy Kenny Juss had been, and suffocating. I choked and sputtered, gasping for air. Someone was shouting obscenities and screaming as my head spun and the grey cracked into jagged black splinters. In my ear a cruel voice I remembered all too well hissed, *'This is what I'll do to you every night, every night, every night ...'*

15: Mary

When I opened my eyes I was lying on my back on the bed, and Mary was hanging over me, eyes wide with concern, stroking my forehead. I panicked and tried to sit up but she pushed me back down. The ragged and torn plastic bag from the exhaust pipe lay in a crumpled heap on my chest, still damp with my spittle, one corner now tied in a loose knot.

'It's all right,' she soothed. 'No-one will get you whilst you're hiding under Rosemary's cloak. Its magic, you see? You've disappeared.'

She seemed quite lucid but I lay very still, waiting, all the same. She continued to stroke my forehead, humming gently. *Rock-a-bye baby.* One of her childhood favourites, I recalled. I held my breath as I studied the ceiling, afraid that if I moved she would transform into a monster again. The ceiling was off-white, ornately plastered, with a small crack trailing away along one wall. Settling – or age. My conscious mind catalogued the surroundings and means of escape whilst my subconscious mind screamed with fear, but I knew from the stabbing in my chest and the heaviness of my body I wouldn't be able to make it to the door before Mary. She'd always been faster than me as a kid, and now I was half-choked, with cracked ribs and feeble, useless legs that felt like jelly. My only hope was to keep her calm so I could slip away later. After a while she stopped humming and peered at me.

'Are you all right, Kenny? I thought you'd be all right after you'd calmed down a bit, but you aren't moving even though you're not dead. Do you want me to get one of the helpers?'

'Maybe,' I answered cautiously. I still didn't move, wary that she might suddenly attack me again. 'How long have you been here, Mary?'

'A little while.' She smoothed a stray strand of hair from my forehead, and started humming again.

'Were you here when I was being attacked?'

She stopped humming. A flash of lightning flickered behind her. I didn't count this time but she'd moved closer by the time the thunder boomed.

'Attacked? Were you attacked? Then I definitely need to call one of the helpers! I just found you lying on my bed when I came back from the kitchen.'

'The kitchen?'

'Yes, I wanted some tea but I couldn't make it whilst it was dark. I had to wait for the lights to come back on. I knew they would. They told me.'

I eased myself onto one elbow and studied her. She seemed completely rational.

'One of the helpers?'

'Probably. It was dark so I couldn't see them, but they sounded nice. They told me to wait in the kitchen until the lights came back on.' My crushed ribs roared as I shifted position. I winced. 'Oh dear – you're hurt. I *will* get a helper.'

Helper, be damned! I had a pretty good idea who *my* helper might have been.

'No!' It came out too sharply and she looked surprised. 'No,' I repeated more gently. 'It's all right, Mary. Someone did attack me but maybe it was one of the helpers, thinking I was threatening you. I'll be all right in a moment.'

'OK.' She still looked worried.

'Was this,' I twitched the ragged plastic away from my chest, 'here when you found me?'

'Yes. You'd got it all twisted round your face.' She studied me, puzzled. 'I thought it was suffocating you so I pulled it away but you wouldn't let go of it so I let you keep it on your chest. I thought you must think it was magic.'

'Ah.'

'Is it? Magic?'

'No, no; not at all.'

'Why is it so important to you then if it's not magic?' She looked wary. 'Are you lying to me? Are you really the devil made to look like Kenny?'

'No! I'm Kenny, your brother – remember?'

'I remember.' She smiled and resumed her humming, but still watching me suspiciously.

'Mary, someone tried to suffocate me. Are you sure you didn't see anyone here when you came back?'

'No, just you, lying on your tummy with that twisted round your face.' She watched me for a while, forehead pinched into a crease. I struggled to muster enough energy to pull myself upright. 'What did you do with my bird?' The change of subject confused me.

'I haven't done anything with your birds. They're all still there.' I indicated nervously towards the curtain of swinging origami creations. She laughed. A squall of rain thrashed against the window pane and the birds seemed to react to it, leaping about on their strings.

'Oh, no. Not those birds. The Win bird I gave you.'

Understanding dawned. 'The birth certificate?'

'Yes. Do you understand now?'

'A little – not completely.'

She looked sympathetic.

'I know, me too. When I take my pills I understand. When I don't – well … but there are times I prefer that to understanding. It's easier. Do you think you might be able to get up now? We could sit over there by the window and watch the rest of the storm. I like lightning – crack! So clean.'

I nodded. Best to humour her, and lying prone on Mary's bed had me distinctly at a disadvantage. She stood up and sauntered over to the window. The rain beat against it and she put her hand onto the pane and stood there watching me as I swung my legs carefully over the edge of the bed and attempted to stand up. My ribs protested again. The attacker's iron grip had undone any tentative steps I'd made towards recovery since yesterday.

'Smash, smash, smash – like smashing china,' she said, to no-one in particular. 'There were times all I wanted to do was smash things when I was little – didn't you? I couldn't, of course. Pop would have been furious and Ma would have suffered for it, so whenever I felt like that I'd imagine the rain smashing down like this. I still do. Come and feel it. Smash, smash, smash.'

My head swam as I straightened and I grabbed at the headboard to steady myself. She watched with curiosity.

'Do you feel like smashing things now?' I asked to deflect her attention from me and my vulnerability.

'Oh, no. I thought you might though. You look very angry, you know.'

The ragged plastic floated gracefully to the floor and lay at my feet like a puddle. I looked at it for a moment, trying to marshal the disparate thoughts racing around in my head before bending painfully to pick it up. I wondered what Heather's mirror would have reflected at me if I'd been able to look in it right now.

'Mary, why did you call the plastic Rosemary's cloak? And why do you say I'd disappeared?'

She was ensconced in the same chair as my previous visit by the time I made it over to the window; arms hanging sluggishly, just as then. They reminded me of vines, draping over their stakes, heavy with fruit at her fingertips.

'It's a story. From long time ago. The rose of Mary and her blue cloak. It's a nice story – unlike that thing,' her right hand waved languidly at the tattered plastic bag before flopping back over the arm of the chair. 'But then sometimes things are made to seem nice just to fool you.'

I staggered to the chair opposite her and dropped into it with a grunt. I lay the plastic across my knees. Hard to believe a short while ago it had been the instrument of my near-suffocation. The knotted corner was reminiscent of how Ma had told us to tie a knot in our hankies to remind us of things. It hadn't ever worked for me; simply made me wonder why I'd knotted my hanky in the first place, but the association lent the plastic an innocence it didn't warrant. I screwed it angrily into a ball inside my fist, then let it go again the way Margaret had taught me to do as a tension reliever, unsure whether to believe Mary's claim she'd been absent when the attack had occurred. From all accounts bi-polar sufferers could be wildly aggressive as well as manically depressive when uncontrolled. On the other hand, logically there hadn't been just one assailant, but two; one to hold me down and the other to put the plastic over my face.

'Tell me the story,' I asked affably.

She cocked her head to one side, like one of her birds, and clicked her tongue.

'Hasn't she already told you it?'

She must be herself, I reasoned. She must think of herself in the third person. I responded in kind.

'No, she's only just mentioned it to me.'

She looked at me strangely.

'Oh. No, no – of course she wouldn't. You weren't there, were you?'

'Where?'

'When we were young. You weren't there. Maybe you already knew the secret of vanishing but hadn't told us about it.'

'No, Mary. I don't know the secret of vanishing. That's for other people. But I do need to know about this,' I indicated the plastic, 'and some other things. Will you tell me her story so I know it too?'

'All right.' She grinned happily. 'It was nice then, although you should have been there too, but Win said no. You'd chosen differently. No-one even knew where you were ...' she broke off to wag an accusing finger at me. 'See, you *had* vanished, you fibber! Sarah was nice though. Maybe I loved her as much as you then because you weren't there. You have to love somebody or you die from loneliness. That would be terrible, wouldn't it? You won't let that happen, will you?'

'No I won't – but I don't think you can, Mary, although I agree it's better to love than not to.'

She nodded sagely.

'Kimmy was there too. Called me mad. *You* know I'm not mad, don't you Kenny?'

'You see things differently when you're a kid.'

'And not when you're an adult?' she added, laughing, but without humour. 'Did you like Kimmy?' She didn't wait for my reply and I was relieved. 'I didn't like Kimmy. She pulled the cat's tail so hard it scratched me once because it thought I'd done it. I cried and so did the cat. Miaow, miaow.' Her cat mewling was eerily realistic. I shivered involuntarily. 'Did you know Kimmy was bi-polar? They say families all carry a likeness, but that was our only one, I think.'

'Yes, I did. I found a letter with the diagnosis in some of Sarah's things after she died.' I hesitated, noticing the use of the past in relation to Kimmy. 'Did you know Kimmy is dead, Mary?'

'Is it true? She told me but I didn't believe her.'

'It's true. Who's *she*?'

She ignored me.

'Poor Sarah. Did I tell you she was nice? Is she dead too? I forget. When I take my pills I don't.'

'Are you taking your pills now?'

'I forget,' she watched me and then roared with laughter. 'Oh Kenny, your face!' I tried to laugh with her but I didn't need Heather's mirror experiment to know what I must look like this time. 'Yes, I'm taking my pills when I need to,' she added when her laughter had died down. 'But you want to know about the cloak story, don't you?' I nodded. She smiled mischievously. 'And about Margaret.' I leant forward involuntarily, despite the discomfort in my chest. She indicated she'd noticed with a small satisfied nod. She recounted essentially the same story as Win, but this time I listened more carefully, as I would have to a client. It's a skill, differentiating between a lie and a truth. They can be made to sound the same but they're not. The lie is practised – crafted, complete – and perfect every time. The truth can be the slightest bit different each time it's told, depending on who is telling it – but still be the truth.

'They diagnosed *her* in childhood. They didn't diagnose me until it was too late for me to be anything but here. Sarah told me that so I'd feel sorry for her because she was like me. But why would I feel sorry for her? The foster carers kept trying with her until she was twenty or more. They must have been saints. No-one did that for me. I would have been nice to them, not treat them the way she did.'

Her face twisted angrily and she reached across and spread her hand against the window pane again. The rain still beat steadily against it and she nodded as if beating time for a while. I waited as the beat settled in my head too. After a while she removed her hand from the window pane and her arm trailed languidly over the armrest of the chair again.

'They kept her back three years in school to try and give her something decent to come out with. Sarah reckoned she had the mental age of a kid ...' she paused again, 'whereas I'm fine!' she shot defensively at me.

'It's OK Mary. I know.' I nodded reassuringly.

Liar.

She looked uncertainly at me and her hand wavered towards the window.

'Really,' I added, anxious to calm her so she would continue with her story. Her hand fell back, fingers twitching.

'The Flowers girls were in her class. They seemed to latch onto each other – or at least Rosemary did. Where Rosemary was, Margaret was always only a few steps behind, but Margaret was my friend. Poor Margaret. She was kind, but a little grey pebble to Rosemary's diamond.' She nodded at me again, sadly. 'The cloak was Rosemary's joke. She'd heard the story at school – about how Mary had put her cloak over a rosemary bush when they were running away from Herod and the magic hid baby Jesus.'

'Well, I don't think ...'

'It did, Kenny – it did! Joseph had a dream about Herod killing all the little boys so they knew to run away. That must have been the cloak too –

magic. Anyway, Margaret told me the story because she knew I'd like it. I did. It was a happy story. Then Rosemary told me she could do magic too because her name was Rosemary and I believed her. I know it seems silly now, but you have to remember that I wasn't on my pills then. Some days I was so happy all I wanted to do was sing. Other days I wanted to curl up in a ball and cry, or shout at everything because I was so angry but I didn't know why. Or smash things. It's how I got this.' She thrust the trailing arm in front of me and I saw the thin white line zigzagging up her arm. 'Through a window. I ran up and down the air raid shelter instead when I was a kid.'

I squirmed inwardly.

'You seem very calm and clear now ...'

She smiled. 'Unlike the last time you saw me,' she supplied for me.

'Well ...'

'I hadn't taken my pills that day. I still knew you had to have Win's bird though – even then.'

'Why Win's bird?'

'So you'd know – and that it's all to do with magic. Magic and disappearing.'

I sighed. This was going nowhere.

'So what did Rosemary do with this claim to magic?' I asked, wondering how much longer before I could call it a day and head back to Win's.

'Nothing. She didn't do anything. Then. It was later. After she died.'

'After she died?'

'Yes, you know she was murdered, don't you?'

'Yes, I know she was murdered.'

'Poor Jonno. It wasn't him. Rosemary would tell you that too, if she told the truth.'

'Rosemary's dead, Mary. You've just said so yourself.'

'Oh, yes,' she laughed gently. 'She was, but she didn't stay dead. She came back to life. That was her magic – see? She put her cloak on and did her magic with it – clever magic. All those lies and everyone believed her, whereas no-one believes me, except maybe you, Kenny, because you would understand. She vanished and came back. You vanished and came back too, so you'd know how she does it. But now you need to send her back where she came from. She's dead and she should have stayed dead.'

I studied her sadly. It was true life had been unfair to her, but when was it ever consistently fair to anyone? I'd done my duty and been to see her, as I'd promised Win. She obviously had nothing of any use to tell me about Sarah or Margaret or the missing box of evidence. The moments of lucidity were punctuated with far too many of confusion. To sort the real from the unreal would be impossible, and surely no-one would entrust vital secrets to this sad and confused figure? On the periphery of my vision the room door opened and closed again. A figure in white approached. Mary ignored her and leaned across to grab my hand urgently.

'You've got to find him before she makes him disappear too, because he won't come back if she gets her way – and neither will you.'

The tall white figure came into focus.

'Mary, you've got a visitor! They didn't say so at reception.' It was a nurse, starched and pristine, but only a portion of her face peered at me through the strictures of her veil. 'I'm so sorry, you're Mr?'

'Juste – Lawrence Juste.' I stared at her. 'I didn't know this was a religious establishment?'

'It's not.'

'But you're a nun?'

'I merely follow my calling,' she smiled at me, amused. 'Don't you?' I looked at the small embroidered logo on the apron covering her habit. Something clanged in my head and then silenced; an alarm bell with its clapper dampened. Win's comment, *No, you got a key, and you got someone telling you it's the key to a box. That's two different things altogether – a pretence.* I opened my mouth to reply but the words remained on my tongue. 'Anyway, I'm so sorry, Mr Juste. The storm knocked the power out and we had to wait for the emergency generator to kick in. The doors might have been unmanned for a moment or two but we didn't think we'd lost any of our residents in that time – or have anyone join us. Security is a must, isn't it?' I was being gently coached.

'I signed in at reception and was told to find my own way here.'

'Really?' She put her hand on Mary's shoulder as Mary started to rise from her chair. Mary sat obediently back down. 'That's not the way we do things here. I must apologise again. I shall have a word with someone about that.' She re-focused her attention on Mary. 'My dear, are you going to have your medication today? It will help, you know.'

'Mary said she'd already had her pills.'

'Did she?' The woman looked surprised. 'Do you know her background?'

'I'm her …' I paused, 'brother.'

174

'I don't recognise you.'

'We haven't been back in touch long.'

'Ah, well in that case I can tell you that unfortunately she's been saying that for weeks now. What stories have you been telling your brother, Mary?'

Mary hung her head sulkily. 'I forget.'

The nun sighed and gave me a resigned look.

'What is the alternative if she doesn't want to take the medication?'

'That will be up to Mary.' She patted Mary's shoulder. 'But no more stories in the meantime Mary – all right? What will your brother think?' She indicated to the bell push on the wall near the door. 'I'll check in later on but when you're ready to go, will you use the door code and ring the bell to let us know you're leaving, please.' She handed me a small slip of paper. 'Hand it back in at reception and don't make it too long. In the light of today we may need to review Mary's security. The lock on the door is automatic as you leave. We like to ensure *everyone's safety.*'

My stomach turned over and I was about to ask her what she meant by *everyone's safety* but she was already heading for the door and Mary was watching me with a gleam in her eye. She waited for the nurse to go, before saying, 'Yes, that is, safe from me.' Her mouth twisted in a mischievous smile. 'So now you'll have to decide who you believe, won't you? Her or me?'

'Maybe I ought to go now,' I started to rise but she slammed her hand down on my knee, making it smart.

'I haven't finished my story yet, Lawrence, who used to be Kenny. You're good at magic too, aren't you? Like Rosemary. You're both someone different now.'

I didn't know what to say. Her face was so close to mine I could feel her breath on my cheek and smell the scent of her hair: sharp and zesty like lemon. She let go of my knee as suddenly as she'd grabbed it and leant back, taking the ragged plastic with her. She rolled it up and threw it back at me. Reflex reaction made me try to catch it but it floated as lightly as one of her birds as I snatched at the air. I balled it into my fist as she started speaking again.

'I know you had your reasons, Kenny, but you can't dip out of your obligations forever. Family's meant to look after each other. I gave you Win's bird so you could look after ours. I thought you'd be smart enough to do that since you'd been smart enough to work out the magic and disappear once already. I've spent a lifetime being left out of everything, so I get to know everything because everyone discounts me. Just like all my little birds, all singing their hearts out for me. They know everything too. Watch out for Rosemary, and her magic, and send her back where she should be. Will you?'

A solitary clap of thunder followed by a thin flash of distant lightning momentarily drew her attention away from me. She banged her hand on the window pane in reply to it. I'd been right all along. Mary *was* mad. I got quickly out of my chair, and alarm got me to the door, ducking awkwardly to avoid the paper birds, before she realised I'd moved.

I stabbed in the code, gabbling my excuses, and rang the bell. 'That's fascinating, Mary, and I promise to sort it all out, but I have to go now.' Nothing happened, no sound, no starched and veiled nurse. Nothing. Mary got to her feet and started purposefully towards me.

'You don't believe me, do you? You think I'm mad?'

'I just really do need to go now. I've borrowed someone's car and they'll be needing it back shortly. I'll come back, though – soon,' I pressed the bell again and pulled at the door handle. She stooped to walk under the birds and stopped just in front of them, shaking her head sadly as my knees began to shake and my bladder weaken at the thought of *everyone's safety*. I pushed the bell insistently.

'No you won't. You'll never come back and then you'll never understand my little mockingbird's spells.'

She didn't attempt to get any closer. I felt a fool for imagining she might want to harm me, but still she was crazy – crazy, crazy, crazy. Pitiful. I suddenly felt overwhelmingly sad. The door lock released and I didn't wait for another nurse to appear. I shot out, leaving Mary still standing by the birds making cooing noises at them as the door swung shut.

There was a different receptionist on duty – far more pleasant than the first. I explained who I'd been to see as I thrust the door code slip at her, and that I needed to leave in a hurry to return my borrowed transport to justify my flustered appearance. She looked bemused.

'There's no entry for you in the book. Never mind, just sign yourself out and presumably that should cover us.'

The book looked the same – had someone removed the brand new page my name had originally been signed on? I signed myself out on the top of another new page, equally bemused. I wanted to examine it closer but the receptionist was waiting for me to hand it back, smiling and gently curious at my hesitation. Or were there two books? And if so, who else might have signed themselves in and out in this book?

The storm had passed over now and the rain had completely stopped. Outside the air was fresh and crisp as if it had been cleaned by the downpour. The gravel drive was already starting to drain and I picked my way through the dispersing puddles, marvelling how quickly a flood could drain away – as incredible as it was to have an insane sister in an otherwise unremarkable – if not ordinary – family. I should have felt relieved to have escaped so easily. Instead I felt depressed.

Win's car stood wet and wan in the parking area. It welcomed me in, and I sank into the driver's black leather seat with a sigh, thankful for the fact that it moulded itself so well to my aching body. I felt as tired as if I'd been battling in court all day; drained and brain-dead. It was only then that I noticed I was still clutching the tattered plastic bag Mary had thrown back at me, crumpled and sweaty. I flung it onto the passenger's seat and it sprang back up like a genie released from a lamp. I could almost have imagined it to have some clever internal self-righting mechanism. Maybe Mary was right and there *was* magic in the air. I looked more closely, poking at its spreading mass. It wasn't a self-righting mechanism. It was the knot in the corner that was forcing it open – the knot that would have reminded me of something I had no idea I'd ever known I needed reminding of as a child. I undid it to reveal its message: a scrappy piece of paper, covered in random letters cut out of a newspaper. A ransom note. I laughed hysterically, struggling to quell the sensation of being on a madly careering rollercoaster about to enter a ghost train tunnel full of my worst fears. And this was definitely one of them.

16: The Prize

It was basic and blunt. Two and a half million pounds in used notes – of course – with the time and place of the drop to be notified. No police. The prize wasn't named but I knew what – or rather who – it must be: Danny. I fished frantically in my pocket for my mobile phone, tapping my fingers on the steering wheel like Mary had to the beat of the rain on the window whilst I waited for Heather to answer.

'Ah, a voice from the void? After getting his brother to do the dirty work and tell me he's disappeared again but needs another favour in the meantime. So where are you now? On your way to the restaurant at the end of the universe?'

'No, much more boring than any of that. I think Danny's been abducted.'

'Silly me. I misunderstood you yesterday when you said he was with Margaret and absolutely fine. In that case he and Margaret must both have been abducted by aliens from another dimension and you need me to get the address of the hotel they're all staying at.'

'Heather, I'm not joking. I've just been given a ransom note.'

'Oh.' Silence, then 'You're serious?'

She sounded doubtful but less hostile.

'Of course I bloody am!'

'Oh, my God! Well, tell me what's going on then. You said nothing about this last night and Kat and I have been stalling all this time because you were so certain.'

'It hadn't happened then.' I rapidly summarise what had happened since my call to her from the pub car park in St Rosemary in the Fields, ending with, 'and I understand from Win that he cut a deal with you that if I returned the stolen partnership money you'd give me a head start. That's not the way it is. I didn't steal anything and nor do I need a head start. What I need is to get my hands on the evidence to prove Win's innocence, and that I'm not complicit in witness tampering or any other duplicity which Jaggers has made me out to be the culprit of.'

'So where are you now? And where's Win?'

'I'm in Oxfordshire – in the car park of Mary's' … I hesitated '… home. Win told me a bit more of what was going on with Margaret and we realised that Mary might know more than I got out of her last time I visited her. I left Win at home so Fredriks wouldn't complain then came here to see Mary again, but someone attacked me and Mary was as mad as ever. I made a getaway, but there was a ransom note wrapped up in the bag someone tried to suffocate me with.'

'And all that without drawing breath! But a ransom note? Are you sure you haven't misunderstood? You were certain Danny was with your loving but regularly dematerialising wife. Or that's what you claimed. Now you tell me you were wrong. What do I believe? And what other little games have you devised to tie me up in knots with?'

'Heather, I don't need sarcasm even if I deserve it. I need help.'

'Christ, you're not joking there,' but she sounded less tart. 'Are you really telling me the truth this time?'

'Would I make up such a sick joke where Danny's concerned?'

'No-o. OK, so what does this ransom note say?'

This time she sounded worried, and conversely, I sighed with relief.

'The usual. Two and a half million pounds, used notes and they'll tell me where to take it.'

'And who is they?'

'I don't know, but I can guess. '

'Well if you don't know for certain, you can't just go along with it. And where will you get the money from? We need to talk to Fredriks. Now!'

'I can't. It says no police.'

'Rubbish! If the child's life's in danger you have to tell Fredriks. This means he's genuinely been missing for hours, and he has a medical condition. He could already be ill, or worse. You were so sure. I really didn't expect this!'

Neither had I. I *had* been so sure …

Just be prepared – and don't be spooked if things happen that aren't quite what you expect.

Shit! Margaret had said it just before she left, after saying Danny was fine. This was what she'd meant, and now I'd gone running to Heather, instead of playing out the little charade. Fool! Now I would have to backtrack – somehow.

'Believe me, you don't need to remind me of that, but humour me just a little longer, will you? I need to establish if Danny really *is* missing, first, or whether he *is* with Margaret. I was sure he was – or at least that was what she implied.'

'I don't understand. *What she implied?* When have you seen her again, then?'

'This could all just be another part of the game Jaggers is playing to throw me off-balance.'

'Lawrence, you need to stop playing games and tell Fredriks. Now! Or I will.'

'No!' I almost shouted into the phone. 'Heather, I know this isn't a game, but please will you let me deal with it my way? I may never be free of it otherwise. I'm sorry, maybe I overreacted at first. I don't think Danny will come to any harm, even if he is being held to ransom. Either Jaggers will need him for a handover to happen, or if it's a scam then he'll be with Margaret, and safe. I need to establish which of those two possibilities it is, though, and then what to do about it. Please?' She didn't answer. 'Heather?'

'I'm considering.' She sounded irritable. 'All right, I'll see what I can do, but for the moment only. What are you going to do now?'

'What the ransom note asks me to, raise the money and then wait for instructions. In the meantime, I'll try to make contact with Margaret, but that will take time and I'll have to wait for her to respond so I need your help again.'

The sigh was melodramatic but I knew she'd oblige. 'What?'

'I need you to persuade Fredriks to allow me back into my house to retrieve some of my personal belongings. It must have been made safe by now, even if it's still sealed off. Under normal circumstances I would have been there to find out myself, if it hadn't been for …'

'My niece,' she cut me short. 'OK, OK.'

'But please don't tell Kat about any of this. If the authorities start chasing then the whole deal's out in the open and I don't know where I or Danny will stand. After that I need you to certify to the insurance company that I'm of sound mind when I make my claim for just a percentage of rebuilding costs, with the land left in trust with them pending finalisation of the investigation. Should I later be charged with anything in connection with the fire, it will be forfeit by me. That should allow them to expedite the claim straight away.'

'Lawrence, are you mad? That's the major part of your assets. You need to wait it out and press a claim for criminal compensation, expenses and God knows what else when they nail the person responsible. It may take a while but at least at the end of it you can start again properly. You're not living in my spare bedroom for the next five years because you're stony broke!'

'Heather, I know what I'm doing.'

'No you don't. You're insane – or up to no good.'

'Whichever – will you do it?'

She sighed. 'I'll *think* about it – all of it – and let you know.' The way Ma had *thought* about it when she wasn't going to agree.

The phone clicked down on me and I debated whether to set off for Win's or to wait for her to ring me back. Ten minutes – that should be long enough for her to hand me over to Fredriks or decide to help. I laid the phone on the passenger seat where the plastic bag was and examined the ransom note in more detail. The nausea I'd experienced when I'd first read it was starting to fade and be replaced by objectivity now I'd realised it was probably another part of Margaret's plan. So this had been the reason behind the attack – not to harm me but to prime me. Maybe Mary hadn't been responsible after all. My assailant had been strong, very strong. Not female strong. Male strong. Even in my current incapacitated state I was a big man, over six foot and no weakling, but I'd been unable to escape. Admittedly the bag over my face and the whispered words, whether real or imagined, had caused sufficient paranoia to confuse me but it still took a man to pin me down. A man and an accomplice, with a plan in mind.

John Arthur Wemmick and his 'sister', Molly?

No – that would mean Margaret was in collusion with Jaggers! That was crazy, and she was on my side – or I on hers; the distinction was no longer relevant.

My head was pounding again and the pain in my ribs felt like small knifepoints piercing me viscerally. A sudden and overwhelming return of the urge to be sick had me leaning my head against the backrest of the BMW and closing my eyes. *Calm, calm.* I tried deep breathing but it didn't work. I switched Win's on-board music system on. Music to calm the savage beast – although what kind of beast Win's taste in music would be aimed at was questionable. The dashboard lit up, saying that the radio was selected. Classic FM, and what sounded like Handel, sweet and melodic, violin rising to flawless top notes surmounting the underlying refrain. My hands lay slackly on the steering wheel, surprised by yet another unexpected aspect of my bully-boy brother. Bemused, I allowed the music to help calm the specific savage beast that was me – ineffectual rage and the battle to quell the rising tide of putrefaction that seemed to be my stomach. I was so intent on the synchronisation between perfect harmony and re-establishing control over my rebellious body I didn't notice the car door open and my passenger slip in until the rush of cool evening air hit me. I opened my eyes abruptly and saw with dismay that my companion was Mary.

17: Magic

'I need to know the boy is safe. You didn't believe me about magic but I'm right – you'll see. For now, you only need to see this to believe me.'

She handed me a small sheet of paper. A drawing. I took it from her, mute with shock. The ransom note fell from the angle between the spokes of the steering wheel where I'd balanced it, and landed, open, on my lap. I looked from it, to the drawing, and then to Mary.

She plucked the ransom note from my lap. 'I told you! I told you she'd take him under her cloak and then you wouldn't see him again. Now she has – but it's not too late yet.'

'Rosemary's dead, Mary.' My voice came out as a harsh croak. 'We've already been over this. This is something else altogether. Her brother – and he wants money. A lot of money, but it might simply be a scam. Danny might not be missing at all.'

'Oh, he's missing all right.'

'How do you know?'

'I heard them planning it.'

'Win and Margaret? They wouldn't plan this. Margaret wouldn't harm Danny and nor would Win.'

'Not *them*.' She was scathing. 'Don't you listen Kenny? Rosemary. Her and the devil. It's what they've always planned.'

I shook my head. I needed to humour her, but I could barely cope with myself at the moment, let alone a madwoman. I looked at the picture she'd given me whilst I thought about what to do to get her back into the institution. Its style was unmistakably similar to the other drawings I'd been sent. This one was of a small boy holding a book. I didn't need to look too carefully to guess what the book's title would be.

'Did you draw this, Mary?'

She stared at me wide-eyed.

'I forget.' I sighed. This was all I needed. 'But I didn't forget what I heard,' she added.

I barely had the energy to ask, but I knew I was expected to. 'What?'

'Drive and I'll tell you.'

I put my head in my hands and bent over the steering wheel. I felt like I was about to burst, spewing out the molten lava of fear that was bubbling away in my stomach.

'I can't. Mary, you need to go back and I need to find out what this is all about – not go on a joy ride.'

'Oh, there's no joy in this, Kenny, believe me.' She clicked the manual lock down on the car door.

I sat back again, praying Heather would ring and I could somehow tell her what was happening so she could alert the institution. In my desperation, all thoughts of keeping my little jaunt to the countryside secret had gone.

'Drive,' Mary commanded. I was about to protest but the little flick-knife glinted in the drowning dregs of the evening sun that had unexpectedly appeared as the storm clouds faded. An angry sunset was giving way rapidly to gathering gloom as the sun sank behind the rolling Oxfordshire countryside. I turned the ignition over, suddenly no longer bilious.

'Where are we going?' I asked shakily.

'It doesn't matter. Just drive for the moment. We need to get out of here first.'

In the background the music swelled in a sweet crescendo of violins.

'Pretty music,' she commented. 'I like it. Is this the kind of thing you normally listen to?' Out of the corner of my eye I could still see the point of the knife, waving. She seemed to be conducting with it. I glanced sideways at the knife.

'Sometimes, but this isn't my car, Mary. I really *have* borrowed it from someone and need to return it tonight. They'll be wondering where I am if I don't.'

'That's all right, you can still do that – I expect. It depends.'

'On what?'

'On you. And magic.'

We crept down the gravel drive towards the exit. I drove as slowly as I could in the vain hope that something – or someone – would stop us from leaving the grounds. Over the rise and fall of the music I tuned in to any kind of alarm emanating from the grandiose building behind us, but there was none. No wailing alarm, no shouting, and no pursuit by white-veiled staff. Nothing. In the rear-view mirror, I watched the building dwindle to a small speck in the distance. No matter how slowly we moved it would be barely seconds before it couldn't be seen at all as the drive curved. I slowed to a snail's pace as we approached the junction with the main road.

'Where now?'

'We need a map.' She looked meaningfully at the car's dashboard and the inbuilt navigation system. 'There. It's a clever car. You can tell it where to go and it will take us there. Set the navigation to Crahan House, St Rosemary in the Marsh.' I stared at her. How did she know about satellite navigation? Or where I'd last seen Margaret? 'I wonder if it's how I've always imagined it. *She* used to talk about it a lot, boasting.' She smiled gently at my dismayed expression. 'I told you I'm not mad – or stupid,' she added softly. I flicked the navigation system on. 'C-r-a-h-a-n. Put it into the magic system. It's in Sussex.' No point arguing. The flick-knife was too close and the point too sharp. At least the journey would be logged on the car's system even if all they found later were my blood-soaked remains, I thought sourly. 'This is exciting,' she continued. 'I've always wondered how they worked in real life. Margaret and Rosemary used to live there before their father became ill. They moved to London then, well, near to London. Near Kimmy. They had to take their dad to hospital a lot. Even Rosemary's magic couldn't *stop* him disappearing.'

I began to understand.

'Mary, when you talk about magic – do you mean real magic, or something you don't understand the workings of?'

'Both, maybe.'

'So tell me something that is real magic.'

'Rosemary,' she said with finality. I could sense her watching me, gauging my reaction. Instinctively I stiffened, unnerved, as I finished tapping in the place name and county. It would be dark by the time we reached St Rosemary in the Marsh – a good two hour's drive at least, and I knew there'd be nothing there. Perhaps she would tire and fall asleep and then I could get the knife from her? I turned the music up a notch and allowed it to roll over us. Perhaps it would tame the savage beast in her too? We drove for all of an hour like that. I didn't manage another surreptitious glimpse at her until a while later. She was still smiling gently, the knife moving rhythmically to the music. I gave up and drove.

Strangely, the music calmed me to the point that I almost forgot Mary. Driving settled me too, not as well as it had in the Austin Healey, but the BMW was pleasant to drive and feather-light-reactive on the accelerator. Handel moved on to Bach and then Mahler. My thoughts followed their tempo and style – from soothing to dramatic and finally sombre. The sombre thoughts were just centring round why I hadn't heard back from Heather and what that might mean when Mary surprised me by breaking in as the music dwindled during a lull between movements.

'Don't you want to know?'

I turned the music down and glanced at her. The knife was now resting on her lap, nestling amongst the folds of her scarf, but she was still holding it tightly.

'Know what, Mary?'

'Why?'

'Why what?' There were too many 'why's' I wanted to know but I doubted Mary had sane answers to any of them. 'Why you're doing this?'

She surprised me again.

'Why I could run faster than you up and down the mound.'

I stumbled over my reply, nonplussed.

'I suppose because you were better at running than me?'

'Oh, no. I'm sure you could have been faster if you'd realised.'

I unexpectedly found myself changing my opinion of my 'mad' sister. Although the question might seem irrelevant to the layman, it had the distinctively shrewd twist to it of the type my colleagues and I would have applied in court when we were softening up a target. My reply, this time, was a gamble – after all, things couldn't get much worse, and I was at least safe while I was driving. Even a lunatic wouldn't kill the person in control of the steering wheel whilst travelling at speed.

'You're very cryptic, Mary. I wonder if you're like that on purpose.'

She laughed. 'Cryptic? Like in the newspaper crosswords? Or do you mean insane?'

'Cryptic,' I replied carefully.

'Maybe it's my condition? Or my way of life.' I didn't answer, sensing she was evaluating me and my question as much as I was re-evaluating her. We drove on in silence for a while. 'I could leave there, you know,' she interjected suddenly. 'I don't have to stay now they know what's wrong with me. If I took the medication all the time, I could leave. They've said that lots of times now – trying to persuade me.'

'Why don't you, then?'

'Where would I go and what would I do? I'm little better than a child. I've never had to be an adult.'

I was taken aback. 'I don't think I understand you at all, Mary.'

She sighed. 'I doubt I understand myself. Once upon a time I wanted to leave. If I could have left when I was younger – when Win first got us all together – I would have. I liked staying with Sarah, but I wasn't a kid, so I would have to have stood on my own two feet even then. But I wasn't on my pills then – not until Sarah explained Kimmy's problem to them and they wondered if I was the same. Then everything changed, but it was too late by then. Sometimes it's easier to be mad anyway. No-one challenges you. They just say, *"Oh, that's Mary for you. She's a bit mad".*'

'But you're not?'

'Not if you don't think I am.' She paused. 'It wasn't long after I started on the medication that it all began anyway. It has nasty side-effects, lithium – did you know?' I shook my head, but didn't say anything, not wanting to interrupt the current flow of sanity. She sighed again. I stole a sideways glance at her. Her eyes were glassy, far away. For a moment I feared she was lost again but she gave a little shake of her head and the sharpness returned. 'Funny how something that's meant to make you better can make you so much worse too.' I felt her eyes on me, studying my profile. I concentrated on the road and not reacting, wondering what might be coming next. She settled more comfortably in her seat and wrapped the knife in the scarf, then opened the glove compartment and put them both inside.

'I could run down the slope faster than you, Kenny, because I concentrated on that and nothing else. It's what athletes do. They focus purely on what they want to do and then do it. You were always casting about to see whether Win was watching, or Jonno was after you – or wondering where Georgie had gone. Or you were sulking about how much faster than you I'd been the last time, and worrying that I was odd. Your thoughts were everywhere but where they should have been – like they are now.'

I laughed awkwardly.

'I'll admit to being a bit distracted, but that's not surprising. I've just been attacked by someone who tried to suffocate me, and now hijacked by my own sister waving a knife at me after being told my so—,' I corrected myself, 'Danny has possibly been abducted.'

'Abducted.' She considered. 'Yes, I suppose you could call it that. I call it vanished.'

'Vanished, abducted – they're the same thing, then?'

'It's all magic,' she agreed. 'That's what my little birds say, anyway.'

I ignored the last comment. It seemed safest to concentrate on what she said that was normal. If I did that, the sane Mary conversed with me. Teasing the meaning out of her cryptic statements encouraged madness for both of us. I changed the subject; back to childhood.

'You really think I could have beaten you down the mound?'

'Actually maybe not. You were very clumsy. Your head seemed to go faster than your feet most of the time. Too much clever in it. Do you remember much about then?'

'A bit.'

'What?'

'Jamboree bags, the rooks at the back of the yard. Sarah cleaning shoes and getting polish on her dress, a day at the seaside – once. Win and Binnie argued about building a sandcastle. Seems like they've always been at war.'

She laughed appreciatively 'Always will be. Just because you're brother and sister, doesn't mean you have to like each other. We went to the seaside when you were about two as well. Just for the day. We got the train there. It was very cold. My fingers were blue but it was the seaside so I didn't care. We even went in paddling. You had a little blue woollen bathing costume that stretched when it got wet. You thought that was so funny. You laughed about it nearly all day. I think you even fell asleep laughing on the way home.'

I couldn't remember that – too far back – only the time when we'd argued over the sandcastle and Mary hadn't really featured in that memory. Perhaps the earlier one was too distant, or I'd been too young. It was depressing to think I had a store of happy memories inaccessible to me. I pictured us how I would have liked us to look: the Juss family, buckets and spades, smiling parents, laughing kids – even with iron grey clouds and icy Atlantic water to paddle in. Then again, us five years later, making a promise to each other I knew I hadn't kept. Both seemed a world away – a world I suddenly wished with such intensity that I hadn't lost.

'Tell me what *you* remember about then?' I asked to mask my melancholy.

She cocked her head to one side.

'Ma was always tired. And she always smelt of milk and powder. Babies. Pop – I stayed away from Pop if I could. He never belted me like he did you boys, but that buckle – it reminded me of a spear, that little sharp point on the pin in the centre. It left a hole in Win's legs once.'

'I don't remember being thrashed – just aware it could happen.'

'Win was always being thrashed – but then he was always up to something, wasn't he?' She giggled like a small girl. 'He stole Pop's Brylcreem once and sold it to the girls on the ground floor as face cream. Said it would get rid of their spots. He wasn't half for it when Pop found out – but nothing like as bad as what he got from those girls.'

I could imagine. They were one element of my childhood, I hadn't forgotten – especially Glynnis.

'I wish I could remember more of Georgie,' I remarked involuntarily.

'Georgie? He's vanished too.'

'Georgie died, Mary.'

'It's the same.' She sounded cross. 'Why don't you get it, Kenny?'

'Dying and disappearing aren't the same, Mary.' I tried not to sound supercilious, but failed. I sensed her bristling irritably. I tried again. 'When people die they don't come back. When they disappear, sometimes they do – like me – maybe with a different name.'

'No,' she shook her head. 'Sometimes they die and they come back too. You'll see.' We were heading into difficult waters again so I shut up and concentrated on the road. Twilight had long since leached what little daylight had been left after the storm and the road was winding from here on, but I recognised the turn-off to St Rosemary in the Marsh from the night before. I indicated left, ignoring the Satnav, but Mary objected.

'No, we're going to Crahan.'

'I was here last night with Win. The landlady at the pub told us that Crahan House is deserted. Derelict.'

'Do you always believe everything you're told? I thought you were a barrister. Don't barristers question what they're told until they get to the truth?'

I hesitated, but turned off the indicator and continued on the main road.

'Facts are facts, Mary.'

'Maybe – but so are the facts you don't know. Turn here instead.'

I almost missed the sign, buried as it was in the roadside foliage. I cornered sharply and we sped down the winding side road, bordered by high banks either side with the occasional passing point dotted along it. Without regular street lighting the place seemed even more forbidding than it had yesterday.

'Slow down,' she instructed. 'The entrance will be coming up soon.'

'It sounds like you've been here before.'

'No, she described it to me so often I feel like I've been here before.'

'She? Margaret?'

'And Rosemary. That's how I knew it was where she'd go when she vanished.'

I shook my head but didn't bother to argue. We were here now and I was curious too.

'Is that why we've come here now, Mary?'

'And so you can see I was right about what she and the devil were plotting.'

I wanted to ask her who the devil was supposed to be in Mary parlance but the entrance to Crahan House loomed in front of us as we turned the next bend in the road. It was barred by heavy wrought iron gates, rusting but still sturdy. I pulled up in front of them. The house itself could just be seen at the end of a long tree-lined drive, squat and solid in dark grey stone, now mainly clad in ivy. Not an elegant house but one that looked as if it would stand the ravages of time, although clearly as deserted as the pub landlady had said it was.

'That's it then. Can we go back now?' I turned to her and waited. She peered into the gloom.

'Open the gates.'

A sturdy looking chain twisted between the iron curlicues, two ends clamped together by an outsize padlock.

'They're locked.'

'So unlock them.'

'I haven't got the key.'

'Yes you have.' She smiled complacently at me. 'One, one, nine. Eleventh of September – the day Kimmy was born and the rest of us went into the children's homes. You've only got the spares though.'

I stared at her and after a while realised that my mouth had dropped open. I swallowed hard and a sweetish taste like pus slid down my throat and settled uneasily on top of the rest of the bile in my stomach.

'That's the key to the deposit box with the evidence in it.'

'Is that what she told you it is?' Mary laughed derisively. 'There's no deposit box with evidence in it.'

'There is! Margaret has it – or knows where it is. And I have the key to it, on the ring with the other keys.'

'Poor Lawrence. Poor Kenny. The keys are for here. Go and try them.'

I struggled out of the car, stiff from driving. The smell of a herby plant was strong – sharp and woody – as I approached the gates. I examined the padlock. It was freshly oiled and the grease stained my hands a dirty green, as if my flesh was decaying. Forgetting I would soil my clothes, I wiped my hand on my trousered thigh and rummaged in my pocket for the bundle of keys with the small ornate one stamped with 119. It was far too small for such a heavy padlock so I selected one of the others. It moved easily in the unresisting lock and my stomach turned with it. Paranoia took hold again. I turned to check what Mary was doing, half-expecting her to suddenly slide across into the driver's seat, rev the car and slam it into me and the gates, crushing both of us. She was sitting serenely just as I'd left her, a small half-smile playing round her lips as she looked back at me. The foliage on either side of the gates rustled in the light breeze that was all that now remained of the thunderstorm – or perhaps they hadn't suffered it here? The disturbance in the leaves released more of the herby smell I'd half-recognised as I'd approached the gate. It came to me then – where I'd smelt that overpowering aroma before; in my study, full of rosemary and the cryptic note telling me facts about the herb itself – and the woman.

'What do you remember now that might have been transformed under rosemary's cloak? Or should be seen differently? A cupboard full of secrets.'

I didn't remember anything, but Mary did. And Mary saw things differently too, including secrets.

She nodded encouragingly at me. I knew even before the hasp sprang open that it would. I disentangled the heavy chain from the flaking, rust damaged gates and tossed it alongside the rosemary bushes. The gates swung open lethargically to reveal the distant house in all its crumbling grandeur. I stood for a moment considering what might await me at the end of the sweeping drive. It reminded me somewhat of the place Sarah had spent her last few days, without the air of studied preservation. No doubt the banks of tumbling weeds, rising towards the house in a series of shallow steps, would once have been filled with an abundance of blooms similar to the beds at the Green healthcare establishment, and the now chickweed-infested gravel drive would have been as crisp and manicured as the approach to the hospice. For now, the grand dame of the local gentry was a mere shadow of her former self; an abandoned tangle of stone and fecund growth, but I could imagine what it would have been like once. Stately without being pompous, impressive without being overstated. No wonder Margaret had told Mary so much about it. No wonder she'd boasted about it. It wasn't only a home, it was a home with substance and a sense of belonging; a home with a mother and a father and a sister – and a brother.

I went back to the car and eased myself into the driver's seat.

'I'm assuming you want me to drive in?'

'You want to see it too, don't you?'

'If it was Margaret's home, I'm curious, naturally, but I don't know what it will do other than show me where she lived as a child.' I realised with wry humour that I sounded like Win had yesterday.

'It'll show you Rosemary,' she replied firmly, staring straight ahead. 'Swing off to the right when you reach the house. There's another way round to the garages and servants' entrance.'

I followed her instructions and we navigated what amounted to little more than an overgrown gravel path until we'd rounded the decaying edifice and taken a one hundred and eighty degree tour to end up at the back as she'd predicted. Opposite the less ornate version of the front entrance – obviously the servants' entrance – was another, smaller building. It looked equally derelict. I surmised it had comprised the garages once, or perhaps the garages and stables. It was boarded over now, hefty planks of wood nailed haphazardly across the shutters, splintered and weather-beaten, but still strong enough to defy intruders.

'There,' Mary said complacently. 'That's where she is.'

I parked up facing it and turned the headlights on to full beam to illuminate the building. I changed my mind about my sister for a third time. This time there was no doubt. She was crazy. The place was falling into ruin and no-one could live here; apart from which Rosemary was dead. And Margaret? Well, she was playing out her role as Molly Wemmick currently, so even if childish nostalgia occasionally drew her back here, those occasions would be rare and brief.

The silence surrounding the place was like a blanket, folding inexorably around us, broken only by a low murmur, which I realised after a while was the radio, not quite completely muted. I went to turn it off but lack of familiarity with the car had me turning the knob the wrong way by mistake. The new channel blared at us, and I jumped and twitched it off, but not before my name had been triumphantly announced by the presenter as this week's hottest news. Mary reached across and turned it back on.

'... development, with details emerging about his dubious involvement in a number of past cases which may need to be re-opened.

His personal links with the criminal element was first revealed after he flouted court etiquette by retaining crucial evidence until the eleventh hour when he defended his nephew against a manslaughter charge. It was then revealed he could claim not only a brother linked to the mob, but a sister with a record for soliciting and an assumed identity for himself. Speculation is now growing about Lawrence Juste's business interests and personal financial background, particularly in view of a recent near-tragedy in which his home was ravaged by fire – now under investigation alongside his sister's murder. A feature in tomorrow's *Court Questions* turns the spotlight on our legal man of the moment, and follows hard on the heels of the difficult questions of morality and social conscience he has yet to respond to in today's article in *Forward Thinking*. There has been no comment so far from Juste or his advisers about his involvement in either, but there's one thing that's not in doubt; times may soon be a-changing too for this year's golden oldie QC …'

The presenter's voice faded and was replaced by Dylan's 1964 hit, 'For the times they are a changing', in his distinctive nasal twang. I turned it off mid-wail.

'Were you expecting that?' Mary asked.

'I wasn't not expecting that,' I replied, shaken nevertheless. So Margaret had been right. Wheels were being oiled and soon they'd be rolling right over the top of me. There could be no turning back now.

'So it's starting then?'

'Whatever is starting, started years ago, Mary. It's completing now.' All the same, she was right in another way – alongside whatever was completing now, worse was starting, and I needed to get back to deal with it. I consciously pulled myself together and took the most reasoned and calm tone I could muster with her. The one I used on my victims in court when I wanted to lull them into a false sense of security before going in for the kill.

'Mary, I know you are curious. So am I. And it's strange that I have the key to the padlock on the gates, but maybe that's just a fluke. Padlocks are often mass-produced so there could be thousands of keys in circulation for any one lock, even though we assume it's unique. We assume far too much most of the time. Maybe you've assumed or imagined too.' I debated adding that Margaret was really alive, and that she didn't need to mourn for her – her friend – but decided against it. It would only give credence to her wild claims that the dead came back. The cat had probably started it. These strange twists of the mind usually had their roots in the simplest of memories, and the one Win had supplied me with probably explained the whole of this particular twist.

She tutted impatiently. 'Give me the keys,' she demanded. I handed them over obediently, eyes more on the knife than her. 'And the car keys.' I obliged again, heart pounding. Was this going to be it? Murdered by my own sister? Perhaps that would solve everything after all. 'Come on then.' She waved the knife at me to indicate I should get out of the car. I slid out, eyeing the knife. She followed and clicked the car's automatic lock. The car beeped and locked. She turned and faced me. 'Time to see some real magic, Kenny.'

She indicated to the path round to the back of the building and that I should lead the way. She walked behind me, knife point to my back, until we found a small black-painted door, almost lost in the dark shuttering and gloom of the shrubs that marked the edge of the cultivated area and crowded up towards the garage block. She held the bunch of keys out to me.

'Never say die, huh?' I gabbled nervously, imagining her disembowelling me with the flick-knife once we were inside. No, it was too small – maybe gouge out my eyes or pierce my heart and leave me to pump out my blood across the dusty floor. She gestured at the door.

'Come on, we haven't got all night and I thought you said your friend wanted their car back.' The lurch of relief almost made me gag. To return the car I had to be alive to drive it. I fumbled amongst the keys and tried the smaller of the two in the lock. Again the lock was well-oiled and turned easily.

'Open sesame,' she announced. 'I always liked that phrase.' The door creaked as it opened. Inside was a cavern of black. 'After you.' The gag reflex returned and this time I heaved, bringing up nothing but an acid burn at the back of my throat. All I'd consumed today had been a few mouthfuls of Win's stewed tea. Inside the door the dark grabbed at me with sly fingers and greedy desire. The air smelled damp, like the cellar had. Icy sweat covered my body and I stepped back, terrified, feeling the point of the flick-knife jab in the small of my back, but not caring.

'Careful,' she warned. The knife point was removed.

'I can't.'

'What do you mean, you can't?'

Not even the image of Tony falling backwards with the knife in his gut and the blood blossoming like a rose round it that I'd carried with me all the way from the children's home could make any difference. Nothing

– not even a knife in my back – would persuade me to plunge into the dark with the possibility of rats lurking within it. Nothing.

'Rats,' I gasped.

'Don't be ridiculous.' She sounded amazed, then suspicious. 'Women are afraid of rats, not men.'

I swung round to face her

'I can't Mary. I just can't. At the children's home. It was my initiation. I thought there were rats in the dark. You can knife me, but I can't.'

She stared at me, open-mouthed. 'You're really scared, aren't you?' I couldn't reply. My voice caught and held in my throat. Her face softened. 'It's all right, Kenny.' She sounded like Ma. 'I wouldn't let anything hurt my little brother. I'll go first.' She pushed me gently to one side and I leaned weakly against the door frame. She stepped into the shadows and was lost. A moment later a light flicked on in the depths of the building and she and it were illuminated. It wasn't a cavern or a cellar. It was a hallway – not unlike the one in Heather's apartment, with stairs rising from the far end. 'Now will you come in?' she asked. She was still clutching the flick-knife but it hung loosely by her side. 'And shut the door behind you. Don't want to attract attention.'

'No-one is here,' I said automatically, but with less conviction. There may be no-one here *now*, but clearly there might have been not so long ago. I followed her upstairs to where the counter top in the kitchenette was untidily cluttered and still displaying remnants of bread crumbs. Dirty crockery was stacked in the sink, crusty-brown gunk congealing on one of the knives and a red lipstick stain making a teasing semicircle on a mug still half-full of cold coffee. Mary made straight for what passed for both dining and lounge area. It contained a small two-seater sofa and a table and chairs, carefully arranged under the window to catch what little light filtered in through the slats nailed across the outside. It smelt musty, but used – soiled.

'This is a hide out!'

'Got it in one, Kenny. Somewhere to vanish.'

'I don't understand.' I was about to ask her if it was where Margaret laid low when I remembered she didn't know Margaret was still alive. I revised the question to, 'for whom?'

She looked up at me and her expression was surprised and then sad.

'I know what you think,' she said. 'Even though you pretend not to. Do you still not understand?' I shook my head, wondering how I was going to manage to get the car keys back and persuade her to let me go.

'Squatters,' I suggested, remembering Heather's response to 27B. And if this was Margaret's hide out, she wasn't here and therefore all the more reason to not be either, but to be where she was, especially now things seemed to be moving so fast. I watched anxiously as she put the flick-knife down on the table. She sighed and shook her head.

'No, no, no!' She started to rifle through the pile of paper that had been left on the table as if searching for something. 'Rosemary didn't die. She merely vanished. I knew as soon as I stopped taking my pills. It was obvious.'

'Mary, you said yourself you forget things when you're not taking your medication. If anything, not taking it would confuse you more.'

'No, Kenny. When I stopped taking my pills was when they started talking openly because they thought I wouldn't understand. They thought exactly the way you do. Stupid Mary. Mad Mary. We can say whatever we like in front of Mary. No one will believe her; no-one will even understand her. So they talked – about everything. What they'd done, what they were going to do and how they were going to do it. And I listened because I always listen – it's what you do when you're always on the outside. You listen. There's nothing else you can do so you listen and hope one day you'll hear something that will put you on the inside instead.'

She sat down at the table and gestured for me to join her. I sat, still nervously eyeing the flick-knife.

She studied me sympathetically. 'Are you all right? You look tired.'

'I'll survive – I hope.'

She grinned unexpectedly. 'That's the Kenny I knew. Yes, you will – if *you* listen carefully too. There wasn't anything for me at *the place* to begin with – I call it *the place* because there's no other word for it really. It's just a place where I am. I exist. The pills made me sick and I didn't like feeling sick so I refused to take them. Then Bill came and everything changed.' Her eyes softened. 'Bill persuaded me to try them because one day, when I was well enough, he said we would leave there together. He must have known even then it wouldn't happen, but he didn't lie to trick me. He did it to save me – to give me a chance at life one day. It just wouldn't be with him.' She stroked the paper her hand rested on, as if caressing it.

'Who's Bill?' I asked, confused.

'He was a volunteer. Came in every Wednesday to talk or play chess, or anything that kept our minds working. We fell in love.' I hadn't realised until then that she was crying. The overhead light threw more shadow than relief. 'He has MS. That's why he volunteered – to do something useful while he could. We were well on the way to making a case for my discharge when he had to admit it to them – and me. Instead of being a volunteer then, he became a resident and I knew I couldn't leave him on his own there. Nor will I, but that means I have to be ill to stay there. Sister Maria knows that and disapproves, but it's my choice, isn't it? It's always your choice – what you do with your life, no matter how menial.'

I watched her tear drops fall onto the back of the hand that was stroking the paper and felt an intense burning anger. She had a lost past, a ruined future and a hopeless present.

'Mary, I …' I put my hand over hers. She shook her head.

'That's why you needn't worry about having to make me to go back. I'll go back willingly all the while Bill is there. But the thing is, once I'd started taking my pills, all those things I'd heard when I was mad Mary started to make sense to sane Mary. All their plans. Now do you understand?'

I didn't, entirely – but nor did I want to break the spell.

'I'm so sorry about Bill,' I hedged, 'but I don't know what made sense to you so how can it make sense to me?'

She disengaged her hand from mine and wiped her eyes on the back of it.

'This is what should be making sense to you, Kenny. If you're dead you don't need to live somewhere do you? But Rosemary lives here. Look – this is Rosemary.' She handed me one of the sheets of paper. It was a list, with a doodle scrawled in the corner. My skin crawled. I'd know that handwriting anywhere.

'I still don't understand.'

'Here you are then. What about this? She scattered the rest of the papers our hand had been resting on. They were a mixture of paid bills and receipts, all in the name of Molly Wemmick, together with little notes and scribbles, but underneath them all was the one that explained everything and nothing. It was a small black-edged funeral card, like the ones I'd sent to announce the details of Margaret's funeral service. No notes on this one, just a series of doodles, a little gallows icon, each with more complete hanging man. She'd been practising.

Mary was watching me closely.

'John Wemmick pays my bills. Has done for years. *She's* supposed to be his sister, but she's not. She's Rosemary.'

Of course. I could see now why she was so convinced Rosemary was still alive, but not why she'd been so insistent we'd find her here. Mary didn't know it was Margaret who was still alive, playing her dangerous game and needing a bolthole to do it from. Her fixation with the dead had alighted on Rosemary, not Margaret. I wondered again if I should come clean, but she pre-empted my confession.

'And that little gallows was the doodle Rosemary left everywhere after ...' she shivered. 'It's a long story, but she could be mean. Margaret understood though.'

I understood too, now. I'd uncovered a truth I didn't want to know.

'I think I know the story – Win told me about it. Sarah's cat.'

She looked surprised.

'Did he? Maybe I misjudged him.' She frowned. 'Well, anyway, "Molly" absentmindedly doodled that little gallows on a piece of paper once when she was visiting and then I knew who she really was. She could call herself Molly or Margaret or whatever she liked but I knew. Sarah told me to hush or I'd get into trouble. Binnie pretended she hadn't heard me, as usual, and I couldn't say anything to Win because *she* was always there, and he was in on some of her plotting anyway; but I knew.'

'Win ...'

She shook her head.

'Just a silly fool – he didn't see, but you do – now.'

'Maybe. Can I really trust him?'

'If you want to. He's only stupid, not bad.'

I gathered the papers neatly back into a pile, whilst the pieces of this particular puzzle blasted apart in my brain, before settling in an entirely unexpected new formation. In one way everything made perfect sense. Margaret had been playing Jaggers off all ways – pretending to be an accomplice in his plotting whilst also plotting her own secret war using Win as her troops. Sarah seemed to have been complicit with both, although I didn't understand why, and Binnie? Well, Binnie had simply done what she'd done since childhood; made herself the conscientious objector and ultimately removed herself from a situation she didn't want to be part of. But the little gallows icon perturbed me. I'd thought it symbolic of me running out of time on everything Margaret had fed me on the breadcrumb trail to find her, but maybe it signified something else altogether. Something, the possibility of which – if Mary really wasn't insane – I didn't like at all. The something I didn't like at all continued to plague me, and even with the lights on, the place was beginning to spook me.

'Why were you so sure this place existed?'

'They talked about it, when they decided she'd have to vanish. They didn't say where it was but I remembered all the stories about it from when Rosemary and Margaret were kids. They used to play hide and seek here until it was converted to servants' quarters and when the servants were out they used to play "house" here. Rosemary got hold of the keys. It was obvious where they meant.'

'So why would I be allowed to have the keys?'

'It's a joke, Kenny – on you. She's mean, I told you that. She likes her jokes. Who better to make a fool of than you by making you the keeper of the castle without knowing it even existed?'

A joke? The *something* did more than plague me now, it worried me; and the rearranged puzzle pieces made no sense unless *I* was insane. Oh yes, I would certainly be a joke if it was true – but the last laugh had still to be heard. In my chest, something cold and hard seemed to have developed. Not anger exactly, but a certainty that I was no longer going to be the puppet on the end of this particular set of strings any longer. I looked at my watch. It was now nearly six hours since I'd left Win at his maisonette in Finchley, promising to be back by the evening, and we still had to get back to *the place*, as Mary called it. I didn't know yet what I would do with this strange and perplexing turn of events, but I had to make the final pieces of the jigsaw puzzle marry up with the odd idea that had begun to twist round my brain in the churchyard and was now intertwining with Rosemary's gallows doodle.

'Thank you for bringing me here, Mary. I think I understand a little better what you mean about magic now.'

'Do you? Then I have one final piece of magic for you, and then I want you to promise that whatever you do with it, you'll make sure the boy doesn't stay disappeared.'

'I intend to, believe me.'

'Take me back now then.' I straightened slowly, wincing; then remembered the knife. She got to it before me, scattering the papers again as she snatched it up. She smiled at me and then held it out, balanced in the centre of her palm, handle pointing obliquely towards me. 'Yes, you might be needing this before long, too.' I took it and flicked it shut before pocketing it.

'Thank you.'

She nodded and shuffled the papers back together into a neat pile alongside the book they'd been covering.

'Jesus Christ!' I swooped on it, horrified. It was a copy of *To Kill a Mocking Bird*.

I opened it up. Danny's name and mine were proudly inscribed on the flyleaf. The congealed sludge on the knife in the kitchenette now made sense. Peanut butter sandwiches were his favourite. Wherever he was now, he'd been resident here until recently, resident or detained – and now I suspected the latter.

18: Confidence

The drive back to Mary's institution was quiet and unremarkable. She slept most of the way and the knife poked sinisterly against my hip from time to time, keeping me wide awake. I would have preferred to have removed it and put it in the glove compartment but a part of me needed the comfort of having it close now the game appeared to have changed again. It was bothering me, too, that I hadn't yet heard back from Heather. The next part of *my* plan – such as it was – was reliant on her beating the pathway to my door for me with Fredriks, and backing me up with the insurance people. If she was actively against me, I was lost. Of course I could throw myself on Fredriks' mercy and tell him the whole sorry tale but that would guarantee me a lifetime in prison for my many and varied infractions of the law, and for Danny? God alone knew what kind of fate.

We arrived back at *the place* just past ten o'clock, with me relieved both that there had been no speed cops and that Win's car was a powerhouse on the road. I pulled into the gravelled car park area and dimmed the lights. As we turned up the drive Mary woke without me needing to rouse her, as if she'd set some internal personal alarm before falling asleep.

'We're here,' she announced.

'Yes. Will they have realised you've been gone?'

'No, I put the "Do not disturb" sign up. They're used to me doing that when I say I'm tired. Sister Maria knows I'm sneaking off to see Bill.'

'Then do we need to sneak you back in?'

'Yes – through the kitchens.'

'Won't they be full of staff?'

'Not now, they won't. They'll all be off duty.'

'And the entrance locked.'

'Of course, but if you know where the key is, what's the problem? Come on.' She swung the car door open and slid lithely out. I marvelled at her aptitude for intrigue. I followed more slowly, back aching, and most other parts of my body complaining. Lawrence Juste – caped crusader! I allowed myself a soft wry chuckle, relieved that I still had that part of me that Mary had recognised to draw on – the Kenny who'd laughed himself exhausted over a stretchy blue bathing suit.

Mary loped off into the dark and I only barely caught up with her as she reached the thin straggle of bushes acting as the demarcation between drive and parking area. She waited patiently until I drew level. 'They bring the coffee round at ten thirty, lights out at eleven. What's the time now?'

'Quarter past ten.'

'Just enough time then, but you'll have to move faster – focus, Kenny – remember?' She grabbed my hand and yanked me after her. I gasped at the effect on my sore ribs, but gritted my teeth and put all my efforts into keeping abreast to avoid her wrenching my arm again. We skirted the parking area until we came to a small break in the bushes. I could see the back of the building through it, eerily lit by a sliver of moonlight as the sullen clouds briefly parted. Mary looked up at the moon. "Ill-met by moon light"[3] she laughed. 'I liked that right from the very first time I read it. I liked that book you put on the back seat too. Mockingbirds – singing their hearts out. Why did you bring it with you? It should have stayed there really. Where it belonged.'

'It belonged to me once – and now it belongs to Danny. That's why I brought it.'

She leaned in close to scrutinise me in the dim light, sighing.

'Oh, I understand you a little better now too. No wonder you're jumping about like a dancing skeleton. He's your Bill.'

'He's my son, Mary.'

The admission slipped out without warning or thought. I hadn't intended telling her, but it felt the right thing to do – to tell this woman who was always listening and had always been on the outside, even when we were children.

'That's what I mean, Kenny. You love him. But thank you for telling me.' She smiled happily.

I opened my mouth to tell her she had to keep it a secret but she grabbed my hand without warning and ordered 'Run!' as the moon dipped behind the scudding grey-black clouds and the world dropped back into darkness. Heart pounding and head thumping a rhythmic accompaniment, my wheezing lungs managed to get me to the back door of the kitchens before the moonlight revealed us only because of Mary's dogged persistence. I collapsed against the wall beside the door, sobbing with pain, whilst Mary, apparently unaffected, fished under a pile of pebbles bordering the herb garden, neatly arranged along the path leading towards the front.

'You can still run faster,' I hissed.

'And you know why,' she whispered back. She returned holding a key aloft triumphantly.

'Should have tried one of mine,' I gasped out. 'I seem to have the key to most things except the answers.'

'You don't need to have all the answers to know the truth, Kenny,' she grinned. 'But you'll know when you do. You'll feel it in your gut.' She slipped the key in the lock and pushed the door open, motioning for me to go in.

'Mary, I've still got to get out again.'

'Go out the front door.'

'How can I do that? I'm not meant to be here.'

'Who says? The receptionist will have changed shift by now and if you sign over your name in the visitors' book again, she won't look. They never do. Too intent on keeping their desk and their nails perfect.' She put her hands on her hips and looked me over. For a moment, in the gloom, she looked like Ma when she was resignedly examining yet another of my set of bumps and bruises from tumbling down the air raid shelter mound. 'If you pretend to be something with absolute confidence, no-one will question you, no matter how crazy the claim. I learnt that quick here. You need to do that too, Kenny. You may be a professional, and a successful one at that – according to Sarah, but you've never really understood the ways of the world, have you?' I was about to reply that surely I was more versed in the ways of the world than she, who'd lived apart from it all of hers, but that annoying little impish voice that was probably my conscience – or that feeling in my gut she'd just referred to – stopped me.

Overhead the floor rumbled as if the thunder had returned. I guessed we were in the basement of the building. 'That's the drinks trolley,' Mary announced. 'We've really got to get a move on now.' She shoved me hard and I catapulted into the darkened kitchens. Along the long range of work surface, catering size pots and pans gleamed dully in the shadows. The hanging rail reminded me ominously of the little gallows man. Mary ducked back outside and then reappeared within seconds, just as I was about to panic and call to her. She clicked the door shut behind her and the kitchen became the rat cellar from my nightmares. I felt the old familiar sense of suffocation and fear rising to swamp over me and struggled against the urge to shout for help. Something – it had to be Mary – brushed past me and light crept back into the room as the door to the inner hallway opened the merest crack.

'Come on!' she urged. I needed no encouraging. I hurried over to the chink of light and was momentarily blinded as she opened the door wide.

'Where did you go?' I asked as I blinked and squinted.

'To put the key back. The door locks automatically from the inside. Give the game away if the key wasn't put back. It's one of the commis chef's tricks – so he can slip out for a fag or get back in late after he's been into town on the booze.'

'How do you know that?'

'I told you, I listen.'

We made it back to Mary's room undiscovered and she pushed me firmly into the armchair facing towards the door. She grimaced an apology, and sat down opposite me, arm trailing over the side of the chair just as it had been earlier. We could have been a tableau – unmoving since the visit from the white-veiled Sister Maria, hours ago.

'This is your debut at pretending to be something with absolute confidence. You can figure out what,' she added mischievously.

Across the room the curtain of origami birds fluttered and swooped. I shook my head and frowned, mind completely blank apart from an almost inconsequential question.

'Why do you call your birds mockingbirds, Mary? Is it because of the book?'

'The book?' she shook her head, amused. 'Oh, I see. No, they're mockingbirds because of what they do. They mock the truth, but only as you see them. They're being something else too. One day I'll let them sing their hearts out for you, if you need them to. They're the other bit of magic. They're ...'

A peremptory knock on the door cut her short. She frowned and pursed her lips. Whatever she'd been about to tell me was important.

It wasn't the white-veiled nun who appeared this time, but a navy-uniformed care attendant. The cloying aroma of cocoa preceded her and suddenly I was ravenously hungry.

'Mary! You shouldn't still have visitors. Visiting finished hours ago. You'll be in trouble!'

I broke in apologetically. 'I'm sorry. It's my fault. We had a lot to catch up on.'

'Still, you'll have to go now, and I'll have to report this. You know the rules, Mary.'

'My brother – I haven't seen him in ages,' Mary smiled dreamily at the attendant. 'Is that nectar for my birds?'

'No, it's your bedtime drink, Mary,' the attendant sighed, then patted Mary's trailing arm indulgently, setting the mug down on the side table nearest her. 'Your little birds don't need feeding.' To me, briskly, 'But I'll see you out right now, if you don't mind.'

I stood promptly, 'Of course, but I can see myself out. You carry on, I know the way.' The attendant shook her head and returned to the door, tapping in the exit code and then ringing the bell, holding the door ajar for me to follow her.

'Nevertheless,' she said, and waited.

I followed reluctantly, ducking to clear the curtain of paper birds, still bobbing in the draught from the open door and cursing that Mary hadn't been able to finish what she'd been about to tell me. Mary called me back.

'Kenny, wait! I need to give you a memento.'

The nearest bird dangled in front of me – so close its beak was almost pecking my eyes out. I brushed it carefully aside from its attack. It had been intricately folded to create the shape of a flying bird, with the text of the paper it was made out folded in on itself. Small portions were still readable and fixed themselves in my mind as I disentangled myself. *"...would appear to be fragmen.... eye stone in place. The unique des... nd stone undoubtedly tally with ... in question ... marking caused by the results of liv ..."*

Mary popped up in front of me, long face impish as my focus switched dizzily from bird to attendant and then back to Mary. She thrust the box at me that she'd asked me to open for her last time I'd visited. The box she'd been afraid to open, but which had been empty.

'There you are. A disappearing box for a disappearing man,' she said. 'It was Sarah's, our sister,' she added for the attendant's benefit.

'Oh, the one who died recently?' The attendant looked sympathetic. 'Don't you want to keep it?'

'No, it was always meant for Kenny. I was just looking after it for her until he could have it. I was her safety deposit person.'

The words swam around my head, and my jaw dropped. Since I'd seen it the last time, she'd scrawled 119 across the top of it. She laughed and my skin crawled with excitement simultaneous with shame at the memory of Sarah and how little I'd done for her. 'You should have it now, Kenny. You don't need to have all the answers to know the truth, remember?' The little paper bird bobbed jubilantly back in front of my face. Could it be that Mary had just handed me what I needed after all?

'I'm sorry to rush you …' the attendant prompted politely.

'No, no – I'm coming right now.' I peered into Mary's face, only a few inches below mine, and the bird buzzed around me more like a hummingbird than a mockingbird.

'Magic. Believe in it, but don't be fooled by it,' and she stepped swiftly aside, ducking back under the bobbing, flapping line of paper birds.

I followed the attendant out and down the corridor, the wheels of her trolley soundless on the plush carpet.

'Are you all right from here?' she asked as we reached the fork which led to reception one way and into another corridor the other.

'I'm fine,' I nodded reassuringly.

'Good. I should see you all the way out but I'm running late now and my supervisor will be on my back if I'm not done by quarter to. Lights out at eleven, you see.' With that she set off immediately down the unexplored corridor, leaving me alone and bemused. Mary was right about the receptionist; she was different – and indifferent. Mary clearly had the workings of *the place* off to a fine art. The receptionist pushed the visitors' book to me, hiding a yawn behind perfectly manicured nails and I over-signed my previous exit record. She pressed the door release button and smiled politely at me, leaving the visitors' book wide open, but only showing the page I'd written on. I still wished I could see who else had signed in before me. It must contain a lot of visitors' details over the past year too.

'Door's open – just push,' she instructed, lazily surveying the box Mary had given me. An idea occurred to me.

'Would you mind?' I brandished the box at her, as if it would impede me doing anything except walking. 119 waved tantalisingly under my nose.

She sighed but slid elegantly out from behind her sprawling but immaculate desk and wiggled her way to the door for me. I balanced the box under one arm so I could flick the visitors' book over to the beginning. It started just over a year ago. I shoved the visitors' book under my arm and repositioned the box to hide it.

'Thank you so much,' I fawned at the receptionist as she held the door open and I shuffled through it, crab-like. She shrugged and turned her back on me, forgotten before I'd even left. The door closed behind me and I walked swiftly back to the car, eager to see both what was in the box and in the rest of the visitors' book. I heaved myself into the driver's seat and pushed the seat back to its farthest reaches to give myself room to unpack the box. At last! Holding my breath in anticipation, I slung the box lid and the visitors' book on the passenger seat and peered inside.

Nothing.

It was empty – just like before. I swore. Jesus Christ – now what was Mary playing at? She was as bad as all the rest! Was there no-one in my life who wasn't manipulating me or playing me for a fool? I gave in to frustration, turning the car blue with the foulest, most abusive language I could think of – the kind the guttersnipes I'd had to defend as I made my way up the ranks had used as common parlance. Eventually I ran out of words, but the anger remained. I looked at who I'd become in the rear view mirror and was afraid. The man who looked back was on the verge of chaos, misjudging even those closest to him, and yet was trying to fool himself he was playing a game that had no rules as cleverly as his opponents. I wasn't playing at all. I was being manoeuvred, absolutely and completely. I retrieved the lid from the passenger seat and put it back on the box, grimacing at the 119 inscribed across its top. Damn fool!

And yet?

I put the box on the passenger seat and leaned my head back against the head rest, clicking down the internal locking system before I shut my eyes this time – just in case. Of course it would be empty. It had been before, and the addition of the 119 had simply been to persuade me to take it and realise without her being able to tell me in so many words that its contents were elsewhere and to not rely on it. She hadn't given me evidence, she'd given me facts: now I knew there was no safety deposit box, but there was someone who potentially knew where its contents were – even if she had teased me with an empty box. I also knew Danny had been with Margaret initially, but had subsequently been coerced to leave because he'd be unlikely to willingly abandon *To Kill a Mockingbird*. The ransom demand must therefore be valid – in some way; or important for me to follow through. And Mary's mad claims? Maybe they weren't quite as mad as they first appeared. The little gallows icons certainly implied that could be the case. I pulled the visitors' book onto my lap, and flipped through it. Win, Sarah, Binnie all featured in it at various stages, officially visiting Mary. So did two other names. Molly Wemmick, of course – and her brother. Now I had the 'they' Mary kept referring to. The devil – John Wemmick and Molly, alias Margaret; the two people really involved in all of the plotting.

I made it back to Win's in record time, via the post box tree. Not the place I most wanted to visit in the dead of night, but the knife bumped comfortingly in my pocket and the common seemed as devoid of attackers as I would have been of conscience if I'd met any. The note was simple and to the point.

'Danny kidnapped. Need to meet urgently. Highgate cemetery: Edith Mary Juss, plot 3159. Thursday 9th 11am.'

Apart from imparting my news, I knew I needed to see my enigmatic wife with new eyes – ones that saw her objectively, not in the heat of passion or exigency. It was already into the small hours of Wednesday morning and she'd need time to pick up the message but I also needed time to collect the stashed partnership funds and negotiate an urgent claim with the insurance company. That part of her plan remained necessary and if my suspicions were right the 'kidnapper' would know exactly when I'd completed those tasks without me needing to prompt. I enjoyed repeating the little numerical joke too. It was time to play out my own angles.

19: Puzzle Pieces

Win woke me with the paper and bad news.

'Heard you come in. Useful day?' I grunted and rolled on to my side before remembering why I'd been lying on my back as my ribs grumbled. 'What did she say?' I grimaced, struggling to pull the events of the previous day from the shroud of sleep. 'And he really don't like you, does he?' he continued, showing me the article on page six. I dragged myself into a sitting position with difficulty. I'd collapsed on Win's lumpy chintz settee on my return, pulling an overcoat I'd found by the front door over me in lieu of a blanket. He'd replaced it with a brown checked blanket some time during the night. The coat was now draped limply over the mis-matched armchair – a dull dun brown – albeit matching the rest of the room, apart from the floral red and orange settee – a lurid splash of summer colour in an otherwise decaying landscape. The article contained a litany of my – now I read a summary of them in the paper – undeniably suspicious behaviours, concluding with the fire at my house. The article the radio presenter had referred to last night, no doubt. I needed Heather to back me up more than ever. The insurance company were hardly going to be deaf to what the press had to say – or dismissive. Win summed it up succinctly for me.

'They always say there's no smoke without fire,' he laughed. 'Get it?'

I sighed melodramatically for his benefit, and then allowed the rest of his whimsical but irritating remarks to go over my head as I read the remainder of the report to make sure I knew the worst before I tackled the insurers. Heather's ominous silence broke with a phone call from her just as I was nearing the end of the article.

'Where are you now?' she demanded. Win mouthed at me – I guessed something like 'who is it?' I waved him away.

'Hello Heather, thanks for not asking, but I'll survive – even though it was bit of an ordeal last night after I told you about the ransom note for Danny.'

Win mouthed at me again. I guessed this time it was about the ransom note. I shook my head and mouthed back 'tell you in a minute.'

'I did try – you must have been out of signal, but lucky for you I *have* been doing your bidding anyway, fool though I am. I've paved the way for a home visit for you later on today and after talking to your insurers to see what they need, I've written a reference for them, claiming you're of sound mind and short pockets. Well, at least one of those is true! I said you were in need of immediate funds because of simultaneous business and personal strictures and therefore were prepared to settle on a disadvantageous basis simply to get back on track. I did also cover myself by saying my statement was based purely on information and representation made to me by you. I wash my hands of the outcome, though. I still think you're mad, and you'll have nothing left to get you out of the shit if you hand it all over – not to mention still having to repay all the partnership monies you've misappropriated ...'

'I promise you ...'

'Yes, yes – we've been there before, although, I suppose on that score, if you're really nice to me, I could let you work for pocket money for the rest of your life in lieu of payment.'

Win's face was contorting with curiosity and I had to ignore him in order not to laugh – which would have almost certainly been the last straw with Heather.

'That is extremely kind of you, Heather,' I said pleasantly, 'but hopefully it won't come to that, although I really appreciate what you've done. When am I allowed into the house?'

'This morning, at eleven. I'm coming with you though.'

'Why?'

'It was a condition that Frediks imposed. Me, and a policeman too, so don't try anything tricky.'

'When have I ever?'

'I shan't waste my breath answering that,' she replied shortly. 'So what was this ordeal you suffered and what's happening with Danny and this ransom business?'

I summarised briefly for her – but not all of it. Win listened pop-eyed, mouthing questions at me, with me signalling I'd fill him in when Heather was off the phone. I wound up with, 'that's why it's imperative I have this insurance claim in hand – in case.'

The noise she made was somewhere between an expletive and a grunt.

210

'You know what I think of that idea but meet us at the house and I'll bring the statement with me. I'll fax a copy to the insurers in the meantime.'

She cut the connection before me – she always did. One day, I vowed, I would beat her to it. I put the phone down on my lap on top of the newspaper and prepared for the next inquisition.

'What the bloody hell was all that about, then?' Win exploded.

'OK, so I went to see Mary, like I said, but I bumped into someone else whilst I was there – in fact more than one person, and at least one of them must be Danny's kidnapper because after they'd tried to suffocate me, I found I'd been given this.' I showed him the crumpled ransom note. He snatched it from me.

'You said it was a ransom note for Danny. It don't say Danny on here?'

'No, that's because the kidnapper knows they don't need to specify their prize, only their price and I will know exactly what, or who, we're bargaining for.'

He sat on the end of the settee, crushing my legs and pinning me in place. I wondered if it was deliberate.

'I may be thick, but I don't.'

'Jaggers wants my money back.'

'Yeah, I know – you already told me that – and who wouldn't? Right bloody fortune you've amassed without us knowing! Jesus Christ, and I thought *he* was tricky!'

'Money isn't everything, Win. I may have amassed a fortune but it seems I've amassed little else except trouble with it. However, trouble or not, Jaggers wants it back, and like I also told you, will achieve that any way he can. Putting me and Danny in court was his first attempt – to force my past into the open. Kimmy's murder was the second, to put me under threat, the fire put me on the run, and now he's discrediting me to back me into a corner and he's using Danny again, just to make sure. But I haven't witness-tampered, played arsonist or been involved in anything to put anyone's life at risk.'

'Take your word for it.'

'Cheers! But he's got me – and you – by the balls with Kimmy's murder, nevertheless ...'

'Which I wasn't involved with, by the way,' he interrupted.

'Take your word for it,' I threw back at him as he bristled. 'And with Danny's kidnapping I have to play ball, just in case. Finally, there's

Margaret herself ...'

'Who's still helping you? '

'Yes, so it seemed. But maybe she's one of those red herrings I told you about.'

He snorted. 'Bloody lawyers – you always talk in riddles until it comes to the pounds signs.'

'OK, in a way, they're all red herrings, that's what I'm trying to say. The only absolute truth is that Jaggers wants that money and he'll do anything to get it. Oh, yes, there are lots of other peripheral truths that have, or will, come to light along the way – Danny, Margaret's identity, finding my family again, but this,' I took the ransom note back from him, 'this is merely the latest in his coercion methods to persuade me to play ball. The thing is, who else is playing it with him?' With difficulty I shifted my legs. He rocked atop them like an outsize boat on a mutinous sea, but didn't move. He wanted the whole explanation, and if I wanted my legs in working order, I was going to have to give him at least part of it – the part I was sure of, anyway. 'It's a puzzle, Win. Think of it as a giant puzzle, with the pieces slowly being dropped into place.'

'I ain't really into that kinda thing.'

'I know.' I remembered Win as a child; the intrepid explorer – always first to try everything. It was how he'd got the V-shaped scar under his chin during an 'expedition'. It was why he'd wanted to compete with Jonno, and why he'd taken over one of the gangs in the children's home. Win was a doer, not a thinker. Whereas I – what was I? A thinker, yes, but maybe not as objective about it as I should have been. I changed tack, hoping that clarifying things for him might also clarify them for me. 'Sarah showed me how to do jigsaw puzzles when I was a kid. You find the corners first, then you add the edges. That gives you a framework to work on. Only then can you fill in the middle, building it up from the outside in. We have the corners and the edges – Jaggers wants his money and Jaggers will do whatever he must to get it. The rest of the puzzle picture is only now gradually forming though.'

'And what does it look like so far?'

'Confusing – but becoming less so.'

He snorted. 'That's a lot of help.'

I smiled. 'What would be of significant help, Win, would be if you got off my legs and let me go and collect that bit of film that should clear you, and maybe reveal Kimmy's real murderer. That would put another puzzle piece in the right place.'

'Now you're bloody talking! When?' He jumped up then, making whatever active springs remained in the chintz monstrosity recoil and ping into me with dire consequences. 'This morning. Heather's got me a pass back into my house from Fredriks.'

'Right! I'm on it,' he grinned delightedly and the boy I'd known before our childish world disintegrated momentarily looked out of the man's face.

'But I think I ought to go alone – just in case.'

'Bloody hell! Here we go again! In case of what?'

'There are any more suggestions of evidence tampering – but this time from you …'

'Oh.' His face fell.

'Win, I've got you covered – all right? I won't let you down.' There was no blood brother pact or swearing involved, but this was a promise I knew I had to keep, as much as I had to keep my promise to Danny. I looked down at the newspaper article still lying provocatively across my lap – the pointing finger of the reporter's words reinforcing what the posture of the man in the image alongside implied: guilt. The picture was of me – caught unawares as I left the court after Danny's case was dismissed, and taking Ella out the back exit I'd thought none of the press would be covering. The headline called me a liar, a manipulator, a thief. The next accusation would be murderer if I didn't make sure my son was safe. *That gives you a framework to work on. Only then can you fill in the middle, building it up from the outside in, until you get to the heart of the puzzle.* I didn't like how the heart of the puzzle was starting to look, but there was no choice now but to complete it, and it seemed I might have to change my role altogether to do so.

Win reluctantly allowed me to take possession of his car again and I rolled sleekly up a few minutes before eleven, as instructed. The double yellow lines had been ignored by the squad car that was already in position across the head of the mews. Heather arrived in a taxi mere seconds after I did. She gave the car and me a disgusted once over.

'I see you take more care of your brother's car than mine, even if you look like you've been enjoying a night on the tiles,' she commented sweetly. I clearly hadn't made enough of a job of tidying myself up after my adventures in the marshes. I pulled my tie straighter, as if that would help. The crumpled shirt and trousers were beyond help.

'I'm really sorry, Heather. I'll pay for all the repairs, I promise.'

'I shouldn't be so hasty with your promises if I were you,' she replied

213

icily.' The car's a write-off and you've yet to repay the partnership money. Where is it all coming from Lawrence?' For a moment her face belied her demeanour, then the worried expression reverted to frosty business bitch. 'The insurance pay out? Or a money tree you've yet to tell me the location of?'

'It will get sorted,' I assured her.

'Really?' She turned imperiously on her heel to command the fresh-faced young policeman in the squad car. Her heel tip had ground a hole in the pavement and I stared abjectly into it to avoid a further dressing down. I glanced back up briefly to find her still watching me as she greeted the police officer. She looked from me to the hole and back to me with obvious meaning. The worm, who might as well crawl into his self-made hole. I took the point, but Heather had already given herself away by even being here. I silently added her to the list of promises I should keep. 'Shall we get started?' she continued briskly. 'I've still got a business to keep from completely collapsing.'

'The fire services have cleared the building for safety, ma'am. It seems there wasn't as much structural damage as you'd have expected from the fireball. More cosmetic – windows blown out, décor ruined, and so on.' The young policeman turned earnestly to me, 'but you still need to be extremely careful, sir.' I hoped the forensics report wouldn't dumb down the cost of refurbishment or the insurance claim might fall short of the required amount. Then I remembered the excessive costs I'd complained about so regularly when the work was being done and silently congratulated Margaret for being a spendthrift, even though this couldn't have been part of the plan then. If I could locate some of the invoices when I looked for the hidden money, they would cut any arguments off at the legs with the insurers.

The policeman looked too young to be out on his own, or maybe that was just age and rampant cynicism on my part. He was waiting uncertainly for my answer – obviously also curious about my dishevelled state but too polite to ask. Not so Heather. She fixed me beadily like a mother hen in designer feathers.

'And you'll need to change before you meet the insurers,' she added.

'Of course, I'll be guided by you,' I replied to both of them.

'That'll be a first time, then,' she grumbled, and allowed the police-boy to lead the way to my blackened front door – not quite as blackened as my name was becoming, but close. He entered first, cautiously testing the floorboards just inside the front door before stepping more confidently into the hall. I walked on past, leaving him and Heather halfway along the hallway. *Pretend to be something with absolute confidence ...*

'If they say it's safe, it's safe,' I said as I passed them. 'Got to believe somebody some time,' I added pointedly. I went on into the kitchen – which was surprisingly unscathed other than for the lingering sour smell of smoke. The fireball had obviously not reached the back of the house. 'It's virtually untouched out here,' I called back. Heather was the first to follow me in. The police-boy hovered behind her, anxiously looking overhead as if he expected a fiery beam to fall on him at any moment.

'You're right. Why's that?' She swung round to the young officer. 'Do you know?'

'Err, according to the report the blast zone was all at the front of the house, and fuelled purely by the petrol leak from the car. Seems there's very little flammable stuff in your house, sir. The gas pipes have been embedded in fire-proof casings, the electrics are all new and similarly protected and the materials used on the doors have been specially treated to be inflammable. Even the walls have been painted with fire retardant coating underneath the emulsion. Very safety-conscious refurb. The fire department were impressed. Because the fire ignited in the study and the windows were already knocked out, the fire probably sucked in air from the front, and when it had burnt off the petrol, only had the interior of the car and some of the furniture to feed on. After a good dowsing it was out in no time. Model fire control, the officer said.'

'Very impressive,' Heather remarked.

'Thank you ma'am.'

'I didn't mean you, I meant how the fire was controlled.' She turned on me as the police-boy blushed. 'Don't you think? Was this what Margaret spent all your money on in your refurb?'

'I hadn't thought about that until now, but I suppose she must have.' The idea intrigued me. 'Can I see the report? It might be useful when dealing with my insurance claim.' I wasn't surprised at Margaret's efficiency, but I was with her attention to fire safety. Why had she been so concerned? I was intensely curious about that now.

'I'll get a copy of it for you, sir, if you come back down the station afterwards. It's all on file, with the rest of the forensics.'

'What else did forensics turn up then?' I was surprised too that the film and the hidden camera hadn't already been spotted. They must have crawled all over the place to put the fire report together. I only hoped the hidden panel at the back of the wardrobe and its fire-proof suitcase hadn't been found during the course of the crawl. 'Not a lot, sir. It was mainly to do with the fire. It was obvious where it started and how, so they concentrated on that, but it did make a note of the fire retardation factors as a matter of course'.

'I see. Well, let's see if we can find this camera then.'

It wasn't difficult because I knew where it was, but a closer examination of the kitchen revealed probably why the forensics team hadn't found it. The power had been shut off with the fire, and the kitchen was virtually untouched. Of course the little green light wouldn't still have been blinking so they wouldn't have looked for it. Its hiding place was almost perfect, but I located it immediately. How to get the damn thing out was a different matter altogether. Try as I might, I couldn't get the panel concealing it to move. After half an hour, I gave up and the police-boy called in one of his colleagues who also puzzled over the unmoving panel, and also eventually gave up.

'I could try and find the contact details of the people who installed it, but that would have been in the paperwork in the study – or if we're lucky – in the stuff I kept upstairs in the spare bedroom. I'd like to find some of the documents relating to the refurb expenses for the insurance claim anyway. Shall I look upstairs since the study is obviously out of bounds?' I asked casually. Yellow and black striped safety markers criss-crossed the study entrance – now with non-existent door, presumably removed by the forensics team.

'I don't know.' The young policeman looked nervously at his colleague for guidance.

'Whereabouts is the spare room situated, sir? If it's over the study, then no. Just in case of structural implications, see? If it's at the back of the house then it might be OK.'

'It's at the back,' I lied, almost joyfully, before tempering my excitement with a more considered approach. As far as they knew I was simply looking for old paperwork, not treasure-trove.

'Do you want some help?' Heather asked, eyeing me curiously. Heather, with her mirror games and astute observance of my inability to control facial expression. Heather – with her knowledge of the floor plan too. Careful.

'That would be good … but,' I swung round to the two police officers, imagining what the face of earnest concern would look like and trying simultaneously to assimilate it into my own. 'Are you sure it's safe up there? It's important we retrieve this evidence since it will almost certainly clear my client of a murder charge but there's no way I'm putting anyone else at risk to get it. There's been enough of that already.' They hesitated. 'Shall I just bring everything down and we'll look at it here.'

The consensus, after a few moments of heated discussion was that they still weren't sure. I swept their uncertainty away with decisive insistence that I *must* try, but that Heather should remain where it was 'safe'. If it hadn't been for the two nodding dogs of policeman applauding my integrity, Heather would have given me the slow handclap. As it was she nodded slowly, clearly amused, in the background. OK, so I hadn't *perfected* the art of pretending to be something with absolute confidence for everyone, but I was improving. I didn't wait for them to change their minds. I swung upstairs and made straight for the small dressing room at the front, directly over the study. Nor did I need to look far for paperwork with the details of the contractors who'd installed the camera system. I knew exactly where I'd find it. If they'd been responsible for organising the fire safety conscious refurb, there was little doubt they would also have had a hand in supplying the false-backed wardrobe and the fire-proofed suitcase.

It was that simple, too. Once you knew the wardrobe had a false compartment, it was merely a case of working out how to open it. I hoped I wasn't going to be as difficult as the access panel for the camera or I was in trouble. It wasn't. Behind the dresses, now sour and smoky, so unlike Margaret's fresh floral perfume, there was a small lever. I pressed it and *open sesame* worked perfectly again. The case itself was surprisingly compact. I could barely believe it contained over half a million pounds, but if this wasn't one of the red herrings that Win was now getting fed up of hearing about, it did. I pulled it out and laid it on the suitcase rest that was tucked into the corner of the room. As I'd anticipated, it had the supplier's seal of approval on the lid of the case in the form of a riveted metal label, sporting name, address and phone number to ring in the event of any difficulty opening the case. It was locked by three spinning digital number locks on either side, but I made a calculated guess at the code, and this time the joke wasn't on me. Inside there was room to spare alongside the stacks of notes. I was surprised that much money took up so little space. I shut it quickly and locked it again, then followed the lead Mary had shown me at *the place* and took the case downstairs to show my appreciative audience the contact details. The younger of the two police officers was immediately in the phone.

'What's in the case?' Heather asked quietly as he negotiated with the security company to come and retrieve the camera, whilst the older one had yet another go at releasing the catch on the panel. Some people never give up, even in the face of impossibility. I admired him, in a way.

'Paperwork,' I replied vaguely.

'What kind?' she persisted.

'The kind you don't want to get burnt,' I replied. 'I'll put it in the car.'

'Don't need to keep a tight hold on it then?' She asked artlessly. 'In case there are more murky secrets in it we should know about?'

'It's just paperwork, Heather.'

I could feel her eyes on me all the way to the car, but I concentrated on what Mary had shown me how to do and this time I could have sworn Heather wasn't sure whether to believe me or not. I slung the case nonchalantly into the boot and clicked the car's automatic lock as I walked away, looking for all the world as if all I'd thrown in the boot was a case full of old receipts and guarantees. She continued to watch me closely until the security operative arrived, but then all eyes were on him. Small, weasly-faced and with greasy hair, the engineer was a far cry from what I'd expected. He reached deftly behind the cupboard trim, jerked at it, grunted, jerked again, face set in concentration, then a slim rectangular panel dropped onto the worktop. His hand reappeared cradling a small black camcorder, remarkably similar to what I imagined a bomb about to detonate might look like.

'Here's your little bugger,' he announced. 'Deluxe model too,' he sounded appreciative. 'Sound as well as vision – someone's got money to burn.' He sniffed and grimaced. 'Careless too - put the panel back wrong, and it got wedged. Easy if you got the knack, of course...' He lowered the camera so it rested in his hand like a baby in a cradle, its tangle of red and green wires like an umbilical cord attaching it to the kitchen unit. 'Will have run out of film by now, though.'

'How do you know?' I asked.

'You the bloke I spoke to – the cop?' He looked wary.

'No, I'm the owner of the property.'

'Oh, don't you remember the training?'

'I didn't take much notice of it at the time.' *Or any other, until now.*

He made a face at me like a downturned clown mouth.

'Don't like being on candid camera then? Not many do.' He placed the camera gently on the work top. The wires stretched taught. 'Turn it on over there and it'll show green if it's ready to record, red if it's run out of film.' He gestured to the general vicinity of the door. 'All you do then is wipe the film and reuse it, unless there's stuff you want to keep on it, '

I walked over to the door and the double light point and flicked the switch. Nothing happened. He laughed.

'Well it won't work now, will it? The power's off. Ain't using your head, are you?'

I stared at him. The truism was almost beyond comprehension. It was so simple, and it applied to everything I'd done all my life. I hadn't paid attention to the simplest, most obvious things – the kind of things even Win noticed. I wasn't using my head, only my inclination. The puzzle pieces tumbled over and another fell into place. Not quite at the heart, but I suspected the next conversation I had would probably take me to within one piece of it.

The security firm operative cut the wires after I assured him I wouldn't be using it again and twisted yellow sticky tape over the frayed ends. With that, the camera and its precious contents were born off to Chelsea police station to be examined. Heather and I were invited to the premiere later on that afternoon, but I had another starring role to complete first – convincing the insurance company that my claim was valid. It involved an urgent audience with the underwriters and signing a document that might as well have been a contract with the devil for all the clauses and sub-clauses it contained should I renege on the agreement, be found to have fraudulent intent or be involved in criminal activity. Strange how easy I suddenly found it to sign my dishonesty away. I signed, but not in blood, and the underwriter agreed to ring me as soon as the proposition had been considered, quantified and sanctioned. I had followed Heather's advice this time, though. I'd smartened up before I went.

With my future potentially in my pocket I rendezvoused at the police station to see Win's returned to him. Fredriks flicked the playback button on the VCR and the film fluttered through my departing back and several minutes of empty, but pristine kitchen.

'Immaculate,' remarked Heather, as if it was a sin.

'Margaret was,' I replied, vaguely defensive, to my surprise.

'In everything but honesty,' she retorted.

'Children!' cautioned Fredriks, eyeing us with amused curiosity.

'Huh!' but I noticed Heather accepted the admonishment without complaint. Interesting. I made a mental note to revisit the changing dynamics between them at some point, but almost immediately forgot as my attention was refocused on the film as the kitchen door opened.

'You must have switched the camera on instead of the light off as you left the room,' he commented to me. 'I understand the switch is positioned next to the light switch?'

'Ah, yes – of course.' A stupid habit of mine, turning lights off that weren't even on. 'I'm always doing that.' It made sense now – distracted, not paying attention as I hurriedly left to visit Sarah and absent-mindedly switching the kitchen spotlights off; activating the camera instead.

The new arrival was Kimmy. She seemed drunk, flinging her bag haphazardly on the counter and banging clumsily into the bar stools. The clatter grated on me, edgy as I already was. Off-screen a door banged.

'Oh fuck off!' she shouted to apparently no-one, and moved in front of the camera so all we could see was her blurry shape filling the screen. She moved aside and in the brief hiatus before she blocked the camera's view again, another form appeared at the door to the kitchen and moved across the room towards her. The shape settled into a person as the camera re-focused. Win. 'I told you to leave me be,' she spat at him.

'Don't be stupid. I ain't letting you get into any more trouble. Come on. Let's go.'

Kimmy moved away from the counter and into the centre of the room, waving her arms about. In her right hand was one of Margaret's prized Sabatiers. She jabbed it at Win and he blundered off to the left, alternately feinting, dodging, and begging her to put the knife down.

'Oh, piss off, will you? This is my business, not yours.'

'You're me sister, you are me business.'

'No, I'm not. Come any closer and I'll cut your balls off – if you've got any!'

'Kimmy, leave it will you? This ain't the way. Trust me! You don't want to tangle with the likes of him.'

'Trust me, don't do this, do that! You don't even know the half of it,' she sneered at him. 'And where's it all got you, being ordered around? Fat, poor and stupid! I want me dues and I'm getting them today.' She swung the knife at him again, face contorted. It looked to have been within inches of cutting him this time. He backed away and his shoulders visibly slumped. I knew my brother's body language well enough by now to know this was the moment he'd recounted to me – the moment he'd given up and walked away. That was exactly what he did on-screen.

'Suit yourself, you selfish little bitch,' he threw back angrily. 'We all suffered for you, and for what? Get on with it on your own then!'

We watched him leave and heard the door bang shut behind him, leaving Kimmy alive, well and high in my kitchen. The film fluttered and snowed out to nothing. The end of the recording, and Win in the clear.

Fredriks was the first to speak.

'So, Mr Juste, it would seem what your brother said was true. We will have to check the film for any *adjustments* that may have been made to it, but subject to that, I'll be in touch to confirm there'll be no murder charge – currently.'

'He'll be delighted to hear that.'

Heather reached across and patted my shoulder.

'Well done for that, at least. One down – how many more to go?'

'Two,' I said and left her surprised expression for Fredriks to sort out.

I collected a copy of the forensics report about the fire on the way out, the young policeman having been as good as his word. Back in the car I rang the security operative to ask about the loose wires.

'As long as you leave them sealed up they're fine. The power's turned off, anyway, but you're right, at the moment it is potentially live when the power's back on, so be sensible. I can come back Tuesday to sort it if you want. Booked out all day Monday. Only came out today because the cops insisted.'

'Tuesday will be fine, thanks. That's all I needed to know for the time being.'

I sat in the car for a while longer, devouring the forensics report, until my conscience pricked. Win would be waiting at home, worrying about what the film had turned up, and I wanted to know if he understood why Margaret should have had such a thing about fire.

His reaction to being cleared was almost anticlimactic, until he did a little jig as he left the room to bring back a bottle of scotch. He poured two large glasses.

'Tits up!' he announced, handing me one of them.

I laughed. 'I thought it was bottoms up?'

'I prefer tits,' he said, between mouthfuls.

I took a sip. 'Tits up then, and arse over tit to the rest of them.'

'Yeah! So what's next – the lad?'

'Yes, after I've seen Margaret again.' I put the glass down on the coffee table and perched uncomfortably on the arm of the monstrous orange and red settee. 'And I'll need your car back for that tomorrow.'

'Take it, mate – I'm going to be nursing one God almighty hangover tomorrow.' He grinned delightedly, and took another swig, downing the remainder in one.

'Well before you drink the rest of that bottle, there's something I wanted to ask you about. Why would Margaret be worried about fire?'

He poured another half glass and raised it to me.

'Dunno. Why?'

'Because it turns out that the reason we were able to recover the film so easily from that camera was because only the study was actually fire damaged. The house had been so completely fire-proofed as part of the refurbishment Margaret was in charge of, the rest of it was untouched. I wondered why it cost so much – even with her expensive tastes. It seems that was probably why, but why go to such lengths unless you have a paranoia about fire, or a hidden agenda?'

Win flung himself down on the misshapen settee and nursed his glass. He was already flushed from the alcohol, but not as lurid as the settee, although in other ways the settee wasn't dissimilar to him – overstuffed upholstery echoing his rounded belly and rucked shirt.

'Didn't think she had any problems, really, except always being overshadowed by Rosemary. Like I said – she was quiet, a bit mousy. Not given to outbursts – only that time over the blasted cat. Rosemary were more interested in that kind of thing – like she was over Emm's scar when she was hurt – burnt. The only time they met too. Bit ghoulish that, wanting to know all about it. Got hold of me lighter and tried to burn herself to see what it was like. Spooked even me with that. She lost interest when she found out it was boiling water, not fire, though.'

'Margaret?'

'No, Rosemary. Sarah banned me ciggies and lighter from the house after too, but we didn't see much of either of them by then – they were grown up, see? And it was then that Kimmy and Rosemary got really into the club so I didn't encourage visits either.' He paused and took another swig from the glass. 'Sort of thing Rosemary would wind Margaret up about, I s'pose, getting burned, like she wound Mary up about the cat – except she weren't around by the time you had the refurb, were she?'

'She sounds quite cruel.'

'I s'pose she was. Yeah – you're right. That's what she was. Cruel.'

I left him carousing with the bottle whilst I completed what I needed to do as I waited for my two bits of news – from the insurance company and from the kidnapper. The forensics report on the fire made fascinating reading. I went back to the part that intrigued me most and made notes. It was a scholarly piece, written by someone as fascinated with fire and its power as with containing it. The glimmer of an idea started to form, as diffuse and confusing as smoke – and potentially as lethal, combined with Margaret's plan to pretend the money I was supposed to hand over to Jaggers was burnt. I went out for a walk, leaving Win gently snoring on the settee as I tested how the puzzle pieces came together round it. If I added all the small, apparently inconsequential comments my family had made to me, and the otherwise seemingly irrelevant facts I'd been steadily gleaning, it fleshed out quite a different person behind Margaret's plan.

The first of my anxiously awaited news updates arrived on my way back, head still reeling. The insurance company had agreed to my proposal. The underwriter disconnected after giving me the good news, leaving me rooted to the spot on the patchworked pavement leading back to Win's maisonette. Long ago, or so it seemed, even though it was barely a few weeks, I'd felt like I was standing on a precipice and deciding whether or not to jump after I'd first slept with Kat. That moment paled into insignificance with the partnership money sitting in the boot of Win's car, and the insurance company sanctioning the full amount of my claim. Now I had the wherewithal to really jump – it was merely a question of where to?

20: Wise Men and Honest Men

I arrived home to find Win still snoring on the sofa, the empty scotch bottle abandoned on the floor next to him. It seemed he'd replaced me there so I paid him the same compliment he'd paid me and draped the checked blanket over him, stuffing a pillow under his head for good measure. His reply was a disrupted snore which I took as a thank you. I sat in the armchair and watched him for a while, remembering as much as I could from our childhood and our reunion since. It was an odd mix – infantile and adult – and at times transposed, so that the child thought as an adult and vice versa. I wondered if siblings thought this way if their relationship continued seamlessly from toddlerhood to maturity, or whether it was a peculiarity of ours, and the necessity of viewing what childhood I'd had through an adult's eyes that had hampered me all my life. I'd lost and found myself, abandoned and reclaimed a family, and found and lost my faith in justice. Where did I go from here?

His snoring returned to a deep and regular rhythm, and I allowed my thoughts to rise and fall with it. The unexpected addition of Danny to my life added to the sense of being lost and found. I had a second chance at getting it right – through him, yes; but could I really make that happen? I'd spent most of my life getting it wrong. I'd fashioned myself in the image of Atticus Finch, but not lived within the spirit of him. Now I potentially had a choice bigger even than the one I'd made as a child when I left the children's home. Far from escaping the past, my life now was made up wholly of a past I'd denied – and feared – and still feared would consume me. I either had to take hold of what remained – the good and the bad, the unsavoury and the desirable – and take the consequences. Or I had to start all over again.

I fell asleep in the chair still debating which, without the benefit of the scotch or the checked blanket. I woke in the early hours of dawn to my mobile phone ringing. It was the vibration against my chest that roused me more than the noise. Win stirred, and then merely turned over again with a loud hiccup. I fumbled to accept the call with the fingers of a dead man, numb and lifeless.

'Just listen. This is your first message.' The voice was muffled. 'You'll receive another later on today. The drop will be tomorrow. Be prepared.' The phone clicked off and the backlight blacked out. Win slept on, but sleep was long lost to me now. I got up slowly, legs stiff and ribs still grumbling. My head swam and my skin crawled. I felt sick but wasn't sure if that was because of the message or my bodily state. I struggled to the bathroom – a modest affair with a chipped enamel bath, chain flush and over-large rectangular wash basin, none of it matching. Surprisingly, though, it was pristine, with a large slightly misted mirror over the washbasin, polished to sparkling. Win was a good housewife, it seemed, even if some of his other habits were less appealing. A wave of dizziness swept over me again and I braced myself against the wash basin. Probably head rush from getting up too quickly and not having eaten properly for the last two days. I would be meeting Margaret in a few hours. Get a grip man! I assessed myself in the mirror – the five o'clock shadow along my jawline, the sunken eyes, the slack mouth. The suave, successful barrister of only a few weeks ago had transformed into a deadbeat. Give me grazed knuckles and a flick-knife, and I'd be the perfect lout. I laughed hollowly. Courtesy of Mary, I already had the flick-knife.

It took me two hours, but I managed to turn the hood back into the maestro of the high court before Win awoke.

'Blimey, you've spivved up. Going somewhere special?'

'I've an important meeting to go to.'

'You did yesterday too, but you didn't get all tarted up for that. Oh, I get it – it's Margaret, isn't it?'

'It is, but smartening up is because I need to be in control, not to impress. It's metaphorical.'

'Yeah, that too – right.' He winked and I was irritated. He yawned and scratched his bald patch, then wrapped his arms round his rolling gut, and added, 'Can't say I blame you, though. She's a fancy bit of skirt – and don't get all arsy with me. That right hook was a lucky hit last time. I'll take you out if you try it again.' I laughed. Neither of us were in any fit state for a fight – he bleary-eyed and hung over, me sleep-deprived and on edge. I just hoped I'd keep my new role going long enough to find out what I needed to know and then conclude my own plan. 'Mind you, you need a bit of a nip and tuck with that shirt. I guess it's mine since you're travelling light. I should roll the sleeves up a bit at least – make yourself look casual, instead of a casualty.'

'Since when did you become a follower of fashion? I'll be thinking you and Heather have been putting your heads together if you're not careful.' I rolled the sleeves of the shirt up The right sleeve still hung over my little angel nevertheless.

'Heather? You mean bitch lady? Blimey – you gotta be joking. She'd bite mine off before she let me put my head anywhere near hers. No, it's what I'd imagine Emm would suggest. Rubs off on you after a while, without you knowing it.'

'Doesn't it just?' I thought of Mary and grinned. I looked at my watch. It was just after ten and I wanted to make sure I arrived at Highgate before Margaret. My grin faded but Mary's influence remained. 'I've got to go now – if it's still OK to borrow your car again? I'll be back later on this afternoon.'

He pretended to consider, a slow smile of amusement spreading across his face at the anxious expression I obviously didn't manage to hide. 'Yeah, go on then – since you got me off the hook. But hey – you make sure you don't need to make use of that, won't you?'

'What?' I thought for a moment that the outline of the flick-knife could be seen in my trouser pocket.

'Your guardian angel, like Ma had.' He looked thunderstruck. 'Blimey! Danny's got one too, just like that. He *is* your kid, isn't he?'

'Yes, he is my kid – and that's why I've got to sort this all out once and for all.'

'You need me to help?'

'Just you stay safe here. Then I don't need to worry about you too.' It slipped out before I could stop it. He looked as surprised as me.

'OK.' He was uncertain. The brotherly comradeship between us was too new for either of us to feel at ease with it. 'Yeah. And don't you bust my car, right? Or I'll bust you.' Back on comfortable footing, I nodded and he nodded back.

I turned to go as the idea struck. I turned back to him.

'Win, do you smoke?

'Nah, gave it up – only vice I ain't got, apart from women.' He snorted. 'Chance'd be a fine thing there.'

'You don't still have a lighter, though, do you?' I thought of the rattling kettle on the gas hob.

'In the drawer – ciggies too, just to prove I can say no. Why?'

'Can I borrow them? Just a theory I'd like to test.'

How strange that we accept without accepting, and acknowledge without believing. I'd been doing it all my life, and so had Win. Simultaneously always thinking about the other distractions in our lives and missing the point that the present moment is making to us; the little clues that explain all the mysteries – like Margaret and her intriguing notes, and Rosemary and her intriguing ways.

***

Ma's grave was untouched since the last time I'd been there. I re-read the lettering on the headstone and for a moment was back to that time and place where everything might have been different – but it wasn't. Face facts, Lawrence. It is as it is, whether you like it or not. I stepped away and into the shadows of the overgrown shrubs that bordered the small clearing her plot nestled in. It was a double plot, dug deep enough to take two coffins, one on top of the other. Pop lay in it with her. I hoped they were happier wherever they were now, genuinely at rest after their turbulent lives. Now knowing that my roots had been as ambiguous as my current place in the world brought them and my childhood into a different perspective. Once I would have sided with Ma on all counts, and judged the man I'd believed to be my father a bully. Now I wondered what personal anguish his heavy leather belt had kept contained, but unleashed when he could no longer bear to look at Win and me and pretend equanimity?

We are never really what we appear to be. There is always something more, something hidden, that the casual onlooker cannot see and will never know. I would never have imagined the feisty little woman who had been my mother, worn out from childbearing and the daily grind of keeping us all fed and cared for, to have been a keeper of secrets herself, but she had – most I would never know, but perhaps some secrets are best taken unvoiced to the grave. I couldn't ask Ma, but I could ask the woman treading lightly and daintily up to Ma's last resting place to share her secrets, despite the fact that I knew she wouldn't.

I watched her for a while, admiring her gracefulness and the proud bearing of her head. The sunlight dappled her hair with gold. If I'd been of a fanciful turn of mind I might have wished those little gold spotlights into tiny lasers, boring into her brain and examining her intentions, but I had another way of doing that now. Whereas I was alive to the nuances of the place and its inhabitants, she seemed blithely indifferent, both to the gravity of the place and the message I'd sent her.

'Margaret,' I tested quietly. She didn't react. She was studying Ma's headstone much as I had, apparently lost in thought. 'Margaret,' I called again. Still oblivious. The third time she started and spun round before making her way across the graves towards me.

'Why are you hiding in the bushes?' she called, amusement in her eyes. The shifting sunlight made them appear to glitter.

'You're meant to walk round them, not over them.' I indicated the graves.

She planted herself in front of me, smiling impishly.

'Are they going to complain, do you think?'

'I doubt it, but it is convention – and a mark of a respect.'

'Respect,' she tilted her head to one side and her smile slanted with it. She swung round suddenly and addressed the graves she had just walked across. 'I'm sorry dead people. I promise not to do it again.' She faced me again. 'Is that better?' she laughed. 'You know, you are *very* conventional, Lawrence – for someone with such an unconventional life!'

'Not really, but I think rules are created for a reason. Go too far outside them and you're at risk. It's why society creates them, isn't it? To make sure we don't go too far out on a limb.'

'Perhaps, but rules are meant to be broken too, Mr Morally Compromised.'

'Are we debating sociology or discussing Danny?'

'Probably both – he's certainly outside the conventions of society, isn't he?' She exploded with laughter.

'Not that far. He's merely illegitimate.'

'Now – but once you thought far worse, didn't you? You weren't on your high horse then.'

'Things have moved on, and so it seems has Danny because he's missing from the children's home. I assume he's still with you? And this ransom note is of your doing? So what plan are we following now?'

'Missing? Ransom note? What are you talking about?' She moved closer.

'You must have read the note I left you or you wouldn't be here.'

'Well, of course I did.' She was surprised. 'But I don't understand.'

Now the surprise was mine. Maybe I'd been wrong after all?

'I put it in the note. Danny's missing and I've been sent a ransom note.'

She pulled away from me and fished around in her pocket. The note read,

"Need to meet urgently. Highgate cemetery: Edith Mary Juss, plot 3159. Saturday 11th 9am."

I handed it back to her.

'It's not the same note – even though the instructions are the same.'

'Damn! I knew I shouldn't trust him.'

'Trust who?'

'The tramp who plays lookout for John. He works for me too – or at least I thought he did. Fill me in – what's going on?'

'I went to visit Mary and whilst I was there, I was given a ransom note. It must refer to Danny. Two and a half million – conveniently identical to what your brother wants from me, isn't it?' I couldn't keep the sarcasm out of my voice. 'The drop is to be tomorrow. I'll be given further instructions later.'

She clapped a hand across her mouth and her eyes widened above it. The other hand pressed hard against my chest. For a split second I lost my balance. Distraction technique – she was good. Her voice was muffled when she eventually spoke.

'Oh my God, this is terrible.' Her nails were painted a deep black-red, much darker than the shade Heather had always hated and on the small snippet that must still be lying in the evidence bag amongst the papers Heather had appropriated from my drawer just before the explosion – wherever they were now. 'It means he knows.'

'I presume you mean Jaggers – John?'

'Who else?' She took a deep breath in and then let it out slowly. Her hand sought mine and squeezed, nails digging into my palm.

'So this wasn't your idea then?'

'Of course not,' she looked horrified. 'Why would you think that?'

'I thought Danny was with you – that's what you implied anyway.'

She shook her head.

'No.'

'Then we need to tell the police everything.'

She shook her head vigorously. 'No, absolutely not! We need a different plan. Damn! This is tricky.' She dropped my hand and paced the graves, still walking heedlessly across them. 'OK, here's what we do,' she announced eventually. 'You get the money as we planned originally, but I'll have to switch sides – or appear to. The game's up with John now if Frankie – the lookout – has told him what's going on. Frankie wouldn't have switched that note, but John would, so it means he now knows we're in contact.'

'Then the game's up altogether.'

'No, it's very much on – just approached from a different angle. John won't hurt him – yet. The danger will be later, after he has the money, so we'll have to be really clever how we play this.'

'We might as well play this out as intended then. Hand over the money and be done with it. At least we'll have Danny back.'

'But with no money,' she added ruefully. 'That's no good.'

'I don't care about the money. It's Danny's safety that's important, isn't it?'

'Oh, of course.' She looked affronted. 'But …'

'And we'll still have the evidence you've got.'

'Ye-s.' She sounded unconvinced. 'Until he comes after you again …'

'Well, we could play that off against him once we've got Danny back. Cards on the table – cold war; stand-off. Probably the best solution all-round, except for clearing Jonno's name.'

'Oh, I'm not bothered about that.'

I reeled inwardly.

'But I thought you wanted justice for him – and your sister?'

'I do, but you have to be realistic. They're not here any more.'

'So justice doesn't apply if someone is dead?'

'Oh, Lawrence, the dead are gone – the living are what matter. I want what's mine. That will be sufficient justice, I think – don't you? Natural justice.' She pulled me to her, taking the words of protest from my mouth with her kiss, as dizzying as the one outside Fulham Broadway Tube Station, but a part of me could stand aside now, observing. It saw the man, the woman, and the reaction; and also why it hadn't been present before.

The lighter was burning a hole in my pocket. I gently disentangled from her and leaned against a gravestone. Pulling the cigarette packet from my pocket, I took one out and put it between my lips, flicking ineffectually at the lighter.

'When did you start smoking?'

'When did all this start?' I replied ironically. 'Just no good with this damn lighter.' I held it out to her. The old Margaret would have treated me to a tirade about the effect on my heath. This Margaret took the lighter and flicked it expertly into life, staring into the flame as if mesmerised before holding it out to light my cigarette. As I dragged on the cigarette, controlling the urge to cough, she flicked it again. I held out my hand for the lighters return. She smiled at me and flicked it again, watching the little orange flame sputter in the gentle breeze for a while before it was extinguished. Only then did she reluctantly hand it back.

'Good job you're not an arsonist, although with all that fire retardant work done in the house, neither of us would be very good at it.' I laughed. She watched me pocket the lighter. 'In fact I've been meaning to ask you, why did you do that, Margaret?'

'What?'

'All the fire retardant work.'

She shrugged. 'Just how it happened - security, I guess.'

'But we weren't at risk.'

'Does it matter?'

'I'm curious.'

'You have to protect what's yours,' she dismissed my curiosity with the arrogance I was now becoming to associate with her.

'Is that all you've been doing all along? Not seeking revenge?'

'Revenge is best served cold, and at a distance, unless you want your fingers burnt.' She laughed sarcastically. The image of our burning house and the newspaper article that had presaged the press's plaguing of me danced in front of my eyes. It was almost too circumstantial – almost.

'And that's why you suggested we pretend the money is burnt – because if we stage it in the house, there's no real fire risk?'

'Ah, at last – you're catching on!' she smiled coquettishly. 'But I think we may have to amend that plan now. Go for something more traditional. And of course, I want what's mine. I lost my inheritance simply because two generations back my grandmother was conceived on the wrong side of the bedcovers. I'm about to lose the possibility of it again now. Danny – and you – are my way to get that back.' The trees bounding the clearing trembled as the breeze whipped up. '*Our* future, Lawrence,' she urged. 'Remember? That's what we agreed. Listen, this is what we need to do …'

I stubbed the cigarette out and listened carefully – like Mary did – and the undernotes of deception finally descanted above the notes of self-delusion. They say realisation breaks like a thunderclap, shattering the world around you. Not so for me. It came like a slow insidious slip of the sun from behind a cloud to reveal an unwanted whole. I stared into the void created by the jagged edge of reality piercing the pretty picture I'd previously created for myself. Truths, once acknowledged – no matter how undesirable – cannot then be undiscovered. I searched her face for proof I was wrong, but it wasn't there. Revulsion replaced disbelief, then anger. Even I, the habitually blind man, finally saw, whether he wanted to or not. My life had been full of graveyards and gravestones, dead and presumed dead for so long, I hadn't seen the living amongst them.

Her plan was to pretend to go along with the handover, then double-cross Jaggers at the last moment. I disputed with her, just to see how far she would go.

'But in that case shouldn't we recover the evidence before I go to the hand-over and simply give it to Fredriks? Our back-up plan in case Jaggers has another trick up his sleeve.'

She ignored the suggestion and addressed the challenge.

'This is my plan, Lawrence. *We* go to the hand-over.'

'But I'm the one paying the ransom – and it'll be dangerous.'

'All the more reason to let me plan it. You can't handle both Danny and the money. Whilst you're dealing with Danny I can keep an eye on the money.'

'You're his mother – wouldn't he be better with you?'

'No. He trusts you. And John will trust me. It will be more risky because John will suspect me after intercepting that note,' she made it sound as if it was my fault, 'but I'll find a way of persuading him to tell me about the kidnap and ransom so I appear to be helping *him* – although really I'll be helping you.'

Helping me. I wanted to laugh.

'And how will you do that?'

She pursed her lips. 'Probably using Uncle George. I'm meant to be monitoring the situation in Dubai – checking whether he gets any worse before John's realised the estate. I could pretend he's deteriorated and we need to act quickly. That'll mean John will either have to liquidate the stocks held in Uncle George's name – at a huge loss; everything's down at the moment because it's a bear market,' she grimaced, 'or tell me what he's up to. Well, of course he won't want to liquidate the stock, so I'll have a way in. I'll tell him I've been keeping an eye on you so you'd cooperate and then suggest he now lets me in on his plans properly – take control of the boy, for instance.'

'Danny,' I corrected.

'Danny, the boy – whatever.' She sounded irritated. 'He's the boy for John's purposes, Lawrence. I have to keep in role if I want to succeed.'

I let it pass, brain racing as well as heart.

'OK, what then?'

'Once you hand over the money, Danny will be handed to you. I will take charge of the money, and we'll rendezvous later at the tree.'

'And how will you explain to John that you have the money and he doesn't?'

'I won't need to. I'll tell him a different version of the same plan and that I'll rendezvous with him afterwards somewhere else.' She laughed wryly. 'You may not get much legal work afterwards, of course, but we'll have the Wemmick empire all to ourselves – via Danny – so who'll need it?' Her delighted trill set the birds fluttering like Mary's little mockingbirds.

'I still think we should collect the evidence now so everything is in place.'

'It's safer where it is.'

'And where is that?'

She shook her head and put her fingers to her lips but didn't reply.

'In a safety deposit box that the key with 119 on it will open?'

'Who told you that?'

'It wasn't difficult to work out.'

She wagged her finger at me teasingly and moved away with her normal exit line, 'Be in touch soon.'

I called her back. One last test.

'Have you got a safe house that you took Danny to when he went missing from the children's home?' I asked.

She stared at me, startled.

'A safe house?' she laughed. 'Are we playing spies too?'

'There's an empty building opposite Heather's. I could have sworn I saw you at the window there the other day. Were you? With Danny?'

'Oh dear, Lawrence – you'll be seeing ghosts next.' She laughed, artificially casual. 'Whoo!' She fluttered her fingers at me.

'There was definitely someone there. I thought it was you.'

'Not me,' she smiled sweetly.

'Or anywhere? Where do you go when you disappear?'

'I don't have a safe house anywhere, Lawrence – nowhere's safe for me, remember?'

'But you took Danny somewhere – you said you had when we met in

233

the churchyard.'

She shook her head vehemently.

'No I didn't. You must have assumed I had. Or maybe that was where John took him? John has all kinds of places dotted round the city. I only have under everyone's nose to hide.'

I let her have her way. She would anyway, and she was right; it *was* time for natural justice to have a hand in the proceedings. I watched her go in the lie with mixed feelings, knowing a turning point had been reached and passed. She'd had her day in court, and at least three opportunities to tell the truth. Now it was my turn to pass judgment. An honest man might assume that he must always act with complete honesty to achieve justice – but then what are little white lies for? A wise man uses all the tools at his command, whether that includes vindication or not, and natural justice is one of them. It's not perfect, but then neither is life. So now I had another choice to make: whether to be the honest man, or the wise one?

21: 27A

There remained just one last thing I needed to do to confirm my crazy theory, and that I wasn't as mad as I'd once thought Mary. Heather wasn't home – probably still in Chambers juggling figures and bottom lines. I felt a twinge of guilt but put it to one side. Anger stiffened my resolve. She hadn't retrieved her spare front door key from me yet so I used it to advantage, slipping quietly into her kitchen and collecting the keys to number 27 from the key rack. The road was as quiet as I could hope it to be, early afternoon home-lunchers having already returned to work and the other residents either settled in for afternoon tea or out teetering around the shops of the West End in designer gear and over-high heels.

I collected the crowbar Win had in his boot – old habits obviously died hard with him too – and let myself into number 27 as unobtrusively as I could, wrinkling my nose at the still present stench in the hallway. I looked apprehensively up the stairs, but that wasn't where I was going this time. I pushed the crowbar into place and trashed the lock to 27A. That was there I found the proof I was looking for.

The smell had pervaded everywhere. I put my hand over my nose and found the kitchen. The blinds were down but the reason for the smell became apparent as soon as I opened the door. Someone had let something go off – meat of some kind probably – and the room was full of buzzing, frantic blowflies and the sickly smell of decay. I recoiled in horror, my overactive imagination turning it into a rat – or worse; a horde of rats. I slammed the door shut just as I caught sight of something hot and red and flaming a warning at me, but it was in the lounge-diner I hit pay dirt. The curtains were drawn and it was difficult to see but it was silent there; no flies, no stinking vermin. Counting to ten to keep the anxiety darkness brought on in check, I waited until my eyes had adjusted to the low light. The table was littered with detritus – pencil sharpenings, a dirty tea plate, some scraps of paper and a small crumpled box. I ignored most of it, but two things confirmed every lie I'd ever been told: the careless doodle of the little hanged man swinging on a gallows, scrawled on one of the paper scraps, and the box. It must once have been home to the pencil I'd picked up off the floor in 27B. The product name was identical and inside, only one small sentinel was missing from the tidy row. A summary inspection of the other paper scraps made the final connection – childish multi-coloured writing. Danny's psychedelic attempts at recording what was happening in his world, just as I'd done once.

I debated whether to read them there and then, but what use was it to know my son's thoughts if he wasn't alive to share them with me? I pocketed the scraps instead – more evidence – and steeled myself to check out the kitchen. I opened the door from the kitchen to the lounge-diner and rushed back out into the hall, slamming the connecting door shut and waited for the exodus to complete. I gave it five minutes then risked opening the kitchen door a crack. The frantic cloud of buzzing insects had mostly diffused into the lounge so with one of Danny's multi-coloured diary sheets across my mouth I plunged into the kitchen and slammed the door between the kitchen and lounge shut again. The hall buzzed lazily with a handful of glutted and dozy bluebottles that had escaped when I first opened the kitchen door and I braved them to wedge the front door open so they could escape. Flies are remarkably stupid creatures. Even when there is an open space for them to escape into, they don't, they circle aimlessly, round and round the same old problem, unable to see any alternative. I'd been doing the same until now. I went back to the kitchen doorway, and there, facing me was an alternative I'd not considered before.

The power point for the cooker had been pulled off the wall and the wires left dangling. Electrician's tape like that on the cut wires of the camcorder in my kitchen was wrapped around them below a large red warning triangle. I squinted to read its cautionary advice, alerting me to the danger of live wires and the possibility of their combusting a local gas supply. I was still clutching the scrap of Danny's writing that I'd used to protect my face from the flies as the idea fell startlingly and terrifyingly in place.

"She told me Mr Big wanted me safe and I wouldn't be safe at the home. I asked her if that was all he said and she said it was. No code word." This was underlined. "But she's Mr Big's wife, even though she's meant to be dead, so she must be all right, mustn't she?

"We played a game called hangman. She won because she kept changing the rules. I said that wasn't fair. That was cheating. She said she wasn't cheating, just playing the game better than me. It's like playing football. You don't just stand there and hope the ball comes to you without doing anything. You duck and dive, trick your opponent and get the ball that way. You have to make your own luck – you don't have a guardian angel to do it for you. I laughed at that and showed her my birthmark and told her I did. She said she'd never seen anything like it before. Maybe I did have a guardian angel then, but I still had to make my own luck. Then she said I should trust her anyway because we were family of a sort – through Mr Juste. I thought about that. I trust him but she didn't say the code word, so I'm going to pretend to play along whilst I wait for it. Duck and dive. Is that all right Mr Big? I think he'd say yes."

He wrote the last sentence in yellow.

'Yes, Danny,' I said aloud. 'Mr Big would say yes. We've both got to duck and dive now.'

I left number 27, still partially numb with dismay. She'd never seen anything like it before? Margaret had seen my guardian angel every time I undressed, every time I merely bared my arms. She knew exactly what it was. On the other hand, the sister who'd supposedly died before I'd even met her didn't. The most unlikely piece of the jigsaw puzzle really did fit perfectly in the centre, and my crazy sister was far from crazy. Margaret wasn't Margaret at all. She was Rosemary, playing the role of Margaret with the same absolute confidence Mary had told me to utilise. Here was the magic Mary insisted existed – the woman who'd returned from the dead. No wonder Margaret hadn't worried about Rosemary's untended grave. No wonder she was prepared to use Danny for what she called natural justice in a way no caring mother would. No wonder she seemed so different to the woman I'd married that I wondered if I'd ever really known her at all. She wasn't the same woman.

So where, then, was Margaret?

My legs suddenly felt weak. The unexpectedly abandoned plan with Win probably answered that. I really had cremated my wife, after all. That meant she'd been murdered too.

I stumbled back to Win's car, sick at heart.

The only place I could think of to go to recover enough equilibrium to even consider my next move was the Common. I set off there unsteadily, thinking about ducking and diving, assumption and deception. The Common was the same as ever – green and peaceful – but everything else had changed. Everything. I found a quiet spot and sat in the dirt of the real world, as far off the path as possible. The birds still sang, the wind still blew, the sun still shone, but my world was as changed as it was possible to imagine. I couldn't bring myself to accept it at first. So Margaret was Rosemary and Rosemary was Margaret. For how long had it been so? Since Margaret had been killed, or longer? Now I came to think of it things had occasionally been oddly uncharacteristic of my dutiful and earnest wife for a while, but by then we were far from close – and definitely no longer intimate; even avoiding each other at times. And Heather had remarked on how Margaret could be plodding and dull one minute, quick-witted and devious the next. Would Margaret have had a fling with Jeremy? Certainly not. Would Rosemary? By all accounts, more than likely. But then where did Danny fit into this? Wasn't it me and my money she was after – presumably hand in glove with Jaggers, not plotting against him as she claimed? But of course – as Margaret's son, he was the Wemmick heir, and the only remaining male in the blood-line. With Margaret gone, someone had to claim him in order to make use of him – and who better than his real father, blindly manipulated by the woman he thought was his wife. The ransom was simply another way to milk me of whatever I had in case everything else went wrong. As she'd said, she had a plan B too, and I doubted either of us would figure in it for long once she'd got what she wanted via plan A. Danny would be milked of his claim on the Wemmick estate and then probably discarded, whether she and Jaggers were working in tandem or alone. He was a haemo-philiac, for God's sake. How difficult would it be to engineer a tragically premature death for him? And me? I was already set up to fail. Why not a tortured suicide note from me, the discredited liar and thief? My heart beat faster and my palms sweated. Then I was angry, head spinning with rage at the trickery, the deceit, the cold-blooded manipulation; the amorality that would use a sister and her child for pure materialistic gain, but eventually the common worked its magic. Rage softened to sadness and finally to one thought alone: I had to find a way to keep Danny safe.

I must stop them at all costs.

Wild thoughts spiralled into even wilder ideas. Maybe there was also vindictiveness in them too; to finish the game in a way that would make Rosemary suffer what Margaret – and Kimmy – had suffered. Subject her and Jaggers to the excesses they and I'd suffered at their hands over the years. I was still trying to figure out how when I finally eased myself to my feet because I had to return the keys to number 27 before Heather noticed they were missing.

Heather had already returned by the time I got back to her home. I cursed myself for not returning the keys before I'd high-tailed it to the Common, but I put Mary's advice to use and pretended self-absorption and there was precisely the Lawrence Juste that Heather, and everyone else, had been seeing for years. My credibility was perfected at last – in the role I'd been playing all my adult life – but Fredriks was playing tricky too, actually seeking my input for once, and Heather wasn't taking no for an answer on his behalf.

'But it's about the film. For him to ring and actually ask to see us is unheard of. Normally he demands. This time he asked. It must be important,' she insisted. I smiled inwardly. They'd make a perfect – if challenging – pair.

'He's learnt the efficacy of charm where you're concerned, Heather. That's all. You've been teaching him well, but sorting the money out is more urgent. You know why.'

The second warning message had arrived on my way back to her, much as I'd expected. The rat trap was set. I just had to walk into it to set one of my own.

'Yes, I know why, and I still disapprove. Talk to Fredriks. He can help.'

I couldn't let him keep me from the ransom exchange and my plan for the sake of good relations.

'I will, but I must do this first. Just this once, please?'

'It's always just this once, Lawrence,' she grumbled. 'Just because your brother's apparently off the hook, it doesn't mean the case is closed.' I shook my head apologetically. 'I haven't said anything about the partnership money to him yet ...' she added meaningfully.

I smiled openly this time. I knew to look beyond outer appearance now. Heather had her business head on, to cover up her private concern. I experienced a brief moment of guilt for not telling her I'd already recovered it and was about to give it away again, but Danny superseded all claims on my conscience. Heather had enough pairs of shoes and Jeremy enough girlfriends to keep them going for a while, and Francis would be looked after by his battle axe – but loaded – wife. All would eventually be well for them because of Heather's determination even if the money was never returned. I shook my head and got up to go.

'The insurance money first.'

She tried again. 'You're jumping the gun using that insurance money.

Unless you're thinking of taking off somewhere?'

I stopped in my tracks.

'No, of course not. I just want to make sure Danny is safe, but maybe it will be time to move on once this is sorted.'

'Where to?' She was incredulous.

'I don't know.'

'You're not suicidal, are you?' she asked suddenly. 'That would only mess things up even more. And we couldn't recover any of the money then. Insurance doesn't pay out on suicides, remember. Unless Margaret's thought of a new angle on that?'

'No angles, Heather. Really.'

The tiny seedling pushed its way through the compost of crazy ideas in my brain.

'Then you ought to hold out for what the house is really worth and talk to Fredriks.' She paused, and as if suddenly thinking of it, 'What does Margaret say about this ransom, by the way – or is she still merely a ghostly apparition?'

'She's playing her part as we speak.'

'Her part?'

'I'll explain when I can.'

The stuck record played again. 'Why don't you just tell Fredriks ...' I sighed. Heather was nothing if not persistent.

'Heather, please! I do know what I'm doing.'

'That'll be a first! Since when? Jesus, Lawrence, Fredriks actively wants to help and you aren't availing yourself of the opportunity even though you say Danny's being ransomed? It doesn't make sense. And on top of that you're rushing your insurance claim through for a fraction of what you could push for so you can hand it over to – who? What *is* going on – *really*?'

'Trust me.'

'Look in the mirror.'

'I have.'

'So've I and I don't like what I see.'

'It'll all be fine.'

'It had better be. The heat's up to boiling point. Careful you don't get burnt.' She pushed the newspaper spread out across her kitchen work surface towards me.

'*Will he, or won't he?*' it asked. Underneath, in the main body of the article was another list – not unlike the one Margaret had given me to begin with. It was composed of more questions I couldn't answer without exposing the whole truth and sacrificing myself on the altar of the press. I didn't need to, though. The reporter had answered most of them for me. No judge or jury. I was already damned, and of course now I knew both sources of damnation. The tiny seedling broke through its hard outer shell. I looked up to find Heather watching me sadly.

'And I ought to tell you there was a letter for you at Chambers. It had a seal on it so I brought it home to avoid snooping eyes.' Gregory, of course.

'Open it, then.'

'It's addressed to you.'

'I give you leave.'

There was a pause. She pulled the letter out of her bag and slit carefully along the top.

'Your HCJ appointment has been withdrawn and they're standing you down from the bar pending investigation.' I wasn't surprised, but she was. Her voice was suddenly small and distant, not the strident, harpy-like Heather of usual. 'Lawrence, you need to fight this. It isn't fair.'

'Natural justice will take its course.'

'Rubbish! I know you've been unwise, but you're not a criminal. Not in the truest sense of the word,' she added as an afterthought.

'So you think I'm innocent?'

'I've always thought you innocent, even when I thought you were guilty, you fool!'

I smiled gently at her, both happy and sad that the gift of clear sight had finally been granted me. I was right where Heather was concerned, at least; all bark.

'It will all work out, Heather. I promise, but I've got to go now. Win's waiting for the car back.' It was a lie, but I needed to be free to intercept the next call from the kidnapper and make some demands of my own. She let me go reluctantly and I drove back to Win's more slowly than I would normally have, savouring everything on the way – even the snarled up traffic, the interminable red lights and the jay walkers around Elephant and Castle. Funny how you only appreciate things when you're about to lose them.

Love is a fire, and it can burn and destroy if it isn't managed with care. I'd failed on both counts so far, but it can also cleanse and renew. Cleansing in order to start afresh; I liked that idea. Fire had been such a feature in my life recently too – the fire of passion and the fire of obsession. Maybe it was appropriate now to use it to clear the ground for future generations, particularly since I now knew so much about it, courtesy of the forensic report on my house. And there was a form of natural justice to it too – for Rosemary, at least, the woman who'd been so fascinated by it she'd even wanted to see what it felt like herself. Illogically it made me feel happier. However, like the papers had said, play with fire and you may also get burnt. Whatever plan I might come up with, inevitably I would have to be in the centre of the inferno to light the spark. The old order would have to be destroyed to enable the new to rise from the ashes, and Lawrence Juste was part of the old order, untrustworthy, shamed, and deceitful too – so the papers said. There was clearly no evidence ready to use against Jaggers. The box it had been in was empty. Maybe it had existed once, but in entrusting it to Mary, it had probably been entrusted to little better than the spirits of fire and air. And my other route to innocence? She was already dead – the wife I'd lost long before I thought I'd found her again. No, the only way out now was to burn off the stubble and allow the new seed to grow in its absence. One plan was intractably elbowing all others out of the way but there would be barely any chance of escaping the inevitable conclusion; accepting death to give my son life, unless I was very lucky – or very clever.

Back at Win's, I pumped him for information. Win thought he was merely reliving old glories, but in reality he was giving me a detailed lesson on how to remove doors from their hinges without resorting to a crowbar and be on the receiving end of a punch with minimum injury and maximum effect. In my head, my new forthcoming role was developing fast. I found the art of listening carefully, as Mary did, wasn't so difficult once you tried. Instead of the man, always partly on the wrong side of the law since youth, I saw the brother I'd lost since childhood, just before I lost him again. Even in my future absence, I knew I had to find a way to make things right with him one day.

'Why do you want to know?' he asked part-way through my lessons. 'Am I on trial? That why you're dressed posh,' he grinned, 'even though you still look like shit?' I cast a jaundiced eye over the now crumpled formal suit and askew tie I'd worn to meet the insurance adjuster. Lawrence Juste was all but gone.

'No, it's an education I should have got years ago. If I'm to become one of the criminal class, I may as well know the tricks of my new trade. And it passes the time.'

'Till what?'

'Till the kidnapper calls with my next message.'

'Oh.' He frowned, and began – somewhere not long after he'd left the children's home. He didn't refer to that, and neither did I.

I'd completed his course of almost forty years of delinquency in just under two hours when the call came through. By then I'd also come up with a working plan how to deliver natural justice to the woman who'd taken my wife and returned to take my son too.

I took the call outside, out of Win's hearing. I knew he'd insist on being at the exchange if he had the slightest inkling where it was to be. The instructions started with the usual preamble.

'Just listen. This is your final message.'

I may have learnt little about real people all those years defending and prosecuting them in court, but I had learnt about strategy, and it was high time I employed some of my own.

I cut across the voice. 'No, you listen. This is *my* final message. The exchange will be at a place of my choosing or I will bring in the police. And not all of it – one million only; the rest to an off-shore account in Danny's name tomorrow, when I know he – and I – are safe.' There a brief silence and I wondered if I'd pushed too hard too fast. I counted silently to twenty, regretting not having brought in Fredriks after all. If I'd told the police, they would have been well on the way to getting a fix on the caller's location by now. On the verge of twenty-one, panic joined guilt. The voice cut through it, irritated.

'If you do that, you won't see the boy again ...' he pause was planned for maximum effect, 'alive.' The threat calmed me. Their response was too obvious and left them nowhere to go if I refused to cooperate.

'And you won't get your money. But you will get the police onto you with three murder charges. Do I need to name the other two victims? And if I'm already damned, it won't matter what I do to make them stick, will it?'

The pause was slightly less this time.

'Where?'

'My place.'

'It's out of bounds.'

'When did that stop you? The back way, so we're not seen.'

'You'll be informed what is decided.'

Be informed what was decided? Oh, no. I knew who was making this call – all the calls in this game – now.

'No, you'll be there.' I sounded more certain than I felt.

'And how is the offshore account going to be set up? Who will the signatories be and the access details?'

'It will be Molly Wemmick and Lawrence Juste as guardians of Danny Hewson. I will sign over my authority when we're both safe.'

'How do I know you won't go back on that?'

'You'll already have a million in cash and you can keep me until it's completed. Do I sound like I have a suicidal tendencies?'

I counted to twenty again in silence.

'Ten o'clock this evening then.' The caller clicked off.

Ten o'clock. Not much time. No dithering now. I had to get on with it.

'So?' Win was on me as soon as I went back indoors.

'Just told me to get everything sorted ready for final instructions.'

'Jesus. This is getting to me! I don't like sitting on me thumb waiting.'

'You don't have to. I need you to help me with something and there isn't much time to do it in.' I sank into the orange-puke-flower settee, pretending exhaustion. 'Can you go shopping for me?'

'Shopping? You need Emm for that – or your bitch lady from hell. They know about clothes.'

'Not that kind of shopping. Toy shopping.' I told him what I wanted and why. A smile of malicious amusement spread across his face, before it overshadowed with worry.

'But what about when they find out?'

'It'll be too late then. And I have another plan to deal with that little problem should it arise before it *is*.' I handed him a hundred pounds from my wallet. It cleared me out, but I had to visit the bank to clear *it* out shortly. 'That should do it.'

'Money for nothing. Like it,' he said. 'Anything else?'

I looked at my watch. It was now a little past four.

'Just be back here by early evening – say six-thirty. Just in case. And I'll need your car again, is that OK?'

'What's mine is yours, as long as what's yours is mine.' He winked and threw me the car keys. 'And given what you got, that's a lot – but I'll still skin you if she comes back dented.' He shuffled off, whistling tunelessly. It sounded like 'Money, Money, Money,' or an off-key version of it – much like my plan.

***

It's surprisingly easy to remove a fortune from a bank. I walked in empty-handed, played my role with absolutely confidence, reminding myself all the time why I was doing it in case at any point I stumbled over my words. We calmly counted and stacked the notes, the bank manager and I; crisp, red, fifty pound notes that made small satisfying thumps as the stacks were dropped into the second fire-proof case I'd acquired from the same firm that had provided Margaret – or maybe Rosemary – with the original. Five hundred thousand in twenty five neat rows each of twenty-thousand; virtually unheard of, but my name and standing still had just enough clout to get away with it – for now. The instruction to wire the remaining £1.5 million to the off-shore account on my say-so was my back-up. The security guard respectfully escorted me to Win's car, even politely carrying the suitcase for me; banks are nothing if not helpful.

I sat in the driver's seat, relishing the moment before descending into hysterical laughter. I could disappear and never be seen again, with a million pounds spread between the two cases in the boot of the car. I felt as furtive as if they contained body parts. And in a way they did. I straightened my tie, reminded myself again why I was doing this, and drove away. As I drove, other questions and possibilities lined up – probably never to be answered. The evidence Margaret had supposedly once had on Jaggers; had it once lived in the other fire-safe case the partnership money now resided in? Was that why Margaret had gone to such lengths to fire-proof the house? Against an accident or arson? A threat from Jaggers or Rosemary? Had that been why she'd wanted Win to look after it and eventually given it to Sarah? I shook my head. Maybe it didn't matter anymore. Like Atticus had found, and Mary had claimed – you didn't need to know all of the truth to know the truth nevertheless.

I spent just over an hour in the library, reading every technical report on the causes and control of house fires I could find. I was surprised to find how it breathed life into almost forgotten lessons from school – the chemical reaction that creates an inferno; hell on earth. Oxygen, carbon, carbon dioxide, water vapour, heat and rage. The way to finally put an end to the injustices that had been with me nearly all my life.

I drove from the library to the mews to meet the Electricity Board engineer I'd persuaded to sanction restoring the power. It was already past six and Win would probably be back before me, but this was my last errand. The mews seemed deserted – certainly the houses in the immediate vicinity of mine did. The neighbours either side hadn't moved back in yet, nor had the ones opposite – police tape still sealing off their doors, apart from the old dear at number six who must have been back to tidy up by the look of the new curtains. I made a mental note to check there was no-one home at number six before ten o'clock struck, just in case. The engineer arrived ten minutes later, checked the forensic report was genuine, isolated the circuit for the study and okayed the rest.

'Be back on in about an hour,' he promised as he left. I followed him out, making a show of locking the front door in case I was being watched and returned via the back way with my newly acquired bag of tricks. Everything was as we'd left it. I put my bag down on the counter top and got to work, feeling cautiously around in the cavity where the security camera had previously sat to find the gas pipes first. My memory of what the place had been like before the refurb was surprisingly good. They were positioned more or less as I remembered them, but before tackling them I stood in the centre of the room and played out the scene in my head. Then I used Win's crowbar to loosen the pipe fixings, re-tightening afterwards. The gas seep was minuscule, but by ten o'clock it would have reached saturation level.

Next came the contents of my bag of tricks. I positioned Win's lighter and the soaked towel where I calculated I would easily be able to reach them later, whatever occurred beforehand. The kitchen door, I took off its hinges, carefully following Win's lesson plan, but left propped shut, every word of the text book explanation of the mechanics of a fireball going round and round in my head. The bulb in the overhead light I replaced with a dud, already blown. Then I completed the final details. Hands sweating and heart pounding, I carefully removed the electrician's tape from the wires of the removed security camera, and exposed the live wires.

Slipping quietly out of the back door and back to Win's car, the last leg of the journey was the worst, soaked through to the lining of the jacket with sweat, and stomach heaving and yawing like a sinking boat as I finally allowed myself to think about what I was doing and the consequences if it went wrong. As it turned out, Win was late and I arrived back ten minutes before he did – just enough time to splash my face with cold water again, and air the sweat patches under my arms, reminding myself again why I was doing this. I owed my wife, I owed Jonno, I owed my son. Not much longer to go.

Win slung the bags on the putrid settee as he came in, still in high spirits.

'They thought I was fucking mad. Thought the shop assistant was going to refuse to serve me to begin with but I told them it was for a fancy dress party, and the theme was gambling.' I smiled at the irony. The theme indeed was gambling. However, I still needed Win out of harm's way, but in position for the role he didn't yet know he was going to play. I let him into the secret – or allowed him to think I had.

'Now we need to put this lot in a suitcase before I get the final instructions.'

'You really going to hand this lot over?'

'Yes.'

He shook his head.

'I hope you know what you're doing,' but he helped me stack the toy money into the fire-proof suitcase I'd retrieved from the mews nevertheless. On the top layer was the real McCoy. Win handled them lovingly, stroking each stack into place.

'Seems a shame to even give him this much,' he commented eventually as the last doctored bundle plugged the gap between reality and fiction.

'Ever heard the phrase "give a little to gain a lot"?'

'Nah, sounds like something fishy you legal boys would say, though. Bit like your red herrings – anything to tie the ordinary bloke up in knots until he's run up a bill.'

I laughed. 'Well this time I'm paying the piper, not calling the tune, unfortunately – but only with a portion of what they're demanding: the little. And I'll re-gain a lot: Danny.'

'You sure they won't check it?'

I looked at the case. 'I'm sure – apart from the top row.'

'But it ain't the whole lot is it? What'll happen when they find out you double-crossed them?'

'They won't.'

He stared at me, disbelieving.

'It's toy town money. Soon as they look under the top row, they'll see that.'

'Who says they're going to get the chance to look?' *Or Molly was going to get the chance to access the off-shore account without Lawrence...*

I clicked the case shut before Win was tempted to remove any of the notes, beckoning him away from it and sending him down the road on the pretext of refuelling the car.

'In case I need to make a quick getaway,' I explained. He believed me. My pretence of being this new Lawrence Juste, no matter how much I was quaking inside, was obviously becoming extremely successful. Whilst he was out I tucked the rest of the contents of my bank account, together with the partnership money, in the new suitcase I'd collected the money from the bank in, with a note for him and Heather. Natural justice to be retrieved later. Now I'd kept my promise - at last materially.

It didn't take him as long to fill up the car as I'd expected and I'd only just hidden the money when he returned. My face felt hot and damp again and my shirt was sticking to my back and under my arms.

'You nervous?' he asked me suddenly.

'Wouldn't you be?'

'Shitting it!' he replied. He grinned sheepishly. 'Bloody coward, me, but I don't think you are, and I do think you're up to something. You wouldn't be me brother – or a brief – if you weren't.'

'Win, I ...'

'You don't have to tell me. I trust you. You're me little brother – and me mate. But I reckon you already know when you're doing the drop, don't you? Just tell me what I've got to do and I'll do it. It's for you and Danny. That's enough.'

The back of my throat ached.

'Drop me off at the mews and wait by the garages at the back of it.' I sounded gruff and hoped he'd attribute it to nerves. 'Ring this number and make sure no-one answers. If they do tell them they have to get out of there straight away because another fire risk has been identified.' I gave him the phone number for number six that directory enquiries had helpfully supplied me with after visiting the mews earlier.

'Has it?'

'I don't want anyone around just in case of trouble.'

'OK.' He looked uncertain. 'What then?'

'I'll send Danny out to you as soon as I get him away from them. Beep the horn three times once he's in the car with you and then drive like stink to somewhere safe. Heather, probably.' He raised his eyebrows and looked comically tragic. 'Sorry.'

He gave me a wry grin. 'Whatever. And you?'

Now would be the time to tell him how things had changed for me and I finally understood what 'family' meant, but maybe that would be too much to ask of him – or me. I clapped him clumsily on the shoulder and he reciprocated.

'I have a different exit route planned.'

22: Game's End

I wasn't sure I was going to be able to walk in there to begin with. Although it was my own home, it was pitch black, and worse, I knew what I was walking into. Worse than rats in the cellar, worse than spectres in the graveyard, worse than losing everyone I loved – worse than death. Fear. The bile rose in my throat and burnt it raw. I repeated my mantra – all the names, all the reasons, over and over again until my breathing steadied and my pulse slowed enough to slip the key in the lock of the back door for the last time.

The torch beam cut a wedge of muted yellow though the black, turning the usually sterile and functional room into a chamber of horrors. The bar stools loomed at me like monsters, waiting to attack, and the long-flexed ceiling lights hung predatorily overhead like vultures. Between them was the place designated for the suitcase and me: the killing zone, and me the bait. I put the case down and touched my hand to my pocket. The bump of steel against my thigh was still comforting. It gave me the courage to step all the way into the gloom, shuffle cautiously past the stools and on to the hall and the front door. I unlocked the door and left it wedged the tiniest bit ajar. The combustion feeder. Then I returned to the mid-point between the stools via the counter top with the bowl and the sodden towel in it. I tested again. It was still at arm's reach. So was the lighter. This was it.

I flicked off the torch and waited for my eyes to adjust to the dark, counting off the seconds in time with the thump, thump, thump of my heart. I recalculated the trajectory whilst I waited, shifting fractionally to one side and then back again. Forget it. A few inches either way weren't going to matter. Was the towel wet enough, or the leak sufficient to combust? Damn. I wished I could have asked someone – but who would I have asked? A professional arsonist? How many of them advertised for commissions? I stopped torturing myself and listened instead, repeating my check list in my head – as if I could forget any part of it.

Footsteps first, then a low voice. Jaggers. I'd know his dulcet tones anywhere. A shadow moved across the door. The figure behind the obscured glass came closer. The key was in the lock, handle turning. The door swung open.

'Come in,' I welcomed.

'Is it Hallowe'en already? He asked sarcastically. 'Or do you like playing games too? Did you ever play murder in the dark as a kid?'

'That would be a good one for tonight.'

'Ha-ha. But who will get murdered?'

'I don't know yet. Shame we haven't a camcorder to record it again this time.' With eyes now fully adjusted to the lack of light, I could make out other figures behind him – one small and hesitant, the other slim and elegant. Danny and Rosemary; or maybe Molly, tonight. I juggled with what to call her in my mind. Rosemary – that was who she really was. Let's have some truth finally. I wondered what she'd told Danny this time.

'Can we have some light?'

'It'll draw attention to us and I'm sure you don't want that, do you – unless you don't trust the colour of my money? But here,' I threw the torch at him, heard it collide and his muffled curse as he fumbled the catch. He turned it on and aimed the beam straight at me, and then at the suitcase on the floor. 'Shut the door please, then we'll get on with things.'

'Mr B...' Danny's small frightened voice cut through the gloom and my heart squeezed in a painful irregular rhythm.

'It's all right, Danny. Just do as I tell you to. Go straight back out the door again and run to the garages at the end of the mews when I say to. There's a big black BMW there with your Uncle Win in it. Get in and go with him.'

'But ...'

'I think we have one or two things to sort out first, haven't we?' Jaggers remarked dryly, cutting across Danny's confusion. Rosemary's slim silhouette moved across the doorway behind him, like a storm cloud moving into position over the moon, blocking the way out. She pulled Danny in front of her and hushed him.

'Let's get on with it then.'

I balanced the suitcase on the bar stool, dialled in one-one-nine and flipped the locks. Their sharp little clicks sent a shiver down my spine, paranoid that even the noise could create a spark.

Play the game. Stay in role. Don't lose it now.

It didn't. I swung the lid up and displayed the contents of the suitcase. Jaggers shone the torch across it.

'And underneath?'

I lifted one of the stacks from the top layer to reveal more of the same, then another and another.

'Trust me, I'm hardly likely to play games, given what's at stake.'

'All right. Hand it over then.' He held out his hand, beckoning impatiently. I ignored the gesture.

'Danny leaves first.'

'I'll take him,' Rosemary volunteered.

'No, you stay where you are. Danny leaves. When he's reached the car, Win will beep the horn three times and then I'll hand over the money.'

'Pantomime! I love it!' Jaggers laughed sarcastically, flashing the torch light directly at me and then at Danny. 'Go on then, kid – you heard the man – run, rabbit, run!'

Rosemary remained blocking the back door, barring it.

'I should go with him,' she said. 'At least until I know you've got all the money.'

'It's OK,' Jaggers threw over his shoulder at her. 'Win'll do what I tell him to if he knows what's good for him, and we've got our *benefactor* here until he completes the deal. He knows what's good for him too. Let the kid go and then find the bloody lights.'

I watched the back door open and shut, a blurring of dark against dark as the small figure paused on its threshold.

'Mr Big?'

I knew his uncertainty was not with me but with leaving me.

'It's all right Danny. This is the right thing to do. Like we agreed in Eastbourne. Go.' He hesitated only a second and then ran. I could hear his feet pitter-pattering across the cobbles on the way to Win's car – or maybe I imagined them in my need for him to be safe. The back door swung shut behind him with a neat little click which signified that it had locked as it was intended to. There was a distant sound of a car door opening and slamming shut and then three blasts on a horn.

'Your signal, M'lud,' Jaggers announced sardonically. He moved closer and held out his hand again. I shut the suitcase with a soft click but kept hold of it.

'So have you always planned this?' I looked past him and the torch light, to Rosemary. The torch sputtered and died.

'What the fuck?'

I could hear Jaggers shaking the torch to try and revive it. I could have told him it was useless. I'd expected it to last marginally longer – but not much. It had been on almost continuously since early afternoon and I calculated that eight hours battery life had long since dwindled to twenty minutes or so, maximum, by the time I'd thrown it to him.

'Margaret? Molly? Or maybe you'd prefer your real name, Rosemary?'

She didn't reply immediately, hovering hesitantly just behind Jaggers – the storm cloud gathering malice. Without the torch light my eyes adjusted quickly to the gloom again. Theirs would take longer – and they didn't know where everything was either. I could tell Jaggers had swung round to look at her by the change in the shape of his bulk. He turned back to me and I marked the position of his hands as a dancer would spot as she pirouetted, bracing myself for the assault. My marker, the lion's head ring, was a dark blip in the ghostly pale on his right hand. I kept it on the periphery of my vision as I waited for her to reply. It came at first as a slow hand clap, then sarcasm.

'So you've figured it out at last. Clever Lawrence – although I must say I think Margaret overrated your intelligence. I'd expected you to work it out much sooner, given your supposed brilliance. But perhaps that's just in court?'

'Maybe we don't see what we don't want to until we can no longer ignore it. But why?'

'Oh dear. You want the whole *mea culpa*?' Jaggers drawled. 'The courtroom drama in your kitchen?'

'Why not? We've got time to kill – and isn't that what is usually granted the condemned man? His last request?'

'And are you condemned?'

'Aren't I? There's only me between you and the money now. How am I going to stop you taking it? Indulge me. Tell me the real truth, not the truth we've all been presented with until now.'

'If that's your last request be my guest. Rosemary, do you want to do the honours?'

She stepped forward then. I couldn't see her face but I could imagine it. The deep blue eyes, the luxuriant blonde hair, the feistier, more determined chin than I remembered on Margaret – perhaps not a prosthetic addition as she'd claimed, but the real Rosemary. Bolder, brighter, more beautiful than Margaret – but cruel. The one you didn't forget when she walked into the room. The one who'd turned my head once she took over where her dead sister had left off, and made me wonder how I'd missed the siren attraction of my wife all these years. I hadn't. I'd missed her sister.

She sighed melodramatically.

'Poor Lawrence. So prosaic. That letter I wrote for you was mostly truth. All the rubbish about how Margaret got herself knocked up and managed to marry you was true. And we are Wemmicks. Jonno was a nuisance, always trying to muscle in on the act, especially when he found out about our little plan to kill me and Margaret off so we could finally get Uncle George to name John as heir in absence of any other male. It seemed appropriately ironic that we should set him up with my murder on the understanding we'd cut him in when we got the money if he kept his mouth shut.'

'The murder was risky, wasn't it? Why invite attention?'

'More like to avoid attention. The death was real enough – some little junkie who'd run out of steam in the night club toilets, and we had to do something with the body. Turn your disadvantages to opportunities, they say, don't they? We turned her into me and got the ball rolling. It had to start sometime – why not then?'

I listened but the words flowed over me, intent on remaining alert for the moment I knew would come. She continued virtually without pause – showing off as Mary had described her doing.

'Margaret became awkward though, going on and on about it not being right. To begin with it was just who was the girl? And who was going to be saddled with her murder? She didn't like our choice – argued with John about it so he had to make doubly sure of the conviction. That shut her up for a while, but then she was back on it after he got knifed in prison. She just wouldn't leave it, but having manoeuvred herself into being your wife, she'd very cleverly put herself out of our reach. It was becoming a problem until I found out about the kid – sly little cow.'

'Through Kat?'

'Yes, the little social worker you lust after so. That was Margaret trying to play me at my own game by turning FFF into a *reputable* charity – and losing. See – it's what twins do. They compete. They say they want to be individuals but that's only true of the stronger one. The weaker one always secretly wants to be their twin.'

I wasn't sure that was true of Emm and Jill. My twin sisters were as different from each other as imaginable, and I couldn't envisage any circumstances under which either of them would want to be each other, but then neither of them appeared to be psychotic.

'Insider knowledge – that was what we needed. By being my dearly-departed sister, I could get it. Dear Kat wasn't sure what to make of us – the composite us, that is. She thought we were both Margaret. She asked me about Danny not long after I'd started to play Margaret/ Molly and then the cat really was out of the bag.' She laughed at her own witticism; the sound of broken glass scattering across a bloodied tarmac road. 'She was easy enough to control once we had the brother in tow. Like a little lamb to the slaughter, although she did start to get a touch tricky after she'd met you, so we had to turn the screw then and drag Fredriks into it. It's amazing what the minutest amount of pressure at the right moment can do to logic. Brother or lover? I'll give you she was torn, but that type of woman caves in to responsibility every time, even if she doesn't want to. She's like Margaret in that. Of course they won't find anything wrong with her brother's case. Your bitch of a partner wouldn't ever countenance anything dodgy, but it set you all nicely at each other's throats for a while, didn't it?'

'Ella set us at each other's throats, not Kat – was she part of your scheming too?'

'She's ambitious. She'd already worked out that with you out of the way there'd be a place just crying out for her. She'll go far with auntie's backing. She didn't need to be part of our scheme. She's merely making hay at your expense, Lawrence. That's what you have to do with people – turn their agenda back on them.'

'Is that what you did to Margaret?'

'Yes, she thought we'd believe she was still going along with our original plan but she could double-cross us; get you to adopt the kid and then – ta-dah! His real identity would be revealed via you, high-profile, and she could come out of hiding and point the finger at us from the safety of being the latest scoop for the press. She was thinking big – I'll give her that. Trying to copy me. She always tried to copy me but never quite managed it.'

'And the hit and run was for real, not the set-up she practised with Win?'

'Of course – once we'd got him off the scene. I had a very convincing 'Margaret' argument with him and sent him off in a huff.' She laughed throatily and I clenched my fists.

'So you killed off Jonno, Margaret and Kimmy, all just for money?'

'A lot of money, Lawrence,' she corrected.

'No amount of money is worth taking a life.'

Her dry sneer slid through the dark at me like I'd imagined the rats would have done in the cellar.

'Hear that, John? The man's clearly forgotten what it's like to be poor, hasn't he – the dregs of society. The Wemmick money should have been mine if it hadn't been for outmoded conventions and male dominance. Now it will go to some snivelling kid simply because I'm a woman.'

'But it's not just the Wemmick money involved here. It's people's lives – your sister, Kimmy, Jonno. What have they ever done to warrant this? What have I, or Danny done?'

'It's nothing personal, old chap,' Jaggers replied smoothly. 'You're just in the way.'

'It is personal,' Rosemary disagreed coldly. 'You fathered the little brat, now you can pay for him too.'

'So now what? When you've got the rest of the money? What happens then?' I didn't need to ask. Jaggers slid himself from his lazy slouch. I could tell he'd moved from the intensification of the shadow near me.

It was now.

In the gloom, I located the two pale shapes that were his hands. They looked like silver butterflies, flitting towards me. I silently let go of the suitcase. Its balance on the bar stool was precarious but only I knew that. Only the thin grey of twilight though the glass panel of the back door lit the room, and that was partially obstructed by Rosemary. I could see both of them in silhouette, but they would barely be able to see me at all in the shadows.

'What difference does it make?'

'I may object.'

'You're hardly in a position to, Lawrence, *old chap*.' Jaggers' voice was silky. I imagined the expression on his face – the same expression as when I'd confronted him in the snooker hall just before Danny's trial. 'The papers are already questioning your honesty. Your charming brother may have got off the hook with that security video, but a little creative editing has replaced him with you perfectly. As he left, now you arrive. Body doubles – so handy, aren't they? Just like they do in real films. Have the police been in touch yet? Might not have spotted it immediately – it was made to look as if it had been doctored to remove you, not insert you, but forensics should be thinking they've discovered a cover-up any time now...' He laughed and it sounded over-loud in the dark. 'So good of you to tip Rosemary the wink about it, by the way.'

The invitation from Fredriks – not being polite; being canny to get me back into the police station without revealing what he'd found ...

The silver butterfly with the dark smudge of tiger claw ring moved towards me. I slipped my hand in my pocket and curled the fingers round the flick-knife, ready for the first blow. *Bastard! Think you're so clever...* His hand reached mine just as the knife flicked open and our combined momentum took the blade clear through his palm. I felt the impact along my arm, jangling every nerve in my body. It happened in complete silence until the bunch of my fist grasping the handle of the knife met the warm flesh of his palm and the knife exited the other side. Then he screamed; a scream that pierced my brain and made my ears ring. In the dark, I knew I was grinning like a maniac. Rosemary's dark outline moved towards us at speed, shouting, 'What's happening?' whilst Jaggers and I were conjoined; Siamese twins bonded by the knife.

He roared and swung at me, the second silver butterfly taking a rush of air past my head, but missing me by inches. I had to get free; duck and dive until I could reach the lighter and the towel. I yanked at the knife, feeling it edge its way grindingly through skin and tendon until it met bone. Jaggers' screaming was making my head spin; high-pitched and wailing, like a banshee, but it still felt good – all the pent-up years of my frustration and anger and fear encapsulated in his screams.

'Christ! John – what's happening?' Rosemary's voice was high and panicky.

I focused all my strength on the knife and we see-sawed until the dull click of metal on metal signified the knife had met the ring. The stool next to me clattered and fell. Rosemary. *Bitch!* Stumbling past me. I ducked Jaggers flailing left hand and grabbed the thin grey slivers that had to be the fingers of the impaled one, catching only his fingertips, writhing and twisting until the knife suddenly jerked free.

'Get the fucking lights on!' he shrieked. I fell sideways, colliding with the other bar stool, and knocking the suitcase onto the floor. Rosemary tripped over it, cursing.

'What the fu— What's this? The suitcase skidded across the floor and rebounded off the base units under the breakfast bar opposite with a heavy thud. 'Jesus, it was the money!' She hesitated and I could smell her perfume mixed with the sweat of fear. 'John, for God's sake, what's happening? Where are you?'

'The bastard's knifed me! Get the fucking lights on,' he shouted, wheeling away from me as I pulled the knife clear and something else soft and wet came with it. 'Ah, my hand – ahh!' In my hand, bone sharp against ragged flesh, ring clamping the end tight like the gasket on a pipe, was what I realised then was his finger. I gagged, but held on tight. 'Forget the bloody money. Get the fucking lights on so I can kill him.'

I heard the sound of her footsteps across the floor. She would reach the switch within seconds. Panic speeded everything up so her footsteps, Jaggers' curses and my pounding heart combined to produce a mêlée of noise and in the middle of it, me; counting down in despair. *I hadn't got the towel yet!* I clenched my hand into a fist and the ring slipped from the finger and stuck to my palm whilst the mangled wedge of flesh slid into the void somewhere. Jaggers was still shouting, 'The lights; the fucking lights!' I retched, and the bar stool on the other side of me clattered against the suitcase as someone – it must have been me – lurched against it.

'I'm trying, for God's sake! Shut up, will you?' Rosemary screamed back at him.

I dropped the knife and pushed the ring on my finger. Evidence. What evidence? It wouldn't make any difference now…

"…would appear to be fragmen…. eye stone in place. The unique des… nd stone undoubtedly tally with … in question … marking caused by the results of liv …"

Evidence, my brain disputed.

The forensics report on the ring.

Mary had it.

It was one of her little birds – her little mockingbirds. The little birds she said one day she'd make sing for me. The moment was simultaneously sweet and bitter.

Too late – all too late, unless...

I reached across to where the bar stool had been to find the empty space. My marker was gone. I felt frantically along the counter top for the bowl and the soaked towel. It wasn't there. Christ! It wasn't there. I slid my hand desperately along the counter as the countdown in my head continued. It came up against the hard edge of the bowl just as the click of the light switch made its icy journey of terror down my back. *But I still hadn't got the towel!* I waited for the world to burst into light but nothing happened.

257

'Come on,' he bawled almost into my face, banging into the bar stool on the other side of me. 'What the fuck are you playing at Ro?'

Now I had it.

My fingers crept over the edge of the plastic bowl and found the wet towel. I grabbed at it and the bowl came too, soaking me with tepid water.

I felt cold and dank, like in the cellar.

It was dark, like the cellar had been.

I was back in the rat hole, shivering and blubbing and desperate to escape.

'There are two. It was the wrong switch. I've got it now.'

No, not the rat hole! The inferno. Focus! I had to get the towel around my head before...

Cool logic slipped into place. My heart still pounded but the determination to survive took over, as it had all my life. I slapped the towel roughly over my head and across my face as I launched myself at what I judged to be Jaggers' middle. My rugby tackle hit him mid-gut like a juggernaut into a shop window and the air expelled from him in a surprised 'uh'. He wasn't expecting it or me. He lost his balance and the force of my momentum took us to the the floor. He landed heavily on top of me, like a felled tree, covering my turbaned head with his torso but dislodging the towel as he fell. One tiny portion of my face was still exposed but his weight crushed me flat. I struggled to free my arm, but couldn't. I buried my face into the floor instead and carried on counting; waiting for her to find the second switch – the one that connected not to the blown light bulb, but to the cut wires of the camcorder. And the spark to the leaking gas.

I reached twenty in muffled isolation before I heard it – or maybe I didn't actually hear the tiny click of the switch, because the towel would have deadened it, but I saw the first flash of the spark light through the gap where the towel had been dislodged. Instinctively I squeezed my eyes shut and held my breath like I had as a child when I was afraid.

At various times in the past I've watched the old films of the first atomic bomb explosions – the blinding white light followed by the mushroom cloud and then the descending darkness as the ash and nuclear fallout cloak the earth below. The part of me that wanted to see if that was how it really happened – the knowing that can only be known with annihilation – battled the vain hope of survival, but the instinct to survive naturally won. I'm only guessing now how it looked; the spark from the current coursing through the live camcorder wire and igniting the floating gas cloud; the spark blooming to brilliant blue flame, and then imploding in on itself. Finally, the ball of white hot rage searing everything in its path; raging along the unprotected side of my face until surely all I could possibly have left was my skull, seared of all flesh. I'd done my best, and played all the odds in my favour with Jaggers sprawling full length across my supine body. My assailant had become my bodyguard instead, and whether I survived or not, all my calculations – even with my head bursting and my blood bubbling – told me that there were two people in the direct path of the fireball who couldn't. Not even with the help of a miracle.

The last thought that slipped through my mind as the flames swept across me and my human shield as hell tickled my feet, accompanied by a satisfaction I hadn't ever felt before, was:

'... *and that, Rosemary, is natural justice* ...'

23: Choices

I was floating and numb; cold – so cold. I touched my face to see if it was still there. It felt rough, fabric rough. Why was I encased in fabric? Then I remembered. The fire. I must be dead and in my shroud ready to be buried. No, not buried, cremated. I'd always said I'd be cremated when it came to it. The irony made me want to giggle, then scream. God Almighty, but if I was conscious then I was still alive! How could I touch what should be my face, or think, if I wasn't? I must be encased in my opulently padded coffin, still conscious, and awaiting the slow slide through the flames into eternity. My legs tingled. The furnace could already be blazing just feet away from me. I tried to call out, shout that they were going to cremate a living man, but the covering over my face made it difficult to make any kind of noise. I struggled desperately against it, finally managing to lift my hand clear of the coffin in protest, only for it to wave uselessly in the air like the Pope's blessing to the masses. I could see it through the bindings over my face. The ring had seared into the skin, embedded like an embossing stamp and the back of my hand was blackened and taut-skinned. I stared at it and the loosely woven bandages extending as far as my wrist, wondering why the ring was on me and not Jaggers. The hand that caught mine and took it gently back down to meet my floating body was white and soft.

'It's all right. You're in hospital. You're badly burned and it's going to be a long way back, but you'll get there.' I didn't recognise the voice. I tried to protest, but nothing came out. She soothed me again. 'Your throat is scorched. You'll find it difficult to talk for a while – and we've only just removed the intubation tube but each day it'll be a little easier. Rest now. It's good to see you awake.'

I focused in on the hand clasping mine and then widened my field of vision sufficiently to see a pleasant-faced nurse, looking kindly down on me before turning to adjust a monitor and tweaking a valve attached to a long snaking tube. A pleasant flow of warmth crept over me and she drifted into the distance, leaving me with my memories and my dreams – or maybe they were the same.

She was right. It did get easier by the day. And clearer. I marshalled all the memories as they came back to me and mentally divided them between fact and confusion until I had two boxes completely filled with them. Then I put the lids on both and lay back to ponder. The form of address the nurses and doctors used for me wasn't the name I thought I'd owned. So who was I?

John, they called me. John Smith? John Doe?

No. It slowly dawned on me as the days passed. John Wemmick. They thought I was John Wemmick, self-styled modern-day hero and philanthropist. The man who'd wanted to destroy me. The irony of it all was that *I* had destroyed *him* – and Rosemary – and now didn't know what to do about it.

24: Supposition

'Seems we'll have to go with supposition then? Shall I tell you mine?'

'Please do,' I invited, steeling myself for my nemesis in the guise of DCI Fredriks. His duck pout pursed into a small round hole I imagined being sucked into. I set the morphine pump apparatus to one side. I needed my wits about me right now.

'OK, you, a female companion by the name of Molly Wemmick, Lawrence Juste and Danny Hewson all met at Juste's house. Danny says you and Juste were arguing about money and that Miss Wemmick had been keeping him hidden. Presumably there was some kind of deal going down and he was the goods? Mrs Trinder says Juste claimed you were blackmailing him and that he had a ransom note from you, although she never saw it. On the other hand, she said Juste was intent on liquidating everything he had, and at precisely the point that his reputation was being shot to hell by you. She thinks, from something he said shortly before the night in question, that he was about to run, possibly also with money he'd stolen from her business. What kept her from handing him over was his claim that his wife was still alive, and that it was she who'd misappropriated the funds. There was also the possibility that he was suffering from a nervous breakdown after his wife's death – because we know Margaret Juste is very much dead – and the shock of his sister's murder immediately afterwards. But she also thinks there may have been some substance to his claims and he was on the thin end of a very clever game. How does that sound so far, Mr Wemmick?'

I shrugged awkwardly. 'Like I said, I remember virtually nothing. Can't Mr Juste help you?'

'Haven't they told you?'

'No-one's told me much at all, Detective Chief Inspector. I think I've been cushioned somewhat …'

'Ah, then I'm sorry to say that this may come as a bit of a shock to you. I'm afraid neither Miss Wemmick nor Mr Juste survived.'

'My God,' I paused, allowing the moment to mature, crystallise, become the past, like the old me was. 'That's terrible.' In the silence a monitor bleeped. I was tempted to push the morphine pump as my bodily aches returned but I knew I shouldn't. Pain would keep me focused.

'Do you need me to give you a moment?' Fredriks asked.

'No, no. It's all right. I probably already knew that was likely.' What now? Play on? I wondered what else Heather had said. I played on, wondering where this angle would go. 'What about the boy – Danny? Is he all right?'

'Yes, I'm glad to say. He was sent out of the house by Juste mere minutes before the fire started. You survived mainly because, ironically, Juste shielded you when he fell on top of you, sir. Miss Wemmick, we believe, was in direct line of the fireball as it exited the kitchen. I'm afraid both bodies were burnt beyond recognition, but of course we know who was present from Danny – and personal effects.' He indicated the iconic ring, still resident on my finger. I considered it silently.

'Shall I continue with my surmise, Mr Wemmick?' I nodded, oddly calm, still anticipating the denouement – the death blow. 'All right, this is what I've pieced together from Miss Trinder. There was an old feud between you and Juste – dating back to your joint time in a children's home in Eastbourne. After you both left there, Juste changed his name and started a new life on acquiring a small fortune via the will of Lord Justice Wemmick – no coincidence in the name, either, is there?' he smiled, meaningfully. *Had Heather told him everything then?* 'Juste's older brother, however, remained in contact with you, and after he got out of prison, you helped him out by giving him a job. It seems your families may even have become close, with your two half-sisters befriending Juste's youngest sister, Kimberley. After your half-sister, Rosemary was killed, her twin, Margaret – later to become Margaret Juste – became obsessed with reconciling all of you, especially with Juste. She somehow managed to get herself close enough to Juste to marry him, but after a while things went badly wrong. Contrary to popular belief, she and Juste were not the happy-ever-after couple. Far from it. In fact, so far from it, it's possible Juste may have eventually divested himself of her via a convenient road accident, only to find himself in an even bigger trap – explaining himself to you.'

I twitched involuntarily, tension getting the better of the already loose control I had over my limbs. I rued Heather and her tricks with mirrors; even with a face masked by bandages, my body gave me away.

Fredriks leaned in, almost conspiratorially. 'But there's more, and that's where it gets really interesting. We turned this up purely by chance, independent of Mrs Trinder, who's been very *helpful*. An anomaly in one of the post-mortem samples kept after Margaret Juste's post mortem indicated yet another connection. The genetic similarities in the bloodwork between her and Danny Hewson were beyond coincidence. They were closely related – like, mother and son related. Amusingly, it was Juste himself that got us curious there, by wanting his sister's genetic structure compared to Danny's. They were supposedly mother and son – and yet they weren't, and Juste must have suspected that to have asked, mustn't he? How am I doing so far?'

'You tell me Detective Chief Inspector,' I replied, trying not to show my anxiety.

'OK,' he smiled, pout expansive. 'Mrs Trinder said Juste also thought his sister Kimberley and his wife had some arrangement between them to eventually foist the boy on him, which he didn't like – to begin with ... but of course, if Danny Hewson is really Margaret Juste's son, and she used to be Margaret Wemmick – leaving aside the various other family names that seem to have swilled around in her past – then the boy is also potentially heir to the Wemmick estate. Even more interesting, huh? So wouldn't Juste have known that too, and wanted to use it to his own advantage, or did he try to use it against you?'

I shifted nervously, blood pressure rocketing sky-high. One of the monitors complained. It brought an anxious nurse in to check on me, and usher Fredriks away.

'My patient is exhausted, Detective.' she cautioned. 'Can't you continue this another time?'

'And when might that be?' he asked mildly.

'Maybe when he has someone else here to stop you tiring him out again,' she replied tartly. 'He's not the one on trial, is he – it's the other one.'

'Possibly,' Fredriks agreed, grinning nevertheless. 'May I suggest I send Mrs Trinder along with a statement of what we've discussed so far, assuming you agree with it? She's well up on the history, so it makes sense to ask her to continue to be involved for the moment – if you agree, of course? Then we can work out where we go from there.'

'But she's not acting for me.' He smiled again. 'Or do I need representation?' I asked carefully.

'I don't know, sir. Do you?'

The nurse waved him away before I could answer, but I knew the reprieve was only temporary. More temporary than I could have anticipated, as it happened. Heather appeared later on the same day, in the guise of the angel of death – or so it felt.

'Here's the statement. Just sign it.' Her face was cold and hard. The monitors continued to click merrily in the background and the morphine pump, currently set on automatic because I hadn't anticipated more visitors, delivered another dose of heaven.

'You're not happy with something in it?' I hedged as I endeavoured to marshal my senses.

'I'm not happy with anything – especially not seeing you lauded as a hero.' She wrinkled her nose with distaste as she watched me sign the document awkwardly with my left hand. I could write with my right hand, but the burns were a useful device to mask the fact that my signature wouldn't ever be anything like the confident scrawl that personified John Arthur Wemmick's written stamp of approval.

I handed the signed statement back. She took it brusquely. 'You're as guilty as hell and you know it, however many statements you sign to the contrary. I just can't prove it. Lawrence was innocent.'

'We're all innocent when we're born and as guilty as hell by the time we die, Mrs Trinder. I'm no different.'

Odd how much I cared about her now, after all these years of discounting her. The temptation to blurt out the whole truth was almost irresistible. Almost, but not quite. If I told her the truth, she'd have to choose.

'Clever words,' was all she said, sourly. 'They don't reflect the truth, even if everyone else is fooled by them.'

Truth versus justice – natural justice – but which would Heather choose? It could go either way at the moment, depending on Heather's input, but she was the one most capable of putting it all together. Now it had to go together in an order that could take me forwards, not back. I still needed her help, but how to get it?

Build bridges instead. Allow for change.

'Words and appearances never reflect the truth. I'm told it's a trick that mirrors do – reflecting back at you what you see, but of course what you see isn't real. It's reversed.'

She paused, door ajar and statement already filed in her briefcase. My heart pounded and my blood pressure rose as my body disobeyed everything Mary had told me about playing out my role. Heather studied me curiously as the monitor sounded and a nurse again appeared anxiously at the door.

'You seem different to the way I remembered you from the last time we met.'

'As you remember me? Maybe none of us are as we are remembered. Or seen as we are?' *Careful – publicly you're Wemmick.* 'Personally, I remember nothing of myself before the accident. I'm a new-born babe in many ways so perhaps I can endeavour to start again and reflect better in your eyes in the future?'

Her lips parted slightly, then compressed again.

'As you wish.' She considered me for a moment longer and my heart continued to race. I nodded. The nurse came over to my bedside, and took my pulse. 'In that case, the man I met will never reflect well for me.' She looked at the monitors and then back at me. 'But what you do with his future remains to be seen.' Suddenly she smiled, a small wry twitch of the lips. 'Privately I maintain what I said just now; John Arthur Wemmick is as guilty as hell and Lawrence Juste is innocent – if a fool. We'll see how we go from there.'

'I'll endeavour to change your opinion of me, then and reflect something better.'

'Do.' She gave a stiff little bow. 'I'll be back with DCI Fredriks later. You can make a start then.'

She left, leaving Lawrence Juste and John Arthur Wemmick apparently still separately contained in their own little boxes. For that I was both grateful and sad. I respected Heather – liked her a lot. I wanted her esteem, but I couldn't have it unless one day I earned it. She'd at least allowed for that possibility. I relaxed back against the pillows and allowed the morphine to muffle the world and its woes a while longer. Heather was the least of my worries. She had a signed statement from me – the new me, and we had a form of truce. Whether it would be accepted by Fredriks remained to be seen. My heart steadied and I breathed easier. The nurse pressed the button on the morphine pump and its dose of happiness surged through me almost immediately. I silently thanked her for its small measure of paradise before hell dragged me back.

***

Of course I didn't have long in paradise. Heather's promise to return with Fredriks happened the next day as I'd guessed it would. They sat side by

266

side. In unison. Almost as if they'd become a team – that was what the change in dynamics between them had indicated when we'd been looking at the film footage recovered from my kitchen.

'Are you up to continuing our little chat from yesterday, Mr Wemmick?' Fredriks asked politely.

'Ten minutes, only' the nurse instructed. She looked at me. I nodded. The moment had to come. Let it be now.

'We were talking about Lawrence Juste, and your relationship with him. I hope you don't mind I've brought Mrs Trinder along this time. As I said, she knows the history – and Mr Juste. She's by way of my chaperone too, in case I become too tiring.' The nurse gave him a black look but he smiled affably back. 'Mrs Trinder tells me you can't remember much. Is that still so today?' I looked at Heather and so did he. She remained impassive, watching me blandly. Fredriks looked back at me and Heather shook her head the tiniest fraction when his head was turned. 'I also shared some of my research with you. Have you anything to add to it?' She shook her head again. She reminded me of one of the nodding dog toys you see in the back of cars. It was hypnotic and I found myself shaking my head as well.

'I'm sorry Detective Chief Inspector, as I said to Mrs Trinder, it's as if I'm starting from nowhere, as of now.'

'Then we have to end up somewhere, don't we sir – for the boy's sake – if nothing else.' Heather nodded beside him. *Was she leading the witness?* 'Good,' he said in response to my inane acquiescence. Heather smiled minutely. Christ, she *was* leading me! 'I'll tell you what we've pieced together then. The Lawrence Juste we knew was a man of shadows – much like you are now, sir.' He grinned engagingly, but there was nothing engaging in his eyes. 'He had an abandoned past, and a manufactured present. He was also probably responsible for helping wrongly convict another person from his childhood for the murder of your half-sister, Rosemary. He seemed to have quite a thing about burying his past – or forgetting it – didn't he? Also rather like you at the moment. You could be peas in a pod!'

'But I haven't buried anything – simply can't remember.' I replied dryly. Heather frowned. I continued more deferentially. 'So your supposition is?'

'That behind all of the recent events is a very clever criminal mind. One that disposed of Margaret Juste to get her out of the way, murdered Kimberley Hewson to shut her up, destroyed or tampered with any evidence that could put him in the frame in the arson attack on Juste's home and all to get to the proverbial pot of gold: Danny Hewson. The perpetrator had just one more trick in mind before he got his fingers well and truly burnt.' He eyed my scorched and swollen hands. 'To get rid of any resistance to his plans for Danny – pay them off, if necessary.' I waited. The axe must be about to fall on me now. 'Who do you think that criminal mind belongs to?'

I looked at Heather. She was still expressionless.

'Who?' It was more croak than question. The silence was excruciating.

'Lawrence Juste.' I could barely speak. 'And you had a very lucky escape. I think you were extremely unlikely to have left his house alive if it hadn't been for that fire – whatever your deal was going to be. The sheer irony of it! He'd disposed of his wife and sister to avoid being lumbered with the boy, only to find he'd just almost killed off his golden goose. To get it back he had to get rid of you, making it look as if it was you who'd killed them, whilst spreading enough evidence around for the boy's origins to be discovered, apparently circumstantially. You stood in the way of everything as Danny's protector under the auspices of FFF and as administrator of the Wemmick estate for your half-sister's uncle.

'My God.' I stared from him to Heather. 'So that explains everything?'

'Unless there's anything you want to add to it,' Heather replied quietly. I shook my head hastily. 'Then, yes – it's the explanation for the whole of the last few months.'

'Well, it's almost everything,' Fredriks interrupted. 'There are just two things we haven't yet established.'

'Which are?'

'What was the deal you were brokering? And who was Molly Wemmick?'

I looked at Heather. She looked blankly back. This one was obviously mine to field, and I had no idea how – apart from...

'I'm sorry Detective Chief Inspector.' I slumped back against the pillows. 'I have no idea. Like I said, it's all a blank. I suppose I must have been paying him off to keep him away from Danny, but ... are there no clues?'

'Nothing – on either score. Miss Wemmick is a complete mystery. There was a name change recorded for your sister Margaret to Molly, but of course we know that's not possible. Other than that, there are no references to her, no dental records, nothing. Even Mr George Wemmick didn't know who she was. Only knew her as Molly and thought she was some kind of PA to you. Same with the staff at FFF, yet you all obviously accepted her as part of the organisation.'

'Well, then, maybe she was?'

'Maybe. We'll keep trying with that.' Fredriks frowned.

'Or maybe it's time to let sleeping dogs lie and the healing begin?' Heather suggested gently. 'If she's not been identified or claimed by anyone by now, maybe it's because there is no-one to do so. Sometimes not having all the answers is for the best.'

Fredriks studied her speculatively.

'Would that be your advice?' he asked, dead-pan.

'It would be my supposition,' she replied, the tiniest of smiles twitching the corners of her lips. Looking at them both, somehow I suspected the supposition would be accepted.

'So where do we go from here?' I asked cautiously.

'That's very much up to you, sir,' Frediks replied, the consummate professional again. 'I believe Miss Roumelia has been talking to Danny quite a lot over the last few days, explaining things to him. As you're the boy's closest relative now, you would of course be first choice for his guardian, but under the circumstances, if you don't feel up to it – or he doesn't want that – it's entirely understandable.'

'But then he'd stay in the children's home?'

'Quite probably. I understand children over the age of ten are less likely to be adopted. Maybe fostered on a short-term basis.'

'Then I need to be equal to the task, don't I?' Heather smiled complacently under cover of shuffling papers into her briefcase and I knew then who I had to thank for my second chance.

25: Centrepiece

My second chance arrived the next day; Danny, reluctant and awkward, Kat accompanying him. She hovered at the door until the nurse beckoned her in. Danny trailed behind her, red-faced and shy. Kat walked slowly towards me, a strange mix of known and unknown, disliked and desired – for both of us, not that she was aware of that. For her I was someone else. For me, she was many others. The woman I thought I'd fallen in love with, the woman I thought had betrayed me, and the woman I now knew had been manipulated and betrayed herself. She stopped at the foot of the bed to encourage Danny to come in. There was some murmured disagreement between them, settled eventually by Kat's calm insistence. I half-closed my eyes behind the bandages, trying to assess them and the situation. The morphine still clouded my head with waves of well-being, fooling me I was well and still me. They approached the bed, diffident and icily polite. The nurse provided two chairs that they didn't sit on and then left.

'Mr Wemmick?' Kat's voice was cool. 'I've brought Danny to see you.' Her perfume filled my senses, still over-sensitive to anything but the blandest stimulation. I battled to keep the unexpected emotions sparked by her proximity and the softness of her voice in the box I'd relegated them to. She was the Kat of long ago – the one whose hair I'd cried into and whose name I'd murmured as I first tumbled over the precipice when Margaret died. She must have thought I was asleep or hadn't heard. *Forget it. Put it in the past. This is the future.* I opened my eyes and peered through the bandages. She leant in closer and repeated my name. Her breath was warm on my face even through the dressings, and for a moment I panicked – back in the furnace of my burning kitchen and the smell of charring flesh. I gagged and with difficulty, swallowed back the bile. She drew back sharply, repelled, no doubt, but continued to study me. I wondered what the face of John Wemmick would be like when he was finally unravelled. Danny scrutinised me curiously too, but from a distance.

'You look like a mummy,' he said eventually, small voice high-pitched and nervous.

I laughed – a throaty cackle.

'I feel like one, but I don't know that I'd be much good at playing one. You're to be my ward. Did you know? What do you think?'

'I dunno.' He looked worried. 'You and Mr Big were arguing in the house before the fire and then he got killed in it. I dunno.' He took a step forwards and was at the foot of the bed. 'What do you look like underneath?' He was appalled by me, yet fascinated too. Typical kid. Just like Win and I would have been.

'I don't know. Would you like to see when they take the bandages off?'

'I guess.' He looked anxiously at Kat. She moved towards him protectively.

'We'll see,' she supplied as get-out.

'Does it matter so much what I look like?'

He considered for a while as the monitors beeped irregularly in the background. The nurse peered in.

'Not too long – he gets tired very easily,' she warned them.

'OK,' Kat said hastily, and edged closer to Danny and the door. Outside a horn blared and she jumped. Danny paused, as if listening. It hooted three times – like I'd instructed Win to. He shook his head vigorously.

'I guess not. It don't matter about looks but it does about what's inside.'

'I hope I'm all right – inside – whatever all right means for you.'

'I thought Mr Big – Mr Juste I mean – was all right, but everyone keeps saying he wasn't; that he wanted to hurt me. I don't know what to think now. Why do you think you're all right?'

This test I had to pass.

'People's actions tell you what you need to know about them. How did he treat you?'

He was wary, looking towards Kat for guidance. She nodded encouragingly.

'It's all right Danny. You can say whatever you think. No-one will hold it against you. You knew Mr Juste as well as anyone who's been saying bad things about him.' Her voice had an edge to it. Her face had a pinched look too – like the moisture had been sucked out of the burnished peach.

'He was OK, then.'

'What made him OK, Danny?' I asked. An indulgence perhaps, but Lawrence Juste deserved a eulogy before being damned forever.

'He listened. And he kept his word. He wouldn't have hurt me, whatever they're saying about him. He wanted me to be safe, that's what he said.' Kat squeezed his arm.

Now the real test.

'He was also involved in some kind of deal including you. Was that telling you the truth, or keeping you safe?'

Kat glared at me. 'That's pure guesswork – we don't know for sure.'

'I'm only repeating what I've been told,' I countered mildly. 'I want Danny and me to be honest with each other, and always say what we think right from the word go.'

She made to reply but Danny cut across her.

'He wasn't like that at all. He was OK.' Kat looked as she wanted to hug him, and I wished for a moment that I was Danny. At the last minute she pulled back, compressed her lips and stared belligerently at me, waiting for a response.

'Then maybe he had his own compelling reasons. But if he was a good man – as good as you say he was, he would have wanted the best for you now, wouldn't he? He'd have wanted you to have a new home and a new start; to be happy and to be cared for. In fact he did once publicly say that he wanted you to have a fresh start via the charity I administer, didn't he? So maybe you're right; he wasn't bad, he was good – in his own way.' Danny scuffed his shoe against the wheel at the bottom of the bed but wouldn't meet my eyes. 'Let's say that of him, shall we? That he'd want you to have – and make – good choices in your future?' He looked up then, squinting to discern what was behind the words – and the bandages. 'Shall we agree that?'

'Dunno.' He was still wary of me and we were at an impasse – neither agreeing nor disagreeing. We had to move on from here. Kat looked from one to the other of us, gauging the situation. Unsurprisingly she didn't help.

'Danny, you don't have to agree to anything you don't want to.'

I cut across her. 'Could we have a moment alone?' She frowned. 'Please?' She shrugged and motioned for Danny to leave the room. 'No, I meant Danny and me – since this is between us now.'

She rounded on me officiously.

'And me because I'm his social worker and responsible for his well-being. We only agreed to this because Heather Trinder said we should hear you out. '

'I know, but everything has to start somewhere, including a truce.' She flushed and her tawny skin darkened a rich plum colour; the colour I'd always wanted to bite into to see if it blanched or bruised. 'Just a few moments. You'll be all right with that, won't you Danny? After all, I'm only a mummy – can hardly do anything more than unravel.'

He laughed involuntarily and there was a spark of genuine amusement in his eyes. I waited. His laughter seemed to persuade her.

'Oh, all right – but just a few minutes, that's all. I'll be right outside.' It was a warning. She left in a cloud of perfume and antagonism and beneath my bandages I smiled because I knew her hostility masked her grief for Lawrence Juste. Danny watched her go and made a rueful face after her.

'Don't you like her?' I was surprised.

'Oh, yeah.' He looked taken aback and then grinned. 'She's all right too. More mum than me mum was. It's just – women …' He sounded like Win and I wanted to laugh.

'She's trying to protect you.'

'I don't need protecting.' The street kid was back, but the vulnerable child still lurked behind his eyes.

'We all need protecting sometimes, Danny. It's good to know there's someone who will do that for you.'

'And you want to protect me too? Because of all the money? You were arguing over that – the money – with Mr Big. He had a case load of it. I saw it in the torchlight. Was he giving it to you, or were you getting it back off him? How can I know which of you I should trust?'

'Sometimes what you see isn't really how things are. You only see a bit of the picture, but not the whole – like a jigsaw puzzle partially completed.'

'Right.' He sounded sceptical. 'So what's the rest of the picture?'

'The rest of the picture is the future and what you – and I – choose to do with it. Your money is yours – protected by the law. It's you I'm interested in, not your money. I've got enough of my own already.'

Ironically, I had – or John Wemmick had. The bear market had turned bull immediately after the fire and the manoeuvred investments had created their own golden goose. Danny's chin jutted and his face took on the mulish set I recognised as signifying he was weighing things up.

'I still need to know whether you're all right or not. Mr Big told me I should always check with him if someone was all right before I trusted them. I trusted Mr Big's wife seeing as she was his wife, but she was arguing about the money too.' His eyes narrowed again and I knew he understood more than a ten year old should. Despite the terse ambiguity of the discussion between Jaggers and me before Danny had been released to run to Win, he'd understood he was the reason for the barter. There was now really only one way our future could have its genesis because, frustratingly and admirably, my son was keeping absolutely to our pact. I could see Kat's nebulous outline through the frosted glass, calculating how much longer a few moments were. Long enough for one word, I hoped.

'I'm going to be in here for quite a while longer, Danny, so you'll have plenty of time to decide what you want to do – no pressure on you.' He hovered near the end of the bed, fidgety to leave. 'When I'm discharged I'm going to have to convalesce too. Somewhere by the seaside.' Kat's shape outside became clearer, pushing the door open. I had to keep going or the moment would be gone. 'The sea air is meant to be good for you, isn't it? Fresh – clears the head, and the past.' The door swung shut behind her like the old fashioned clapperboards in films. She stood proprietorially beside him. He glanced up at her and then studied the floor again. I pressed on. 'Do you like the seaside, Danny?' His eyes shot to my face and his lips parted. I knew what word they were forming without being able to lip read.

'I skimmed a fiver there. On the beach.'

'Maybe it'll be a sixer next time.'

'Yeah, maybe. Can you skim stones then?'

'I used to be able to. Might be a bit difficult now.' His eyes dropped from my face to my bandaged arms, resting uselessly on the bed covers.

'I s'pose I could teach you.' The inflection was slight, but I caught it – the emphasis on the 'I' and 'you'. He could become my teacher where once I had been his.

'I'd like that. By the sea, then.'

He nodded and shuffled along the edge of the bed, still examining me. Kat stiffened; the panther ready to pounce. I could tell she wanted to pull him back – away from what she perceived as danger.

'Where d'you reckon?'

'Oh, I don't know – somewhere not too far from London so Miss Roumelia can bring you to visit for my lessons.' I tried to sound casual.

'There's more to raising a child than playing games by the seaside, Mr Wemmick,' Kat interjected sharply. 'Shall we leave the make-believe for now? Time to go, I think Danny.'

Danny ignored her and moved closer; close enough for Kat to be unable to see his expression.

'How about Eastbourne?' I asked disingenuously.

Our eyes locked. I held my breath. Behind the bandages I felt exposed – more vulnerable than I'd ever felt before as I let my son decided whether to give me the second chance Heather had engineered, or to be my downfall. His eyes dropped pointedly to my right arm, and then back to my face. He grinned delightedly.

'I already been there,' he said eagerly. 'You'll like it.'

'That sounds like a plan then.'

'That will have to be the subject of formal discussion when you're convalescent,' Kat's social worker persona cut across us.

'Oh no, Miss. It's my choice now, ain't it?' Danny swung round to her, and I could see the truculent street kid I'd first met and had despaired of getting through to in the set of his body. She looked from him to me and her eyes narrowed.

'Only if it's in your best interests. We'll talk about it on the way back to the children's home.' She gathered him to her like a bundle of paperwork, lips pursed in disapproval, and nodded curtly at me. Danny pulled a face again and then grinned at me as he raised his right arm in salute – exactly as he'd done when we'd returned him to the children's home after the trip to Eastbourne and our secret pact. I managed to move my right arm the smallest amount in response – the arm with Jaggers' ring still embedded in the skin of the fourth finger, and now freed of some of its bandages as the skin healed, but it wasn't playing ball today. It merely waved wildly and flopped back onto the bed, inner arm exposed. The purple of now healing burns surrounded the little angel who'd flown with me all my life and had amazingly managed to escape the worst ravages of the fire. I realised now why Danny had been studying me so intently as we'd been talking. He must have spotted it. Kat's eyes followed the uncoordinated failure on my part and I felt as if I'd been thrown back into the flames for them to complete the job of devouring me.

She didn't say a word, simply turned on her heel and hustled Danny out of the room, still protesting. The door banged shut on them and I closed my eyes, unsure where I was now in my raggedy life. Exhaustion swept over me like a black cloud and I lingered on the edge of unconsciousness for all of a minute before I felt breath on my face again and a hand on my arm, turning it over until it lay fully exposed – a collaged pattern of fire, revenge and salvation. The whites of her eyes gleamed round dense black pupils. The panther had pounced.

I tried to shake her off but was too weak.

'I need to know who you really are.'

'And who am I?

She looked intently into my eyes and I saw the recognition in them.

'Danny's guardian angel, I hope.'

Epilogue

'Dad?'

There was a wheedling tone to his voice as we pulled into the lay-by outside the crematorium. We'd agreed the name was easier than John Arthur Wemmick, *guardian.*

'Danny?' There was a smile in mine.

'When you're finished here, can we go for a drive before I have to do my homework?'

'We'll see. Just sit tight. I won't be long.'

We'll see. How many times had that been said to me as a child? How many times had it been said to any child? And seeing was so hard to do. *Really* seeing, that is.

It took me a while to locate the place where Margaret's ashes had been scattered. I didn't move fast these days, and the stick often hampered more than it helped me. I was leaning heavily on it today, the pain of memory as bad as the pain of bodily malfunction – but both would pass in time, I was assured by the medical profession. Once I'd found Margaret's last resting place, it was easy to find the other two. Molly Wemmick and Lawrence Juste. A small wooden plaque, lettered in black, named both spots. I placed the black-edged card – identical to the ones I'd sent out for Margaret's funeral, and Rosemary had sent to me with her cryptic clues on – between the two plots. There wasn't much on this one – it was in memoriam.

'For Margaret, Jonno and Kimmy.'

I placed the rosemary on Margaret's small space of earth – for remembrance. For me, I was glad just to be alive, and one day, to forget. I stayed there longer than I'd expected. Saying goodbye is strange when you've barely said hello. Or maybe I was saying goodbye to much more than lost souls.

As John Wemmick I now officially paid Mary's residential bills. The visit I'd made to her in my new body had been official too, offering my condolences. For the future to exist the past had to be lost. She'd simply smiled kindly at me and nodded. She had the window wide open this time and the little origami birds fluttered and dipped in the autumn breeze. I wondered if she would set her little birds free now Lawrence was gone. She watched me watching them.

'They're mockingbirds,' she said quietly. 'They sing their hearts out when they need to and just listen when they don't.' She plucked one from its string and gave it to me. 'A memento of your visit,' she added mischievously. 'Do come again. I like visitors.'

I unfolded the bird in the car. It was a blank sheet of paper apart from a number and the address of a bank. It was a security box number, and this time I didn't need to check to know the 119 key would fit and that it would contain all the other little mockingbirds, should they ever need to sing for me one day. You don't need to know everything to know the truth. *I will, Mary. I will visit again.*

I hadn't followed up on Binnie – what was the point? She had walked, like she'd always walked when she wanted out. Nor Emm – but with a great deal more regret. She had Jill, and their twin relationship was all that Rosemary and Margaret's was not. They'd been complete before I'd reappeared. What was left in my life now was what was necessary to the future.

When I got back to the car – the replacement Austin Healey 3000 in racing green that Danny and I both relished for different reasons – he was playing with the steering wheel as if he was a rally driver.

'You took ages,' he accused.

'Sorry, I'm not much of an athlete these days.' I'd probably never been, in truth – running up and down the air raid mound had been my bid for self-belief; a self-belief that had been won in an entirely unexpected way after all.

'I was just a bit worried that's all,' he added sheepishly. 'Win said to look after you – make sure you didn't overdo it.'

'What's Win – my nursemaid?' I winked with difficulty.

'No,' he grinned. 'Your mum,' he added cheekily. 'Or as good as – old mother hen!'

Old mother hen indeed! But one I knew wouldn't ever squawk, however much anyone pushed him. He was family – albeit old family – and family stuck together. I grinned back.

'Could be worse! Could be Kat grounding both of us.'

'Yeah – but she never means it.' He grinned, 'or not where you're concerned. What were you doing, anyway?'

'I had a message to deliver.'

'What?'

'About natural justice,' I smiled lopsidedly. The scar tissue on my face still felt hard and uncomfortable, like I was wearing a mask – not that it mattered. Danny smiled back, uncertainly. Not because of me, but what I meant. We both knew that what was underneath the mask was what mattered. 'Come on, I'll steer and you can change gear.'

I turned the ignition over and paddled the accelerator to make the car rev throatily.

'Is that allowed?'

'No, but who will know other than you and me if between us we drive this beast perfectly, and with absolute confidence?'

'Yeah!'

The outcome would be good even if the method was bad. It was a twisted logic, but what of this nightmare wasn't twisted? And he had to start learning the ropes some time; that life was a patchwork and it was only our belief in each other that kept the patchwork cobbled together.

Bibliography:

1. 'For now we see through a glass, darkly; but then face to face: now I know in part; but then shall I know even as also I am known.' 1 Corinthians 13:12
2. 'You never really understand a person until you consider things from his point of view ... until you climb into his skin and walk around in it.' *To Kill a Mockingbird*, Harper Lee
3. 'Ill-met by moonlight' *A Midsummer Night's Dream* – Act 2, Scene 1, William Shakespeare

The Patchwork Trilogy

PATCHWORK MAN

Have you ever met a patchwork man?

Lawrence Juste is one. The QC with a conscience - privileged, reputable and emotionally frozen. The perfect barrister.

But Lawrence hasn't always been who he is now. When he is glaringly in the public eye after his enigmatic wife is killed in an apparently random hit and run, he could do with his hidden past surfacing like a hole in the head.

Unfortunately the past has a way of finding its way back to you, just like betrayal. His dead wife has helpfully left him a sinister resume of his, and she just keeps adding to it...

Patchwork Man is the first book in the trilogy.

PATCHWORK PEOPLE

The second book in the trilogy.

Lawrence Juste QC has already had to face the public appearance of a long lost and criminally inclined brother, the renewed attentions of a boyhood bully, threatening to ruin him professionally and financially, and the machinations of his dead wife apparently keen to do the same. What else could go wrong?

Plenty.

It seems it can only end one way for Lawrence - disaster; unless his dead wife can help...

PATCHWORK PIECES

Patchwork Pieces is the third and final book in the trilogy.

It seems Lawrence Juste's life is so disassembled it would take a miracle to put it back together without losing himself in the process. And even then the picture wouldn't be pretty. Murder. Blackmail. Revenge. And the living dead. It sounds like fantasy. In reality its fate, and the past finally catching up with not only Juste, but anyone who's ever cheated, lied or betrayed alongside him.

It's going to be one hell of a party when the patchwork is completed...

About D. B. Martin

D.B. Martin writes adult psychological thriller fiction and literary fiction as Debrah Martin, as well as YA fiction, featuring a teen detective series, under the pen name of Lily Stuart.

You can find more about her work and sign up for updates on forthcoming publications on www.debrahmartin.co.uk or by joining her newsletter list at http://eepurl.com/3-965.

Printed in Great Britain
by Amazon